Tom F. Dodd

I0649075

Other Great Novels by Tom F. Dodd:

THE MUSE ALSO WEEPS —

A riveting, page-turner involving the murder of a ninety year-old, Nazi SS Officer, stolen artworks, buried Nazi gold and the Amber Room that combines a masterfully wordsmithed whodunnit mystery with a romantic tale that is nearly impossible to put down.

THE MUSE ALSO WEEPS is selling worldwide to unanimous critical and reader acclaim. Available from www.Lulu.com and from on-line book seller's world-wide.

THE DEVIL'S ORACLE -

As mankind moves closer to a terrorist confrontation with a dirty nuclear device, clues emerge that propel Chief Inspector Paul Soria and his associates on the hunt for an elusive jihadist- a demonic man who plans the ruination of international economic stability.

THE DEVIL'S ORACLE is shocking, spell-binding and compels the reader to eagerly discover how it all ends. It is both timeless and timely in its subject matter. Something the reader cannot ignore in today's world of terrorist threats.

Other Books by Tom F. Dodd:

"The Adventures of MONTY, the Kelped Crusader" –

Beautifully written with co-author Pamela Schmidt, the story is a delightfully illustrated children's book about three adorable and cuddly otters who realize the importance of obeying their parent's instructions as they pertain to their safety and welfare. The book is a valuable teaching aid for children between the ages of 4 and 11, and has received glowing reviews from both parents and professional educators. The book is available at Pamela Schmidt's website at Lulu.com.

THE STRANGE CASE OF THE NOAH'S ARK CONCEPTION

A NOVEL

TOM F. DODD

Copyright - 2008

Tom F. Dodd Publications, L.L.C.
ALL   RIGHTS   RESERVED

ISBN: 978-0-615-25355-8

www.Lulu.com

Printed in the United States of America.
This is a work of fiction. All incidents and dialogue, and all characters with the exception of some well-known historical and public figures, are products of the author's imagination and are **not** to be construed as real. Where real-life historical or public figures appear, the situations, incidents, and dialogues concerning those persons are entirely fictional and are not intended to depict actual events or to change the entirely fictional nature of the work. In all other respects, resemblance to persons living or dead is entirely coincidental.

This book is dedicated to my son, Thomas F. Dodd Jr., and my brother, Michael J. Dodd who have always encouraged me to continue writing adventure and mystery stories. And also to my mother, Margaret (Peggy), who read to me many stories as a young child.

ACKNOWLEDGMENTS

I also wish to take the time to acknowledge several people who have encouraged me to continue writing. First of all, my fans, who have been very supportive and have enjoyed all of my stories.

In addition, the following people have motivated and encouraged me and I will be forever grateful to them: Pamela Joan Touch Schmidt, Andy and Marilou Nuzzi, Bill and Julie Dormandy, Tom and Nori Treichler, Richard and Debbie Roof, The Blackhawk Museum Guild and my wonderful fans and friends who have enriched me beyond measure.

"Man has mounted science, and is now run away… science will be the master of man… Someday science may have the existence of man in its power, and the human race may commit suicide by blowing up the world."

Henry (Brooks) Adams – 1862

"Man's destiny is to be the sole agent for future evolution on this planet. He is the highest dominant type to be produced over two and a half billion years of the slow biological movement affected by the blind opportunistic workings of natural selection; if he does not destroy himself, he has at least an equal stretch of evolutionary time before him to exercise his agency."

Julian Huxley - 1964

The Noah's Ark Conception

THE STRANGE CASE

OF THE NOAH'S ARK

CONCEPTION

Tom F. Dodd

Preface

In the decade leading up to the Second World War, German scientists, biologists and zoologists had been secretly busy with the pursuit of a fantastic dream: the reconstitution and resurrection of extinct species of animals. It would have been a scientific achievement of major implications to pull off such a fete, and another validation that German science was superior to that of the rest of the world – an achievement that would have reflected positively on the "Master Race". Minimally, a Noble Prize in Biology or Genetics would have been awarded if the German's had decided to publish the results of their experiments. But theirs was a super-secret operation. They referred to it as "Die Arche Noah Projektierung".

And while genetic technology, particularly the elucidation and description of the DNA double-helix, by James Watson and Francis Crick, would not occur until 1953, it was a German biochemist, in the 1940's that had discovered deoxyribose sugars and long-chain polymeric sequences of nucleotides, and suggested further that this DNA sequence might actually be functioning as a "gene". For it is the gene that ultimately determines the specific characteristics of all life forms; and by manipulating the human genome one could engineer a smarter, stronger Aryan race with bluer eyes and blonder hair – thus ensuring the preservation and the Aryan purity of the "Thousand-year Reich".

By implementing the reconstitution of extinct species of animals such as the powerful Auroch, a giant cow from the Pleistocene Era that had died out in the 17th Century, and had purportedly possessed nearly mythological strength, then enormous credibility would have been underscored to the long, ancient Germanic fokelore and the physical and intellectual superiority of the Aryan godmen. The Nazis, therefore, endorsed and funded this clandestine genetic research. But there was another, more sinister reason for breeding long-extinct species of mammals. Because, if these animals could be turned loose in the countrysides of the enemy, then surely the disruption and the havoc created by the sudden appearance of such huge and rapacious beasts such as Aurochs, Cave Lions, Cave Bears or Sabre-tooth Tigers would offer strategic advantages to the armies of the conquering Nazi horde.

In 1937, the Nazis constructed a super-secret, underground laboratory near the town of Rottweil, in the hilly area of south-western Germany. Ironically, this sylvan setting had been the source of the "seven dwarves" fable.

Situated on the steep banks of the upper Neckar River, Rottweil enjoyed excellent railroad and surface roads servicing the historic town. The inhabitants of Rottweil had no idea what the strange, imposing complex of concrete buildings and the high, crenellated, electrified walls were to be used for. Research facilities of all types had and were being constructed all over Germany, and were manned by wermacht and "SS" personnel. The average German citizen cared little about what the fanatical Nazis were up to.

The area immediately adjacent to the facility was patrolled by heavily armed guards, and at night, intense floodlights illuminated every blade of grass within one-hundred meters of the exterior walls. Incongruously, the areas enclosed by the walls of the complex were not illuminated. It was thought that perhaps the Nazis did not want overflights of Allied surveillance planes to capture on film what was being accomplished inside.

Dr. Ludwig Heinrich Heck, nicknamed "Lotz" was born in April of 1895, and was a trained zoologist, animal researcher and the director of the Berlin Zoo. He also bathed in the good graces of the Nazi party's propaganda machine. A favorite of Adolf Hitler, Hermann Goering and Josef Goebbels, Lotz Heck became influential in persuading the Nazis to underwrite his peculiar genetic research experiments, as well as transporting to

Germany perfect specimens of animals liberated from the major zoological parks of Europe.

For his research, Lotz surrounded himself with like-minded German scientists: Men like, Dr. Hans Antonius, Karl-Heinz Heck, Dr. Franz Ziegler and Dr. Otto Warnung. They all shared Heck's vision of bringing to life animals that had not been seen on planet earth for thousand's of years. It seems a cruel irony that the same Nazis who wanted to eradicate every Jew from the face of the earth, so passionately wanted to repopulate it with lesser order mammals that had not managed to survive.

Lotz Heck was a rare visitor to the research laboratories in Rottweil. Instead, he preferred to manage the Berlin zoo from his offices there; remaining close to the Nazi center of power, or he travelled to distant countries in pursuit of novel animal species that his zoological park did not possess. In addition, history documents Heck's involvement with trying to restore extinct sub-species of horses and zebras in places like Poland and South Africa. As a result, Heck delegated the responsibility to his older brother, Karl-Heinz, to supervise the goings on at the research facility in Rottweil. He carried out all of his duties with the full authority of Reichsmarshall Hermann Goering himself – the self-professed head game keeper of all lands that Germany had occupied.

On several occasions, the townspeople of Rottweil reported bloodcurdling and very loud screams and roars coming from behind the walls of the dimly-lit research complex. They never inquired as to the source. Instead, they were content to assume that whatever was going on bore an unsettling resemblance to the Roman custom of throwing Christians to the lions in the amphitheatre. Oftentimes, gunshots were heard in the middle of the night; followed by the agonizing cries of some poor dying creature. One elderly lady who lived near the facility made a sinister comparison to H. G. Wells', "The Island of Dr. Moreau".

The research group purportedly tried, in addition to their experiments with extinct species, cross-breeding contemporary species such as male lions with female tigers (offspring – Ligers); and male tigers with female lions (offspring – Tigons).

Similarly, they attempted a cross with a large Kodiak bear sow and a Polar bear boar. The impregnation occurred while the sow was anesthetized. But the entire operation proved too dangerous, and fertilization did not take place. As a result, these exercises in many cases proved tragic, as lions and tigers are natural enemies and the potential parents killed each other before the mating process was ever consummated. This experimental approach was quickly abandoned.

History did not document what level of success the research experiments at the complex in Rottweil had achieved, as the Nazis deliberately destroyed all records as the end of WWII approached in the spring of 1945. A reconnaissance company of American troops from the 813th tank destroyer battalion happened upon the hastily abandoned research facility while on their way to take Memmingen and Munich. Anecdotal information about the strange laboratory in Rottweil was passed along by an eyewitness, SSGT Douglas Fernandez, who maintained that the research facility resembled an enormous veterinary hospital from the inside, and that there had been preserved in huge vats of formaldehyde, the fetuses of animals, some of which no one could identify – "and we had a lot of experienced farm boys in our outfit." In addition, there were skulls and the rotting carcasses of large animals that resembled bears and lions, but seemed too large to be real. Later, all of the large animal carcasses were burned with gasoline to eliminate the nauseating stench of decaying flesh.

Lotz Heck died in Berlin, in 1983. He only spoke about his genetic research and experiments with Poland's Tarpan horses and the selective breeding "Quagga" project using the Plains Zebra in the Etosha province of South Africa. He never mentioned or hinted at "Die Arche Noah Projektierung" experiments that went on in Rottweil.

Scientists today ridicule Heck's work as nothing more than a fanciful pseudo-science. Unfortunately, the truth may never be known about how successful the extinct species resurrection program may have been, as no records of those original experiments were ever recovered.

PART   ONE

ANACHRONISM

<u>Chapter One</u> – April 27, 1946

The rider's horse jerked nervously, as the unfamiliar odors and sights of this high, alpine valley caused it to fear this place. Gripping the reins tighter now, the man dug his heels into the horse's flanks urging it forward. It resisted. Then it advanced cautiously, moving forward at a reluctant pace. It was at that moment the rider realized that his horse might have become lame. It might have been due to the additional weight of the gold that he carried – a lot of it.

The man's steel blue eyes quickly surveyed the meadow that spread out ahead of him for any sign of movement; his right hand moving aside his riding coat to allow rapid access to the pistol that he always carried. He had never ridden this high on the mountain before, and his horse's strange, uncharacteristic behavior and its labored breathing at this altitude imparted a feeling of foreboding.

Alert now, the man's eyes continued to scan the granite walls that ascended abruptly from the valley floor and towered high above to the northeast. Spring was late coming to this meadow, and the snow had melted away only in those places where the sunlight could warm the ground unimpeded by the tall pines and the massive boulders. There was a biting chill in the air. He could almost feel a palpable stillness – it was ominous; and combined with the high altitude, his mouth became very dry. He was also wary of an ambush, as he was now a very wanted man.

After riding for several hours, some of it at a rapid pace, Alex Van Traubben was becoming tired. He understood that his horse badly needed some rest. The sun warmed him as he halted his grey mare in an open patch of meadow grass. He allowed his animal to relax and nibble on the new shoots for a few minutes. The horse's head continuously poked upward, as if reconnoitering warily. The man looked backward scanning the trail from whence he came. Nothing or no one seemed to be following him, and he decided to rest for a while before pressing onward. It would be several hours, perhaps a day, before they would be coming for him. He had given himself the advantage of a long head start.

Alex Van Traubben, seven hours before had robbed the Brig branch of the Credit Suisse Bank, and had gotten away with nearly forty-thousand in swiss francs and gold. The loot was safely ensconced in two large, leather bags that were attached to his saddle and draped over the horse's rump. The dead weight of the gold added to the horse's irritation, stress and burden.

Alex had stolen a car, robbed the bank and then ditched the stolen vehicle where his waiting horse had been tied. His plan was simple: He would make his escape via horseback over terrain that motor vehicles could not possibly follow, thus avoiding all potential road blocks and ensuring his escape. Methodically, he had planned every detail and thought out every possible contingency – and so far, his daring plan was working flawlessly.

The sky darkened and a light snow began to fall. Van Traubben directed his horse to a small stream from which to drink. Once in the stream, he dismounted and refilled his canteen as his horse drank eagerly. The water was only a few inches deep; running swiftly and very cold. The melting snows had given birth to this rivulet, and the man could feel the bracing bite of the frigid water through his leather riding boots. Then he heard what seemed to be a deep growling sound coming from somewhere in the dense thicket of trees ahead. Leaping back on his horse and grabbing the reins, he sat upright in his saddle and looked around quickly, craning his neck to see if he could locate the source of the noise. He saw nothing and did not hear any further sounds. He slung the strap of the canteen over the pommel of his saddle.

Fifteen kilometers away and four thousand feet down the mountain, eight deputized men and a persistent Federal Inspector driving a medium sized truck now realized how the crafty thief had made good his escape. In was impossible to follow him with their vehicle, and they would have to resort to using horses to negotiate the difficult, roadless terrain.

"We're dealing with a clever fellow here," the Inspector noted. "Now it looks like a couple of us will have to track him on horseback," he declared with a sense of frustrated resignation.

"I guess that we have no choice now except to go back."

The snow storm had begun to intensify. The meadow had become church quiet. He needed a cigarette. Van Traubben decided that he would have his smoke under a dense stand of conifer trees that would shelter him from the falling snow. Afterwards, and considering the abrupt change in the weather, he planned to cut short his escape and find a suitable shelter for the night. If it did snow, then the snow would have the additional benefit of covering up his horse's tracks. If anyone was pursuing him, they were going to find it difficult to track him beyond this point.

Confident that no more mysterious sounds were coming from nearby, he lit his cigarette, inhaled deeply and enjoyed the relaxation that came as the nicotine invaded his bloodstream. As he continued to enjoy the cigarette, his eyes scanned over the boulder and broken tree festooned area near the base of the cliff wall. The entire area was dimly lit and shadowy apparitions were created by the boulders and the rotting stumps of fallen trees. The twisted and dense mass of rocks and trees seemed impenetrable. Siezing the opportunity for dense natural cover, he eased his horse further into the thicket for a better look. His horse protested, and Van Traubben dismounted to get a better look at the horse's right front leg. It had become swollen. The animal was clearly worn out and could travel no further. He hadn't counted on this.

There was a bone-chilling dampness and a musty smell in the air. All of the fallen trees were covered with a thick, green carpet of moss and sprinkled with fresh snow. The scene would have been beautiful in the sunlight.

No sound of any kind emanated from the thicket – no birds, no wind, only the sound of his horse's deep breathing, and the occasional snapping of twigs as the mare pawed the ground nervously with her hoof. The light of day was rapidly yielding to the inevitability of dusk, and Van Traubben suddenly realized that he needed to make camp in this the high alpine valley for the night, and doing so would mean that he would have to find shelter very soon.

He slowly led his horse by the reins deeper into the thicket and soon they were passing through a small clearing. It was there that he noticed the first of the unusual scratch marks high up on the side of a large pine tree. The bark had been scratched and scraped away at a site about ten feet above the ground. The underlying yellow-white wood was exposed, and that too had been scratched and bore deep scars in the wood. There were two sets of four, nearly parallel deep scratch marks. The tree was oozing sap, its lifeblood, through the gaping wounds. Sap was collecting in the crevices of the bark in large, amber teardrops. A small bird had become trapped in the sticky ooze and it's sap-matted, feathered body hung grotesquely by one leg. It had broken its wing in terror while attempting to free itself. Colorful feathers were strewn about in the snow below.

Catching an unusual dark shape out of the corner of his right eye, Van Traubben spotted what looked like a cave opening in the rock wall. He would have to pick carefully around the broken trees and rocks to get to it, but it might make the safe cover he required as shelter for the night. He led his horse as close to the cave as it could get without risking any more damage to its front leg, and then tied off the reins around a large, fallen tree limb. Loosening the cinch of the saddle, he pulled it free from the horse. The animal's back quivered after being released from its burden. The man placed the saddle carefully over the limb, and took the blanket and the saddle bags containing the stolen loot with him.

When he arrived at the opening in the rock, he peered inside cautiously. It was indeed a good sized cave but the internal darkness precluded him from seeing how far back into the mountain it went. At the entrance he also noticed the remains and the incomplete skeleton of a red deer. Parts of it were dismembered and tossed about. He guessed wolves were the cause, although he couldn't remember reports of wolves living in Switzerland. He drew his pistol. If there was anything or anyone living in this cave, he was not going to be taken by surprise.

Entering the cave slowly, he allowed time for his eyes to become accustomed to the darkness. The cave had a particularly musty smell – a pungent mixture of bat droppings, decaying flesh and dampness – thousands of years of rot and death. There was also something else about the smell, but Van Traubben couldn't identify the strange odor.

It was a very deep cave; well high enough to stand inside. He could get accustomed to the smell – the cave would do well for the night's shelter. Besides, he had lived near stockyards as a child and he remembered that nothing could smell as bad. Then he returned to the mouth of the cave, satisfied that no wolves or other threatening creatures were living inside.

He fed and watered his horse, examined the horse's foot and assumed that by the morning, the swelling should have gone down sufficiently to lead his animal down the mountain and across the frontier border into Italy. Van Traubben gathered dry, broken pieces of wood for a fire, which he ignited on the damp, clay floor of the cave – the warmth felt good. Sitting on a large, flat rock, he became mesmerized by the orange-red flames devouring the logs and reducing them to glowing embers. Nearly seven hours of hard riding, much of it in the thin atmosphere of ninety-five hundred feet had taken its toll; his exhausted body demanded rest, and sleep was already overtaking his nervous system. He felt that he had chosen a safe shelter – at least the cave kept him out of the harsh elements.

He rolled out the horse blanket on the damp earth near the fire and removed his riding boots. Rubbing the circulating blood back into his feet, his eyes wandered around the dimly lit walls of the cave. Hulking shadows created by the flickering fire loomed ominously everywhere. On one wall he noticed petro-glyphs engraved into the rock. Figures of large cattle, buffalo, horses, eagle-like raptors and large ferocious bears succumbing to the spears and arrows of long-dead, but brave hunters and warriors. One drawing depicted three men attempting to kill an enormous bear. The bear had four lances in his side and chest, and it was crushing the head of one of the men in its great jaws. The bear had bitten off the leg of another hunter, and a third man was lying in a grotesque position on the ground; his chest was ripped open. The cave wall was tinted with a dull, faded red-ochre dye.

Must have been one helluva fight? Van Traubben mused.

Exhausted, Alex Van Traubben pillowed his head against the rolled blanket top, and he covered up as best as he could with the remainder. As he reached out and felt the saddle bags containing the gold coins, bullion and the cash, he believed that his financial future was now secure. Sleep quickly overtook the watery-eyed man. Outside his cave, it was beginning to snow heavily and the big wet flakes were being driven by a stiff breeze.

The night became increasingly cold and the snow came down from the northwest and formed deep drifts that piled the snow high against the rocks and tall trees. Then, remarkably, almost as quickly as the storm arrived, the freakish blizzard departed with a suddenness that left a full moon as witness to the winter wonderland on the valley floor. The ice-encrusted snow glistened like diamonds on pure white lace in the pale moonlight. The valley had an unearthly stillness as the wind abated. The tall pines stood in frozen attention – silent sentinels in green uniforms with white epaulets.

Inside the cave Van Traubben slept soundly. No dreams disturbed his rest. The campfire had consumed itself, and red-orange embers, their warmth receding, transformed into grey-white ash on the cave floor. Illumination from the fire was quenched by the darkness that expanded outward in tentacle-like shadows, consuming more and more of the evanescing light in the cave. The cave's entrance was bathed in moonlight, and its brightness soon competed with the dying fire for dominance.

Outside, the horse dozed under the shelter of the branches of a large conifer – hidden from the ghostly eyes of the night. Tied securely to the limb, it grunted and fidgeted reflexively. The only motion in the valley was the occasional dropping of snow in pillowy clumps from a drooping pine bough disturbed by an owl making its nocturnal rounds of meadow mousing.

The great beast entered the valley from the northeast side, and reared up on its hind legs to better examine the air for the scent of food. The animal's massive head jerked up abruptly as it detected a new scent; one that was not present the last time that it had hunted in this meadow. It was a very complex scent: part of it enraged the animal, but another part revealed the welcomed traces of sustenance. The huge animal ambled along steadily in the direction of the odors – stalking quietly. Having no natural predators, the massive animal was fearless, but still, it moved cautiously, testing and retesting the air.

The horse detected the movement first. Filled with an overwhelming sense of dread, the horse thrust its neck backward repeatedly against the secured reins in an effort to get free. Now in a panic, the horse bucked and kicked wildly in all directions and managed to snap off the limb that restrained it.

The giant carnivore lunged from the trees with its long claws exposed and huge jaws agape. A loud roar announced the attack. The sight of the animal caused the horse to attempt to escape, but dragging the severed tree limb still attached to the reins through the broken rocks and tree stumps caused the horse to slow in painful, neck-jerking stops. Before the horse could reach the open meadow, an enormous, razor-sharp claw penetrated its neck and tore it open from the ear to the shoulder. Spurting blood from a severed artery sprayed the trees and the ground, forming contrasting patterns of red and white in the snow. The horse never made another sound as the predator's other claw crashed down across its neck, shattering and severing three vertebrae instantly. The horse was dead before its corpse collapsed to the ground.

The great animal seized the horse's neck in its immense jaws. Then using its powerful front legs and paws it raked open the horses belly and chest. Blood, viscera and entrails spilled onto the ground. The horse was shaken violently from side to side until the predator's ferocity subsided and it was satisfied that the equine prey was dead.

Half of the horse was devoured within an hour. The great animal carried what was left of the headless carcass into a dense briar thicket and buried it in the soft earth – excavating the ground easily with its powerful forelegs. Then, scanning the thicket with cold, black eyes, the animal made sure that no scavengers witnessed where it had hidden the kill. It rose up on its hind legs and re-sharpened and cleaned off its claws against the side of a pine tree; ripping off huge chunks of bark. The tree swayed violently as its trunk was being assaulted. A flock of sleepy pine jays protested about having their perches disturbed. Van Traubben was sleeping soundly, completely unaware of the savage drama that had taken place outside the cave.

He woke late the next morning. In an instant he understood from the sun's brightness that some of the precious time required for him to get home had been lost. The Federal Police were undoubtedly searching for him, and he had lost valuable time. He gathered up his things and moved towards the cave's opening.

He squinted hard as his eyes were not use to the strong sunlight, particularly as it reflected off the brilliant, fresh white snow. Bracing himself against the mouth of the cave, he peered outside. No unusual sounds were present – only the raucous sounds of feeding, scavenging crows and the slight rustle of the branches of nearby tress.

Venturing out of the cave cautiously, his eyes searched the area where his horse had been tied. Fear shot through his nervous system as he realized that it was gone. He withdrew reflexively back into the cave and tried to collect his thoughts. Could the police be waiting for him?

Perhaps the horse had wandered home by itself?

Horses were known to do that, he thought.

He quickly reviewed his alternatives: He could stay inside of the cave and wait for the police to come and get him, or risk exposure by wading through the deep snow and walking down the mountain.

Van Traubben was hungry and grabbed some lamb jerky from his saddle pouch. The taste of it refreshed him, and he decided to light a cigarette to claim his nerves. Confused by the unfortunate turn of events, Van Traubben attempted to clear his head and to try making some sense out of his new situation. This alternative was not part of his well thought out plan.

He exited the cave, and this time he inched his way down to the thicket. By the time he reached the spot where his horse had been tied, he was confronted with a horrible sight. The ground was torn up, indicating signs of a great struggle. Blood, viscera, mud and snow were churned up everywhere; the trees and the snow were stained with splashes of blood. He had to chase away a flock of scavenging crows to obtain a better look.

The leather rein still attached to the broken limb was connected to what remained of the horse's head. The head had been severed behind the ear. Bone, flesh and internal tissue protruded where the neck had been. The horse's eyes projected a terrible fear.

"Mein Gott! What could have done this?" Van Traubben uttered aloud.

Sickened and frightened by the carnage on the ground in front of him, Van Traubben felt his knees weaken. Fearing the worst, he drew his pistol and surveyed the thicket – **nothing**.

He surmised that the horse had attempted in vein to escape from whatever had attacked it.

"What the hell kind of an animal could do this?" he considered. The pistol began shaking in his hand. He holstered the weapon and ran back up to the cave.

He had seen animal kills before. But what kind of an animal could carry off the largest part of a thirteen hundred pound horse? His mind conjured up and considered images of an escaped lion or a tiger – some huge bear, or maybe a family of bears. A bear had the power to drag away a large carcass; but bears were solitary, except a sow with cubs. Maybe the cause was wolves?

"That's ridiculous!" he exclaimed, as his words echoed in the cave.

"There are no such animals roaming freely in Switzerland."

Nothing made any sense, and so he chose to remain in the cave analyzing his alternatives.

Four thousand feet down the mountain, the Inspector had returned with only two deputies and three horses. They were mounting a search and capture mission, as they had discovered the abandoned, stolen car and had deduced that Van Traubben had affected his escape on horseback. His tracks were clearly visible, as the weight of the gold he was carrying added to the depth of his horse's hoofprints. The authorities were also aware of the ferocity of the previous night's snowfall, and what it might mean in terms of the dangers of exposure for anyone trapped in that kind of weather overnight. Unfortunately, the police had no idea where Van Traubben was headed, and the surrounding countryside offered the thief a myriad of escape avenues. They all hoped that he had managed to take shelter somewhere, and that the snowstorm would have slowed him down. They believed that the advantage was now theirs.

The sunlight had provided little illumination inside of the cave and Van Traubben was becoming restless, cold and anxious to be home in his warm chalet across the Italian border. He imagined how welcomed a good hot bath, coffee and a shave would feel. He was a very wealthy man, but at this moment he couldn't buy a horse, a shave – anything.

He decided that his best option would be to leave the cave and to try and make it on foot as far as he could down the mountain and then across the Italian border. He considered burying the heavy gold in the cave, and then returning at another, safer time to retrieve it. He was completing the thoughts of his plan, when he heard the noise outside of the cave's entrance. The sound of something or someone crunching through the snow grew louder. It sounded like two, perhaps three men. Maybe they **had** seen his tracks in the snow? He dashed to the entrance of the cave, his pistol was drawn.

A large shadow eclipsed the light entering the cave, and scratching could be heard near the entrance. An immense dark-brown paw penetrated the opening first; the wet claws glistening like steel sabres. Then a huge head burst through. Growling and snarling, the great beast sensed that prey in the form of the hated man-creature was near. Fear iced Van Traubben's veins as this was the largest bear he had ever seen.

The bear forced its great bulk through the cave's opening; clawing the ground with powerful strokes as it pulled itself through. It hesitated, sniffing the air to detect the location of its quarry. Van Traubben hunched down, motionless, behind a rock.

The bear found the saddle pouches and the horse blanket, tearing them asunder in seconds. The money and gold coins were scattered in all directions. The sound of leather being ripped to shreds by the great claws was unnerving. Van Traubben fired his pistol into the ceiling, hoping the noise would frighten the bear out of the cave. Instead, the enraged carnivore let out a deafening roar and charged the area where it had seen the flash.

As the huge brownish black mass of fur came around the rock, Van Traubben fired his pistol again and missed. He understood that a .38 calibre slug would not be effective against a large bear, and the man fled in terror.

Despite its enormous size and ponderous gait, the bear caught Van Traubben easily with its right forepaw and sent him crashing to the ground. He screamed and fired four shots into the bear's chest and shoulders, but the hideous monster kept coming at him like a runaway locomotive. The last thing that Van Traubben saw in his life was the terrifying sight of an immense snarling head; cold, unfeeling black eyes; long, white canine teeth and jaws streaked with foam.

The bear pierced Van Traubben's groin with eight-inch claws and lifted him high into the air, and then smashing his body against the roof of the cave. The man felt his body being ripped open from belly to neck, and his intestines spilling onto the floor. Hurling his body against the ground, the great bear seized the man's head in its mouth and crushed it like a grape. The bear's incisors penetrated the man's skull easily. His taste was bothersome to the bear, and so it took more than two hours to consume Van Traubben's body.

The Noah's Ark Conception

Neither Alex Van Traubben's body nor the stolen money was ever recovered, and no sign of his horse was ever found. The police team searched the mountains for a week. They were able to follow Alex's horse's tracks as far as the stream at the entrance to the meadow, and then the falling snow had erased every suggestion of a trail. Afterwards, the Federal Police officially changed the nature of their mission to one of recovery.

Frau Elise Van Traubben passed away in Italy, in1967, twenty-one years after her husband had disappeared. She never remarried nor learned of her husband's fate. She had filed a missing person's report, and described her husband as tall, having deep blue eyes, and a birthmark in the form of a crescent moon over his left eye. Later in her life, despairingly, she assumed that he had just abandoned her.

The townspeople of Brig talked about the brazen, daylight robbery for years afterwards, and the fact that the thief had never been apprehended. More tantalizing was the fact that forty-thousand swiss francs in gold and cash might be lying around somewhere up there in the mountains. One of the young deputies who accompanied the Swiss Federal Police Inspector on the pursuit was Gina Ann Schmidt's uncle Mario, and he talked about his adventure and the lost fortune in gold until the day that he died.

<u>Chapter Two</u> – May, 1997: First Attack

"**B**ravo, alpha, one… This is central control… come in, bravo, alpha, one… are you there, over?" the woman's voice barked from the speaker of the police cruiser. A few seconds of unmodulated static noise was followed by the same voice repeating the same message. The police cruiser sat, parked by the side of a small, newly paved mountain road; the red and blue flashing lights on the roof projected their silent warning.

"Paul, can you hear me?" the insistent female voice pressed.

Chief Inspector Paul Soria was about fifty meters behind the vehicle examining a dead Holstein cow that obstructed one side of the narrow, winding road. The animal had been struck by a power company truck at approximately two-thirty a.m., and the Swiss Federal Policeman was checking out the report given by the driver of the truck – a routine assignment. Chief Inspector Soria noted a large hole in the left side of the cow where the vehicle had struck, breaking the animal's back, and the pooled, drying blood on the roadway. Short skid marks attested to the driver's futile attempt at breaking, and a quick measurement taken of the marks indicated that he had not been speeding. The wandering cow was simply at the wrong place and at the wrong time – and so was the truck.

The driver indicated in his report that the cow had walked out of the meadow, directly onto to road in front of his truck. He had no time to maneuver sufficiently on the narrow road to avoid hitting the poor beast. The cow's footprints in the mud by the roadside indicated the direction from whence it came.

"Well, everything checks out." Soria said softly to himself as he noted the extent of rigor mortis. Then he headed back to his police cruiser to answer the call. He made a mental note to notify someone to remove the dead cow quickly, and before it could become a road hazard all over again. He had placed two orange warning cones on the road at a distance of twenty-five meters on each side of the dead bovine.

"Central control, this is bravo, alpha one. What do you have for me, Maria... over?" Soria responded eagerly.

The voice at the other end responded in a relieved tone.

"What's your location, Paul?"

"I'm on Schnell road, investigating the cow impact report that occurred early this morning. Aren't you on duty a little early today Maria, it's only seven forty-five on Monday morning?"

The girl's voice suddenly appeared more serious, and she ignored his question.

"Paul, there's been some kind of an accident up on west face of the Alpenkopf ski area. They need to see you up there right away," the dispatcher announced urgently.

The policeman thought for a moment before answering.

"No one should be skiing up there at this time of year. What was it... an avalanche?" Paul inquired. "And why do they need me to go up? The rescue team should be able to handle it," he insisted.

"The people who called in the report were deliberately vague about exactly what happened. They almost made it sound like a homicide." Maria clarified. The voice clicked off.

"A homicide!" Paul let out a low whistle.

"Okay, that's a different issue altogether. Tell them that I'm on my way, and then contact the Brig cornoner's office and have them meet me at the scene. Tell them to keep everyone away from the immediate area, and I'll be there in twenty-five to thirty minutes. Do you copy?"

"Thirty minutes, chief... I'll let them know," Maria confirmed.

"Oh, and Maria," Paul added. "Get a hold of Johan Edel and have him remove his dead cow from Schnell road, and to finally fix his goddamn fence, please... this is the fourth time I've asked him to do that." Paul insisted, his voice betraying annoyance.

"Right, chief! Central out." The channel went quiet.

The Chief Inspector got back into the cruiser, turned on the siren and motored at a moderate speed in the direction of the Alpenkopf ski resort.

Chief Inspector Paul Soria had served as the chief police officer for the Swiss Federal Police jurisdiction of Brig for the past three and a half years, and in that time there had never been a homicide. Brig was a quiet agricultural and winter resort community of approximately five-thousand residents, nestled in the picturesque northern Simplon valley in the Alps. The gentle, meandering Saltine stream passed along the banks of the town. Its older buildings were decidedly Italian in appearance, but the town's prominent castle was a former Jesuit college and Ursuline convent.

Brig had seen its share of drunk and disorderly people; fatal skiing accidents, motor vehicle accidents and the occasional vandalism caused by impetuous youth, but the last felonious act in Brig hadn't occurred since long before Soria had been appointed as the town's Chief Inspector. In fact, he had just been thinking that the jurisdiction may have been just a little too quiet for his liking. But all of that was about to change, and change radically.

It was a magnificent May morning in western Switzerland. The azure sky was ornate with billowy cumulus clouds, and the high mountain air was clear and smelled sweet. Flowers in myriad colors blanketed the embankments adjacent to the roadway right up to the line of pine trees. It was the kind of day that didn't deserve to be sullied by the gore that Paul Soria anticipated that he'd have to witness by nightfall.

A barrage of questions surfaced in his consciousness as he drove west towards the ski resort: How did the person die? Who might have killed him or her? What could be the motive? Were there any witnesses? What was the time of death? He reviewed a checklist of questions that needed to be answered. A checklist that he used regularly when he had begun his career twelve years ago as a policeman in Geneva; a list that had become rusty and perhaps out of date in the context today's high-tech police procedures. Paul had come to realize that cop shows on TV taught him more about up-to-date police methods than he had ever learned from his days at the police academy. But Paul was a highly decorated police officer due to the cases that he had solved brilliantly in the big city. His promotion to Chief Inspector and reassignment to the jurisdiction of Brig had been his "reward". He had accepted the assignment reluctantly.

After forty-two months in his current position, Paul felt that the time was ripe for requesting a more exciting assignment – somewhere with a resident criminal element that could be more challenging to his police detective skills. Paul had concluded that Brig might be better suited for a senior Federal Police Chief Inspector who had put in his twenty plus years on the "job", and who needed a quiet place to serve out the remainder of his police career before turning in his "papers" and collecting his gold watch and Federal pension.

Well, Paul mused as he drove, *maybe this situation at Alpenkopf will either turn out to be a homicide or nothing significant at all. But at least it's the most exciting thing that has come along in a while. I may as well enjoy it.*

Twenty minutes later, Paul turned into the ski resort area and headed to the main lodge where the administration offices were located. He picked up the microphone of the car's radio and announced, "Maria, I just arrived at the Alpenkopf lodge… copy?"

"Ten four, Paul. I copy. And there's one more thing."

"Go ahead," he responded.

"Gina Schmidt called, and asked what time were you going to be coming by the Brauhaus Café for dinner tonight."

Paul smiled and felt a warm glow. Thoughts of Gina's pretty face and warm personality always made him feel better.

"Tell Gina thanks for the invitation, but under the circumstances I can't make any plans for dinner tonight. I'll try to be there. If not… well, I'll make it up to her," he said apologetically.

"Is there any specific way that I should tell her that you'll make it up?" Maria quipped. She loved to tease Paul about his relationship with Gina.

"Yes," Paul responded. "Tell Gina that I picked up that special book she wanted, and that I'll give it to her as soon as I see her."

"Sounds exciting," Maria continued to prod him.

"You should see what's in this book, Maria… Paul out!"

He deliberately hung up the microphone before Maria could respond, knowing that her inquiring nature would drive her crazy as she tried to imagine what kind of "special" book that Paul had acquired for Gina.

Maria had a secret fondness for Paul, and envied the attention that he paid to Gina Schmidt. Gina was the kind of zesty and free spirited woman that Paul found attractive. While Maria, with her provincial upbringing, which she resented, could not bring herself to do the things or dress the way that Paul found provocative in Gina. Besides, Paul's feelings for Gina Schmidt had obviously evolved into strong bond – as they lived together.

Paul arrived at the administration office of the Alpenkopf ski lodge, and was greeted by a somber-faced and very upset facilities manager who introduced himself quickly by requesting, "What happened up there cannot be allowed to get out… certainly not in the newspapers, because it will just destroy our business and our…"

"Hold on a second," Paul interrupted the jumpy manager's rant.

"First of all, what is your name?" Paul asked politely.

"Fritz Auklund," was the surprised manager's hesitant reply.

Paul stared into the man's eyes. Fritz wore a grey business suit with a clashing orange-pink bow-tie. He looked decidedly out of place in a ski lodge.

"Look Fritz," Paul immediately assumed command of the situation. "I have no idea what we're dealing with here, and I need to see for myself what's happened. Someone mentioned a possible homicide."

Fritz immediately went on the defensive.

"Who said anything about a homicide? I didn't say that! It looks like a horrible accident to me, and..." the manager studdered.

"**Fritzy**," Paul yelled to stop the man's ravings.

"Until I determine precisely what we are dealing with here, I am in charge of the situation now. And in the meantime, none of your staff is allowed to leave the facility until I say so. Do you understand? And no one is going to say anything to the Press."
Paul's intense stare bored into the manager's eyes. Fritz calmed down.

"Meanwhile, I need somebody, namely you, to take me up to where the accident or whatever happened and allow me to begin my investigation."
The manager stared at Paul wide-eyed, without responding.

"That means right now or sooner, Fritz. Verstehen Sie?"
The man snapped out of his trance when he understood Paul's sense of urgency.

"Ja, sure, Ja." Fritz stammered. We have to use the Snow-Cat, because it's a long way up the mountain.

"Then let's get going." Paul insisted.

After a twenty minute bouncy ride uphill on the snow and ice, they arrived at a spot away from the main ski trail and near the border of the dense pine forest. Two ski patrol men and a woman were standing over an area that was reddened with blood, and looking down into a depression in the deep snow. Paul, a case hardened veteran of years of police work, was shocked at the sight that greeted him.

At first glance, the body appeared to have been shattered outward by an explosion, as internal pieces of the corpse were strewn in all directions. Then Paul entertained the idea that the body had been mangled by a big machine or perhaps might have been dropped from the sky after falling, or having been tossed out of a helicopter. One thing was certain: he had never seen human carnage or anything like this before.

Chapter Three

The upper part of the corpse of a human male that seemed to be in his early thirties, appeared to have been severed from the legs by a chain saw. But closer examination revealed that one leg looked to have been pulled out of the hip joint, while the other was more likely to have been bitten off or severed by some kind of rotary blade.

But bitten off by what? Paul considered.

Large tracks of some kind of animal could be seen heading out, and then back into the pine forest. On the surface, the situation resembled a wild animal attack. Half of the man's face was missing, and his bare skull protruded from the lacerated facial tissue. No one said anything as Paul continuously looked over the situation.

"Has anyone touched the body, or has anyone walked close to the body? I need to know that so that we can eliminate your tracks in the investigation." Paul inquired and explained.

All three members of the ski patrol shook their heads.

"This is as far as any of us came," the girl said.

"Does anyone recognize who this guy was?" Paul asked. Then he rephrased, "Or do any of you think that you recognize anything about this man?"

All of the employees indicated negatively.

"Who discovered the body?"

"I did, earlier this morning; when we were setting the explosive charges to create small avalanches," the ski patrol girl admitted.

Paul inquired further, "Is there some kind of heavy machinery that you guys use up here than can mangle a human body like that?"

"Not at this level," the manager answered. "We have snow grooming equipment down below, but we never use it on the slopes or off the main trails at this level... there is no need. Besides, we'd notice something obvious like a body part or blood

25

when we brought the equipment back to the storage barn for the night."

"There's one other thing," the girl redirected. "Both legs are missing and there are no skis, poles, boots or bindings around to indicate that this man was cross-country skiing by himself up here."

Paul realized that the facilities manager and the ski patrol girl were probably both correct.

He decided against searching the man's clothing for identification until the coroner arrived. And while his keen eyes searched the immediate area for clues that might offer a lead or an avenue of investigation, Paul resigned himself to be patient until the coroner made his report.

Then he had an idea.

Picking up his walkie-talkie he radioed Maria,

"Maria, do you copy? This is Paul," he spoke into the mouthpiece.

"Ten-four Paul," was the response.

"Maria, I'm up here on the west slope of the Alpenkopf, has the coroner left yet?"

"He said that he'd be there in about an hour. That was fifteen minutes ago. Why?"

"Do me a favor Maria, contact Wilhelm Redman. He's the local game warden for the district. Would you ask him to join us up here, please? Tell him it's very important. He can get a ride with the coroner."

"I'll take care of it immediately, Chief. I'll let you know what he says."

"Thanks Maria, Soria out."

The manager was curious about Paul's request for the assistance of a game warden.

Paul had anticipated his question.

"I want an expert to identify what kind of an animal made those strange tracks, and to tell me if there's some kind of predator that could do that kind of damage to a grown man. Maybe there are wolves loose up here," Paul postulated.

"Wolves?" the manager responded with a sense of disappointment. "That's all we need is the rumor to get out that we've got killer wolves running around attacking skiers up here. Bye, bye skiers and tourists."

Soria looked up, surprised at the manager's myopic response.

"Look, Fritz," Paul almost sounded reprimanding. "Whatever or whoever did this to this man, needs to be apprehended. Obviously, this guy didn't do this to himself... so I have a big problem and so do you. Namely, your ski area is now officially closed until I determine what we are dealing with up here. And whether that problem is a pack of wolves, a homicidal maniac, the Abominable Snowman, vampires or a horde of rabid field mice, no one skis on your slopes until we identify and capture our perpetrators - whatever they turn out to be. Are we clear on that, Fritz?"

The manager grudgingly shook his head in agreement.

"Good! Now," Paul continued. "I am asking all of you not to reveal to anyone what you saw up here today. If anyone asks you, just tell them that a body was discovered on the slopes and the police are investigating. Don't mention the condition of the body. It's no one's business. Besides, were going to have to notify the next of kin at some point, and I want them to hear about this from me... and not some street rumor that has been exaggerated and distorted to the nth degree."

Paul watched their eyes to make sure that they had understood the import of what he was saying.

"In addition, I'm going to need your names and addresses before you leave, just in case that we have more questions," Paul insisted.

"I can supply those when we get back to the administration building," the manager responded officiously.

Paul considered that the three ski patrol assistants had seen enough and could not be any more use to him. He also didn't want them around when the coroner arrived.

"One more question before I let you three leave," Paul announced.

"Did any of you see or hear anything unusual when you came to work this morning? Did you see any strangers in the area or notice any unusual activity?"

The ski patrollers all shook their heads negatively.

"Okay, you three can go, now. Thank you for your help. You've obviously got the rest of the day off anyway. Just notify everyone else down the hill that all skiing is closed for the day."

Chapter Four

The Valais canton coroner, whose authority includes the township of Brig, Dr. Serge Francois, and the game warden, Wilhelm (Willy) Redman, arrived on the upper slopes of the Alpenkopf ski resort in a Bell, Jet Ranger helicopter at 10:45 a.m. The pilot skillfully brought the craft down on a bare rocky outcropping about three hundred meters from where the body had been discovered. A plume of billowy white snow engulfed the landed craft until the pilot disengaged the powerful rotor.

Two men climbed out of the aircraft followed by the coroner's assistant, a younger woman with reddish hair and wearing a white lab coat. As the trio approached the site where Soria and the facilities manager were standing, Soria intercepted the group before they reached the edge of the depression where the body lay. Soria didn't want the manager to overhear their conversation.

"Thanks for coming up here on such short notice," Soria greeted.

"What have you got here?" the coroner inquired.

"It's a partially dismembered body of an adult male, and no one has any idea of how he got that way, Serge." Soria began. "None of the staff saw or heard anything; the ski patrol just happened upon the body this morning. No one has been down to the body, so all of the tracks around it have not been disturbed."

Soria turned to Wilhelm Redman, the game officer, and explained to him in a low whisper.

"Willy, I need you to tell me if an animal or animals of some kind were responsible for this man's death, or is there the possibility that the body was scavenged after the time of death. And, if some beast did kill this man, what was it and where is it

now? Also, please don't make any comments in front of these ski resort people. They are leaving soon anyway."
Soria then indicated that it was okay to begin the investigation with a motion of his hand.

As the coroner came to the side of the depression, he muttered almost reflexively, "Jesus Christ! What the hell happened here?"

"Wait, before you go down there doctor, please allow me to take a look at those tracks for a moment," the game warden requested; a sense on strong concern was evident in his voice.

Warden Redman walked around the depression carefully, taking care not to step near the tracks. Then after he was satisfied with what he had seen, he motioned for Dr. Francois and his assistant to begin their examination as Redman began following the tracks back towards, and then into the forest. Redman disappeared into the forest and then emerged about ten minutes later... he said nothing. Soria noticed a strange look on Redman's face. It was if he were at odds with himself about something. His expression betrayed traces of deep concern and confusion. Soria stifled his urge to question the game warden at that moment. He would pick a more opportune time later.

Meanwhile, Dr. Francois and his assistant, clad in latex gloves and plastic booties, were busily examining the body and removing items from the man's coat and tattered pants. The items were placed carefully in clear plastic evidence bags that were labeled with a black magic marker. The coroner's assistant took photographs with a Canon digital camera as she worked. She meticulously placed plastic bags over both hands of the body, and another one over the head to preserve any evidence associated with the facial wounds. She executed her tasks with efficiency and an attention to detail that Paul couldn't help admiring.

While the two coroners continued their examination of the scene, Paul went over to warden Redman and pulled him aside to get his appraisal of what had befallen to the dead man.

"What's your take on what happened up here, Willy?" Paul asked.

Willy Redman with a worried, hesitant expression on his face stared at Paul and answered tersely, "I'm not completely sure, Inspector. It's difficult to say under the circumstances."

"What do you mean?" Paul attempted to clarify. "Was this man killed by an animal or not?" Paul pressed his question.

"First, I'd like to wait for the coroner's estimation of what killed this man if you don't mind Chief Inspector. But there was definitely some kind of large animal up here feeding on that corpse."

"What kind of animal, Willy?"

"Well, I'm not exactly sure. The tracks resemble those of a bear. But there's something distinctly different about them, and this would be the largest bear that I've ever heard of," Willy stressed.

"What are you saying?" Paul continued to probe the warden.

"By my estimations, this bear would have to be nearly four meters tall standing on its hind legs, and weigh nearly a ton. The only bears that come anywhere near that size live on Kodiak Island in western Alaska, and are not indigenous to the continent of Europe. And unless a huge specimen has escaped from a nearby zoo, and I haven't heard of any Kodiak bears that have escaped from a zoo, then what is this animal is doing running around up here in a forest in Switzerland? This is a complete mystery to me, Paul. In all my thirty years of experience, I have never seen tracks like that, or animal fur like this."

The game warden produced a dense tussock of brownish-black fur from a plastic envelope in his pocket and showed it to Soria.

"Where did you get that?" Paul asked.

"It was stuck in the bark of a tree back there in the forest where the bear, or whatever it is, passed by," Willy pointed out.

"What are you going to do with it?" Paul inquired, while feeling the course hairs with his fingertips.

"I want to send this sample to a lab I know of in Basel. They should be able to identify what kind of an animal this came from. Meanwhile, I want to make plaster casts of a good representation of front and rear paw prints. Then I'll need to do a little research, and I should have some solid answers for you by the time that the coroner's report is completed. Will that be okay?" the warden requested. "I don't want to guess at anything, Paul. I need to be sure."

"Sure, Willy... no problem," Soria responded with professional understanding.

They were interrupted by the coroner's voice, "Chief, would come here for a moment, please?"

Soria walked over to the edge of the depression and Dr. Franscois handed him the bag containing the dead man's wallet.

"This should identify your victim, Paul," the coroner said.

"Thanks doc," Paul responded as he reached into the bag for the wallet.

Paul removed the wallet from the coroner's plastic bag and was drawn immediately to the initials tooled into the expensive leather: "A. W." The letter "A" was formed by a cross bar tooled into the lower middle area of the "W". It reminded Paul of a branding logo that was used for cattle.

Opening the wallet carefully, Paul looked for a driver's license. He found it without much effort. It was an international driver's license, issued in Zurich to an Arthur Weigel, born February 29th, 1948.

A leap year baby, Paul thought.

The address indicated that the man lived in Geneva, and was a member in good standing of the Swiss Banker's Association. The wallet contained several pictures of what Soria assumed to be his wife and children, and there were more than fifteen hundred Swiss francs inside.

So robbery was not a factor in this case, Soria concluded.

"Okay, we're ready to turn over the body now Chief Inspector," the coroner announced.

Soria replaced the dead man's wallet into the plastic bag, and then observed carefully as Dr. Francois and his assistant turned the body on its back. Except for the impression of the corpse in the snow and the pooled, dried blood underneath, the only thing exposed was a long, curving sharp object that resembled a piece of claw.

The coroner's assistant picked it up, and after examining it, handed it to her boss without a word of comment.

"Doesn't she ever say anything?" Soria addressed Dr. Francois.

"She can't Paul. Celeste is a deaf-mute. She was born that way," the coroner replied.

Celeste had read Dr. Francois' lips, and had interpreted Paul's question from her boss's answer. Then she turned and smiled at Paul. It was at that moment that he realized for the first time how stunningly beautiful she was.

"And what have we here?" Dr. Francois called out. "It looks like a piece of animal tissue – or a claw, and what a claw!"

Soria immediately noticed the very concerned looks on the faces of the facilities manager and his staff.

As Dr. Francois held up the strange object discovered under the body, warden Redman requested, "Can I take a look at that please, doctor?"

The coroner tossed the object to the game warden as Soria walked up next to him to get a better look.

Wilhelm Redman examined the object carefully; turning it over and over in his hand. The broken piece of claw was about four inches long and weighed about a quarter of a pound.

"Is that what I think it is?" Soria asked, in a hushed tone.

"I'm afraid so, Paul," the warden responded with a pronounced sigh.

"This piece of claw only adds validity to what I'm afraid could be running around loose up here, and it also verifies that its size is massive... virtually unbelieveable," Redman added.

"I guess this animal must be really big?" Paul asked glibly.

"Definitely! We've got some kind of a bear on steroids," the game warden emphasized.

"Wilhelm doesn't think that it is a claw," Soria called out aloud as he jabbed the warden furtively in the ribs. "He says that it looks more like a piece of ivory jewelry... like a pendant or a souvenir of some kind."

Soria clearly did not want the Alpenkopf staff to believe anything about a huge claw or the possibility of the animal that it once belonged to.

"Okay, gentlemen," the coroner called out. "We're going to tag and bag the body. And I'm going to need your help carrying it over to the helicopter and getting it secured to the skid gurney."
Paul and the warden nodded, indicating that they'd help.

"Also, Paul, I think that you should put a barricade with a three meter radius around this site, just in case we find the need to come back here and sift through the snow for more evidence," Dr. Francois cautioned.

Paul made an arrangement with Fritz, the Alpenkopf's manager, to cordon off the area with fencing. The manager readily agreed to cooperate.

"How long will the barricade have to be maintained?" the manager asked.

"As long as we decide that it's required," Paul replied.
The manager was not happy with Paul's response.

Chapter Five

It was nearly three in the afternoon before Chief Inspector Paul Soria arrived at his office in Brig. He soon discovered two of his detectives, Meeker and James, were busy fielding questions from vociferous newspaper reporters. The office was a cacophony of dissonant noises: ringing telephones, clattering teletype machines and people shouting to be heard over the racket. He walked into Maria's dispatching cubicle and sat down unobtrusively before he was spotted by any of the reporters.

"What the hell is going on out there?" he asked her. "Who are all of those people?"

"Reporters," she answered in a scoffish tone. Had you not turned off your radio on your way down here, Chief, I could have warned you," she answered, half admonishingly.

"Okay, point taken… so, warn me now." Soria said dryly.

Maria paused and gathered her thoughts. She wanted to put the events in proper order so that Paul didn't have to waste time by having to compose unnecessary questions. She took a deep breath.

"A woman was found, dazed, and wandering on Kugler Road today; she was pretty beat up and she had lost a lot of blood. Someone found her and drove her to St. Boniface Hospital. At the hospital, she tells the emergency room staff that she and two other people that she had been hiking with up in the mountains, were attacked by a large bear." Maria raised her eyebrows.

"Oh shit," Paul gasped.

"Anyway," Maria continued, "detectives Ferrigno and Haustein went up to Kugler Road to check out the woman's story. They are up there right now. The woman is still in the hospital." Maria finished her briefing.

"Thanks Maria." Paul patted her shoulder. "Let me know the minute that our guys call in; and tell them that I don't want them out there after it gets dark. I want to see the two of them back here because we have to talk."

"Yes sir." Maria acknowledged. "Shouldn't I call them in now?" she asked, her voice displaying an obvious concern.

"No, give them another hour, and if you don't hear from them by then, start calling," he answered.

Paul stood inconspicuously outside the men's room door listening to detectives Meeker and James fielding the reporter's persistent and annoying questions.

"We told you guys," Meeker emphasized with a dismissive wave of his hand, "we have no proof that anyone has been killed. For Christ's sake we don't even have bodies to substantiate that anyone has died."

"But what about what the woman in the hospital claimed," one reporter pressed his point.

"Look!" This time detective James fielded the ball.

"All we have is an injured woman that someone picks up on the side of the road; who tells the nurse in the E.R. that the two people she's been hiking with up in the mountains were attacked by a large bear. Are you guys following me so far?"

James paused for a few seconds.

"The woman may have been delirious… on drugs… in shock."

"Look detectives, we're just doing our jobs here, and we want some answers for a story… that's all," one reporter urged.

Exasperation was evident on James' face.

"Now, and get this right this time boys… until we find bodies and confirm this woman's story, then all we've got is just that… **some woman's story**. Am I making myself perfectly clear?"

The explanation wasn't enough for one of the persistent and disappointed reporters.

"But detective, the woman in the hospital **was** pretty beat up. Now who or what do you think did that?"

"For all we know she might have fallen half way down the mountain in her shock and panic. The doctors will tell us more about her condition later," James retorted forcefully.

"Then you **do** believe that something up there terrified her," one reporter asserted in an obvious attempt to obtain a printable direct quote.

"Listen to me you damn word twister." James was now becoming very short on patience.

"I'm going to tell you leeches for the last time. We have no bodies, no evidence, no missing persons and **no facts**. We're done!"

James stood up signaling that the interview was over.

"Now, if you distinguished gentlemen of the press will get the hell out of my way, I can get on with the work that the good townspeople are paying me to do."

"One last question, detective, please… Who picked up the woman?"

"Thar person asked not to be identified," Meeker added.

"Okay, then where's the Chief Inspector? And why isn't he here anyway?" one reporter insisted.

Paul, still standing by the men's room door answered aloud, "I think that he's pulling up outside right now."

The reporters stampeded out through the front door of the police station and into the parking lot; seizing the opportunity to pounce on someone from whom they might obtain more quotable information.

"Nice move, Paul," the detectives noted approvingly. "You managed to get those story hounds off our necks for a while anyway. Thanks!"

"Let's all go into my hidden private office where we can talk," Soria suggested.

Paul led the detectives to a back room that was used as a storage area for old furniture and file cabinets. As they entered, Soria turned on the light and shut and bolted the door behind them. Soria relaxed his usual tough demeanor. He seemed a little relieved that they could not be interrupted.

"What's the hard evidence on this case so far, Meeks?" Soria inquired.

"Well, it was Doctor Solis who picked up the lady on the road while on his way to work at the hospital this afternoon. He didn't want to be identified, but he called in here directly from the emergency room at the hospital."

"What's the injured lady's name?"

"Her name is Hilde Kroner or Kroners, and her driver's license indicates that she's from Denmark. She told Dr. Solis that she's here on vacation with her two male friends. I asked Maria to call Interpol and get more information on her and her friends."

"Anyway, Dr. Solis told me that in his estimation, she was not under the influence of any drugs or alcohol, and that technically she was in a state of shock when he found her lying by the side of the Kugler road. She was just sitting, propped up against the guard railing."

"Did she say anything to him?"

"All that she said, so far, is that a bear killed them both. At this point we have no idea who **they** were, and we don't even know where they were hiking. That's why we sent Ferrigno and Haustein up there to take a look around. Unfortunately, there's a lot of real estate up there," Meeker emphasized.

"We'll probably need a 'copter to search for them," Soria added.

"Yeah, except that we don't have one of those." James noted.

"I'm aware of that. But the lumber company **does** have one. The director of that company owes me a lot of favors for keeping some of his boys out of jail. I think that I can prevail upon him to borrow his aircraft and a pilot for a day." Soria stated as he scratched his head. "But first, we'll need to get a better idea of where those two guys were attacked from the Kroner woman."

Meeker cautioned, "The doctor said she's sedated, and that she'll probably sleep until tomorrow morning."

"That's okay, because I need to brief Ferrigno and Haustein as well as you two on what happened up at Alpenkopf today. I'm afraid that the two cases may be related, which is why I'm bringing Willy Redman in on this." Soria revealed.

"The game warden?" detective James commented with a sense of surprise.

"Correct," Soria confirmed, "the game warden."

Chapter Six

Chief Inspector Soria went back to his office, while waiting for Ferrigno and Haustein to come back from their search in an effort to confirm the injured woman's incredible story. Well trained and well organized, he stood in front of his desk and stared at a framed topographical map of his geographic police jurisdiction located on the wall behind his desk. There was also a push-pin laden corkboard, hanging on the wall next to the map, whereon Paul kept important facts about various cases and current investigations in progress. The board helped him organize at-a-glance the work flow in his command; apportioning out the case load to his cadre of detectives. He felt that he couldn't function efficiently without the aid of his corkboard.

After a few seconds of reflection, he removed a lone, red push-pin from the corkboard, and placed it on the topographical map at a point where the Weigel body was discovered at the Alpenkopf ski resort. Next, he removed another pin, and placed it on Kugler Road, at a spot where he believed that the Kroner woman was found, although he recognized that where she was found was not the site of the bear attack. Then, assuming that the Weigel attack had occurred first, Soria estimated that the bear was probably headed in a southwest or westerly direction. And that would put it on a course aimed directly for the outskirts of Brig – assuming that there was only one bear.

He still had one more distasteful job to do. Soria had to notify the Swiss Federal Police authority in Geneva that Arthur Weigel's remains had been found, and that they in turn would have to notify the next of kin about the man's death. There would be the obvious questions about the cause of death and the disposition of the remains, for which Paul had few answers until the coroner's office completed their investigation. He wasn't looking forward to making the unpleasant call as he picked up the telephone.

Detective Inspectors Peter Ferrigno and Phillip "The House" Haustein arrived back at the police station at nearly six-thirty in the evening. They were both very hungry and grabbed coffee and picked-over, stale donuts from a box in the break room before reporting to their chief's office. Ferrigno was a solidly built Italian. Resembling a fire-plug, he stood only five feet, six inches tall. He had shiny black, wavy hair.

Haustein was German-Irish, stood six-four and was built like a giant commercial refrigerator... which is why he was nicknamed by the other policemen as the 'House'. The two men had worked efficiently as a team for the past two years, and got along surprisingly well. Prior to that time, no one wanted to work with Phil Haustein because he had a violent temper, a huge ego and was generally contradictory and unfriendly. His reputation as an unpleasant partner and an arrogant malcontent caused the other officers to shun him. But Ferrigno seemed to have figured the big man out, and avidly maintained, to everyone else's disbelief, that Haustein was actually just a big softy at heart.

They knocked on Paul Soria's office door and then let themselves in. Meeker and James saw the pair enter the office, and they joined them in the room. After exchanging a few pleasantries and some funny anecdotes about their daily experiences with some of the town's more eccentric residents, Chief Inspector Soria got down to business with an abrupt seriousness.

"What did you guys find up there?" he asked, turning to Ferrigno.

"Essentially nothing, Chief. We started at the place where Dr. Solis said that he picked up the woman. We scoured the woods for at least half a mile on the high side of the road, trying to pick up her trail or some clue as to what happened to her, and then we drove up and down the road for two miles in either direction. We saw and heard nothing; there was no sign of the two men that she claims she was hiking with...niente, nada...zilch... sorry."

He shrugged his shoulders and shook his head.

Soria listened patiently, knowing full well that Ferrigno and Haustein were two of his most experienced detectives who possessed great instincts for police work. He also understood that neither of them were experienced animal trackers – a skill set that wasn't in their job descriptions. He decided that it was time to tie the two cases together, formally.

"Gentlemen, I'll put this bluntly. It appears, at least for now, and until the coroner confirms this theory in the next few days, that the man who was killed up on the Alpenkopf, a mister Arthur Weigel, may have been dismembered by a huge bear."
Soria paused and watched the faces of his men. Meeker let out a low whistle, as Paul continued.

"This Kroner woman's story about a bear attacking her friends is very disturbing, 'cause it is far too coincidental to be dismissed as a hallucination or deliberate fabrication."

"Chief, maybe this guy Weigel you found this morning was one of the Kroner woman's companions," Meeker postulated.

"I doubt it Meeks, because the man was found more than fifty kilometers away from where the woman was located on Kugler Road. She couldn't have travelled that distance in so short a period of time in her condition. Besides, Dr. Francois, the coroner, said that it appeared from his initial examination that Weigel had been dead for at least twelve hours before his body was discovered," Soria emphasized further.

Ferrigno offered a tentative conclusion, "Then it appears that either we may have more than one bear or two separate attacks by the same bear."

"That's the way I'm seeing it too, Pete," Soria added. "And that's why I've asked Willy Redman to join our investigation on this case."

"Why is that, Chief?" Haustein asked.

"Willy got a look at Weigel's body just as we had found him. He says the tracks around the body were those of a very large bear, and he even found clumps of fur, which he's having positively identified at a special lab, and which preliminarily seems to confirm that we may have a rogue bear running around up there. Anyway, all of this evidence seems to indicate that there is real substance to the Kroner woman's story." Soria paused for questions.

"So that means we've got to find those two men she said were attacked and purportedly killed by this bear." Meeker concluded.

"Exactly right, Meeks... and quickly; before scavengers remove all of the evidence. I am planning to interview the Kroner woman at the hospital tomorrow morning to see if she can give us a better idea of where the attack occurred. And if we're lucky, I'm going to get the lumber company to loan us a chopper, and then me and Willy Redman are going up to that place and take a look around."

"Meanwhile, what do you want us to do, Chief?" James inquired.

"Stay close to the fort, keep your ears open for any reports that might be linked to a bear incident; put a pin in my map as to where the incident reportedly occurred. But whatever you do, do **not** say a word about any of this to the press or any civilians... understand? I don't want to give the media anything that they can print until we know exactly what we are dealing with."

"Absolutely, Chief," the four men chorused.

*   *   *   *   **TUESDAY** *   *   *   *

The next morning, Willy Redman, the local game warden, pulled into the parking lot of the Brig police station in a faded green, noisy Toyota pickup. The dense blue smoke, belching out through several holes in the exhaust system, testified to the paroxysms of a dying engine. He turned off the ignition by pulling two wires apart that were sticking out from under the dashboard; but the engine continued to sputter on for a few seconds before coughing to a stop. Willy remained in the front seat for a few minutes; his mind focusing on the possible task before him. Something inside him dreaded his involvement with this case, but another part compelled him to learn more. He was curious about this strange bear that was not indigenous to this part of the world and moreso, to the odd set of footprints that suggested something a lot more sinister than a normal bear.

Willy was a local boy. Withdrawn and aloof, he had just turned fifty. He was a man with a purposeful economy of words that made people uncomfortable in his presence. His bathing habits left something to be talked about furtively as well. Willy always said, "God gave me only a limited amount of words to say in my life, and I have to make each one count." He also had a personal detent going with human society. He shunned the company of people, television, movies and newspapers. Instead, he was attracted by the forest and its denizens – all who lived together in a kind of natural harmonic balance that he could relate to. Willy was a simple man, and took only what he needed to survive. He was a poor student in school; always daydreaming about the splendor of the outdoors, and he cut classes routinely or would disappear into the alpine forests for days. A caring and perceptive school guidance counselor had recommended that Willy obtain his secondary school diploma, and then go to work for the Swiss forestry department, as the counselor felt that it was the kind of a job that was best suited for Willy's personality.

He resented the human habit of polluting the environment, and the compulsive need of society to take more than they gave back to the world. But Willy was pragmatic, and understood that although he cared little for human society, his reality dictated that he still needed to interact with them – in the same way that the eagle lived with the hawk.

If some bear was indeed responsible for the death of Arthur Weigel, then Willy's fear was that the bear would ultimately have to be destroyed. The police would ask for his help in tracking down the animal which they would eventually decide to shoot. This was another example of the conflict and paradox which raged frequently within him. He had an entirely different regard for the bear. It had qualities that should be admired and studied. If the bear **had** attacked, then the victim had probably done something to provoke the attack. *Revenge was never an appropriate justification to kill any animal*, Willy thought as he sat in his truck, watching people go about their business.

The Noah's Ark Conception

Willy enjoyed a good relationship with Chief Inspector Soria. Paul had always treated his fellow law enforcement officer despite the fact the he was a game warden, with respect and friendship. Further, Paul seemed to make allowances for Willy's eccentric nature. Paul Soria was different than most people that Willy knew, as Paul seemed to be compassionate and understanding. He seemed to accord Willy a unique form of respect and appreciate for his contrarian point of view, and so a tentative but evolving bond of friendship slowly developed between the two men.

Sometimes they went trout fishing together. And on those long journeys into the high country, Paul would seek out Willy's companionship and opinions.

When he received word that Paul needed his help with this case, Willy anticipated that it might strain their relationship. But he also hoped that the strength of their relationship would prevail. He trusted Paul's judgment, and respected his tendency to seek advice and not be afraid to admit that he didn't have all the answers – a rare trait in anyone.

Willy got out of his pickup, pushed the creaking, rusty metal door shut and walked up the short flight of stairs to the front door of the police station. He entered and looked around for Paul. He had spotted Paul's police cruiser parked outside, as well as Paul's red, "87" Porsche Carrera. Willy knocked twice on the door to Paul's office. Paul was glad to see him and invited him to sit down.

Soria spent some time explaining to the game warden exactly what had transpired relative to the Kroner woman's story, and how Paul felt that it tied together with what they had concluded in the aftermath of the Weigel attack. He explained further the need to interview Ms. Kroner at the hospital, and then attempt to find the site where she claimed that her other two hiking companions were assaulted. Paul asked Willy to come with him to the hospital, and then to the site where she and her friends had encountered the bear.

"Willy, I really appreciate your help on this case," Paul sincerely stated, "because we street cops are really way out of our element on this one."

Willy nodded his head and added, "You can count on me to do what I can, Paul."

"Excellent, thank you," Paul offered, as he extended his hand to the game warden. Willy's grip was powerful and genuine.

As they were leaving the police station to drive to the hospital, Maria informed Paul that Interpol had called to answer his inquiry. She told him that Hilde Kroner's mother had revealed that Hilde, her brother Dirk, and a friend named Sven Oosterlund had departed three days ago for Brig, and were not due back until the end of the week.

The detectives told Interpol that they suspected that Hilde had become separated from the two boys, and that she must have gotten lost. And the Brig Federal Police were out searching for the boys now.

"Thanks Maria," Paul said gratefully. "We're headed over to the hospital to interview the Kroner girl. I'll notify you when we leave the hospital."

Paul and Willy left the police station and got into Paul's cruiser.

Chapter 7

The huge bear ambled menacingly to the edge of the pine forest and looked out across the adjacent flowery meadow. A wide but low stone wall halted the animal's forward motion temporarily, and it used the pause to scrutinize the area ahead carefully. There was an old chalet in the middle of the clearing, built in the late eighteen hundreds out of field stone and hand-hewn pine boards. It stood, as did most chalets of that vintage, on stone piers that lifted the building about a meter above the level of the earth. The underside of the building was used for storage, and five wooden planks functioned as steps to the front door. A metal stovepipe chimney emanating occasional whisps of white smoke protruded in a twisted arc from the roof. The same family descendants were currently occupying the structure as who had, generations before, constructed the building and farmed the surrounding pastureland.

The bear instinctively understood what the man-made structure represented – a source of food and prey. It focused its cold, black eyes in an effort to obtain a better look. But this bear did not have the keen peripheral and forward vision that had evolved in contemporary bear sub-species. Instead, its eyes were situated more forward in its head along a flat plane, like those of a baboon, and that ran perpendicular to the length of its great body. It needed to turn its head to obtain better detail on its left and right sides, and the animal's depth perception was far less acute than that of modern bears. With objects that were up close, the bear was a formidable killing machine. But objects farther away presented unique problems of recognition. Under those circumstances, the bear turned to its incredible senses of hearing and smell.

Standing upright on its hind legs to gain a better perspective, the bear put it forepaws on the stone wall and sampled the air. The wind brought the scent of cooked bacon, fresh made bread, curing meat and cow's milk. All which immediately stimulated the bear's salivary glands to work overtime. Food was inside that structure – the bear's food, and she wasn't going to share it with anyone. The huge animal let out a low growl.

Fortunately for Felix Ostermann, the old dairy farmer who owned the chalet, he was working in a distant section of the meadow, tending to the delivery of a Holstein calf. The mother had given birth during the night, and the farmer was busily checking the calf for any signs of an abnormality or a disability, and making sure that it was nursing properly. The young animal seemed to be healthy in every way, and the farmer was pleased.

The bear lept over the stone wall easily, charged across the open field and reached the chalet quickly. First it ripped the decorative latticework that concealed what was stored under the house. It was rewarded for its efforts with only farm implements, old rusty milk cans, grass seed and stored fuel supplies such as chordwood and red plastic containers of gasoline. Unsatisfied, frustrated and uncertain as to how to get inside, the enormous bear placed its front paws against the side of the chalet and began rocking its great weight against the building; using its huge feet and claws to gain purchase in the soft earth.

At first the building did not move. But the decades old mortar that held the rocks of the stone piers together- mortar that had survived freezing temperatures and the ravages of melting ice and snow, suddenly began to fail. The grinding pressure of the motion of the bear's efforts caused the mortar to turn to powder. Then excessive play developed between the foundation stones. And with one huge effort, the bear finally succeeded in pushing the small chalet off its eight foundation piers and toppling it, on its side, and onto the ground with a great crash. The old building crumbled to pieces immediately.

The farmer, kneeling nearly a quarter of a mile away and out of sight of his house, heard what seemed like a strange low rumble and felt a curious vibration in the ground under his knees. He looked around briefly and noticed nothing out of the ordinary, and then resumed his task of cleaning up the cow and her newborn calf.

The Noah's Ark Conception

The great bear methodically began to pull apart what remained of the chalet as it searched for the source of the food odors. Ancient wooden planking and stones began flying in all directions as the bear raked the structure with its huge claws. It paused for a while when it found a small box of sugary chocolate mix. The animal enjoyed the unusual treat.

Under the pile of twisted debris that used to be a chalet, the small wood-burning stove had fallen over and the hot ashes from the morning's cooking fire spilled out and underneath the aged, pine wood of the chalet walls. The seasoned wood was tinder dry and quickly caught fire. In minutes the fire was growing rapidly and consuming anything combustible within reach.

Acrid black smoke and flames began to spill out of the rubble, but the bear continued its foragings, attracted by the odor of curing meat and paying no attention to the portion of the chalet that was now ablaze. It glanced at the flames, growled menacingly at the billowing smoke and continued to tear apart what was left of the building.

The pungent smell of the fire was carried away by a gentle cross-breeze and wafted in the direction of the farmer. When the odor registered in his brain that a fire was nearby, he stood up rapidly, scanning the horizon in the direction of his chalet.

"Merde! Merde!" he shouted as the smoke cloud indicated that his home might be burning, and he began running as rapidly as possible back towards his house. As he ran up a grassy incline and reached the top of the small hill, what he saw caused him to stop abruptly.

Aside from the fact that his chalet was no longer standing, and smoke billowed from the portion that was now fully engulfed in flames, the sight of the enormous animal that was busily destroying the remainder of his home was awesomely terrifying and surreal. The sight of the great bear and the emotional impact of his destroyed homestead almost made Felix believe that he was having a bad dream. He dropped to his knees reflexively and stared, mouth agape, as the bear, oblivious to Felix's presence continued to savage the chalet remnants for food.

Felix Ostermann contemplated his next move – he had few options, and chasing the bear away was not one of them. He decided to run downhill, away from the carnage of his old homestead, and towards his neighbor's house. There, he would use the telephone and call the Swiss Federal Authorities for help.

PART   TWO

A   QUIET   LITTLE

TOWN

Chapter Eight

Chief Soria and Warden Redman sat down in Paul's shiny, new police cruiser that was parked next to Redman's worn out and dirty pickup truck.

"I see that you're still driving around without legal tags for your truck, Willy," Soria pointed out. "I'm guessing that your driver's license still hasn't been renewed either."

Soria had no intention of harassing Willy; only to offer a gentle reminder for him to straighten out his affairs with the Swiss Federal DMV. Willy seemed to have a selective disregard for certain types of regulations.

Paul deliberately changed the subject.

"Why don't you join Gina and me at the café for dinner tonight, Willy?"

Willy politely declined by shaking his head, "No thank you, Paul," he responded in his usual terse manner, and not feeling that he had to offer a reason as to why he had declined Paul's considerate offer.

Soria started the police car and headed for the hospital. As they drove out of the parking lot, Paul couldn't help thinking that Willy seemed uncharacteristically troubled by something, his mind appeared to be overwhelmingly occupied, but then Wilhelm Redman always seemed at odds with himself.

*　　　*　　　*　　　*　　　*　　　*　　　*　　　*

The town of Brig is nestled in the Valais Valley, near the Simplon Pass. The Simplon Pass is an ancient glacier-carved passage hewn through the Alps Mountains, and traversed as far back as ancient Rome – used by humans as a convenient conduit between Italy and Switzerland. Hannibal and Napoleon and their armies both used the Simplon Pass on their way to conquest. Today, many resorts, principally used for skiing, have sprouted in the mountainous area of about 650 square miles. Most of the area is very remote, and that land is accessible only to skilled climbers and backpackers.

The valley is surrounded by the Alps, with more than fifty major mountain peaks, some over fourteen thousand feet. Several glaciers still rest within the mountains, supplying melt water run off that feeds the streams and reservoirs of the nearby towns and fills Lake Geneva.

Aside from being the hub of a major vacation resort area, Brig had done little to distinguish itself over its century or so of existence. Throughout the years, the only record of the town's history had been chronicled, in detail, by the resident monks and friars who once occupied a large monastery near the town. The monastery had survived a devastating fire in the early nineteen hundreds, and in 1940, the monastery was closed by the Vatican. The departing friars donated the records to the town's library. The library had the records bound and published and sold to raise money for renovations for a more modern library.

The friars had recorded in high detail each day's events: Births, deaths, weddings, baptisms, accidents and less laudable occurrences, all the way back to the early 1800's. The historical records of the area were kept in such minut detail that the reader could feel the evolving personality and stresses of the maturing territory. It was this book that Gina had asked Paul to obtain.

*   *   *   *   *   *   *   *

Gina Ann Schmidt was born in Lake Como, Italy, to a stunningly beautiful Italian mother, Ann, and a tall handsome German father. On her twentieth birthday, Gina left Italy to live and work with her uncle, Mario, the proprietor of the only café in Brig. Six years later, at seventy-nine years old, he died. And

Gina, having grown fond of the people of Brig – and the townspeople of her, remained to run her uncle's café business. Now, eleven years after emigrating to Brig, she managed a comfortable existence. Although her café was barely breaking even. Her costs were increasing, and the town's senior citizens who frequented her café were dying out. She made out well, but only during the tourist season. She had to take out a loan to modernize the café and stay competitive with numerous other bistros that had opened in Brig over the past three years.

Gina's Italian personality was well-suited to her business. She loved to cook, and was superb at anything she made. Always cheerful and possessing an arresting smile, she thoroughly enjoyed interacting with people; going out of her way to catch a snippet of gossip offered furtively by one of her customers.

Gina could be found humming this song or that as she busily went about her daily chores in the café. She adored music and it played continuously from speakers positioned strategically around the café. She was also a big fan of American, German and British films, although she said that Italian films had too much gratuitous sex and French-made films put her to sleep. She spoke four languages fluently.

Generous to a fault, she would occasionally support, with a meal, one of the townspeople who may have fallen on hard times, or a stray dog or cat. If she was able, she'd attempt to lure the animal into a pet carrier, and then take it to the local veterinarian for a check up and shots.

Her attractive, five feet – five inch body glided smoothly around the counter and tables. Gina had shoulder-length brown hair with blonde highlights which she kept restrained during business hours. Her legs were shapely and slightly muscular; toned during many hours of hiking or cross-country skiing in the mountains. At times when she wore a dress to work, the male customers would linger, sipping their coffee, and enjoying the sight of Gina bending over to clean off a table, or having to reach up to remove something from one of the high shelves.

Her soft, brown eyes were large and round – "bedroom eyes", as Paul had once described them.

The Noah's Ark Conception

Marriage was not in Gina's immediate plans. She valued her independence, and was not interested in sharing her space with anyone else. Although there had been a number of relationships over the years, none of them approached a level where she would consider "the big commitment" as she referred to it. Her major interest, other than the cafe, was researching Brig's history, collecting rare orchid plants and redecorating her diner with local relics and antiques. Naturally, when she found out about the book chronicling the friar's detailed history of the area, she understood immediately that the book was required reading. She was anxious to corroborate her Uncle Mario's tales about a very clever thief who had made off into the mountains with a lot of gold, and who had disappeared forever.

Uncle Mario had made one unsuccessful attempt to locate the lost gold when he was sixty-five, and it nearly killed him. To his knowledge, no one else had ever tried to recover it. The brazen, day-time theft was reduced to a local legend that endeared grandparents enjoyed relating to their awed grandchildren.

Paul Soria entered Gina's life through the side door, literally.

As a the newly assigned Chief Inspector to the jurisdiction of Brig, and a bachelor, Paul insisted on meeting and introducing himself to all of the business owners in the town. He arrived at Gina's café on the one day a week that it was closed – Monday.

She was inside the locked café taking a physical inventory of supplies that were needed when he noticed that the side door had been left ajar. Perpetually suspicious from years of duty in the big city, Paul entered the café and discovered Gina removing the weekend's cash receipts from the store's safe in preparation for making her bank deposit. Naturally, he assumed the worst.

"**Freeze**," he commanded as he confronted her with his 9 mm pistol at the ready.

Gina screamed and dropped the money which scattered all over the floor behind the counter.

In that split second, Paul recognized that Gina's beauty didn't fit the description of any thief that he had ever apprehended, and she had noticed his uniform (which doesn't fit him today, so he doesn't wear it) and concluded that whoever this man was, he wasn't a thief coming to relieve her of her money. Five minutes later, after some awkward introductions and apologies all around, they were laughing like old schoolmates at a class reunion.

One of the first things that struck Gina about Paul was how familiar he seemed. It was almost as though they had known each other for years. His cheerful and self-assured manner attracted her, as did his self-effacing humor. Paul's honesty was refreshing and reassuring at the same time. He did not come across as trying to impress her with his authority or false bravado. Other men did that, but not Paul. Instead he was down to earth, sensitive and very considerate. He had volunteered to pick up all of the money she had dropped, counted it out for her and put it into the bank's deposit bag. Afterward, he offered to escort her safely to the bank. Gina developed a school-girl crush on him immediately, and emerging feelings were beginning to let her know that there might be a place in her heart for this handsome policeman with the attractive smile.

Paul's feelings for Gina evolved at a slower, more purposeful pace. He recognized almost immediately that he was physically attracted to her; it would have difficult for any man not to be. But Paul recognized that he had been attracted to other women in his past, but once he was able to get beyond the sexual compellings, he found most of them shallow and self-absorbed. Needless to say, those relationships ended up on the trash heap of his "been there, did that, got the T-shirt" experiences.

"All looks, and no substance", as he liked to categorized them.

Paul found himself dining more frequenty at the café – particarly after working late and the dinner hour had passed. As the frenetic pace of serving her customers slowed and the evening grew late, Gina would often sit with Paul in his "usual" booth, and discuss whatever they both felt like chatting about.

The Noah's Ark Conception

Their communications were always carefree and light-hearted regarding what was going on in their little hamlet. She was very intelligent and passionate about her feelings which she always articulated impressively. She was knowledgeable about a variety of subjects, well-read, and always current on contemporary world political events. And Gina always made sure to have his favorite dessert on hand at all times: French-crumb apple pie. He always ordered it warm, and with two scoops of home made vanilla ice-cream.

Paul needed Gina in ways that he couldn't define. Yes, she was very easy on the eyes, but she was much, much more than that. She was often on his mind as he fell asleep at night, and he wondered if she was the "one". Still, his experiences cautioned him to take baby-steps with their budding relationship, but he was contemplating asking her out formally.

One evening, as he exited his red Porsche that he parked in front of her café, delicious aromas wafted through the night air hinting of the delicious epicurean treats that Gina had prepared for his late night dinner. And there was a new feeling - a feeling that suggested coming "home" as he walked through the side door; a feeling that Paul found honest, welcoming and comforting. He wondered if Gina and the café represented the sense of stability he so greatly desired, but until now, he hadn't realized that he needed in his life – and further, that his profession rarely permitted.

He found it easy to imagine coming home to her warm smile and welcoming arms at the end of his long day: A refreshing contrast to policing up after the havoc and the pain caused by the area's occasional miscreants.

As he entered the cafe, the scent of rosemary mingled with the sensual, woody fragrance that Gina had seductively and strategically sprayed on her body, and Paul felt that he could easily make passionate love to her right there in her kitchen. But they had not crossed that threshold before. Still, something in her eyes tonight hinted that she was having similar feelings for him. That happened over three years ago.

Chapter Nine

Paul drove his police cruiser into the oval driveway in front of the hospital and found a parking place in the visitor's lot. The morning had started out clear, but grey clouds were moving in from the northwest, darkening the sky. The weather was always fickle at this time of year.

They walked to the reception desk and Paul asked the cheerful, rotund volunteer behind the desk, "Hilde Kroner's room, please?"

"Are you family?" the lady with the friendly smile asked politely.

Paul flashed his police credentials.

"Oh," the woman responded as her face turned very serious.

"Third floor... room three-oh-eight," she answered promptly.

Paul and Willy headed for the elevator.

"Wait, you'll need a pass," the Candy-Striper called out. "Oh, sir...?"

Paul ignored the lady and got into the elevator with Willy. After reaching the third floor, the two men walked to the nurse's station and Paul announced that he was going to question the Kroner woman about her accident. The medical resident, standing nearby, heard the conversation and walked over to address the two men.

"Miss Kroner had a very bad night," the doctor interrupted. "According to the night shift, she woke up screaming at approximately three a.m. She appeared to be terrified from a bad dream; shaking and sweating profusely. The attending physician on duty last night prescribed a medium-strength sedative for her. We injected her at three-fifteen this morning."

"How is she now?" Paul inquired.

"She is awake and coherent, although she is very tired and groggy."

"Can we interview her?"

"Yes," the doctor answered, pointing the way towards her room, "but I'm going to ask you not to say anything that will upset her emotionally. She's in a very fragile state. She is also a diabetic. I completely understand your need to question her, Inspector, but please keep your questions simple. If she becomes too agitated, I'm afraid that I'm going to have to cut your interview short, for her sake."

"We understand, doctor. Thank you." Paul acknowledged. "We'll make this as easy on her as possible."

The three men walked quietly into the Kroner woman's cheerfully bright, blue room. Willy stood close to the door while Paul and the doctor took up positions on either side of the woman's bed. Her eyes were half open and glassy. The medication had done its work well. She was aware of their presence in the room; her eyes attempting to focus on the unrecognizable shapes that moved near her.

"Hilde, I'm Doctor Karl Metzler, and these gentlemen are from the Federal Police and would like to ask you some routine questions. It's okay to answer them, and they will not take up too much of your time or upset you, I promise."

She moved her head slowly and with great effort to accommodate the direction of his voice. She nodded faintly to indicate that she understood and that it was alright to procede.

The doctor motioned for Paul to begin.

"Hilde, my name is Chief Inspector Paul Soria. Can you tell me anything about what happened to you and your friends?"

There were a few seconds of silence as the woman struggled to organize her thoughts. Then her words broke the hushed quiet of the room with the impact of a small explosion.

"The bear tore both of them to pieces," she managed to blurt out. And then the room went silent again.

Dr. Metzler winced at her graphic description.

Paul felt the full force of her words and felt sorry for what she had to have witnessed. He understood the role that he would now be expected to play out in the unfolding scenario until it was finished – the bear or bears had to be destroyed. The responsibility was now completely his. He was grateful that Willy had overheard the description firsthand, and in the girl's own words.

"Hilde," Paul asked, trying hard not to lose his composure, "can you tell us, please, where this horrible thing happened… and when?"

She seemed to take a deep, but labored breath before she answered.

"We had left our hotel, Die Schweizerhof, in Brig early Friday morning to go camping near the Fletschhorn Mountains. We parked the car in a clearing next to the eastbound side of the Italian road, about seven or eight kilometers from the border. We hiked into the mountains, following a broad stream for most of the day."

"What kind of a car were you driving, Hilde?" Paul interrupted.

"My brother, Dirk, was driving a rental car… I think it was a Renault – a blue Renault sedan… a cheap model."

"Who was with you?"

"Only my brother Dirk and his friend, Sven," she answered weakly as her voice began to crack. She rubbed her eyes and tears began to weep out of the corners.

"They were only twenty years old," she managed.

"We're very, very sorry," the doctor managed in a compassionate voice as he placed his hand gently on her shoulder.

They stopped the questioning for a moment, allowing Hilde time to recover from her emotions.

"Do you want anything to drink?" Paul asked.

Hilde nodded yes, and the doctor retrieved a glass of water from the nurses' station. Hilde drank the entire glass.

"Can I ask you to continue?" Paul inquired with a gentle urgency.

"We set up our little tent at four o'clock in the afternoon, while there was still plenty of daylight left. After we finished eating, I took a short walk into the woods to…."

The Noah's Ark Conception

"We understand Hilde; please continue."

"Suddenly I heard an unearthly roar and growling, and then screaming... lots and lots of horrible screaming."

She clutched at the doctor's arm.

"I will never forget those sounds for as long as I live," she stammered, as her tears were flowing profusely.

The doctor squeezed her hand in a comforting gesture.

"And then... all of the screaming stopped. I could hear something thrashing around near the campsite. It was making grunting noises. I was scared... very scared. I started to shake uncontrollably... I just couldn't stop shaking. I thought that the thing – whatever it was, could hear me. I stayed there, hidden in the bushes for a long time. As it got darker and more quiet... then I heard the cracking sounds... like a small branch or a twig when you step on it. I thought that maybe someone was hurt; crawling along the ground."

"What did you do then?"

"I had stopped shaking, and I thought that maybe they needed my help. So I went back to the camp. I went very slowly, so that I wouldn't make the thing come back." Hilde broke into long sobs, followed by almost hysterical crying; her breathing became heavy, spasmodic and irregular.

"I couldn't do anything to help them... I swear it. They were dead... all in pieces. The bear was eating them. It had been cracking their bones with its teeth. **I hate that sound! I hate that terrible, terrible sound!**"

The doctor interrupted the interview, because Hilde was becoming incoherent, and he was afraid that the emotional stress would send her into shock again. Any further attempts at questioning her would be dangerous in her delicate condition and probably futile.

"Gentlemen, I'm afraid you're going to have to leave," the doctor ordered as he pushed the button to summon assistance from the nurse.

"This woman is in no condition to continue with your interrogation."

Paul and Willy recognized that the doctor was right and left the room immediately. They asked the nurse who was running in their direction if there was some place that they could speak privately. She indicated a vacant office down at the end of the corridor. They found it and closed the door behind them.

"Well, what do you think, Willy?" Paul appeared shaken.

"Assuming that the girl wasn't hallucinating, and I don't believe that she was, we now have the corpses of two boys in the mountains and an extremely dangerous animal to deal with. I think that we need to find that blue Renault, and from there, pick up their trail along that stream to their campsite. It shouldn't be too hard to locate, especially if it's been all torn up. But I'm really curious about something," Willy said.

"I don't know any bear to eat a man the way that she described."

"I don't understand, Willy, what do you mean?" Paul pressed.

"When a bear gets old, his eyesight gets bad... his claws broken... he gets arthritis, just like people. If he gets ravishingly hungry, then he might take food that way. But a healthy bear will not eat people. It might attack and kill them... but when they no longer move, the bear loses interest and leaves. If a man stands between a bear and his food, or a sow bear and her cubs, the man will almost certainly get mauled... but not eaten."

"Then you believe that this is very unusual behavior for a bear?" Paul attempted to clarify.

"Unusual? It's downright unnatural." Willy emphasized strongly. "First of all, bears are a rare occurrence in our country. However, the Alps have always provided a natural migration corridor to allow Brown bears to wander here from Italy, France, Germany, and from other countries to the east. Other animal species that were thought to have vanished from Switzerland have recently reappeared: the lynx and the wolf, for example."

"Willy, suppose that the bear was sick... diseased, had a brain injury or a tumor of some kind. Could that cause a bear to behave that way?"

"I have studied ursine behavior in my training, and I have never heard of such a story... except."

"Except what, Willy?" Paul sensed that Willy had hit upon an idea, and that he might be holding back something important. He pressed him for his thoughts.

"In my studies of the history of ancient wildlife indigenous to this region there was a bear, called a cave bear that supposedly died out long ago; the animal was huge and very powerful and could easily have killed a horse or man with a single blow. This bear would eat a man. That fact is clearly depicted in old petroglyphs on cave walls in France. It stood almost as tall as two grown men."

Paul considered for a moment what Willy was suggesting.

"But Willy, let's be realistic here. What are the odds of something like that surviving until the present without being discovered, and then showing up in our mountains today?"

"You're right, Paul. I've been struggling with that myself ever since we discovered those tracks around Weigel's body yesterday morning. I guess the lab report on the fur sample will confirm or deny what I'm postulating." Willy responded.

"Meanwhile," Paul added, "we have the use of the lumber company's chopper and a pilot, and they are ready to go as soon as we get over to the mill headquarters. We need to find that campsite.

Paul and Willy left the hospital and headed northeast to the lumber mill.

Chapter Ten – Tuesday Afternoon

The manager of the Helvetia Lumber Company greeted the two men in his well appointed office just after noon. Paul and Willy politely refused his invitation to lunch; emphasizing the need to pursue their investigation with haste. Paul also considered quickly that Willy would never agree to sitting down at the same table and breaking bread with a man that made his living by destroying the great forest. Consequently, Paul concluded that it would be better for everyone that they should procede with the search for the missing boys with all dispatch.

The manager escorted them to the helipad, where a light blue, Bell Jet Ranger rested with its motor idling. The pilot was going through a stepwise protocol of a pre-flight check and was examining the tail rotor when the three men approached. Willy regarded the helicopter with a combination of awe and suspicion. He had never flown in such a machine before, and his attitude about anything that defied gravity was apprehensive. He was unable to comprehend how a machine could fly without wings – it appeared unnatural.

"Paul, this is your pilot, Bill Dormandy," the manager said as he introduced Paul and Willy. "Well gentlemen, I've got a lumber company to run, and Bill has instructions to take you anywhere that you require." The manager offered his best wishes for a successful search.

"Thanks again for your help," Paul said gratefully as he extended his hand to the manager's.

"Don't mention it Chief Inspector. You've helped us out many times."

Paul completely understood his meaning.

Willy and Paul climbed into the helicopter and strapped themselves into their seats. The pilot, after securing the doors, buckled himself in and placed a radio headset that was suspended from the roof of the machine over his ears. He threw a few switches and engaged a lever. Slowly, the main rotor began to turn. Vibrations in the craft diminished into a constant hum as the machine came alive; the rotating blades diffused into a blur. Willy grew tense and gripped the arm of his seat firmly. The helicopter began to rise slowly from the concrete pad.

"Where to?" the pilot shouted over the din of the rotor.

"Head east over the Simplon Pass road, to a point about eight kilometers from the Italian border, Bill," Paul directed. "We are looking for a blue Renault sedan that is parked in a clearing on the eastbound side. We are trying to pick up the trail of a couple of lost boys."

Paul didn't want to give the pilot any more information than was necessary. He wasn't going to be embarrassed if the search turned out to be a wild goose chase.

Willy hesitated, and then he ventured a glance out of the window. His insides felt strange – queezy. They flew over streams, powerlines, tall trees and deep chasms and finally reached the concrete roadway of the Simplon Pass. Occasionally, he spotted a car or a truck far below. They appeared insignificant. The forest and the snow-capped mountains appeared to spread out as far as the eye could behold – the lush, green carpet of nature's living room. Willy soon began to experience the exhilaration of flight.

So this is what it's like to feel like a bird, he thought.

As his confidence about the stability of the helicopter increased, Willy began to enjoy the flight more. But a sudden downdraft of turbulence reminded him brusquely of his mortality. He gripped the arms a little tighter.

Half an hour passed quickly. Paul, seated in the right front seat of the aircraft, alerted the pilot that they were nearing the area described by the Kroner girl in the hospital. They passed over several clearings; all were empty. A quarter of a mile beyond the next right hand bend in the road, a large clearing appeared on the eastbound side. Two cars were parked there – one was a blue Renault sedan.

"Can you get in for a closer look at that sedan, Bill?" Paul asked.

"I can land this thing on the roof if you'd like Inspector," the pilot responded with a confident grin.

The pilot skillfully maneuvered the craft into the clearing. Sand, dust and gravel were whipped up by the rotor's wash, and their vision was obscured by the flying debris.

"I'm gonna put her down here, Inspector," the pilot confirmed.

"Good idea!" Paul added.

The pilot skillfully brought the helicopter to rest gently in the clearing. Willy noticed how white the skin on his fingers had become, and the pain of the cramps from gripping the seat so hard.

After all of the suspended dust began to settle, Paul could read the license plate on the Renault sedan. The tags designated a rental car.

"Bill," Paul requested, "Would you radio in a request to DMV to confirm license tag "47046HHQ" as a rental car, and ask them who was it recently rented to?"

"Roger, Inspector."

Paul and Willy climbed out of the helicopter to examine the vehicle. Paul felt the hood – it was cold. Meanwhile, Willy examined the ground the the car.

"This car has been here a long time; three, maybe five days,"he noted. The tracks around the car indicate three people. The driver was a man... 180 to 200 pounds. He wears hiking boots. The smaller man's right foot is turned inward... maybe he limped... he's wearing sneakers. They had packs in the car and they put them on while sitting on the rear bumper – here. The bigger man is very strong," Willy rattled off his observations like a data dump.

"You can tell all of that just by the tracks?" Paul was amazed at Willy's acumen.

The two men peered inside of the locked car. Willy noticed the cigarette butts in the ashtray.

"The driver smoked too much... not a good idea for a man who is going to be climbing around in the high mountain passes."

Willy continued to follow the tracks out of the clearing northeast, towards the densely forested mountains.

"Inspector," the pilot summoned, "I just got a confirmation on that license." Paul trotted over to the chopper.

"The car belongs to the Alpin-car Rental Company, and was rented four days ago to a Dirk Kroner. Does that make any sense?"

"That's the one," Paul acknowledged. "Tell them to notify the rental agency that we found their car, and that we're going in to search for the two boys."

After a few minutes Willy returned.

"They could travel maybe three or four miles a day – no more with those heavy packs and the man with the limp. The stream is over there, and it looks like they went the way the girl said they did," Willy estimated.

"Okay," Paul said, "let's see if we can locate their campsite by following the stream."

Both men climbed back into the helicopter, and this time Paul motioned that Willy should ride in the front seat, as he was the better tracker.

"You navigate, Willy. Be sure the pilot follows the course of the stream. I'll watch for signs of a campsite."

The helicopter climbed back into the air and advanced carefully up the mountain at a constant height of two hundred feet over the ground. Willy could follow the path of the meandering stream easily. Along the way he saw two red deer, fox and and several hawks. He enjoyed seeing the animals from his vantage point and wondered at the marvelous machine that enabled him to soar like the birds.

The stream twisted left and right, and at some points it doubled back on itself. They were following the stream at approximately five miles per hour, affording ample opportunity to search for the campsite.Close to the seven thousand foot level, the mountain leveled off into a narrow plateau. The stream had widened and backed up into a small pond. They spotted the campsite at the far end of the pond. Paul and Willy saw it simultaneously.

"There!" Willy indicated with his finger.

"It looks like a dump. There's litter strewn everywhere," Paul noted.

"I can't land there," the pilot noted. "I'll have to look for a clearing closeby."

Paul gave the pilot the "thumbs up" sign, indicating that he understood. They found a clearing sufficiently wide enough to accommodate the helicopter about three hundred meters to the south. The pilot sat the aircraft down with great care, making sure that the rotor blades were well clear of any overhanging branches. He turned off all the power to the engine.

The three men climbed out of the chopper and headed through the dense woods towards the campsite. Fifteen minutes later, after picking their way through the tangled undergrowth, they arrived at the perimeter of the camp. The three men stood rigid, in absolute silence; their eyes trying to comprehend the devastation spread out before them. It was obvious that something horrific had occurred. Paul tried to imagine what could tear apart a camp with such thoroughness and apparent viciousness.

Paul's eyes quickly picked out the remains of a human arm. Three fingers were missing. Willy saw the huge paw prints...an icy spasm shook his spine. He had never seen such large, perfectly formed tracks. Clearly, it was those of a bear of immense proportions. It appeared to weigh over a ton; with claws six inches long. Bits of human bone were scattered about everywhere.

Paul was the first to break the pensive silence.

"Willy, I want you to go in first an examine everything. I want to know what happened here, and in as much detail as you can provide."

Willy entered the campsite, and for the next twenty-five minutes, he inspected each piece of shredded bone, clothing and equipment and all of the ground in and around the camp. He felt the ashes where the fire had been and removed a tuffet of the strange fur from the bushes. It was then that Willy noticed a large, moist patch on the ground. Crouching, he picked up some of the damp earth and rolled it between his fingers. His fingers turned red. He was startled by a red drop that fell on his shirt sleeve – blood. The game warden looked up and saw the lower torso of a man's body, with one leg still attached, wedged tightly in the crotch of a tree twelve feet above the ground.

All of the men saw the remains, but the helicopter pilot lost his lunch in a reflexive action of stark nausea and horror. The leg, mangled and partly eaten, was hanging grotesquely from the limb. A white Nike tennis shoe attached to the foot added to the macabre impact of the scene. The bark on the trunk had been stripped away in a series of parallel groove marks augered into the wood. Strips of shredded wood were hanging everywhere.

Willy made a few short trips into the surrounding brush and then returned to join the other men. They waited as Willy formed his thoughts. He continued rolling the strange fur-ball between his fingers and smelling it. His face conveyed an inner conflict: a struggle to sort out the natural from the unnatural. Then he looked up at Paul.

"What happened here was an act of nature. These men were attacked and killed by a very large bear... a very large and healthy animal. The bear had stalked them, and then attacked from that thicket. Both men were killed and eaten. The big man was eaten first. The man who limped is in that tree. The bear stored the body there... it will come back to eat."

"You said that it was a healthy bear, Willy, why?" Paul was intrigued by his deliberate statement that contradicted what he had said earlier that morning.

"Because healthy bears just do not eat people," Willy answered emphatically.

"Then why did this animal eat them?" Paul pressed his point.

"I don't know," Willy replied, dropping his eyes to reinspect the fur which he continued to roll compulsively between his fingers.

Paul could not help noticing the game warden's movements.

"What is that Willy?"

"It's another piece of fur from the bear… like the one I found yesterday at the Alpenkopf accident."

"What kind of a bear are we dealing with…a grizzly or a brown?" Paul questioned.

"Not a grizzly; not a brown," Willy responded confidently.

Paul had never known Willy to be inaccurate.

"Willy, are you trying to tell me that this bear is not a native animal? And are you suggesting that it might be a bear from another country… maybe an escaped animal?"

Willy did not answer. He simply did not know.

A number of possibilities emerged in Paul's head. An escaped bear: a circus train wreck or animal cargo that was bound for a zoo. All were within the realm of possibility.

"I'll submit this sample to the same lab where I sent the other one." Willy offered. "They should be able to clear up the mystery of what kind of an animal that we are dealing with."

Chief Inspector Soria started picking carefully through the shredded debris, looking to confirm the identity of the two men. He discovered what he was looking for under the tattered remains of the tent. Paul opened a brown, leather wallet, noted sixty-five swiss francs in cash and removed a driver's license.

"Sven Oosterlund, date of birth: 8 July 1977."

"I think this pretty well confirms who the boys were, Willy."

Paul seemed satisfied.

"And robbery certainly wasn't a motive here," he added.

"Yeah, just like the Alpenkopf killing," Willy agreed.

"Now we need to positively identify the other boy."

"Look under that bush," Willy spoke solemnly.

Paul walked over to a small juniper and pushed the shrub aside.

"Jesus fuckin' Christ!" Paul jumped back, repulsed. The parted shrubbery revealed the head of the second boy – the one stuck in the tree, and Hilde Kroner's brother. The eyes were open and sunken deep into the skull… staring forward without focus or comprehension. The expression on the face betrayed a snap-shot of a last conscious perception of unearthly horror. All of the insects gorging themselves on the head did not mind its gruesome countenance.

"We'll head back down to Brig now and get the coroner's people up here. I've seen enough," Paul stammered in disgust.

"What do you make of those marks, Willy?" Paul said, pointing to the deep scratches up in the tree.

"Woodpeckers," Willy answered, in a futile attempt to create some levity in a difficult situation.

"Seriously," Willy corrected himself after he realized that his attempt at humor had failed. "Those are the marks of the weapons that the bear used to kill these boys."

The remark had a stunning effect on the pilot.

The three men returned to the helicopter, each absorbed in the conjurings of their own mind's eye, the likely yet horrible events of the deadly attack. They tried to comprehend the horror experienced by the two boys confronting the jaws of death; and that of the young girl witnessing the consumption of her brother and friend. And how she would retain and more importantly deal emotionally with that macabre image for the rest of her life.

Why had the bear attacked them? Paul wondered.

Willy's assertiveness about bears not eating humans was an apparent contradiction in view of the facts at hand. The size, viciousness and possible alien nature of the animal disturbed him. He knew now that the animal would have to be hunted down. Willy's uncharacteristic uncertainty about the bear bothered Paul most of all. The three men discussed nothing on the flight back to Brig.

Paul asked Willy to come into the office, as he wanted to construct a situation map, and to plan the next step actions that needed to be implemented.

Chapter Eleven

When Paul entered the police headquarters in Brig, he immediately began barking orders at the inspectors on duty. What was a relaxed, routine atmosphere seconds before suddenly surged into frenzied activity; much in the same way as a hornet's nest comes alive after being pummeled with a baseball bat.

"Get me the Coroner's office on the phone. Get in touch with Interpol and tell them that we've got two Danish citizens, in pieces, up in the mountains and we'll need someone to positively I.D. the remains... whatever it is that they finally end up with. Now, somebody call the news services... Reuter's... I don't care, and quietly... I repeat, quietly, determine if there had been any reports of escaped large, predatory animals or any accidents involving transported animals. Get a tow truck out to a clearing on the eastbound side of the Simplon Pass road and retrieve a blue Renault sedan that is parked approximately eight kilometers from this side of the Italian border. Somebody get me pictures of all the goddamn bears in the world from the library or somewhere. If any more freakin' reporters show up tell them that I'm in a meeting and can't be disturbed. I'll issue a written statement at six o'clock tonight...any questions?"

"Chief," one of the Inspectors timidly attempted to slow down the runaway train that was Paul's vociferous diatribe.

"**What?**" Paul roared back, annoyed that one of his subordinates might not have understood his orders.

"I've got the Valais Coroner's office on line 2," replied the Inspector.

"I'll take it in my cage. Willy, come inside with me, please."

The men entered Paul's private office and shut the door. Seconds later, the door flew open and Paul yelled, "House!"

"Yes sir, Chief," the big detective snapped to attention.

"Do you enjoy working for me, House?"

"Well, uh, sure sir," he replied hesitantly, not sure that he understood the gist of the question.

"Then get me a fresh pot of coffee and some push pins from the supply room," Paul ordered, uncompromisingly. "And while you're at it... get a haircut."

"Yes sir; right away, Chief."

The office door slammed shut again.

Everyone in the office was startled. They had never seen Paul lose his composure like that before. He certainly had their attention as well as their surprise.

Paul picked up line two.

"Hello, this is Chief Inspector Soria," his tone was much more professional now.

"Two boys have been mauled and killed by a bear, while camping up in the Fletschhorn Mountains, a few kilometers from the Simplon Pass. We just came back from there. Yes, we're pretty sure we know who they were, but they were both torn to pieces and chewed up badly. One of the bodies is hanging out of a tree," Paul recounted.

"Of course I know that bears don't usually eat people... maybe this one's a gourmet... what the hell do I know?" Paul's voice showed signs of his agitation and strain.

"Look doc, we were out looking for two lost boys... so we didn't bring any body bags. If you call Bill Dormandy, the helicopter pilot for the lumber company, I'm sure that he'll gladly take you and your ghouls up there," Paul snapped.

"Sorry, doc... yes, you're right... I apologize. It's been one helluva day here... I **was** outta line," Paul said contritely. "I take back the word ghoul... you're right...I was outta line."

Paul listened respectfully for a moment.

"I'm sure you've never seen anything like what we found up there. Pieces of bodies are strewn all over the place... it looks like a freakin' war zone...and yes, I'll forward a copy of my report to your office tomorrow afternoon. Oh, and doc, make sure you bring a ladder with you to get that body out of the tree. That's right, the tree... you'll understand when you get there."

Paul hung up the phone and walked over to his map and corkboard which hung on the wall behind his desk.

"Now," Paul began by scratching his head, and looking for a spare pushpin, "Where the hell is House?"

At that moment the office door flew open and the doorknob struck Willy in the backside. House looked surprised, as he stood there dutifully, with the coffee pot and the pushpins in his hand. The door bounced off Willy's butt and headed back toward's House's nose. There was the clattering sound of objects falling to the floor, and the sight of fresh, hot coffee oozing under the office door.

Phillip "House" Haustein opened the office door slowly and carefully, reluctantly peered around it; not knowing what to expect. At a minimum, he expected another verbal tirade from his boss. Craning his neck around the door, he held out the coffee soaked box of pushpins. Paul glared at him for a second, and then broke out in raucous laughter. House had managed to break Paul's mood and all the tension in the office with a totally spontaneous piece of comedy right out of a slapstick film.

"Willy," Paul began, "I have a lot of paperwork to do this afternoon, and some important phone calls to make. You and I need to make plans to hunt down this rogue animal. What do you think, as the game warden of this jurisdiction, should be our plan of action before this bear kills again?"

"First, Paul, I think you should officially close the forest and the mountains to all hikers, campers and cross-country skiers. Second, I think that you should issue a strong warning about the attack and advise people to keep a sharp eye out for any bears and avoid them at all cost. Third, I think that your men should post these warnings at all major trailheads, resorts, hotels…anywhere that people might be tempted to wander into the woods."

Paul listened attentively and responded, "I'll issue a statement to the press tonight at six; have it printed and broadcasted immediately. I'll try to get some extra help from Federal Police Headquarters in Bern on the search for the bear."

The Noah's Ark Conception

Chief Inspector Soria understood that his department bore the lion's share of the responsibility in managing this situation. Willy's uncertainty about the animal's origin added to Paul's feelings of isolation and aloneness. He knew that this situation was going to demand the limits of his physical endurance and professionalism.

Paul had one more question.

"Willy, when do you expect to hear back from that lab on what kind of an animal we are dealing with here?"

"Tomorrow at the earliest, but more probably the next day. If I don't hear by that afternoon, I'll call or go over there myself," he declared.

Willy drove home that afternoon, his mind absorbed with a deep sense of dread for his friend Paul. He also feared for the bear. The animal had violated human law, and thus had condemned itself to death. In the act of being itself, the bear had committed no crime against nature's laws. Willy was profoundly troubled by the conflicting motivations he felt. On one hand, Paul had to discharge his sworn duty as a law enforcement officer and to follow the orders of his superiors. If Willy failed to provide his help, his good friend or one of his associates would surely die in the attempt to implement his responsibility. On the other hand, this bear was a great animal, and put on the earth by God in the same way that was man. In conspiring to help destroy the animal he would be guilty of murder in God's eyes as if he had destroyed one of his fellow men. Willy's mind searched unsuccessfully for a solution to his dilemma. He needed to seek the guidance of someone far wiser than himself.

At six p.m., Chief Inspector Paul Soria appeared before the members of the press and announced the details of the terrible tragedy to the world. During the course of fielding the reporter's questions, it became apparent that what had occurred was indeed unusual, and that the public was expecting a quick and finalized resolution to the problem. The summer vacation season was nearly upon them, and no rebellious and uncooperative bear should interfere with the commerce.

Gina Schmidt watched Paul's news conference on TV. When it was over she switched off the set and began to prepare one of Paul's favorite dinners. She sensed that he would be very troubled and stressed out when he came home tonight, and she had some very special TLC in mind.

Gina always described herself as a simple person with simple needs, and yet those defining characteristics were rich in the core family values imbued in her as a child: Honesty, spirituality, taking complete responsibility for her actions and an unquestioning acceptance, devotion and above all love for those around her. She was a hard worker, a frugal spender, a bit of a worrier and she was well read and fluent on issues pertaining to the nutritional value of her meals. She didn't believe in entitlements, possessed a strong sense of personal confidence in her innate abilities and she exercised her body and mind daily. Fiercely independent, she passionately believed that no woman should ever become dependent on a man and even moreso, she was cautious and guarded against becoming vulnerable, and she understood her weaknesses well. Until she was thirty-five years old, the only men who ever lived under the same roof as she were her father and her uncle Mario; both were now deceased.

When Paul came into her life three years ago everything changed dramatically. He was the first man who ever accepted her as a complete human being, and he never once attempted to impose his masculinity on her. It was apparent from the beginning of their relationship that a very special chemistry existed between them and that he accepted her as an equal. She wasn't just another pretty face or an attractive or shapely body, but Gina was someone he could confide in – unburden his mind with her in confidence, and they seemed to have so many things in common. Both were fans of all kinds of music and they liked the same kinds of films. On many a rainy or snowy Sunday afternoon, Gina would make up a batch of hot buttered popcorn, and they'd watch a rented movie together: she with her head on his lap and a box of tissues by her side. Paul didn't mind watching "tear-jerkers" as he put it. They became a conduit that allowed him insights with which to better understanding Gina's emotions, and the way that she perceived and evaluated her world. He called them VIP's: "Virtual Impersonal Personals", because together they could experience and discuss difficult emotions without having to live or to suffer them in real time. No man had ever before appealed to Gina's deeply emotional side nor come close – but Paul was the exception – and maybe the "one".

He was a real "man" in her lexicon, and she realized that he was potentially a real catch. Paul attracted Gina with his warm smile, outgoing personality, can-do approach to life and most importantly, the way that he sought out and respected her opinions.

Their relationship began with instant infatuation, followed by a brief but intensely emotional phase of testing each other; not unlike two wrestlers entering the ring as opponents for the first time. Their cautions and their wariness were the ground rules – each yielding little at first in admitting that there **were** feelings of attraction between them. They communicated paradoxically: in a circumspect, yet at times in a head-on manner. The resultant confusion nearly broke them apart, until one day they finally admitted to each other, after not speaking for over twenty-four hours that neither of them enjoyed the lonliness. Paul sat down and after a detailed and honest confrontation of his feelings he took the time to write Gina a poignant love letter wherein he delineated all that she had come to mean to him. After reading his revealing missive, she undertood that he had fallen in love with her, and they promised themselves that they would discuss all future issues, no matter how difficult, openly an honestly. As a result their relationship cured and solidified. The way it seemed to be with two very strong personalities.

Together, Gina and Paul discovered the meaning of synergy: When they were together, their lives were better than their best days apart. And six months later, Paul moved in with Gina in the cozy apartment above the café. The two of them could never remember being happier than at any other time in their lives. Paul discovered to his profound delight that Gina had been a previously untapped wellspring of intensely passionate sensuality, energy and deep flowing love. She became his soul mate and his refuge. Exactly the way that she hoped it would be.

Paul arrived home at seven-thirty. He was thoroughly exhausted. He held Gina close and kissed her tenderly on the mouth. She could see the toll that the day's events had taken on his soul. She could read it easily in his eyes. She always could.

"Why don't you grab a quick shower, Paul," she suggested tenderly, "and when you come out, I'll have dinner ready for you. I told Consuela to close down the café tonight because I thought that you'd probably need me here when you got home. I saw your TV debut at six, tonight."

"I love you, Gina," was all that she heard him say as he began running the water in the shower.

She never asked him about his day, as she deliberately did not want to reinforce any bad habits of bringing work home to their comfortable sanctuary. He referred to it as their "inner sanctum sanctorum". It sounded good, so she never asked him to define what that meant exactly.

When Paul had finished with his shower he felt much better and refreshed significantly. He put on his pajamas and robe and sat down at the kitchen table. Gina placed a bowl of her best, home-made, chicken with barley soup in front of Paul, and he waited politely for her to sit with him. She augmented the broth with ditalini pasta, and chopped fresh basil and parsley…his favorites. Then she shredded some fresh Parmesan cheese until he indicated the right amount had been added. She placed a slab of sliced garlic bread, wrapped in aluminum foil, next to the bowl.

Gina, her brown hair in a pony tail, was wearing a black, button-front Moroccan caftan, with large, embroidered silver roses across the bodice and on the sleeves, and she had deliberately left the buttons undone from mid-thigh to the brocaded hem. She wore her favorite "pontuffles" – bedroom slippers with padded, furry lining that nearly covered her ankles. "My feet get cold easily," she always maintained.

When she sat down next to him she crossed her legs, permitting Paul a generous glimpse of her shapely thigh; its' milky whiteness in stark contrast with the black caftan. She saw his attention shift immediately.

"See something you like?" Gina articulated with a seductive whisper.

"Yes ma'am, as a matter of fact, I do," Paul emphasized with deliberately raised eyebrows and a broad smile.

She toyed with him.

"No, silly boy... I meant in the soup." Gina couldn't stifle her own broad, impish grin.

Without warning, Paul slid the book that Gina wanted so badly off his lap and placed it on the table next to her.

"The Chronicles," Gina exclaimed gleefully. She picked up the friar's volume of the town's history, examined it quickly, and then realized that this was not the appropriate time to review its contents.

She kissed him on the cheek hard.

"Thank you, darling," she said gratefully. I'll look at this before I go to sleep tonight.

Paul completely understood the power that Gina had over him sexually. In one moment she could be soft, casual and very feminine, and in the next second she could be powerfully seductive, incredibly sensual and a passionate, full-throttled lover; bringing into play all of the allure that her incredibly attractive body commanded. And Gina could flick that switch with a turn of a phrase, a seductive motion or with a nod of her head. She was an amazing woman. She understood exactly how to please him.

But tonight, Gina had sensed that Paul needed a tender loving companion (Gina's definition of TLC), and she would allow Paul to have her in any way whereby she could assuage his needs.

He would feel like a new man before they fell asleep, entangled in each other's arm that evening. Gina would feel satisfied, very loved and complete. What had happened during the day suddenly didn't seem to matter – for the moment.

Despite their intense happiness together, Gina and Paul never discussed marriage. And while everyone in the town who knew the two of them believed that nuptials were a foregone conclusion, Gina and Paul understood that whatever fates had brought them together were also testing them.

There was no question about the depth and quality of the love and respect that they shared, but they also understood the necessity for small steps as their relationship intensified. Neither of them was given to making rash decision or "jumping to concussions", as Gina liked to put it. Instead, they envisioned their relationship as akin to navigating in a maze. Recognizing the complexity of their personalities and their fierce sense of independence, they regarded each day as a new adventure: one that was to be shared, enjoyed and experienced, and one that tested their bond. And while they both hoped for the same outcome – lifelong togetherness, the legal piece of paper brought with it imposed limitations that both of them would rather live without for the moment.

Paul recognized that Gina had the responsibility and her love for the café in her life long before she met him. He was not about to insinuate himself into that part of her life. Similarly, she recognized that his police responsibilities were stressful and very demanding and as such, she couldn't expect him to keep regular hours. They would simply have to work all of that out as part of the dynamics of the relationship.

They did derive tremendous satisfaction from their uncanny compatibility and their commitment to one another. That seemed to be what mattered most from an overarching perspective. They both felt confident that everything else would work itself out, and they would arrive at a point together when the appropriate timing for the "big step" would become very evident. Such was their relationship at that moment.

Chapter Twelve – Wednesday

Paul awoke at six-fifteen a.m., after some early morning dreaming that left him feeling unrested. Intervals of waking and sleeping throughout the night had done little to replenish his strength. His clouded mind – the incessant video tape of his experiences, kept looping visuals of the previous day's events at the ravaged campsite. He needed to focus his thoughts.

His hand crept across to the other side of the bed. He found it empty and cold. Gina had been gone for a while and was already at work downstairs in the café. Adjusting the water temperature for his shower, Paul could feel the gnawing hunger pangs in his stomach. He deliberately spared Gina from an unburdening of his experiences from the day before.

Why ruin two people's days? He thought.

Besides, he would get to see her again before he went to work when he showed up downstairs in her café for breakfast.

The outlook for the day is already improving.

Buttoning his khaki shirt, he picked off a long strand of Gina's hair. Suddenly, his mind connected with the strange fur sample that Willy had discovered and had sent to the laboratory for identification. Paul wondered what secrets the sample might reveal. Paul couldn't understand why the fur sample seemed to have such a peculiar effect on the game warden, and Paul was anxious to have the results of the lab's analysis as quickly as possible.

Paul walked into the café at ten past seven a.m., and looking down the aisle he could see Gina scurrying with the coffee cups full of hot liquid caffeine balanced precariously in her hands and forearms. It was no wonder that she had so many burn marks, he deduced.

Gina saw him walk in and motioned for Paul to sit at the counter, where she could chat with him as she worked. She put a fresh place setting in front on him, followed by a cup of coffee and a large glass of fresh-squeezed orange juice.

"Good morning, Kemo Sabe," she greeted him with a quick kiss and placing her hand on his shoulder as she came around the counter.

"And what would my favorite lone ranger like for breakfast today? It seems to this heroine that you are gonna have to replenish a lot of **ammunition** in that gun of yours before you go out and fight the bad guys today," Gina quipped, her innuendo clear enough.

"You seem to be in a spirited and cheerful mood this morning young lady," Paul noted approvingly.

"As if you had nothing to do with it, I suppose?" she retorted.

"Guilty as charged, you gorgeous creature! Now, how's about ya rustle me up some grub… make it the usual, pardner," Paul tried his best western accent.

"Comin' right up thar sheriff," Gina rejoined.

Paul turned sideways in his chair and quickly scanned the legion of customers in the café. The usual gang of devoted regulars had shown up and more were arriving in the parking lot. It was a genuine testimony of the townspeople's loyalty to Gina and their love of her good home cooking.

When Gina came back to Paul's end of the counter her eyes betrayed an excitement that he had not seen earlier.

"Paul," she began excitedly, "I found a passage in the town Chronicles that deals with the robbery."

Gina could barely restrain her enthusiasm.

"What chronicles, and what robbery are you talking about?" Paul shook his head in emphasized confusion.

"My uncle Mario told me a story several times about one of the major historical events that happened here in Brig…in 1946 to be exact." Gina slid in the seat next to him and grabbed his arm.

"Oh good," Paul exhaled. "I thought that I had yet another case to work on in addition to everything else that's happening in my area of responsibility right now."

"Well, wouldn't you like to solve a robbery and perhaps a murder that's been on the books for over half a century?" she inquired, her eyebrows raising as she touched his arm.

"Not particularly, Gina," Paul chuckled. "If the case has managed to stay unsolved for half a century, I think that the resolution can wait for a few weeks more...don't you...at least until we get this current problem resolved. Besides, I'm guessing that the prime suspect is probably dead by now."

"Hey Gina, can I get some more coffee?" One of her customers inquired impatiently.

She looked up at him.

"You know where it is, Luke. Would you mind helping yourself?" she shot back.

"Paul, please listen to me, the Chronicles confirm that there was a bank robbery here in Brig, on April 27th, 1946. The thief got away on horseback with nearly forty thousand in gold and swiss francs. That was a lot of money during the post war era," Gina emphasized by squeezing his arm.

"That's still a lot of money today," Paul confirmed matter of factly.

"Anyway," Gina continued, "the police had chased this guy who robbed the bank all the way up into the mountains, and then they lost his trail in a freakish, spring blizzard. It just ended near a stream." Gina raised her arms in emphasis.

"Why do all great adventures have to end near streams or ponds?" Paul quipped, a clear reference to the previous day's carnage.

"But Paul, you're not listening. No one ever recovered the gold or the money. It was never seen again. It must be still up there somewhere."

"And I know why," Paul added in the facetious spirit of one upsmanship, "A giant bear came along, ate the thief, devoured the gold, and all we have to do is find a big wealthy bear with brand new gold fillings and we've solved the case...right?"

Gina stopped herself. "Paul, I'm sorry," she said with a twinge of embarrassment. "I've been running off at the mouth about my discovery in the book that you were so nice to get for me, and I've ignored your problem with this bear. I heard about the two boys last night. I guess that maybe I've been a little insensitive to what's been going on. I mean... everyone here at the café has been talking about it in one way or another," she said apologetically.

"You have also forgotten to bring me my breakfast, my darling, and I'm going to have to leave here in about seven minutes," he chided her as he kissed her on the cheek.

"Oh rats!" she exclaimed and headed into the kitchen.

Paul couldn't help but smile as Gina raced off to retrieve Paul's breakfast.

That's my Gina. He mused. *And that's why I adore her so.*

Gina returned quickly with Paul's bacon, eggs and toast, and dutifully refreshed his coffee.

"Paul, just one more thing on the robbery issue," Gina renewed her conversation. "I found no reference in the Chronicles to indicate that the gold was ever recovered. I believe that if the thief managed to get away, he did so because he buried the gold up there somewhere; hoping to come back for it later. But I'll bet he never returned."

"That's a pretty big assumption, Gina," Paul insisted.

"Look, I know this sounds strange but I can feel it," Gina said emphatically. "I know it's up there somewhere, buried near that stream and I'm going to find it."

At that point alarm bells went off in Paul's head.

"Be realistic, Gina. There's an awful lot of ground to cover up there... hundreds of square miles in fact. It would take months of constant searching. You can't just abandon this business. And besides there's a dangerous bear prowling around up there that would love to develop a taste for female gold prospectors. In fact, he just love to snack on your..." Paul reached over and pinched her buttock. Gina let out a short but loud scream followed by a giggle, and half the customers in the café stopped what they were doing or looked up from their morning papers to see what had just transpired. Gina turned beet red.

"Serves you right, miss," Paul chided her.

"Paul," Gina began after recovering her composure, "I'm very serious about this." Her expression had changed and an intense look covered her face. Paul could see clearly that she was adamant about the treasure hunt.

"Look Gina, who is gonna run this cafe while you're off digging around the countryside on this wild goose chase?"

"I'm going to close the Café on Sundays and Mondays, and I've asked Karen Aultschuler to run it for me during the week. She's helped out here before, and I'm confident that she can handle it. Besides, I need a vacation and most of my customers know where everything is anyway."

"Gina," Paul grabbed her arms firmly with his hands. I am considering closing off the entire area until this bear is either killed or captured. I don't want you hiking up in those mountains alone with a dangerous rogue bear on the loose."

Gina was deeply touched by his concern for her safety. And in his place, she would want the same thing for him.

"Paul… I'm sorry."

Gina moved behind the cash register to take money from a man who wanted to settle his bill. As she counted out the man's change, she observed Paul's facial expression. She began to understand the magnitude of the dilemma that he faced.

After the delicious breakfast that Gina had prepared for him, Paul began to feel the numbing tentacles of a disturbed night's rest slipping away from him. His strength and vigor were slowly returning. His mind was sharper, clearer now and he began to sketch out what he had to accomplish today on a paper napkin.

First he would call the print shop and have the warning posters made up. He was also interested in the Coroner's report on how Arthur Weigel had died. Although he expected the report to confirm a bear attack, Paul hoped that perhaps the medical examiner would find something which might shed some light on why the attack had occurred.

"This morning's paper just came in," Gina announced as she placed it on the counter in front of Paul. The headline caught his attention immediately.

"BEAR ATTACK KILLS THREE MEN"

The next line bothered him even more. "Warnings to be posted, but local forest grounds remain open; Federal Police to mount a search for rogue bear." The pressure was being turned on.

"Gina, I'm off." Paul felt the sudden urgency to start his workday and get something accomplished. It was as though everyone in the café was staring at him; wondering what he was doing sitting there instead of hunting down the dangerous animal.

"Thanks for a wonderful breakfast, sweetheart," Paul called out as he opened the front door.

"You're most welcome, Paul," Gina said, waving at him across the counter. Then she had a feeling of foreboding, and she ran to the door to kiss him goodbye.

"Please take good care of your self," she said as she threw her arms around him and as her eyes searched his.

"We'll get this problem solved," Paul stated with hopeful conviction.

Gina did understand who Paul meant by… "we".

Chapter Thirteen – The Third Attack

For those people who enjoy trout fishing, no other country as comparable in size to Switzerland is as rewarding. Many of its streams over six thousand feet in elevation offer some of the best angling action in Europe, and many people have come there to discover the thrill of fly-fishing. Lake trout have been caught weighing up to 10 kilos (22 pounds). Most rivers and streams meander through spectacular mountain scenery, affording an idyllic setting for lovers of the great unspoiled outdoors.

Three men, camped on the west side of the Rhone River, woke at dawn and wolfed down a breakfast of fried, fresh trout and eggs. They quickly donned rubberized waders, snatched their fly rods and selected from a vast assortment of tied flies, the appropriate nymph or adult fly which might tempt a large rainbow trout out of its well concealed lair. Excitement ran high as each man viewed the new day as a new opportunity, and they negotiated their bets for the largest fish caught. Each man had selected a choice fishing spot, and eagerly anticipated the first strike as they waded into the cold, fast moving tributary streams several hundred yards apart.

One of the men, whom they called Ernst, was acknowledged by the other two as the master fly fisherman. Purportedly, he could drop a fly right on the nose of a trout at fifty meters, and Ernst usually caught the legal limit of fish every time out. The other men often tried to keep Ernst in sight when fishing; carefully observing his technique and seeing which type of bait that he preferred. Today however, they had each selected fishing spots well away from each other.

Jurgen, an overweight truck driver from Innsbruck, Austria, went far upstream to a secluded pool that he had spotted the day before. The water was deep and fast moving, and the fallen trees, rotting in the pool provided excellent natural cover for a hefty fish. Jurgen had also observed some feeding activity on the surface, and had caught sight of a pretty big trout. The dense thicket of brush and trees around the pool would make casting difficult, but he would work carefully around them.

The third man fished between the other two, about a half a mile downstream and well around a steep bend from Jurgen. Ernst counted on the fact that Jurgen's awkwardness and the way that he always splashed into the stream would chase the trout downstream in his direction. Ernst's casting was always executed with a relaxed, fluid motion – a masterful example of control. His technique imitated perfectly a fly landing on the surface of the water.

The third man was a medical technologist from Wein, Austria, and fly fishing was, for him, akin to going to a spa for a massage. It soothed him greatly. He enjoyed the fresh air and could almost feel its purging effect, eluting with each breath the toxins of the city air from his lungs. Being out in the woods made him glad to be alive – he witnessed too much disease and death every day at the hospital.

Far upstream, Jurgen selected a reddish-brown larva, with a barbed hook from his tackle box. He lit a cigarette, tossed the match into the pond and secured the bait to the end of a short piece of clear, monofilament line. He opened his creel, slung it over his shoulder and pulled the aluminum tab off a can of Pilsner. He splashed into the stream and headed towards the pool, bulldozing his great bulk through the water. Mud and silt, stirred up at the bottom swirled to the surface behind him in the wake of each footstep. He felt awkward and silly with the waders on. He frequently considered how simple that it would be to toss an explosive device into the pool, and then gather up the fish as they floated to the surface with their air bladders ruptured. No one would be the wiser, and then he could return to camp and immerse himself into some serious lager trinken.

"Here I come you little bastards," Jurgen said as he waded forward. "Uncle Jurg has a nice tasty meal for you, "he muttered menacingly.

His ungainly, clownish form continued to plod through the water, which was now waist deep. He stopped near the pool and began playing out line. His first cast hooked over the branch of a small bush growing out of the embankment.

"Fuck!" He said as he began reeling in the line, and the hook caught the branch firmly.

"Oh shit!" He tugged at the line hard, rapid jerks; whipping his fly rod violently to the left and right. The hook suddenly came free and shot past his right ear, in recoil, with a sharp hissing sound. The big man reached into the creel for the can of beer and consumed more than half of it in one giant chug.

""Uurrrpfff…" he belched so loud that a pair of house wrens flew out of a nearby tree.

He impatiently retrieved his line and rechecked his hook. It was bent outward by the force of his tugging.

"Just what I fucking need!"

He attempted to bend the hook back into place by pressing it between his thumb and his hip. The hook suddenly jerked flat against his side and the barbed point penetrated and stuck fast into the rubberized material of the wader and would not come loose.

"Sonova**biiitch**!" Jurgen was livid and ready to toss rod, reel and creel into the deepest part of the pool.

"Oh, fuck me!" He headed towards to embankment to remove the hook with the pliers that he kept inside of his tackle box. Then he would tie on a new one.

Two large, cold, black eyes watched Jurgen's movements from the seclusion of a dense briar thicket. It sensed that the man's awkward, jerky motions indicated weakness, not unlike those of an unhealthy animal. The bear sniffed at the air; taking in great quantities of it to sample – to try and discern a profile of its prey.

The bear continued to stare, transfixed, as the man removed the hook and fastened a new one to the line. The man waded back into the stream, stumbling and losing his balance. The bear sensed more weakness. As Jurgen tipped over, propelled by the inertia of his own bulk, water flowed over the top of his waders.

"Goddamn sonovabitch!"

The massive head of the bear turned quickly; ears cocked in the direction of the sound emanating from the injured, splashing creature.

Slowly and quietly it inched forward, crouching down and moving through the dense brush. It had begun its stalk.

Jurgen regained his balance but the added weight of the water inside of his waders made his movements ponderous. This added to his overflowing sense of frustration. His second cast landed in the upstream side of the pool and was immediately snatched by a small rainbow trout. Jurgen could see easily that the fish was under the legal size limit, but vindictively, he was determined to make the little fish pay for all of his discomfort and inconvenience.

The huge bear saw the flickering dance of the fish on the water and became enraged that this strange, injured man should steal a meal.

Jurgen reeled in the tiny fish easily. Then, grasping the exhausted trout in his meaty hand he wrench the barbed hook out of the fish's mouth extracting flesh and gill tissue along with it. Blood ran profusely out of the fish's gills and down over Jurgen's fingers.

"Served you right, you little scaly fucker!"

Jurgen tossed what was left of the trout onto the embankment.

The bear sprung from its concealment with a thunderous roar and lept into the stream.

"What the fu…"

The man never completed the expletive as the massive animal landed on him, taking his neck in its powerful jaws and breaking it instantly. The furious bear smashed down on the lifeless body with its powerful front legs; the claws penetrating the rubber waders and hooking the dead man's rib cage.

Thrashing the body back and forth like a toy doll, the bear tore great pieces of flesh and clothing from what used to be Jurgen until the pool was whipped into a froth of red foam. The bear turned the pulpy, lifeless form upside down and bit through one leg with a single snap of its vicelike jaws. The lower portion of the leg circled slowly, trapped in the current of a reddish eddy, then seized by the flowing water it was carried downstream. The colossal bear ignored the escaping limb and proceeded to drag the man's carcass onto the embankment.

The great animal chewed through the rubber waders, spitting the indigestible pieces and consumed most of the body in the next hour.

Downstream, Ernst was enjoying a brisk battle with a two pound rainbow trout. The fish was trying instinctively to swim towards safety, under the tangled roots of a large tree. The early morning sun sparkled on the surface of the stream as hundreds of bright, twinkling reflections made it difficult for the fisherman to see.

Suddenly he felt increasing pressure on the line. The drag increased until he could no longer feel the jerky movements of the fish. The smart trout seemed to have wrapped the line around an underwater root, snapping the nylon and setting itself free.

Disappointed, Ernst began reeling in his line. He thought that he could detect a subtle vibration as though the fish was still attached. The pressure on the line did not yield easily. Trying not to break it, he maintained a steady pressure as the line inched slowly around the spool.

A snag, he thought. Whatever it was, it moved slowly downstream. The line was probably entangled on a piece of water soaked branch bouncing along the bottom of the stream.

Slowly, he played the snag until the heavy object was almost within reach. Backing up into shallower water, he reached down into the murky stream, his fingers sliding along the nylon monofilament until he felt the solid object.

Grasping it firmly, he lifted the heavy object clear of the water. The water around his feet turned crimson as blood rushed out of the bottom of the rubber wader. He froze in horror as the full awareness of what he held in his hand struck.

Half a human leg, torn off above the knee – the femur was protruding in jagged, splintered pieces. Ernst regurgitated his breakfast in involuntary spasms, and mixing with the blood in the water. He tried to cry out for his friend downstream, but the back of his throat burned from the bilious retch. He choked and coughed, gasping for breath.

The trout, still fighting at the end of the line, broke the surface in front on him. The surprise sent the fisherman into a panicked state and he fled the stream; dropping his rod into the water. He ran, encumbered by his waders, as fast as his legs would carry him towards the camp; slipping and falling several times on the moss covered rocks.

The third man looked up and caught sight of his friend running at full steam along the river bank. It was as though he was being chased by the devil himself, but he could not see anything or anyone in pursuit. He waded out of the river, set his rod down on the bank and headed off to join his terrified friend at the campsite.

When he arrived at the camp, Ernst was sitting on the ground in front of the tent and removing his waders. His eyes darting wildly back and forth, scouring the trees and bushes for signs of movement – although he didn't know from what.

"Ernst, what's wrong?"

His friend could see that Ernst's face was ashen and beads of perspiration trckled down his forehead. Ernst's hands were torn and bleeding from his falls.

"Ernst, answer me. What the hell happened?"

The terrified man blinked his eyes several times as if to flush away the vision of the severed, bloody leg. Then he focused on the concerned expression on his friend's face.

"I found a man's leg back there," he stammered.

"What? You didn't see anything else... a body?"

"No, but I touched it... picked it out of the water. It was snagged on my line. It was wrapped in a rubber boot... like a..."

"A wader?" the other man offered.

"Jurgen!" Fear for their friend jolted them as the realization struck simultaneously.

"We've got to search for Jurgen. Christ, I hope that he's all right," Ernst blurted out.

"Couldn't you see him from where you were?"

"No. he went around the bend in the river."

"I think that we'd better go find him. We'll have to report this to the police."

"Okay," Ernst agreed. "I'll show you the spot where I found the leg."

He felt a little calmer now; in control of himself. But he was still a little nauseous, shaking and breathing heavily.

The two men walked along the river, back towards the place where Ernst was fishing. Their eyes continued to scan the forest on both sides of the stream for any unusual signs of activity. After a few minutes they arrived at the site. Ernst could barely make out his rod, lying underwater on the bottom of the stream. The other man waded in and retrieved it. He could feel the heavy resistance offered by the severed limb ensnared on the line.

"Don't pull it in yet."

Ernst wasn't interested in seeing the horrible sight again.

"Let's find Jurgen first," Ernst suggested.

Setting the rod against the embankment, they continued walking upstream. Neither man was sure what they would find, but hoped that they would come around the bend and see their friend splashing through the stream in characteristic fashion.

A quarter of a mile upstream, the two men spotted the enormous beast. They stood transfixed, mouths agape – their feet paralyzed in cementine terror. The bear was standing on its hind legs, sharpening its gleaming claws, catlike, against the side of a large hickory tree. The bark was being lacerated and fell off in shards. The tree shook violently from the animal's assault.

"Get down Ernst," The two men took cover behind a fallen tree.

"Jesus Christ, just look at the size of that bear! I had no idea they grew to that size," Ernst whispered.

"I've never seen a bear like that one before," the other man affirmed. "It's strange looking. The head is unusually large for its body and the snout appears to be too short to be a bear... but its size is incredible."

"It must be nearly twelve feet high standing up like that."

"Oh God, I hope that's not what happened to Jurgen."

The men remained under the log, afraid to move, and watched the animal for several minutes. Finally, the bear lumbered off into the trees and disappeared out of sight. They walked back to retrieve Ernst's fishing rod as unobtrusively as possible, and then relunctantly hauled the leg out of the river. Ernst couldn't look at it. The medical technician recognized the pants and socks immediately.

"Oh God, no!"

There were several minutes of silence.

The third man concluded the obvious, "Ernst, I'm afraid it's Jurgen."

"Are you sure?" Ernst voice began to tremble and break up; tears forming in the corners of his eyes.

"Yes, I recognize the socks he put on this morning, and I'm reasonably certain about the pants."

"What are we gonna tell his wife? Wait a minute! What if Jurgen's still alive up there… and bleeding to death?"

"The femoral artery in that leg was severed; he would have bled out in fifteen minutes, that is, if the shock didn't kill him first. Besides, an animal that large would have severely mauled him."

"Are you positive?"

"Pretty damn positive. I've seen a lot of injuries at the hospital."

"We have to get down and notify the authorities quickly."

"Right! Forget the fishing gear and the tent. We've got to get the hell off this mountain," Ernst recommended strongly.

Two shivering and very frightened men quietly, and with a great sense of urgency moved rapidly down the mountain. That evening their campsite was shredded to pieces. The full moon illuminated the area with an eerie, colorless luminosity. The stream flowed on, perturbed little by the day's occurrences. The trout rested on the sandy bottom and slept peacefully, not too far from where the men had left Ernst's severed leg.

Chapter Fourteen

Paul arrived at the Brig police headquarters by 7:45 a.m. The headquarters were housed in an old red, brick building constructed in the early 1900's. He walked up the marble stone steps and noticed the hollows worn into the steps by millions of feet passing over the last century. Today, he felt like millions of feet had been passing over his own body as well.

As he entered the musty-smelling interior hall, the wooden planked floor creaked, seemingly protesting his every step. He stopped in front of an oak door that framed a frosted glass center panel. The lettering stenciled on the glass read, "Chief Inspector". Some of the lettering was wearing off, as was much of the drab green paint inside the building. The entire place, including the electrical and plumbing, was in serious need of a facelift if not a complete remodeling. The room had high ceilings; tall, massive, poorly insulated windows and oak plank flooring held in place with dowels. There was a moldy, stale odor that imparted an antiquish aura to the place. Federal Police headquarters in Bern had denied his budget request for modernization – twice.

Detective John Meeker sat at an old metal desk in the far corner of the main room busily pounding out a report on his rattling typewriter. When he saw Paul, Meeker ceased his pecking and walked over to greet his boss.

"Guess what, Chief, "he began, "some dairy farmer reported over the phone last night that a big bear had pushed over his house... he claims that the wooden structure was completely destroyed."

"What?" Soria was incredulous. "Did you send someone up to check out his story? And how big does a bear have to be to push over an entire house?"

"Pretty gigantic, and not yet... I thought that maybe we'd take a ride up there together this morning," Meeker answered. "I put a push pin in your map at a place where the incident purportedly occurred. Wanna see?"

Meeker quickly pointed out the location of the newest push pin, and it was apparent that the bear appeared to be foraging in a westly direction; arcing slightly to the north. Paul realized that if the bear continued to maintain its present course and heading, then it would migrate deeper and higher into the mountains.

"At least the beast doesn't appear to be headed into town anymore," Soria observed, his voice reflecting a sense of relief.

"Looks like it, Chief," Meeker agreed, and then he added, "Let's hope that something doesn't cause it to change its mind."

Soria nodded in agreement. "No shit!"

*   *   *   *   *   *   *   *

In a laboratory in Basel, sitting at a lab bench, a short, chubby man was hunched over a microscope, adjusting the focus to get a better look at the strange hair follicles sandwiched between the clear, optical grade microscope slides. Specimen jars filled with grotesquely compressed objects immersed in formalin lined the shelves from floor to ceiling on one wall. There were two parallel rows of laboratory benches in the room, with tops made of one inch thick slate. A long, trough-like drain was inset into the center of each lab bench. One bench supported pH meters, microbalances, electrophoresis equipment, gas chromatographs, flame spectroscopy equipment and gel-plate chromatography tanks. The other served as a work station for experiments in progress. Metal cabinets around the room held an assortment of Pyrex glass Erlenmeyer and Volumetric flasks, beakers, retorts and mechanical distillation apparatii.

The lab technician appeared to be in his mid fifties, but grey to white hair on his temples, a generous belly and a prematurely receding hairline conveyed the looks of a much older man. The surgical mask hid the rest of his face from view. His fingers moved efficiently, adjusting the slide traveler mechanism on the microscope so that he could scan along the individual hair sample of interest. His name was Dr. Morris Levin, and his associates called him "Mo".

A world renowned expert in the field of animal hair and tissue identification, Dr. Levin knew all of the latest scientific techniques to elucidate the origins of nearly all organic material, including plantlife. Using a pair of microfine tweezers, he meticulously pulled the strange hair follicles apart. He used a polarized light to illuminate the samples and made cross-wise cuts to obtain a view inside the follicles. Normally, he could identify the hair or fur from any animal within an hour. Completely stumped by what he was seeing, he decided to employ the use of a powerful electron microscope to help him identify the samples. He ruled out DNA analysis, as the sample was not of sufficient size to extract the minimal amount required for amplification.

His first impression was that he was looking at fur samples from either a bear or some kind of sloth-like creature. But the coloration and the coarsness of these follicles were different from any bear that he had ever seen. The data suggested a new species, but he couldn't substantiate that fact scientifically, so he withheld judgment.

It was possible that this animal might have suffered from a nutritional or genetic malady which caused the fur to take on the strange consistency and morphology. Perhaps its protein diet lacked some essential amino acids. However, he needed to see conclusive data before he could infer anything specific.

Willy Redman walked into the lab at eleven that morning and went looking for his friend Mo Levin. Their greeting was warm and cordial. The game warden inquired as to how much progress that Dr. Levin was making on the identification of the fur sample, and then handed Mo the fur samples that he had discovered and retrieved from the ill-fated trio's campsite.

"Willy," Mo questioned, "Just how important and relevant is it to know what kind of a bear this is," Mo inquired. "And does it really make a difference? I mean, you still have to stop it from killing more people, regardless." Mo looked at Willy searchingly.

"You're right, doc. But still, I was hoping to get a solid reason to explain this animal's unusual behavior that might create the necessity to capture it as opposed to simply destroying the beast."

Mo detected Willy's feelings of frustration and inner conflict.

"Willy, I'll tell you what I'm going to do for you. I have a friend at a DNA lab nearby. I'm going to send this new, larger sample of this fur over to him and ask him for a quick I.D. I'll take this over to him this afternoon, and with a little luck, we'll have an answer for you by Friday... how's that?"

Willy was touched.

"I really appreciate your help, Mo," he responded gratefully.

"Good, then that's settled. Now you can buy me a cup of tea and a donut from our cafeteria."

Mo separated the new fur sample into halves and then slipped one part carefully into a glassine envelope to take to his friend for DNA analysis. The other half he placed into a specimen bag; marked it with a felt-tipped pen and secured the sample away in a drawer.

Meanwhile, Willy browsed around the laboratory and examined some of the large bone fragments in the display case.

"What are these, Mo?" he inquired, picking up a large scapula.

The older scientist peered over the top of his wire-rimmed bifocals and noted where the game warden was standing.

"Those are Auroch bones."

"What's an Auroch?" Willy inquired, his curiosity piqued.

"It's and extinct species of cattle... Bos Primigenius - that roamed Europe before the last ice age. It was an immense animal with long horns, and was probably the ancestor of modern cattle that we know today."

"How old are these fossils?" Willy became more intrigued by the bones.

"Oh... about twenty thousand years... give or take two thousand."

Willy let out a low whistle. "Where did you get them?"

"On field trips," Mo responded as he got up from his desk and walked over to the display case. He put the second envelope containing the fur sample into his pocket.

Mo explained further, "I received my doctorate degree in Paleobiology, and I recovered these and lots of other fossils from my field work and excavations in France."

"What is Pal-e-o...?"

"Paleobiology: It's the study of ancient plants, animals and ancient humanoids and how they interacted with each other. The field doesn't pay very well, and jobs for paleobiologists are very scarce... and so I took this position. I've been doing this for twenty-three years now." Mo answered reflectively.

Later, Mo and Willy chatted for a long time, in a very relaxed manner in the break room next to the cafeteria. Willy admired the older man's philosophy on life. With a cherubic face and a short, grey beard, Mo seemed to exude a feeling that everything man experiences today is a repeat of similar events that have taken place hundreds, if not thousands of times in the past.

"History, does in fact repeat itself again and again. And it would seem that every new generation fails to learn that lesson, that is, until they have to learn it the hard way. So, if we come to better understand the past, then the present and the future would become less of a mystery and consequently less intimidating to everyone," Mo maintained. "We might even make fewer mistakes!"

"Willy," Mo continued as he took a long sip of his tea, "there are many immutable laws of nature. These same laws were operant thousands... millions of years ago, and they continue to provide order in our universe today and will continue to do so in the future. The more we truly understand these laws, the more that we will understand ourselves and our relationship with our environment. Humans share this planet. We don't own it, as many of us often like to think that we do."

Mo paused and reflected.

"There is always a time when the laws of nature collide head-on with the habits of man... and when man's activities run cross-grain to nature's laws, then man loses out inevitably. It may take a while, but Mother Nature always, always prevails.

Our universe, at least the last iteration of it as we understand it, is about ten billion years old... the earth... four billion. Man has been around, depending upon whose theory you accept, about a million years. Civilized man, and I use that term guardedly... about five thousand of those years. **Five thousand years...**one ten-thousandth of the age of the earth – an eyeblink in terms of geologic time. And yet in man's short tenure here on earth, we've managed to muck up the environment; not only for ourselves, but for our cohabitants. Other species have vanished forever or have become nearly extinct as a result of man's tampering."

Mo's voice was becoming louder and more passionate as he spoke, and as he emphasized each point. Several patrons, enjoying their lunch, regarded Mo with curiosity or viewed the senior scientist as mildly eccentric. His animated gestures were almost comical as he delineated each point with vigorous arm waving.

"You remind me in many ways of my friend, Paul, the policeman," Willy commented. "He feels that same way that you do... except he is a lot less vocal about it."

Mo thought for a while and relpied, "Police officers have a very seasoned, realistic and pragmatic view of life... not unlike Pathologists... they get to see the end results of all of man's shortcomings. No wonder there is such a high incidence of alcoholism and divorce among those professions in our society.

Willy couldn't help thinking that Mo Levin would get along well with Paul Soria.

"Well, Mo," Willy stood up, "I've got to be getting back to Brig."

"I hope that I haven't done too much pontificating, my friend, and bummed you out," Mo apologized as he stood up.

"Not at all, Mo. You are very enjoyable company," Willy assured him.

They shook hands.

"As soon as I hear something about your bear, I'll ring you up."

The Noah's Ark Conception

"Thanks again for you help, Mo. I really appreciate it."

"Good luck with your problem. Remember, nature always prevails."

Ten minutes later, Willy Redman was heading back to Brig on the main highway; his truck belching a foul-smelling, blue smoke all the way.

Chapter Fifteen

Paul had decided against making the trip to see the destroyed Ostermann house, because no one had been killed and he made the decision to send Ferrigno and "House" to investigate instead. He preferred to stay near the office to handle probing questions from reporters, and to worthsmith the updated status of the police investigation into a report that would ease everyone's mind back at police headquarters in Berne. In the back of his own mind he worried about Gina. Despite the fact that she was a very capable, driven and headstrong woman, Paul never believed that she would just 'take off' and go gold hunting in the mountains, given the dangerous prevailing circumstances.

He switched on the radio that rested on a shelf near his desk. Paul enjoyed listening to classical music while he worked, and his favorite local station played that particular genre of music 24-7. To Paul's surprise, the local radio station was sensationalizing the latest attack on the two young boys; hyperbolizing and maintaining that a half a dozen people had already been killed by the our-of-control, blood-thirsty carnivore. The announcer went on to say that more people would likely be killed unless the Federal Police took immediate, purposeful and effective steps to capture or kill the crazed beast. There was an inference in the news copy that the police were basically asleep at the switch, and had absolutely no idea how to proceed with the bear's extermination. The newscaster went on to speculate that the bear's next victims could quite possibly be the naïve townspeople of Brig itself, and suggested that innocent, defenseless children could be snatched by the bear in their own backyards while playing.

Paul snapped off the radio in the middle of the announcer's sentence.

101

The Noah's Ark Conception

"Wonderful! Just fuckin' wonderful! That's all we need now is to panic the townsfolk and scare the hell out of the tourists. I never liked that whining, bleeding-heart, commie, pinko, bed wetting, where's my mommy, runny-nosed, snivelling bastard of a radio announcer anyhow," he muttered to himself.

Now that felt better, he thought.

He understood that the police station's switchboard was about to light up like the Eiffel Tower because of that news announcement, and he needed to supply Maria with some kind of an official statement. He went to work crafting one.

He glanced once again at the push pins on the map, so that he could maintain with certainty in his statement that the bear was at least thirty-five kilometers from Brig and safely confined to the deep forest. But he also understood that realistically, the situation could change overnight. Paul prayed that the animal continued on its guestimated northwest heading. Keeping a close eye on the pattern of the bear's movements was the key to keeping the populace informed and avoiding new attacks.

Willy had informed Paul that the bear would most probably climb to higher elevations as spring progessed into summer; driven by the need to feed on the newly emerging grasses. With that fact in mind, and given the apparent direction that the animal seemed to be headed, Paul began to plan where he might intercept and destroy the man-eater.

His thoughts were interrupted by the sound of someone knocking at his office door.

"Come in," he called out, and two men, wearing denim pants and down vests entered the room.

Paul was surprised to see the strangers, as usually one of his detectives intercepted and interviewed all visitors. It was police department protocol.

"Can I help you gentlemen?" Paul greeted them warmly but officially.

The medical technician initiated the conversation.

"Good morning, Inspector. My name is Christoph Jena and this is Ernst Scheimann, were both from Austria, and we're the trout fishermen who reported the bear attack by phone this morning from our hotel." Both men shook hands with Paul, and he noticed that both men seemed very uncomfortable.

"Would you gentlemen like some coffee," Paul offered.

"That'll be fine, thank you." The smaller man seemed to be doing all of the talking.

"If you don't mind, Inspector, we would really like to get this over with quickly. We've got to get home and explain to Jurgen's family exactly what happened, and quite frankly we're anxious to get going."

"I understand," Paul said compassionately, "I'll be brief. Keep in mind that the local police in Austria is responsible for breaking the news to his family, and we have already alerted them," Paul added as a point of information.

"We understand that. But also keep in mind that our families will also hear of the news, and Jurgen's family will want to hear from our own mouths exactly what happened. Let's face it. This is all too incredible and shocking to be believed."

Paul handed the men their coffee and motioned for them to be seated. He took a moment to introduce himself.

"My name is Paul Soria and I'm the Chief Inspector for the Federal Police in this district. We had posted signs on every road, in every local hotel and trailhead alerting campers that we had a rogue bear in these mountains, but apparently you gentlemen didn't see them... you were already out camping. I am very sorry about your friend."

"What are you doing about killing or capturing that bear," Ernst broke his silence for the first time.

"Mr. Scheimann, I am going to have to hunt it down, and probably destroy it. And I would like to get some information from you two, which I hope might give me a lead as to the direction that this bear seemed to be headed."

"We'll help you with any information that we can provide, but I gotta warn you Inspector, the animal you are looking for is bigger than any bear I've ever seen or heard about."

"Then you **did** see the bear?" Paul leaned forward in his chair, closer to the men.

"See it? We're damned lucky to be alive to tell about it. In all my years of camping and fishing, I've never seen such a huge animal."

"Would each of you describe the bear for me, please?"

Christoph began by telling his story of seeing his friend Ernst running down the river bank, and then the two of them going back to look for Jurgen.

"It didn't look like any bear that I've seen on TV, zoos or in the movies. It stood between three and four meters high on its hind legs. It was scratching the side of a tree the way that my wife's cat uses a scratching post to sharpen its claws. The bear's head seemed like it was bigger. Bigger, compared to the rest of its body than most other bears I've seen. It's almost as though it had no neck... the head appeared to be mounted right on its shoulders. The other thing peculiar about it was the muzzle."

"What do you mean?" Paul attempted some clarification.

"Well, the snout seemed shorter... but wider in the jaw. It didn't protrude outward as far as normal bears I've seen."

"Normal bears!" Paul exclaimed. "What does that mean?"

"This may sound a little strange, but it had something of a retarded look about it... you know... not normal. Do you understand what I'm trying to say?"

Paul shook his head and directed his attention to Ernst.

"Is there anything that you can add to what your friend has said?"

"I agree pretty much with what Christoph has told you, except that the bear had long, shaggy fur. I guess I'd have to say that it was blackish-brown; and it had claws like the tines of a pitchfork. I can still hear the sound they were making as it was scratchin' away at that tree. I'll tell you Herr Inspector that is one powerful animal. You're gonna need a tank or a heavily armed infantry squad to go up against that beast."

Paul listened carefully to the men's descriptions, and then handed each man pictures of all the bears that Paul could find in the encyclopedia.

"I'd like you to look at these pictures carefully; take your time, and see if you can identify the one you saw."

The men examined each picture closely, and after a few minutes, came to the same conclusion.

"I do not see the bear that we saw in these pictures."

"Neither do I," the second man confirmed.

"Gentlemen, I'm going to have to ask you to look at those pictures again. These are all of the bears that exist in the world. You must be absolutely certain. Except for polar bears, which are white, these are all of the identifiable species of bears... there simply are no others." Paul began to feel as though things were slipping out of his control.

Both men cooperated and glanced at the pictures a second time.

"The closest thing you have here to what I saw up there in the forest is a grizzly or may be this Kodiak Island species."

"Why do you say that?" Paul pressed.

"Because the grizzly has the high arch over the shoulder, moreso than the other bears; the one we saw had a similar back. But that's the only resemblance... the bear we saw is not in this stack of pictures, and that's all there is to it."

The man's description was interrupted, as Willy walked into the Inspector's office.

"The bear that you are looking for is not here," the other man affirmed, as he handed the stack of pictures back to Paul.

Willy waited patiently as Paul completed his interview of the two men. Then Paul asked the men to indicate, on his map, where the attack occurred and in which direction the bear headed. Ernst obliged by indicating the exact point, and using a push pin, located the spot. Then he used a grease pencil to indicate the direction of the animal.

"It was just about here," Ernst pushed the pin into the map.

"We were about four and a half kilometers northwest of this lumber road, on the western fork of this river. When the bear left the river bank, it headed north, as best as we could tell."

"I appreciate you time gentlemen, and once again, I'm very sorry for the loss of your friend. Your information has been very valuable to us," Paul stated genuinely. "I understand that the Coroner's office is sending some people up there to gather Jurgen's remains.

The Noah's Ark Conception

"Yes, we heard that too," Christoph explained, "We gave them detailed directions on where to look. I just don't know what they are going to find when they get up there."

"Listen, Inspector," Christoph looked at Paul and then glanced at Willy; his eyes had a beseeching look.

"There's an animal out there, and it's not like any bear you've ever seen. I'm dead positive of that. You've got to keep people out of the woods until you either catch it or kill it. But whatever you do, I'm tellin' you to be damn careful."

Paul immediately thought of Gina.

"We appreciate your advice. And as of midnight last night, the forest was officially "off-limits" - closed to the public. Signs have been posted everywhere. We have also informed all local merchants and hotel managers to inform their patrons."

The two men shook Paul's hand and departed. He watched them get into their car and drive in the direction of the main highway. After their vehicle was out of sight, he turned to Willy.

"Good to see you Willy," Paul felt awkward. He knew that the time had come to tell his friend that the bear had to be hunted down and destroyed, just like a convicted, escaped murderer. But Paul needed to buy a little more time; wait for the appropriate moment to break the news to the game warden.

"What do you think of what the two men said, Willy?" Paul asked, "In particular about the bear being different than any shown in these pictures."

Willy studied Paul's face for a few seconds and then walked over to the large wall map. He examined the spots on the map that indicated the three attacks and where the house was pushed over. Willy made some mental calculations about the animal's direction and speed. He turned to face his friend.

"Those men were right. This bear **is** different. It is not a grizzly… it is also not a black or brown bear. I know that now."

"What are you leading up to Willy?" What do you mean: You know that now?"

Paul noticed the agitation that his friend had displayed two days before, was now gone. And now Willy seemed more like himself. The air of quiet confidence had returned, and Paul was relieved to see it.

Willy could see easily that Paul's mind was racing, and that the pressure of his responsibilies was getting to him. He was probably blaming himself for the death of the trout fisherman. Willy also knew that what he was about to tell his friend would be difficult to believe, and that it was critically important for Paul to take him seriously.

"Paul, you are my friend and have been for a long time. You understand that when I tell you something, it is the absolute truth as I believe it to be."

Willy stopped and waited for Paul to mentally digest what he was saying.

Paul realized that Willy, who rarely revealed his thoughts about their friendship, was being very sincere and wanted Paul to know that what he was going to reveal meant a great deal.

"This bear is a species of animal that was thought to have died out thousands of years ago – hundreds of generations in the past. It has different habits and patterns of life that are significant from any other bear on this planet. It is very, very dangerous and highly unpredictable; and yes, it is a ferocious man-eater."

PART   THREE

THE CAPTURE PLAN

<u>Chapter Sixteen</u> – Willy's Plan

Paul stood perfectly still, stunned by his friend Willy's powerful words. Had it been any other person, Paul would have probably thrown him out of his office. But instead, the Chief Inspector just stared at Willy incredulously. He studied Willy's face for a long time, searching for any sign of doubt that the game warden might have; some flicker of doubt that would betray his ernestness or his passion. But he saw none. The expression in Willy's eyes told Paul that he was deadly serious, and believed with his whole heart and mind the words that he had just spoken.

"How can you be so sure, Willy; what you are telling me is a scientific impossibility?"

Willy saw in Paul's face that his friend was trying hard to believe him. And he detected further that Paul was wrestling with the same paradox that he had faced when he found the bear's fur sample. Simply, what was improbable to exist actually **did** exist.

Willy patiently explained to Paul about going to see Dr. Mo Levin, and how the fur sample defied immediate description. He then offered the trout fishermen's corroborative observations and inability to compare the bear to known ursine species as further proof. Then, Willy came to a point that Paul found the most difficult to accept.

"There is a definite reason that this animal is here **now,** at this moment in time. I don't pretend to know why that is, but I feel that some human hand or hands are at work behind the existence this living anachronism."

Willy's assessment of Paul's receptiveness to his last statement was correct. His latest hypothecation was, for Paul, the proverbial last straw.

"Have you lost your mind, Willy? I don't give a shit what kind of ancient museum piece we're dealing with here. It's already killed four people. The animal's trial has been held in the local media, whose editor's have been playing judge and jury. They're calling for the death penalty, and if we don't act as executioner, and damn fuckin' quick, then you will soon read about the loss of our jobs in the newspapers. Now... you come to me with this fastastic idea that this living relic was put on this earth... in my jurisdiction... by someone other that God!"

Willy was taken aback; hurt not only by his friend's use of expletives, but struck by his myopic self-centeredness. He lowered his eyes to the floor.

The emotion that Paul had just vented had been building for several days: The multiple attacks, the criticism in the press, Gina's dogged insistence on going treasure hunting and Willy's fantastic revelation that had catalyzed Paul's emotional outburst. It was too much of a strain and Paul had finally exploded.

Paul saw the hurt in Willy's face and he hated himself for using Willy as the whipping boy for his frustrations. Now, feeling contrite, Paul reached over and touched his friend's shoulder.

"I'm very sorry, Willy. I was out of line saying those things to you in that tone of voice. I know that you're being genuinely honest about the things you told me, but I was feeling a bit overwhelmed, and I got a little out of control." Paul paused, allowing his words to sink in.

"Please try to understand Willy. I've never encountered a problem like this before. This job has always been one of routine police action in the past. And now, suddenly, three people are dead and I feel as though when I walk down the street that everyone is silently accusing me of contributing to their deaths. I guess that the strain of this problem is beginning to get to me," Paul declared, the weight of his present situation obvious in his tone.

Willy looked up and managed a meager smile and nodded in reluctant assent. At that moment Paul understood that all was accepted, and Willy had put Paul's truculent mood swing into perspective and context. He walked over and re-examined the wall map; noting again where the bear attacks had occurred.

"The bear travelled approximately twenty-five kilometers between the first attack on the Alpenkopf and the second attack on the two boys. Another seven kilometers were covered to get to the Ostermann house, and finally the trout fisherman was killed here… eight kilometers further. If we assume that the first attack occurred sometime on Saturday… that would mean the bear is travelling northwest, up into the mountains at the rate of approximately eight to ten kilometers (5 to 7 miles) a day. That's a relatively slow foraging pace to a huge carnivore with a big appetite," Willy concluded, scratching his chin.

Then he analyzed the bear's directional pattern. He noticed one of the dirt lumber roads, denoted as a dotted line on Paul's map.

"If this bear continues travelling at the same rate of speed and in the same general direction, Paul, then it may cross this lumber road, somewhere between here and here, sometime in the next few days," Willy indicated the probable crossing on the map with his fingers bracketing the spot.

Paul, using a red grease-pencil, marked the edges of the spot with two parallel lines.

"We might be able to get a clear shot at it," Paul formulated.

"That's not practical," Willy corrected. "The bear would get across that road in a second, and then disappear into the forest on the other side. You would never have a chance to aim and fire."

Paul realized that his friend was probably correct.

"Do you have a better idea, Willy?" Paul asked, sensing that Willy had another type of plan.

"Yes, we will make sure that the bear stays around one area so we can get a good shot at it… maybe several good shots."

"How do you propose to do that?" Paul inquired.

"We need to bait a trap for the bear," Willy responded quickly. While Paul had asked Willy the question with the presumption that the game warden was genuinely offering his help, part of him couldn't believe that Willy was resolved to destroying the animal. It was uncharacteristic behavior for Willy. Paul sensed that perhaps Willy might have something else planned.

"We'll take a large pig and secure it to a tree by the side of the old lumber road, at a point where we think that the bear will cross. You and I will take up positions on either side of the pig where we can get a good clean shot at the bear. The bear will most probably kill the pig and spend some time consuming it. It is during that time that I hope we can tranquilize the animal," Willy explained.

"**Tranquilize it?**" Paul answered incredulously.

Paul thought that Willy had taken leave of his senses.

"You can't tranquilize a two-thousand pound bear."

"Sure you can. Veterinarians do it all the time with elephants and other big game animals, and they weigh considerably more than a ton," Willy emphasized.

Paul retorted, "And even if you were successful, what are you planning to do with it?"

Once again, Willy stood silent and stared at his friend. He understood now that he would have to assume control over the operation, gradually, if Paul and the bear were to be spared a deadly encounter.

Willy resumed outlining of his plan carefully and slowly.

"We would have to winch the animal into a large cage and transport it to a distant place where it couldn't endanger anyone, and it could live out its existence in peace."

Paul began to see some of the merit in the game warden's plan, and also a way to placate the townspeople as well as to maintain his friendship with Willy. He was amazed that he hadn't thought of the idea and chided himself for the oversight. But Paul was an empowering man and if Willy, a season game warden, could conceive of such a creative notion then Willy should be given a chance to implement his plan.

"I like your idea Willy. But where would we get a winch and a sturdy enough cage large enough on such short notice?"

"That's the part I haven't figured out yet," Willy replied, shaking his head. I was hoping that I could obtain one from the Interior Department."

Willy thought for a few moments.

"They do have portable cages for transporting large animals… perhaps we can borrow one from a nearby zoo or some other place that deals with transporting large creatures. I'll make a few phone calls and find out. The only problem is getting the device here before the bear crosses that old lumber road."

For the rest of the morning, Willy phoned agency contacts in search of a suitable cage. He finally made contact with a forest ranger in Norway who had cages sufficiently strong and roomy enough to transport polar bears, and occasionally a moose. The moose, being a very tall, heavy animal with broad antlers, required a very large cage to transport. His only concern was would the cage be strong enough to hold an animal as powerful as a one-ton bear.

The cage would have to be airlifted from Trondheim, Norway to Geneva, and then transported by truck to Brig, and to the proposed capture site. Willy would make arrangements to load the crate on a tilt-back of a flatbed truck, normally used for transporting cars. The tilt-back would permit the tranquilized bear to be winched into the cage, and the cage in turn winched onto the back of the truck. Leveling the tilt-back would facilitate easy transportation to a larger, more secure holding facility until the bear could be shipped... somewhere. There were a lot of **ifs**, but Paul and Willy concluded that the plan was certainly worth a try.

Chapter Seventeen – 7:00 p.m.

Gina Ann Schmidt, multi-tasking as she was, was simultaneously examining a geodetic survey map of the Fletschhorn Mountain Range; checking and rechecking all possible escape routes available to the Brig bank robber that she could assume from the story as it was outlined in the Chronicles. She was searching for a reasonable starting point from where to begin looking for the gold. The corroborating evidence in the Chronicles fortified her belief in her Uncle Mario's tales about the well-dressed thief who had escaped with nearly forty grand in 1946. She was now more convinced than ever that the gold was hidden somewhere in the mountains and just waiting for her to find it. Gina had been severely bitten by the treasure hunting bug.

In addition, she was in the process of preparing a romantic dinner for Paul and herself. Wearing her apron over a form-fitting, embroidered denim skirt that ended just above her knees; her hair was pulled up and gathered with a large, tortoise-shell hair clip. Her wispy bangs framed her face and her soft, brown eyes beautifully. A pair of two-inch gold hoop earrings, and a topaz ring on her pinkie was all the jewelry that Gina wore. Her medium-heeled shoes were black and casual, and her shapely legs were freshly groomed and lotioned. Her top was a long-sleeve, black turtleneck with the sleeves hiked up to her elbows – one of her trade mark looks, commented on often by her café patrons. But tonight, her looks were all about Paul and their happiness together.

Turning her attention away from the map, she pulled a large pan out of the oven and rested it on top the stove. She had prepared four, stuffed chicken breasts; filled with chopped spinach, pancetta and asiago cheese. After sampling a quick taste and nodding in a gesture of satisfied approval, she went to the refrigerator and retrieved a large bowl of salad that was keeping crispy fresh under a moist paper towel. With the salad in one hand and a wedge of cheese in the other, Gina shut the refrigerator door with a well-directed nudge of her shapely backside.

She calculated in her mind the approximate value of gold bullion coins in today's swiss francs. With gold at 75 francs to the ounce in 1946, she estimated the value today at over half a million swiss francs, or approximately three hundred thousand Amercian dollars. However their numismatic value, as freshly minted, uncirculated coins, might attain nearly double that amount. In Gina's mind, the reward was **certainly** worth the effort and the danger she would risk to find the hidden treasure.

She heard the door open to the garage, and knew that Paul would be walking into the kitchen momentarily. Quickly, she gathered up the geodetic map and the copy of the Chronicles because she didn't want him to see what she was researching. Gina wanted nothing to spoil the mood that she was trying to craft for their evening together. She hid the map and the book in the hutch; dimmed the lights in the dining room and put on some of her favorite Andrea Bocelli and Harry Connick, Jr. selections. She completely transformed the room into a warm, cozy, romantically stimulating environment in seconds – a fete that she performed regularly, and with great skill.

You cannot help yourself, Paul Soria...I'm Italian, she thought, congratulating herself as she returned to the kitchen.

When Paul walked inside, he was immediately struck by the incredibly seductive ambience of their home – an amazing contrast to that of his office, he considered for an instant.

Now free of her apron, Gina walked over to him with a bottle of chilled Chianti Reserva, 1995, in her hand and they kissed tenderly. He allowed his hand to come to rest on her buttocks, and he understood immediately that she was not wearing any underwear.

She deliberately moved away his hand… "**Not now**… eat first, dessert later," she whispered with a sly smile.

"Here," she handed him the wine, "you can open this and let it breathe. We're just about ready to eat. I just need to put a few finishing touches on the salad."

The Noah's Ark Conception

While Paul uncorked the wine and poured it through a "Venturi" into the decanter, Gina was slicing a large, Beefsteak tomato into the salad. She sprinkled on some Gorgonzola crumbles and accented the salad mixture with some chopped cashews, pignoli and pistachio nuts that she had prepared earlier. She garnished the salad with six, tiny orange sections and headed for the dining room. She placed the salad bowl on the dining room table, and next to the bowl she set down a Waterford crystal and sterling silver salad serving set. Gina poured over the salad mixture what she considered to be the perfect amount of her homemade balsamic vinaigrette. After lighting the two red candles on either side of the oak bistro dining table, Gina put her hands on her narrow hips and said, "Perfecto! Mangiare!"

Paul entered the dining room after washing his hands and slipped them around Gina's waist from behind her.

"May I escort my beautiful hostess to her seat?" he asked.

"You may kind sir," she responded with a smile.

He pulled out her chair and seated her gracefully. Dinner was served.

During their delicious meal, the conversation was kept light and bouncy. Paul commented on how well everything tasted, and Gina took the compliments graciously but spiced with a decidedly, 'of course it tasted good' connotation.

Paul brought up the subject of how nice it would be if they had a dog as a pet. He went on to say how much that he admired one of his police inspector's Samoyeds, and what a pristinely beautiful white coat it possessed. Gina tentatively welcomed the idea, favored Golden Retrievers, but cautioned on the possibilities of stray dog hairs finding their way into some of her cooking in the cafe – and **that** she couldn't tolerate. Consequently, with no common ground immediately in sight, they decided to drop the subject of adopting a canine.

Paul and Gina deliberately avoided any conversations that could envelope them in a discussion about Paul's work, the bear or maulings. Both of them seemed to understand that any such discussions, even tangential ones, could potentially spoil the harmonious and warm qualities that the evening had developed. Gina served Paul's favorite dessert: warm, French apple crumb pie, ala mode, with vanilla ice cream. And when their meal had been completed, Gina pulled out her chair and moved it around the table to be closer to Paul. She deliberately crossed her magnificent legs slowly, providing him just enough time for a fleeting glimpse between her thighs. Then they sat and enjoyed the background music, which had shifted to some romantic ballads by Ella and Diana Krall.

The candles had burned to nearly two-thirds of their original height when Paul suggested, "Why don't we adjoin to the couch."

Gina loved that suggestion, because it always meant that Paul would allow Gina to lie on her back, lengthwise on the couch with her head in his lap. As they chatted casually, he would always caress her hair and kiss her forehead; holding her hand or allowing his hand to rest on her breast with her hand on his. She so thoroughly enjoyed that because it was so sensual and romantic at the same time, and she always felt that those were their best "bonding" moments together – a time when all seemed right with the world, and they they were insulated against the rest of their worries and responsibilities. It was simply, "their time".

"Where do you see us in five years, Paul?" Gina asked in almost a matter-of-fact way.

"Hopefully, right here on this couch," he answered with a grin, although he knew that was not the complete answer that she was after.

"You know what I mean," she pressed as she prodded him gently in the ribs with her elbow.

"Of course I do, sweetheart," he acknowledged, gently squeezing her breast.

"I would like to see us living together… possibly married; living here above the café or in a house of our own, a white Pickett fence… and with two dogs in the yard."

"Really!" she responded.

"Absolutely," he chuckled, "I see no reason why we can't have two dogs."

"Oh… stop it with the dogs. Would you really like to see us married?"

"In five years? I don't see why that isn't possible, especially if our relationship has survived that long?"

"Now, what do you mean by **that**?" Gina rose up on one elbow and faced him. "What's wrong with our relationship?"

"There's absolutely **nothing** wrong with our relationship, Gina. What are **you** worried about?" his voice betrayed a little surprise and concern. I never implied that there is something amiss about our relationship… now don't go jumping to… how do you like to put it… concussions again," he chided.

"**Again**! This is the first time that we've ever had a discussion about marriage," she stated defensively. "What are **you** referring to Paul?"

Paul could easily see where the discussion might be evolving, and the wet-blanket effect that it could potentially have on their evening, and so he decided to take the high ground.

"Look, Gina… I didn't mean anything by anything. I would love to see us married in two years not five. In two more years we should have a pretty good handle on our compatability index. After all, we've known each other for three years, and we have been living together for the last two. I see no need to have to wait for a total of seven years to make a decision about becoming man and wife, that's all. I meant nothing other than that."

Gina allowed herself to rest on his lap again, but she wasn't completely satisfied with his answer. But she too, was not going to allow a little verbal miscommunication to ruin their evening together, especially after she had worked so hard to prepare for it.

"Paul?"

"Umm hmm?"

"Can I ask you to do something for me?"

"Sure, go right ahead?"

"Before we go to bed tonight, would you take a look at a map that I bought today and tell me if the area I point out is off limits to campers and hikers?"

"**What?**" was all that Paul could manage.

<u>Chapter Eighteen</u> – Thursday

The next morning, after Paul had departed for work, Gina was back at her cafe table estimating the maximum speed that a rider and a horse laden with gold could attain while headed uphill in a snowstorm. Following the route outlined in the Chronicles, she traced the path following an old lumber road that was indicated as a black dotted line on her survey map. The trail wound its' way upwards, along the northeast side of the Simplon Pass – precisely in the area the Paul had forbidden her to go. There appeared to be a broad, flat plateau in the area, as indicated by the wider contour lines and bisected by a small stream. She wondered if the thief had managed to make it that far.

Gina recalled last night's conversation with Paul, and how he emphasized two points very clearly: the improbability of the outlaw's survival during a severe blizzard; and that she shouldn't go exploring in that area alone under any circumstances. But the more she thought about the outlaw's chances of surviving a blizzard in the higher altitudes, the more she convinced herself that the thief never left that valley alive and neither did the gold.

She began to organize in her mind the equipment she would require to help her locate the gold, and to camp out in the mountains for two or three days. From the map, it appeared as though the lumber road was passable by jeep to the place where it was intersected by the closest point to the plateaued valley. The issue became, were there any rocks or fallen trees strewn across the old road that would serve as an impenetrable barrier. It would make sense to follow the lumber road as far as possible in a jeep, and then to attempt the rest of the trip on foot. Once she reached the valley, Gina believed that her best tactic would be to search for a natural shelter, or some kind of man-made one, such as a cabin or a lean-to. The shelter would have to be large and strong enough to provide a safe haven from a raging blizzard. At

119

that place, she would begin her search for the gold and the skeletal remains of any corpse nearby. She remembered reading somewhere in a treasure hunter's guide that outlaw's and prospectors frequently buried items of value under large natural formations that stood out against the surrounding countryside: large trees, boulders and other objects that would mark the burial site and survive years of weathering.

Gina had purchased a metal detector to help her locate buried objects such as gold. The electronic device claimed to be able to detect a piece of metal, no bigger than a paper clip, nearly one meter below the ground's surface. The longer the item had been buried in the ground, the stronger the signal because the soil around the object became charged with metal ions that had leeched out into the dirt. A large amount of gold that had been buried for half a century would give off a very powerful signal.

Gina had made up her mind despite Paul's vehement objections that she would make her first reconnoitering trip to the mountains this coming weekend. The recent events pertaining to the bear attacks had concerned her somewhat, but she was convinced that the probability of encountering the animal was remote. She had become very excited in anticipation of testing out her theory. And like a schoolgirl on her first date, nothing was going to dampen her enthusiasm about the gold. But just in case she ran across any animal bent on spoiling her fun, she packed her uncle's .45 calibre pistol and a dozen rounds of ammunition to help discourage its interest.

Gina thought very hard about Paul and what he might say about her little excursion into the mountains. Weighing her relationship with him, she knew that he would be angry with her, and probably upset about not following his advice. But she felt that she was a "big girl", and responsible for her own actions. It was something about her nature that he would just have to accept. She would leave a note for him on Saturday morning, and she knew he wouldn't find it until late Saturday afternoon. By then she would be well up into the mountains, pursuing her quest.

<u>Chapter Nineteen</u> – The Hunt

A copy of the Coroner's reports on the death of Arthur Weigel, and the two boys, Dirk Kroner and Sven Oosterlund was delivered to Paul's office by late-morning on Thursday. Inspector Haustein intercepted the plain brown envelope, labeled "Confidential", and handed it to Chief Inspector Soria with his usual pompous flair. He stressed that the contents of the envelope were classified, official police business and that it was for Paul's eyes only.

Paul rolled his eyes at the inspector's "Barney Fife" forced affectative demeanor.

Inspector "House" enjoyed driving around in the police cruiser. It made him feel important and powerful. He kept his blue-grey uniform heavily starched, and every accessory was polished to a dazzling shine. Paul often thought that House must have spent hours caring for his uniform, buttons, buckles and shoes. House wore a .44 cal Magnum, pearl handled pistol as his service revolver, and he kept it turned backward, Wild Bill Hickok style, in the black leather holster that hung on his left hip. House's swaggering gait completed the affectation. That particular gun made Paul very nervous. The townspeople enjoyed the buffoonery, making unflattering comments behind House's back.

Paul was headed out to lunch when the envelope arrived, and he reversed direction and headed back to his office to read the contents. It contained several pages of double-spaced, typed verbiage that included dozens of clinical references in medical-speak to attached photographs that he didn't quite understand. Paul's eyes scanned to the paragraph entitled "Cause of Death", and read the Coroner's official description.

"The subject Caucasian male, indentified as Arthur Weigel, died as a result of massive blood loss caused by multiple injuries sustained in an attack by a wild animal, presumably a

large carnivore. While the remains of Arthur Weigel, as presented at the scene, were incomplete, teeth and claw marks visible on several bones suggest that the missing body parts were consumed by the subject animal."

Paul continued to read the gruesome report, but what he found under "Additional Remarks", particularly surprised him.

"Bite and teeth marks on the victim's thorax measured twenty-six centimeters (10 ¼ inches) between the left and right side of the animal's jaw..."

Paul measured the distance out quickly on his desk.

"Holy shit!" he muttered.

The bear's jaws were wide enough to accommodate a grown man's skull. There were no bears on earth that had a bite that wide. Slowly, a picture of a fearsomely huge predator was forming in Paul's head. The pieces were coming together.

The description of the bear provided by the two fishermen and Willy's story about a surviving, Pleistocene Era species of bear appeared consistent with Coroner's observations.

He continued to sit quietly in his office chair for several minutes, allowing his mind to comprehend the implications of the mounting evidence. All of the information so far pointed to a unique species of bear, but he couldn't announce his suspicions publicly until he was certain. This bear was an animal of astonishing size and power, with immense jaws and an acquired taste for human flesh. It was moving north-northwest, up the mountain; and while it posed no immediate threat to Brig, the bear could alter its course and stray into the town limits at any time.

Paul understood Willy's concern about not killing this bear. If it was truly some kind of throwback, or the surviving sub-species of an extinct race of bear, then the scientific community would want the animal kept alive and unharmed. Trapping the beast was his only option. He could turn it over to government scientists for study, and then it would become their problem.

His concentration was interrupted by the telephone.

"Paul Soria," he answered curtly.

"Inspector, this is Oscar Prescott down at "Heavy Wheels" equipment rental." The voice on the other side sounded very uneducated. "You are the person who ordered a large flatbed truck for a week?"

"Actually, I didn't, but I know who did. Do you have one available?" Paul inquired.

"One what?" The dull witted voice questioned.

"A flatbed truck," Paul answered impatiently.

"Oh, yessir," the slow-minded man made the connection. "In fact, we got two brand new Volvos."

"I only need one, Oscar. How long are the beds?"

"Beds? I thought that you wanted a truck, not a camper." Oscar was becoming confused again.

Paul grasped the receiver tightly; maintaining control of his temper and reminding himself that God occasionally overlooks the intelligence genome in some people.

"Oscar, listen to me carefully," Paul directed. "Exactly how long is the flat cargo deck on the back of the new Volvo truck?"

After a few seconds of silence, "About 8 meters long, I guess."

"Are you sure?"

"Pretty sure, I think." Oscar responded.

"Great! Now, tell me Oscar, is there a power winch on the truck?" Paul had remembered Willy's plan to winch the tranquilized bear into the cage, and then winch the entire cage onto the back of the truck.

"I don't know about no winch, but there's a roundy thing with a long cable on it for dragging cars up onto the back of the truck."

Paul smiled to himself, *surely no one could be that simple minded,* he thought.

"How long is that cable, Oscar?" Paul continued with his questions.

"One half of an inch; it's solid steel."

"No… that's the width. How long can it reach from the truck?"

"Wait a minute, and I'll go and measure it.

Paul was rapidly reaching the end of his patience.

"No, no Oscar…Oscar are you there?" Paul yelled into the receiver.

"Yes, I'm there," the voice responded.

"Is there somebody else there that you can go and ask?"

"Ask what?"

"How long the goddamn cable is," Paul yelled. He was rapidly losing his self control. He didn't want to hurt Oscar's feelings.

The boy on the other end put down the receiver, and after a few minutes of silence Oscar announce proudly, "Two hundred feet long."

"That'll be just fine Oscar. Now tell me, what's the rental charge?"

"For how long?"

"One week."

"I have to check with the manager because he won't let me quote prices over the telephone. I'll be right back."

"**That** doesn't surprise me," Paul said, covering the mouthpiece with his hand. He could hear a muted conversation in the background between Oscar and his boss.

"Five hundred francs a week… no mileage charge… you pay for any diesel fuel that you use up."

"You do take plastic, don't you?" Paul immediately realized his blunder the moment the question had passed his lips. There was another moment of silence followed by, "Plastic what?"

"It's really not important, Oscar. Thank you for the information. You've been a big help. I'll be over to your station this afternoon to rent the truck."

Paul hung up the phone and checked his wallet, locating the credit cards that he assumed would be required.

He returned to reading the Coroner's report on the two boys. The cause of death was the same in all three cases – **"…massive loss of blood as a result of an attack by a large predator resulting in loss of body parts resulting in shock trauma and death."**

Again, Paul's thoughts turned to Gina. Why she wanted to risk her life on a foolhardy treasure hunt was unfathomable. She obviously didn't care for him as much as he did for her, or she would heed his warning.

After paying his deposit, Paul drove the rented flatbed truck to the Brig airfield, parked the vehicle and strolled over to the control tower. A helicopter was delivering the cage from Geneva airport, and was scheduled to arrive within the hour. He had explained to the pilot that he would meet his craft when it landed, and they could drop the cage directly on the back of the flatbed truck.

The sky was a robin's egg blue with high cirrus clouds. A gentle cross-wind occasionally nudged the airport's windsock. The mountains began abruptly at the north end of the field, and were covered with green up to the point where the tree line yielded to the snow-capped granite cliffs. Paul couldn't help thinking what a peaceful place Brig was. The bright sun felt warm on his face and chest.

The popping chatter of the Huey's massive rotor could be heard in the distance. Paul squinted, searching the sky in the direction of the approaching aircraft. A dark speck appeared at first, and grew larger as it began its descent. Banking sharply to the left the helicopter approached the airport at a ninety degree angle and then entered the traffic pattern. Paul walked towards the helipad.

Fifteen minutes later the large, heavy steel cage was secured by strapping on the back of the flatbed. The pilot landed the craft on the helipad, and two people emerged from the Hughes UH-1H.

"Paul Soria?" the pilot inquired.

"Yes, I'm Paul," he answered as he extended his hand. "Did you have a good flight?" He offered the question as an ice-breaker.

"Sonny, any flight that you can walk away from is a good one," the man said as he broke into an unexpected laugh that illuminated his fearsome face. Then he slapped Paul on the shoulder. Paul wondered how the man acquired the ugly scar on the right side of his face.

"This is my daughter, Jean. She is also my co-pilot. I'm Sam Faber."

Paul was surprised as the girl doffed her helmet and then her N.Y. Mets baseball cap, freeing curls of golden blonde hair which cascaded down below her shoulders. Her face was tanned and beautiful, and her eyes were a deep blue. She wore no make up and her radiant smile revealed remarkably straight, white teeth. Her oil-stained green coveralls masked her trim figure, but her full breasts made their presence known against the constraining fabric.

"Nice to meet you, Paul," her greeting was warm, and her manner made Paul feel comfortable immediately. Their eyes maintained contact for several seconds.

"That steel contraption that you had us lug up here weighs almost seven hundred pounds and it has a lot of wind resistance. It slowed our airspeed by nearly thirty knots; we had a devil of a time getting it here," Sam continued laughing. "But Jean here can set this chopper down on a dragonfly's backside if'n she had to. She's the best damn helipilot around, if I do say so myself, Marshall."

"Inspector," Paul corrected. "You're from America, right?"

"Correct!" Sam answered forcefully. "Tell me, there, Inspector Paul, what the heck are you going to do with that contraption we just delivered?" Sam scratched his head.

Paul hesitated before answering, "We're going to try and catch and transport a rogue bear with it."

"A bear… with that?" Jean replied, the surprise evident in her voice.

In Paul's mind, something about Jean's presence caused the importance of the bear to be diminished temporarily.

"I heard on the radio that a few people had been attacked up here. Are you going to kill it?" The expression in her eyes revealed a compassionate nature.

"That's not our intention, Jean." Paul purposefully used her name to bridge the awkwardness he felt about talking about the bear.

"We would like to be able, assuming that the bear cooperates, to relocate it to a remote area where it will be safe, and will not harm anyone."

"I'm glad," her tone sounded genuine. "I wouldn't have wanted to be a part in any animal's destruction. I don't feel as though I could kill anything unless my own life depended upon it."

Paul found Jean's simple honesty and her manner attractive. He decided to change the subject.

"What are you guys doing here in Switzerland... so far from the States?" he inquired in a light-hearted way.

"We go where the jobs take us, Inspector," Sam relied with another laugh. And right now there is more call for our services here in Europe. We're based in Geneva, but we'll fly anywhere, Russia, Africa, Iceland... you name it, if the pay is right." Jean added.

"Can I buy you and your dad lunch...a coke or something?" Paul asked. "It's starting to get a little warm out here."

"No thank you, Inspector," Jean responded. "I wish we could."

"Paul, please call me Paul," he insisted.

"I don't think we can, Paul. But thanks. We're anxious to get gassed up and headed back to Geneva." Jean clarified, her blue eyes sparkling as she smiled at Paul. "Perhaps another time," she teased.

Sam regarded the exchange between Paul and his daughter with amusement.

"Ha, ha," he chortled. "She's just like her mother; more than a match for any man, Inspector."

"I'll tell you what, Paul," Sam offered in a conciliatory fashion, "we've got another big job up here in three weeks; when we come back you can take us out to dinner...agreed?"

"Agreed," Paul declared, as he extended his hand to both of them.

After he left the airport, he drove back to his office where he was scheduled to meet Willy at four o'clock. On the way, he kept thinking about Gina and her hair-brained scheme to go treasure hunting at the very worst time.

Willy's, beat up truck was parked in front of the police station when Paul arrived, and he was still sitting in the front seat. He saw Paul pull up in the Volvo flatbed. Willy got out of his pick up and walked around to the rear of the Volvo truck, inspecting the cage and examining the tension on the restraining straps.

"What do you think?" Paul asked after turning off the engine of the truck.

"I'm not sure if it will hold the bear."

"It should, Willy. Those are 3/8 inch steel bars reinforced with welded braces. That cage weighs seven hundred pounds.

"You have to remember, Paul… no one here has ever trapped a bear like this one before."

Willy's words were taken as a warning as Paul realized that they had little or no information on the disposition or the strength of the creature. And while he was certain that the bear could be tranquilized effectively, he had no idea what to expect when the bear recovered from the effects of the sedative.

"This cage is the largest and strongest on that we could locate," Willy said resolutely. "If it doesn't hold this bear, then I don't know what we can do."

Paul could see that Willy had some misgivings about the cage. But he believed that if they kept the animal sufficiently tranquilized, it would not pose too much of a problem.

"We have enough of the tranquilizer to sedate a small herd of elephants," Willy stated confidently. "The bear shouldn't cause us much trouble providing that we are close enough for a good, clean shot."

Willy and Paul reviewed the checklist of items that they would need for the hunt. They decided that two days and night would be sufficient time to make contact with the bear, providing that they were correct in their assumption that the animal was headed north and west, and that it would be attracted by the scent of the pig bait.

Six tranquilizer darts were packed. Each dart carried enough sedative to knock out an adult Kodiak bear. Willy believed that two darts would be more than adequate. He was also concerned that over-sedation might result in the animal's death by shutting down his autonomic nervous system and suffocating him. Too much tranquilizer could cause the arrest of the bear's unvoluntary muscles, resulting in asphyxiation. Willy packed two syringes containing a powerful stimulant which would counteract the effects of the tranquilizer. He hoped that he would not have to use them.

The two men packed everything, including their camping gear in waterproof boxes. The equipment would remain at the police station until they could load it onto the truck early next morning.

"We'll... did we forget anything?" Paul always relied on Willy's advice when preparing for trips into the high backcountry.

"What we really need cannot be packaged into these boxes," Willy stated.

"What's that?"

"A lot of luck," Willy answered, emphasizing his point with his fist.

Willy was not given to jesting, and Paul understood the game warden's skepticism. He never doubted Willy's instincts in matters pertaining to animals or terrain. Willy seemed to have a sixth sense; an almost unnatural sensitivity to the vageries of nature and a remarkable track record for reading sign.

Willy thought about the danger to his friend as well as to the bear. He understood further that this was perhaps their only chance to take the animal alive. If anything went wrong, it could mean the death of Paul and almost guarantee extermination for the bear.

"Willy," Paul began hesitantly, "I think there's something you should understand. I do not want to be guilty of keeping this from you." He waited for a change in expression in his friend's eyes. It didn't come... Willy was focused and stoic.

"If we capture this bear, and it turns out to be a species which was, until now, thought to be extinct, then there are going to be a lot of people who will want to study it. That's going to mean permanent capture... and not relocation for the bear. It'll be the same as if someone walked into Brig with a live dinosaur. It's an object of scientific curiosity... a once in a lifetime opportunity to study a living fossil. It will create more publicity than the discovery of the Coelacanth or a Tasmanian wolf. Do you understand the implications?"

"I understand... very well, Paul,"

The Noah's Ark Conception

"When the word gets out that we've captured a rare species of bear, this town will be invaded by an army of reporters and scientists," Willy acknowledged. He understood that people's insatiable curiosity and their innate ability to rationalize any activity or pursuit in the name of scientific discovery would mean permanent incarceration for the bear. Minimally, the animal would never be permitted to return to the wild. Willy had made up his mind that he was not going to permit anything like that from happening.

PART   THREE

APPREHENDING   A
ROGUE   BEAR

Chapter Twenty

Five a.m. seemed to come early as Paul was awakened by the persistent buzzing of the alarm clock. Gina mumbled something unintelligible as Paul reached over to shut off the annoying clamor. His first thoughts were of the great bear that was also awakening at this hour, and how both of them had a rendezvous with destiny.

Paul arose, showed and dressed quickly. There would be little opportunity in the mountains for his ritual of personal hygiene. He gulped down a cup of coffee, made himself a bowl of Frosted Mini Wheats and kissed Gina on the cheek.

"Be sure you take the lunches I made for you and Willy. They're in the refrigerator," she managed to say through her sleep induced haze. Gina was definitely not a morning person, and getting her mouth to form coherent words and sentences was difficult for her a five a.m. Paul kissed her again and headed for the police station. Willy would be waiting for him there.

As he walked out of the house, he noticed the eastern sky was tinted a light indigo, indicating that the sun was not far behind. A few early birds were chirping, but other than that it was dead quiet. Starting up his Porsche, he allowed the oil to come up to pressure and then he headed to the station.

Willy was loading the water-proof boxes they had packed, the day before, into the Volvo truck when Paul arrived. In the early dawn light, the truck with its unusual steel cargo on the back resembled some kind of secret weapon. Willy waved a brief acknowledgement of Paul's arrival as he parked the red sports car.

"Mornin' Willy," Paul greeted his friend. "You're up bright and early."

"Willy managed a quick smile. "It's chilly now, but it's supposed to heat up today."

"I'm willing to bet that our bear has been up for a while and is looking for breakfast right about now."

Suddenly Paul heard a squeal coming from the back of the truck.

"I see that you brought a pig, Willy."

Paul walked behind the truck and saw a medium-sized boar tied to the rear bumper.

"Where did you get him?" Paul inquired with a chuckle.

"He's on loan from a friend."

"**On loan**?" Paul shouted. "Don't you think that there's a pretty good chance that you might not be able to return it?"

"We shall see," Willy replied. Once again Paul began to get the feeling that Willy wasn't revealing everything on his mind about his capture plan.

"Willy, what do you really estimate that our chances are of catching this bear?"

Willy answered with conviction, "I think the chances of capturing it are good. I think the chances or holding on to it are something else again."

Paul went inside to his office and retrieved the checklist. Everything that they would need appeared to have been packed. He turned off the lights in his office and locked the door. He left a note for Maria to find when she came on duty. He brought a portable transceiver radio with him so that he could maintain communications with Maria. The pig was the last thing to be loaded. Paul and Willy stepped back and looked at the strange assemblage of items on the truck. Willy was glad that they were leaving Brig before sunrise. He didn't want anyone to see or inquire about what they were up to. The two men climbed into the cab, started the engine and then headed northeast towards the Simplon Pass Road.

After turning north, they drove for about ten miles until they saw the exit for the old lumbering road. Turning left onto the road, the truck banged along northeast. The road had been paved for the first three miles, with ample clearance on both sides. After the asphalt ended, the road narrowed and they found themselves motoring on potholed, red dirt with two ruts on either side, worn deeply by years of passing lumber trucks and pooling water. The foliage on either side of the road was overgrown;

leaves, pine needles and branches smacked and scraped against the sides of the vehicle. The red dirt, churned up by the vortex created by the passing truck deposited a fine patina of dust on the windshield and on the dashboard.

Five more miles and many pounds of red dust later, the truck crossed the crude, but sturdy wooden bridge that spanned the fork of the river. Willy indicated that they were within two kilometers of their planned interception point.

When they arrived, they choose a straight section of roadway where they could command a clear view for at least a quarter of a mile in either direction. Then Willy backed the truck off the old lumber road into a small clearing.

"This looks like as good a spot as any. What do you think Paul?"

"If the bear is headed uphill and northwest from the spot where it had attacked the fisherman, then it will probably stay on that side of the river. I think that this is a likely spot where the bear will attempt to cross this road."

The two men off-loaded the pig, and secured one end of the leash rope to a large tree next to the road. Clearing away some additional undergrowth, they made sure that they had a clear shot if the bear approached from any direction.

Next, they unloaded portions of their gear, including a portable tree platform that Willy would set up next to the road near the downwind side of the pig. Paul helped Willy setting up the platform; placing it high in a conifer tree, about six meters above the ground. It had a canvass cover to protect Willy in case of rain. Willy also carried a short-range walkie-talkie to maintain contact with Paul. Paul would hunker down in the cab of the truck – his shooting position in the stakeout.

Paul picked up his walkie-talkie and pressed the switch, "Testing, testing… Willy, can you hear me?"

"Loud and clear, Paul," Willy replied.

"How about we take turns at these positions? Two hours on, a quarter of an hour break and then we'll switch…" Paul suggested.

"Sounds okay to me," Willy agreed. Then he added, "Listen Paul, the pig will probably sense the bear's presence before we see it. Watch for any erratic behavior and let me know right away...copy?"

"Ten-four." Paul placed the walkie-talkie on the seat and noted the time... nine-twenty nine a.m.

The late May sun climbed higher in the sky, and the temperature inside the cab of the truck reached a sweltering eighty-eight degrees. Even with the windows cranked wide open, there was no breeze and little relief as beads of perspiration trickled down Paul's face. He wiped his face with a handkerchief and sipped some water from a canteen. The pig had settled down and was dozing in the shade near the base of the tree. It seemed to be enjoying its temporary home, and its tail, jerking spasmodically, was the only sign of life. It became so hot that the bugs, usually a nuisance, had sought out the coolness of the shady undergrowth.

At twenty minutes past eleven, Paul picked up his walkie-talkie.

"Willy?" he said in a low voice into the radio.

"What's up?" he responded.

"How're you makin' out up there?"

"Except for the heat and a few bugs... okay."

"Are you ready for a break yet?"

"Good idea! My legs are getting a little stiff."

"Okay, come on down and I'll break out the lunch that Gina made for us."

Willy joined Paul inside the truck, and together they consumed four sandwiches, and an equal number of diet colas. They enjoyed their lunch immensely, and at noon, Paul decided to call into Maria.

"Central control, this is bravo alpha one, come in Maria."
A few seconds later he repeated the call.

"I hope this portable radio works okay, and that they can hear me from way up here," Paul said to Willy. Then he checked the auxiliary antenna magnetically mounted on the roof of the truck.

Maria's voice came through but it was partially masked with static.

"Bravo alpha one, this is central control; I can hear you, Paul...over."

Maria, Willy and I are staked out up here on the lumber road, about a mile and a half from the west fork bridge. The area is marked on my wall map. We believe that the bear may be headed in our direction. Do you have anything for me? Over!"

Maria's voice broke through the static after a few seconds, and Paul assumed that she was checking through his messages.

"Paul, Willy got a phone call this morning from a Doctor Morris Levin. He said that a sample that Willy had given him created quite a stir with the local DNA laboratory, and that they and Dr. Levin wanted to have a meeting with Willy and yourself as soon as possible.

Paul glanced over at Willy and read disappointment in the warden's face. Willy had figured out exactly what such a meeting would conclude and mean for the bear.

"Maria, you'll have to call back Dr. Levin and tell him that I won't be back until tomorrow afternoon... probably very late. It makes no sense for him and his associates to come out here from Basel until Monday morning."

"Roger, Paul. I'll get back to him right away. Is there anything else?" Maria asked.

"No, that's it for now. I'll be off the air until three or three-thirty this afternoon. Bravo alpha is off and clear." Paul hung up the microphone.

Willy said nothing, as he continued to finish his sandwich. He kept alert; looking out of the truck and watching for any unusual movement from the pig.

"Willy," Paul broke the silence. "I guess that sample of the bear's fur stirred up some excitement at the lab. I guess that our ursine adversary out there truly is unique. I hoped things wouldn't have gotten this far, but it looks like scientific interest in this animal is building already."

"Are you ready to climb up the tree?" Willy asked.

"I guess so," Paul responded hesitantly.

Willy helped Paul up into the platform, and handed him the tranquilizer rifle and the walkie-talkie. Then Willy took his position in the cab of the truck.

The afternoon passed slowly in the tortuous heat, as the pig continued its undisturbed slumber. It was a little after two-thirty when Willy heard the sound. A sharp crack alerted him first, like the breaking of a twig underfoot. A few seconds later another was heard followed by a third – each time the sound grew louder. Willy glanced quickly at the pig.

The boar raised his head, and had one ear cocked in the direction of the sound. The sounds had come from the south side of the road; in the direction of a dense tangle of briars and small deciduous trees. Willy picked up the walkie-talkie and pressed the transmit button.

"Paul, Paul... do you copy?" he whispered into the microphone.

"Roger, Willy. What have you got?" Paul replied, sensing tension in Willy's voice.

"I heard some noises... like something moving through the thicket about fifty meters to the southeast of us. Can you see anything?"

"Not a thing. There's too many branches in my way to see that far unobstructed. The pig seems to be behaving normally, though."

Willy answered slowly, "The pig heard it too. But it doesn't seem to be paying any attention to it now."

Suddenly, a crashing sound came from the same area. This time the boar rose to its feet, staring into the woods and sniffing the air carefully.

"I heard it that time Willy," Paul transmitted. "But I still don't see anything."

Paul carefully loaded a tranquilizing dart into the chamber of the rifle, and sat the weapon across his lap. He scrutinized the area where the sound had emanated but detected nothing. Without warning, an explosion of sound occurred as a large covey of grouse-like birds burst from the thicket. The loud beating of their wings caused Paul to jump reflexively.

"Paul?"

"Those birds scared the shit out of me, Willy."

"Something is in that thicket and it spooked those birds," Willy warned. "Whatever it is, it's headed in your direction so get ready."

Paul shouldered the rifle; training the barrel at the place where the birds had emerged. He continued to see nothing.

A few more twigs cracked, and something large moved slowly through the brush. Willy watched as the tops of some small trees and tall brush vibrated as if brushed by some unseen animal. He followed the trail of the disturbed trees with his eyes, and plotted the course of the unknown creature.

"Paul… it's headed right for you and should be under you in less than a minute."

The pig was now fully alert and pacing nervously. It continued to sample the air and snorted while pawing the ground. From his vantage point in the tree, Paul caught sight of the moving bushes, and aimed his rifle directly at the center of the disturbance. He knew that he would only have time for one quick shot.

Then he saw glimpses of reddish-brown as the animal moved through the tall, dense underbrush. He took careful aim, but there did not seem to be enough of the animal visible in order to obtain the perfect opportunity for a shot. Brown-black shadows splattered through the thicket and acted like camouflage, Paul did not want to take a chance wasting a dart on a poor shot. Because if the bear sensed that it was being hunted, it would probably charge off into the forest at thirty-five miles an hour.

Meanwhile, Willy believed that he had a good shot if the bear emerged out of the brush and onto the road. He picked a point on the road near the tree where Paul was hiding, and at a level about shoulder high for a large bear.

Suddenly, as he was sighting through the scope, it appeared. It lumbered out of the bushes and into the full light of the road. Willy relaxed his grip on the trigger as the red deer buck glanced up, surpised, and froze in its tracks as it stared at the strange animal tied to the tree. The deer remained frozen for several seconds as it continued to peruse the pig with a guarded and wary curiosity. Then, trotting down the road for about twenty meters, the deer disappeared into the forest on the north side of the road.

"I'm still shaking," Paul spoke into the radio.

"False alarm," Willy responded.

"I'm coming down," Paul answered. "I need something cold to drink."

A few minutes later, Paul was removing a cold can of soda pop from the cooler on the back of the truck.

"What are you thinking, Willy,"

"I'm thinking that our bear may be following the same game trail that the deer used. There's a very good chance that the bear may not be too far behind."

Paul glanced at his watch: Two-forty. He decided that now was a good time to call in again. He turned on the radio and pushed the transmit switch on the microphone.

"Central control, this is bravo alpha one, come in Maria...over."

He released the button and waited for her response. All he heard was static. After several repetitions of the call, there was still no response.

He rechecked the connection in the back of the radio, and followed the antenna coaxial up to the roof of the truck where it disappeared into the base of the antenna mount. Everything looked in order. He double checked the tuning on his radio, verifying that he was using the correct frequency. He could not find anything wrong with the set. He repeated the transmission.

"Central control, this is bravo alpha one... can you hear me? Come in Maria." Only a raspy, static hiss poured out of the speaker.

"Maybe she's out to a late lunch, Paul. After all, it is a bit earlier than you told her that you'd call in again."

Paul tried one more time to raise Maria and failed.

"I don't know if the problem is with the transmission or with the reception down at the station," Paul stated in a frustrated tone. "I'll guess that we'll have to keep trying, every few hours or so."

Paul and Willy switched positions again. Willy climbed back up into the tree platform, while Paul maintained vigilance from the cab of the truck. The high afternoon temperature had dropped significantly, making the waiting somewhat more comfortable. But the coolness also brought the pesty bugs back out of their hiding places in the deep forest. The winged attackers kamikazeed relentlessly into Paul's and Willy's exposed skin, and buzzed into their ears. They kept swatted them away.

As the sun began to descend below the mountain peaks, visibility into the deeper parts of the forest became a problem. The evening grew quite cool and by six o'clock, Paul estimated the temperature at sixty degrees. He decided to make dinner and to set up camp before they lost the light completely.

"Willy, have you seen or heard anything?"

"A few small animals, but now it's getting too dark to recognize anything."

"Why don't you come on in for the night and I'll get dinner going."

Willy climbed down out of the tree and walked back to the truck, his rifle and canteen slung over his shoulder. Paul was already busy making a fire.

Willy removed a bag of swine chow from the truck and emptied on the ground in front of the boar. He devoured the pellets ravenously, making deep grunting sounds as he pressed his sensitive snout into the dirt. After ten minutes, there wasn't a single pellet remaining.

Paul started to grill hamburgers on the fire, and the scent of the cooking meat filled the air. Willy located the sleeping bags and inflated two air mattresses using a portable compressor hooked up to the truck's battery. He set up the sleeping bags, on the ground under the truck. In the event of rain they would at least have some cover, he estimated. He took both rifles and leaned them against the rear axle, where they would be within easy reach.

The food tasted good, as it always does when a person has been outdoors camping all day. They consumed the first round of hamburgers, and then went back and cooked more. It was dark when Paul threw three more large logs onto the fire. Paul always enjoyed this time of day outdoors, and he took the relaxing opportunity for a casual chat with his friend.

"Willy, I've been meaning to ask you," Paul initiated the conversation, "How did you figure out that this bear was a separate sub-species? Was it when you discovered the fur sample?"

Willy thought for a few seconds, poking the glowing embers of the fire with a long stick.

"When I saw the way Arthur Weigel had been chewed up, I suspected that something was very different about this animal's habits. But when I found the fur sample, I knew that the bear… or whatever it was… was not a grizzly, a brown or a black. It had a different length and texture; different than anything I have ever felt before. At the time, I reasoned it might have been some other kind of escaped alien carnivore. It was only after I witnessed Dr. Levin's reaction to the sample did I understand clearly that we were dealing with something very unusual."

"How do you think that this animal has managed to survive, without man's knowledge of it for all of these years?"

"Europe and Asia are enormous continents… joined together. The wilderness is vast, some of it still unexplored; extending all the way to eastern Russia, Manchuria, Siberia and Southeast Asia. Modern man has lived there since the end of the last ice age. It's just possible that this species had been secretive and wary enough to have avoided himans. And any man that wasn't lucky enough to have avoided this bear didn't live to tell about it. That's all I can surmise," Willy explained.

"Then how do you account for the sudden and localized rash of attacks? Why hasn't someone reported attacks like these before?"

"I can't answer that intelligently. It is a curious behavior. Perhaps this bear happened upon humans for the first time, or maybe it is really sick. Whatever the reason, it must be studied… learned from… and not executed."

"What convinces you to believe that this bear will be killed, Willy?"

"Its inherent violent behavior dictates that it will probably have to be killed outright. The bear will be very fortunate if we can successfully capture and study it. In either case it will die."

"Why?" Paul pressed his friend.

"Because you cannot take a wild animal out of its natural environment and expect it to survive. It will lose the will to live. All wild animals behave that way."

Paul contemplated what Willy had said, and was inclined to agree with him.

Willy continued, "In the 1800's, man hunted the elephant seal to near extinction. A group of scientists were sent to the west to try and locate and to study the remaining, dwindling population... assuming that they could locate any remaining specimens. They finally located eight adult elephant seals off the coast of Baja California. They immediately shot seven of them, so they could take the bodies back to Washington, D.C. for analysis. These men killed seven because they assumed that there were more elephant seals around somewhere. Fortunately, they were correct. But that is the kind of mentality that I despise so much in so many men... that arrogance. To take such a foolhardy and myopic risk in the name of scientific advancement now, and worry about future consequences later is just so wrong. Some people just don't seem to get it, and it angers me to no end."

"Unfortunately, Willy, I can think of so many instances where you are correct," Paul supported his friend. "And I agree with you. When they confirm that this animal is a rare species, people, and not just scientists, will come swarming all over this forest."

"That's why we cannot tell them what we have discovered and where it is," Willy emphasized fervently.

"But what about those friends of yours who are coming out here on Monday, aren't they are going to be asking a lot of questions? My report and the Coroner's reports on the attacks are now public knowledge."

"We must make people believe that we have killed the bear, and then we can relocate the animal to a safe place where it will live in peace," Willy concluded.

Paul did not like his friend's idea. He could see far too much risk in Willy's plan.

Chapter Twenty-One

The night air was cool and sweet smelling. Paul and Willy lay in their sleeping bags, relaxing and waiting for sleep to overtake them. The campfire cast an eerie, orange glow on the trees and stimulated flickering shadows on and around the nearby brush that lined the perimeter of the clearing. The orchestra of the evening: owls, tree frogs and insects made inharmonious music from unseen places which resonated through the stillness. Occasionally, the snap of a twig betrayed the scamperings of a rodent moving furtively along with its nocturnal foragings. Willy understood that as long as those noises continue to persist that everything was normal and as it should be.

By two a.m., the moon had risen forty degrees above the eastern horizon. It waned to three quarters from full a few nights before, diminishing each night. The fire had collapsed into a dull, red-orange glow and the moonlight bathed the forest in a blue-white light. The two men slept peacefully under the truck, oblivious to the total and ominous silence that now surrounded them.

A few meters away, in the forest, two large black eyes stared through the dense underbrush at the strange glow in the center of the clearing. It had experienced fire before and knew instinctively to avoid the hot, yellow-orange flickering thing and the tell-tale odor of the smoke that always accompanied it. It regarded the truck with fear because it was big and it smelled unnatural. The bear's predatory brain had sensed the presence of the pig, now sleeping soundly under the tree. The huge bear's eyes scrutinized everything in the clearing carefully, but failed to detect the men's forms; obscured by the sleeping bags and lying very still under the rear of the truck.

Two additional pairs of eyes joined the surveillance of the campsite. Silently they stared, wide-eyed, and stimulated by the unusual sights and scents. The largest of the three animals sensed prey nearby and was very curious; anxious to explore the clearing and get to the pig. Using its huge head and forepaws, it prodded the other two and forced them back into the safety of the forest. The mother was not comfortable with the strange objects in the clearing. Instinct had warned it that danger was present, and despite the proximity of an easy meal the sow bear was compelled to retreat. Still, the scent of the pig made the huge bear's mouth lather with saliva. But it was the stronger reaction to the truck and its hulking cargo which inevitably frightened the trio away. The mother noted the location of the pig and it would return later – alone.

Willy's eyes flashed open. Something had alerted and awakened him. Adrenalin shot through his body as he perceived the abnormal stillness – the strange, foreboding silence. Something had frightened the smaller creatures of the night. His nose detected a lingering scent. It was the same fetid odor as that of the fur sample he had plucked from the bark of a tree. A powerful realization electrified him. The big bear was nearby!

He lifted his head slowly and carefully from the sleeping bag; his eyes darting about, searching for any sign of movement. He glanced over at the pig and saw that it was sleeping contently, unaware of the potential danger. Willy raised his arm slowly and his hand found the rifle, leaning where he had placed it against the rear axle. Except for where the moonlight penetrated, it was nearly pitch-black in the forest. He understood that the slightest detectable motion or sound on his part would send the bear smashing and clawing into their sleeping area. He was afraid to awaken or startle Paul, who would surely alert the bear to their presence.

The lingering odor was heavy and musky and Willy judged that the bear was within ten to twenty meters of the clearing. He tried to get a sense for the wind's direction, but was not able to detect any. He listened carefully for any sound that might betray the great animal's hiding place, but he heard none. His hand began to tremble and he let go of the rifle, allowing it to rest against the truck. He remained absolutely still for another five minutes.

The Noah's Ark Conception

Soon, the bear's pungent scent began to dissipate and the forest creatures resumed voicing their nocturnal cacophony. Willy knew that the beast had departed, and he wondered why. He glanced over at his friend sleeping peacefully beside him. It was a long time before Willy fell back to sleep.

Willy awoke at first light and carefully sampled the air for the bear's scent. It was clear. The background sounds of the night forest had yielded to the early communications of the daytime denizens. The night shift was scurrying to their secluded lairs where they would sleep away the daytime heat. A few birds had begun to flutter and stir. He carefully wriggled out of his sleeping bag so that he wouldn't disturb Paul and restarted the fire.

The ground was damp with the early morning condensation and Willy retrieved some dry kindling from the floor of the truck. Within five minutes he had a strong fire blazing, and the smell of fresh coffee began to permeate the clearing.

Paul stirred, opened and rubbed his eyes and detected the smell of coffee. He had been dreaming of Gina. They had been making passionate love when a great bear charged through their bedroom window and snatched her, screaming from their bed. He had drawn his gun but was afraid to fire for fear of hitting the woman he loved. The bear had dragged her into the woods and he never saw or heard from her again. It was a true nightmare.

"Shit," he mumbled to himself as he recalled the horrible dream, and he began to slip out of the bag. He had to pee badly.

The first birds were now active and greeted the brightening daylight with their morning spring mating songs. Paul glanced over to the boar, and watched it defecating where it had slept.

Wonderful creatures, he thought to himself as he climbed out from under the truck and stretched. *They shit where they eat.*

He noticed that Willy had walked down the road, about twenty five meters, and appeared to be looking for signs that the bear had crossed the road during the night.

Thirty meters to the north of where the pig was secured, Willy halted abruptly. His feet froze in place, as he could not believe what he his eyes were telling him. There were three sets of tracks in the dirt, and now he completely understood the reason for the bear's savage behavior.

After tending to nature's morning urgings, Paul poured himself a cup of coffee and then walked up the road to join and greet his friend. Willy saw Paul approaching, and his feet scratched the ground, obliterating the tracks.

"What are you doing, Willy," Paul said in a cheerful, good-morning style voice.

"I was trying to determine if the bear had crossed during the night."

"What did you find?"

"Just the tracks of a lot of little animals and some deer, but no sign of our bear," Willy answered hesitantly.

Willy seemed to be in a hurry to get back to the clearing, and he began walking back without further explanation of his actions. Paul detected strangeness in Willy's behavior, but dismissed it as another one of his friend's personal idiosyncrasies.

Paul made breakfast, as Willy fed the pig.

They consumed their food, cleaned up quickly and prepared to resume their shooting positions. Paul wanted to attempt another call to Maria, but he knew that she would not have been in the station house that early in the morning.

Chapter Twenty-Two

Gina Ann Schmidt woke up early and lept out of bed with a sense of urgency. The sun was rising fast and she admonished herself for getting a late start. She stood in the shower, allowing the steaming water to invigorate her and rouse every cell in her body. Her thoughts were on the gold; following the old map and recreating the movements of the outlaw. She was convinced that the thief had required immediate shelter from the unexpected blizzard, and grinned as she analyzed the events that had occurred over half a century before. She believed that she had figured out the secret of the story, and that the loot was waiting for her to come and retrieve it.

She dried herself, dressed hurriedly and walked to the barn. Gina rarely ate a big breakfast – she never seemed to have the time. She started up her Land Rover which she had gassed and loaded up with her equipment the night before; allowing the engine to warm gradually. She returned to the house and removed the map from its hiding place in the hutch. Stuffing the paper into her shirt pocket, she went to the dresser and removed the pistol and holster that was her uncle's. She strapped the holster to her belt.

Gina returned to the barn and reved up the engine on the 4 x 4. As the rpm's came alive, the fuel needle climbed to the full mark. With two, five gallon gasoline cans straped to the back of the vehicle she knew that she had more than enough fuel for a three-day excursion into the woods and back. She put the car in gear, released the hand-brake and eased the Land Rover slowly down the driveway and onto the main road towards the Simplon Pass.

She felt her excitement build as she gripped the steering wheel. She loved her sense of adventure and independence, and wondered if she had gotten that trait from her mother or from her father. Gina often visualized herself searching for, and then locating, the remains of an old prospector's shack, and finding sacks of gold coins buried beneath the floorboards. She could see the coins sparkling brilliantly in the sun, as the rotting canvass sacks burst under the weight of the treasure. Her fantasy was now becoming a reality as each mile of the Simplon Pass Road ticked off on the Land Rover's odometer. She was listening to Mary Chapin Carpenter singing, "Late ForYour Life", one of her favorite songs. It gladdened her that she was seizing the moment. She believed avidly that Uncle Mario would have been proud of her for taking her shot at the brass ring – the "gold" ring. She had conveniently rationalized and forgotten about Paul's warning – it didn't seem to matter now. She was a woman with a purpose.

Gina mentally reviewed the checklist of things that she would need. But she knew that even if she had forgotten anything, turning back was not an option. She suddenly realized that her speed was approaching 110 kilometers and hour and she eased her foot off the accelerator. In her euphoria, her focus was becoming distracted.

She located the service road turn off, and executed a quick left turn. The road wound uphill, through groves of tall hemlock and pine trees. As the hill steepened, the turns and switchbacks became tighter and more frequent. She downshifted several times and felt her ears pop as she approached a sign that warned, *"Forest Closed due to Bear Attacks"*. She ignored the sign and three quarters of a mile uphill the road was blocked with a sturdy, locked chain. A sign hanging from the center of the chain read, *"Area Closed to the Public"*.

Gina parked in a small clearing to the right of the sign and began unloading the gear that she would need for the rest of her journey up the mountain. Bear or no bear, she was on her way.

*   *   *   *   *   *   *   *   *

At midday, Paul and Willy had concluded their first shift. Paul had positioned himself on the tree platform, while Willy maintained his watch from the cab of the truck.

"Willy, it is twelve-oh-five. Let's take a break."

"Roger that!"

"Paul climbed from his perch, dropping to the ground and leaving his rifle on the platform. For a brief instant, he thought that he heard the telltale sounds of something moving on the other side of the road. He stopped and concentrated on detecting additional sounds from the same area. There were none. After a few seconds, he was satisfied that nothing was lurking in the dense tangles of brush, and he continued walking back to the truck. He was very anxious to contact his office.

Willy was busy breaking out their lunch as Paul walked past him and opened the door of the cab. He picked up the microphone and turned up the transceiver's volume control.

He repeated his call signs to Maria twice; each time releasing the transmit switch and patiently waiting for a response. As it had done earlier, only static noise emanated from the speaker's box. One more final attempt at calling resulted in the same static of unmodulated, dead air.

By now Paul was convinced that there was a malfunction in the communication's electronics, and he hung up the microphone in disgust.

"I wish I knew what the hell was wrong with this thing," he protested, stepping out of the cab. "It worked okay yesterday morning."

Realizing that his comments weren't going to change the situation, he became distracted by the rumblings of hunger coming from his stomach.

Suddenly, Paul caught the sight of a hemlock tree shaking about twenty-five meters away, in a thicket directly behind the spot where the pig was tied. From the size of the tree, Paul knew that it had taken a powerful force to disturb it. There was a slight breeze, but not of sufficient power to shake the tree and nothing else stirred.

The pig seemed calm and unafraid, hungrily staring at the food that Willy was unwrapping; it demonstrated no indication of impending danger. The boar was upwind of the hemlock tree and wouldn't have smelled anything.

Paul detected another movement, followed by a cracking sound. This time it came from the holly bushes that were closer to the pig. Ignoring the food, the pig spun around quickly, startled by new sounds behind it. Icy fear gripped Paul as he called out an alert to Willy.

"Willy, behind you!" Paul yelled the warning.

The pig suddenly began to cry out, squealing loudly and attempting to back up; struggling violently against the restraining rope that secured it to the large tree. Willy sized up the rapidly developing situation instantly.

"Grab the rifle," he yelled at Paul.

Paul opened the truck's door and reached into the cab, feeling for the weapon. He didn't take his eyes off the unfolding drama under the tree. The pig was struggling so intensely against the rope that in its terror, blood was beginning to spray out of its nose. The pig coughed as the tightening rope suffocated its air supply.

The bear's massive head, with jaws agape, mouth frothing and long white fangs gleaming, burst throught the dense brush with a deafening roar. Its eyes were wild as the incensed animal focused on the helpless prey. Paul jumped at his first sight of the bear. He had never seen such fierceness in an animal before. But its massive size was stupefying.

The pig continued its futile struggle; helpless, as the ravenous, dark brown beast crashed out of its hiding place and charged the terrified boar. Dust flew in all directions as the bear slowed its charge, the powerful claws digging into the earth. It reared up on its hind legs, lowered its head and walked forward, menacingly with mouth open and fangs exposed. The bear's front, razor-sharp claws were extended. It looked for an opening where it could move in for the kill. With a lightening quick motion it surged forward, seizing the pig behind the head with great jaws and crushing the pig's neck instantly. The bear shook the dead boar violently with the sideways motion of its huge body, separating the pig's head. The remainder of the carcass bounced off the ground, blood flowing from the gaping hole torn between the shoulders.

The attack was over in a matter of seconds, and the bear began dragging the kill into the bushes. Paul's fingers found the rifle and he yanked the weapon out of the truck. The bear's left side was facing Paul as he aimed the rifle at the animal's shoulder. He used the fender of the Volvo to stabilize the rifle and waited for the precise moment to fire.

The bear hesitated for a moment, letting go of the pig's carcass and glanced over at the truck with a wild, vicious expression on its face. Using the hesitation to his advantage, Paul squeezed the trigger, and the rifle recoiled hard as the drug-laden missle was propelled home. The great beast howled as the impact of the pneumatic dart drove the plunger forward, injecting fifty milliliters of the potent chlorate hydrate sedative.

The angry bear reared up on its hind legs; staring at the truck, enraged by the loud noise that had caused the sharp pain in its shoulder. The bear became confused, alternately changing its gaze from the truck to the dead pig on the ground. It decided to continue dragging the pig into the safety of the forest. Willy and Paul watched in amazement as the bear snatched the entire corpse of the pig in its huge jaws and moved towards the underbrush.

"Where's the other rifle?" Willy inquired. "We're going to need another dart."

"I left it up on the platform," Paul answered, embarrassed by his oversight.

"Then reload this rifle with another dart." Willy was clearly taking charge of the situation.

Paul removed another dart from the case and reloaded it into the CO2 rifle.

"Wait, look at the bear," Willy interrupted.

The bear was staggering and shaking its head as if fighting off the effects of the sedative. It dropped the pig and began turning wildly in different directions.

"We do not want to risk the possibility of over sedation," Willy reminded Paul. "Let's wait and see what happens before we fire another dart."

As the two men watched, mesmerized by what they were witnessing, the bear lost control of its left hind leg which it seemed to drag useless, behind it. Then suddenly, the front legs gave way and the bear collapsed on its chest. Its roaring quieted to deep grunts as the bear rolled over onto its right side, succumbing to the potent sedative. All movement from the great animal ceased as it lay partially in the bushes and partially in the clearing next to the decapitated pig. The immobilized bear was now quiet except for an occasional grunt. A strange stillness followed. The two men stopped to catch their breath.

After a few seconds had passed, Willy and Paul approached the sedated bear cautiously. Paul kept the second dart chambered and ready in case the bear rose suddenly. The head of the beast was as big around as a fifty-five gallon drum. The tongue lolled out of the open mouth as if in a drunken stupor. Willy noticed the bear's lethal fangs. They were nearly six inches long. He confirmed his suspicions about the animal's sex – definitely female.

"We must hurry to get this bear into the cage quickly; before it recovers. We have no idea how long the tranquilizer will remain effective," Willy advised.

Paul jumped on the back of the truck and removed the steel cable from the floor in front of the cage. He released the brake on the winch and handed the end of the cable to Willy, who unwound the cable from the winch and pulled it over the bear.
Meanwhile, Paul began tilting the bed of the truck and the cage slowly slid to the ground, but still resting against the tilted truckbed. Paul drove the truck forward slightly, and the cage came to rest on the ground. The cable passed directly through the center of the cage.

"Tie the bear's hind legs securely with the rope, and fasten the cable to the rope, between the animal's hind legs." Willy instructed. "I hope that this rope will be strong enough to take the weight of the bear," Paul said.

With the steel cable's hook secured to the rope that bound the bear's hind legs, Paul powered up the winch and began to take up the slack in the cable. As the cable became taut, Willy double checked all of the connections to make sure that nothing came loose as they were winching the enormous animal into the cage. He directed Paul with hand signals, and indicated that the power to the winch could be applied carefully.

Paul engaged the clutch lever and the winch began to retrieve the cable. The load on the truck was apparent as the rear wheels began to slide backwards. After the rear wheels had sunk sufficiently into the soft dirt and gained traction, the bear began to move towards the cage. Paul maintained a steady force on the cable and the bear's sedated body began to move slowly across the ground and out of the bushes.

Willy lifted as much of the bear's muzzle off the ground as he could, to prevent the face from dragging and causing eye or mouth injuries to the animal. The weight of the great head was enormous and Willy struggled against it. As he was reaching around under the animal's head in an attempt to gain a better purchase, Willy suddenly felt something very hard, about the size of a cigarette pack.

"Paul, hold it a minute," Willy called out. "I think you should come over here."

Paul put the winch in locked neutral and hurried over to see what John had discovered.

"There's something attached to the bear's neck," Willy said incredulously.

"You can't be serious," Paul responded skeptically. "Except for the people that were attacked, we are probably the only humans to see this animal alive and live to tell about it."

Willy elevated the bear's head as Paul reached under it, feeling for the mysterious object.

"What the hell...," he exclaimed in disbelief as his right hand found the object buried in the animal's dense fur. He felt around and determined that the object was fastened to the bear's neck with a braided nylon chord which was joined in the back with two metal links bolted together.

"What the heck is this?" Paul inquired, completed mystified by the discovery.

"I'm not completely certain, Paul, but I think that it's a telemetry collar. The kind that they use to keep track of an animal's migratory habits," Willy explained.

"Migratory habits! Then someone else is aware of the existence of this creature," Paul responded, his anger building inside him.

"Look for the name of the manufacturer on the transmitter, and see if there is a serial number," Willy advised.

"I don't see any identifying marks on the transmitter or on the chord," Paul answered after a few seconds. "I'm a lot more interested in getting this thing into the cage before it wakes up."

Willy commented, "Usually, the agency that collars any animal provides identification in case the animal dies, is captured or the collar falls off. In addition, the animal is usually marked or tagged in some manner, so it is easily recognized from a distance. There doesn't seem to be any markings on this bear," Willy observed as he searched both of the bear's ears for a tag and its lips for an identification tattoo.

"Willy, can we please get this the bear safely into the cage," Paul insisted. "We can search for tags later. Christ, this is a unique animal of immense size. Why the hell would anyone need to paint a sign on it that says, I'm a fucking "BEAR", when you could recognize this monster from a mile away?" Paul stated sarcastically and impatiently; still having a difficult time accepting their new discovery.

"I'm sure the appropriate agency will come looking for its missing **pet** soon enough," Paul quipped.

The bear's feet were nearly at the entrance to the cage when Paul resumed powering the winch. The metal door to the cage had been lifted, and secured with a metal pin that prevented the door from coming down. The retrieval of the cable seemed to be going well.

The bear's legs entered the cage first, and the smooth wooden floor of the cage made the final few feet of the retrieval go quickly. A few minutes later and the bear's limp body was entirely within the confines of the steel and wood paneled cage.

Willy jumped inside, disconnected the cable and untied the ropes that bound the bear's hind legs. Inside the cage, the bear's breathing sounds were amplified, and Willy could hear that its respiration was strong and rhythmic. After completing his cursory examination of the bear, Willy stepped out of the cage and closed and secured the door.

"Nice work, Willy," Paul congratulated his friend with a combination of satisfaction and relief. "If I knew how large that bear was before I came up here, I don't think that I would have been so confident that we would have ever captured it in this manner.

Suddenly a thumping sound came from inside the cage as the paralyzing effects of the chloral hydrate began to wear off.

"I think the drug's beginning to wear off," Willy noted. "Now we'll find out just how well this cage is constructed."

The animal's grunts grew louder and morphed into low moaning sounds. The bear was slowly regaining consciousness and control, and made feeble efforts to rise to its feet.

"Attach the cable to the cleats on the rear of the cage, Willy, and I'll winch it back on the truck and level the cargo bed."

Willy connected the steel cable's hook to the metal cleats on the rear of the cage and gave the "thumbs up" signal for Paul to begin hauling it up on the back of the tilted truck bed.

Suddenly a deafening bellow emerged from the cage as the bear became aware of its imprisonment. The cage began to shake violently, as the huge animal smashed its head and great bulk against the inside of the cage.

"I guess that the bear is fully awake now," Paul yelled, as he continued to apply power to the winch.

The enraged bear roared and continued to beat the inside of its prison with its massive and powerful paws. Willy noticed the impressions of the claws on the metal door and signaled to Paul to stop the winch.

"I don't think that we should put the cage on the truck just yet, and I don't think it's a good idea to transport it until we're sure that it will hold our friend in there."

Paul knew that Willy was right, and he killed the power to the winch. Together they watched the effects on the cage of the animal's struggles; still amazed at the incredible power of the beast.

"Maybe we should give it another injection of the sedative," Paul suggested.

"**I vould not do dass if I vere you, Herr Inspektor**," a very deep voice ordered from behind them.

<u>Chapter Twenty-Three</u>

The afternoon sun felt delightfully warm, even at seventy-five hundred feet. Gina had loaded up her hiking and camping gear and with great enthusiasm, urged herself to take the first steps up the rutted, partially washed away, dirt logging road. She had her walkman's earbud in one ear, and she had selected great travelling music. There was another seven miles to travel before she would reach the high alpine valley by late in the afternoon, and with sufficient daylight remaining, have enough time to set up camp for the night.

She had made her pack as light as possible, minimizing her burden. The metal detector hung awkwardly from her left shoulder, and she balanced the weight with the canteen that was slung on her right. She understood that she would require frequent rests on her journey up the steep mountain trail, and at one mile intervals, she would stop for thirty minutes to replenish her water and her strength with high-carb and fiber bars.

Despite the grueling ascent, her excitement for the treasure hunt had not diminished. To the contrary, she fully expected that each step forward brought her closer to her goal of wealth and perpetual security from insolvency. In addition, the knowledge that she was approaching the place where the outlaw, fifty years before, had probably hidden the stolen gold served to revitalize her with every difficult step. Her strong thighs began to burn from the lactic acid buildup, but she plodded ahead despite the annoying pain.

The mountains were beautiful; resplendent in their late spring greenery. Small animals and birds scurried and flew everywhere; most of the time busily preoccupied with the responsibilities that rearing young families required. The high mountain air was clean and pine-scented. Brooks and streams bubbled, their banks overflowing in a vain attempt to accommodate the spring snowmelt cascading from the higher elevations.

Gina imagined the clinking sounds of each of the gold coins with every step she took. It was at that point that she suddenly realized that she might not be able to recover all of the gold at once. A thousand ounces or more of gold would definitely be an overwhelming burden for her to carry. It would be a better option if she concealed part of it, and then returned later for the remainder. She wondered if the thief had struggled with the very same decisions.

At first she chastised herself for not considering that consequence of her success, but afterwards she decided that she could cope with the situation easily. Clearly, her primary objective was to locate the gold, which she was absolutely certain was waiting up the mountain, just a few more miles ahead.

It was nearly four-thirty in the afternoon when the terrain began to level off and Gina ventured her first steps into the valley. She sat her pack down against a large log, and double checked her location against the geodetic survey map using a compass and some landmarks. According to her calculations, she was entering the same valley where, according to the police officials in pursuit fifty years ago, they experienced the blizzard and lost sight of the outlaw's trail. She looked up, allowing her eyes to scrutinize the valley ahead of her.

This is definitely the place, she convinced herself.

The valley was created by a steep granite wall that climbed and formed a high mountain to the right, and a smaller, dome-shaped mountain, covered with fir trees bordering to the left. Sculptured and augered out by some extinct, receding, glacier thousands of years before, a flat meadow garnished with a multitude of wildflowers spread out for nearly a half a mile in front of where Gina stood. The meadow was surrounded by a dense thicket of tall pines, firs, and aspens that carpeted the perimeter of the valley, and appeared to go on forever on the other side. The meadow was partitioned by a stream that snaked along toward the right side. The water in the stream was shallow and occasionally collected in pools less than a meter deep as it wound its way to the southwest.

Gina concentrated and forced herself to believe that she was desperate outlaw, attempting to flee with her ill-gotten loot from the pursuing lawmen. She looked around carefully, but saw nothing that would serve as an effective escape route or an obvious shelter from a late-season blizzard. She forced herself to concentrate harder; to feel the meadow's subtle vibrations and to sense what the valley was telling her.

Suddenly, she realized that it was the wrong kind of weather today. Fifty years ago it was probably freezing, and the snow was already falling when the outlaw had entered the valley. His first concern, other than to find shelter, would have been to cover his tracks – especially if he was going to hold up. Clearly, he would not have wanted the posse to ride right up to his hiding place. And riding a horse, he would have left specific hoofprints, which would have been easy to follow in the snow and give away his retreat. The outlaw would have looked to hide any trace of his passing.

Gina looked around, hoping to find a rocky outcropping through the earth where a horse could pass without leaving tracks. She saw none, but felt that if one existed, it most probably would have been located on the right side of the valley. She reasoned further that the right side of the valley would have afforded more protection from the icy wind and the blowing snow. She turned right and began walking eastward across the meadow. A quarter of a mile later, she came to the edge of the stream and readied herself to wade across. The water, while flowing swiftly was not deep and she could ford easily. She moved up the embankment on the opposite side and headed in the direction of the aspen thicket. Once she arrived in the grove of aspens, she realized that they would have been too dense and impenetrable on horseback. Their low hanging branches would have made a difficult obstacle for a rider on horseback to negotiate. It would have dramatically inhibited their progress. Gina felt that she had made the wrong choice.

Mindful that the daylight was ebbing, Gina decided to make camp on the edge of the aspen grove. It was a dry and level spot, and the availability of firewood was ample. She unloaded her burden and began to unpack her equipment that would be needed for the night's camp. She made a clearing for a fire, gathered rocks from the stream for the perimeter and spread out her bed roll. Fifteen minutes later, a warm fire was burning and Gina was roasting three hot dogs impaled on pointed sticks.

The sounds accompanying the enveloping darkness became more audible as the creatures of the dark began to communicate. The wind had died completely, and a damp coolness gripped the forest quickly as the final glow from the sun disappeared in the western sky. Gina felt a slight chill and put on her eider-down blue vest to help her ward off the evening's cold. She climbed into her sleeping bag and rested her head against an inflatable pillow. Sleep arrived without warning – it had been an exciting but an exhausting day.

Chapter Twenty-Four

Paul and Willy wheeled around and found themselves looking down the barrels of two, 9mm parabellum Lugers. A tan colored Mercedes SUV was driving slowly up the road towards them. It had no official markings or insignia, and with all of the noise that the bear was making, they did not hear the vehicle drive up.

"Who the hell are you?" Paul demanded in an official sounding tone.

Both men holding the guns were very tall and powerfully built. They had military style cropped blonde hair and blue eyes, and except for their camouflage hunting outfits they reminded Paul of stereotypical "SS" men.

"Who ve are ist not important to you, policeman. What **ist** important ist dass you release dis animal right away… schnell," one of the men ordered in a calm but firm voice as he gestured with his pistol.

"Listen fellas," Willy tried to be reasonable, "I'm the game warden in charge of this area, and this is official Swiss Federal business. If you guys are hunters, then you should know by now that this area is closed to hunt…"

BOOM, the sound of a pistol being fired into the ground in front of him was deafening, and Willy jumped.

"Ve are nicht going to tell you again, herr warden. Release that bear immediately, or be prepared to pay zee consequences. The choice, of course, ist yours," the leader threatened calmly.

Paul took note of their accent, and he suspected that the duo was from Germany or Austria. The person who drove up in the Mercedes was unrecognizeable through the tinted windshield and did not get out of the car. The license plates were foreign tags.

"All right, you win… I'll let the bear go," Paul said reluctantly; not wanting anyone to get hurt. "But tell me, who are you guys and what organization is behind this?" Paul asked, only half expecting to receive an honest answer.

"Later," came the reply, "just let das gottdam bear go free."
The two men were in control, but were beginning to lose their patience with Paul.

"Okay, okay, I'm going to open the cage. But you had better take cover. When this animal gets free, we're all going to be in a shit-load of danger here."

Willy climbed on top of the shaking cage. The bear sensed the warden's presence and roared in angry disapproval. The two, blonde-haired gunmen retured to the Mercedes and Paul climbed into the cab of the truck. Willy released the locking pin and opened the metal door of the cage. The bear hesitated for a few seconds and then shot out of its confinement. Ten meters past the cage the great animal stopped, turned around, roared at the cage and then charged into the forest. It ignored the dead pig in its haste to escape. For the moment, Willy was worried that the bear would charge the cage and knock him to the ground. He was very relieved when the carnivore disappeared into the trees.

Now very angry, Paul climbed out of the truck and approached the three men who were seated inside of the car. As he approached, the man in the passenger seat lowered the window.

"Who the hell do you think you guys are, anyway?" Paul demanded to know. The man pointed his pistol out the window and directly at Paul's chest.

"Das ist far enough," the man ordered brusquely. "If I vere you, herr policeman, I vould forget that zis entire affair ever occurred... verstehen sie? How do you say... count your blessinks that the bear did not get you first. As you have no doubt noticed, dass ist no ordinary bear. It's almost twice as large and five times as dangerous as anything else in das vorld," the man explained as he stepped out of his car.

"Now, you and your friend are going to find out what it feels like to be caged.

"Get in," the man ordered.

"Into the cage?" Willy attempted to confirm in his astonishment.

"Ja," the guman's answer was swift and terse.

Willy and Paul climbed into the cage; the pungent scent of bear still permeated the inside. Once inside, the man lowered the door, and Paul heard the locking pin being set into position.

"Hey, you guys can't leave us in here. How will we get out?" Paul called out.

But the man did not reply. The next sound they heard was the door slamming on the Mercedes and that of the vehicle driving away.

"Sonofabitch!" Paul exclaimed. He was livid. "What the fuck is going on here? Who were those bastards and how are they connected to this bear? And what about that radio collar? Somebody is going to have a lot of explaining to do when we get back to Brig," Paul said angrily, his frustration apparent.

"First we're going to have to find a way out of here," Willy retorted in his usually calm manner.

It took about a half an hour before Paul and Willy figured out that they had to implement some kind of escape plan; one that would solve the problem of their unexpected and forced confinement. After a few minutes of discussion, they arrived at a workable plan.

Using their combined weight, they had managed to turn the cage over on its side. And as they had calculated, the locking pin which prevented the cage door from opening was jarred out of position by the force of the cage hitting the ground. Paul was then able to work open the heavy, metal door, a few inches at a time, until they could get their hands around it. He opened the door sufficiently, permitting them to squeeze through.

Paul was furious. He decided that the best thing to do would be to drive back to town immediately. He was determined to find out who was responsible for collaring the bear, because he believed that it would lead him to the trio in the car. He also made a mental note of the tan-colored Mercedes. He had never seen that one in Brig before.

He felt as though his professionalism had been compromised, and that his authority had been ridiculed. The entire incident had been a blow to his ego and he was personally going to find and arrest the persons responsible for releasing the bear. He wished that the radio was working so that he could contact Maria. It would not have been too late to set up a roadblock and apprehend the men in the Mercedes.

Willy was struggling with his confusion about the recent turn of events. His beliefs were reinforced that scientists, in some fashion, had been tampering with nature. The bear had been collared, hunted and tormented – for what purpose? It was now obvious that many people were aware of the existence of the unique creature. But what else was there to know about this strange sow bear. Were they aware that she was travelling with two young cubs; and where was the father? How had this species managed to reappear after thousands of years of extinction? Whatever the reason, Willy understood and believed that the bear and its' family had to be protected at all cost. He was now going to handle the situation his own way.

Willy and Paul worked hard, in near darkness, and managed to reload the cage onto the truck. Willy took the decapitated remains of the pig and buried it. It was after ten p.m. when the duo arrived back in Brig.

Paul shook Willy's hand in the parking lot and thanked him for his valuable assistance. He assured Willy that the law would handle the affair, and that he would need Willy's assistance again to identify the men once or if they were caught.

"I might not be available," Willy answered, his eyes focused straight ahead through the truck's windshield.

"What do you mean?" Paul responded with surprise, taken back by Willy's remark.

"I think that I'm going to take a little vacation time… do a little hunting and some fishing… I need a break," Willy responded without a trace of emotion in his voice.

Paul stared at Willy for several seconds, searching for some clue to his friend's true feelings. Willy continued to focus his gaze straight ahead, purposefully avoiding Paul's eyes. He started his pickup truck and backed out of the parking space. Paul knew his friend well enough to know that he had other plans in mind. He ran up to the door of the pickup, and this time Willy looked at him.

"Be very careful, my friend," Paul cautioned.

"I'm always careful," Willy said assertively.

After Willy had driven away, Paul parked the Volvo truck at the rear of the police station and went inside. He bounded up the steps of the building. Inspector Haustein was on duty, sitting behind Paul's desk in his office, in the large swivel chair that Paul like so much and with his feet up on Paul's dcsk. As Paul burst into his office, the sudden commotion startled "House" who dropped a copy of "Police Gazette" on the floor, and nearly fell over backwards attempting to recover his balance.

"**Jesus Christ**, Chief!" House stammered. "What the heck are you doing here so late at night? You scared the shit out of me."

"Listen, House," Paul came directly to the point. "I want you to immediately get out an alert to detain any tan-colored Mercedes sedan with out of country plates and driven by one of two, blonde-haired men with German accents."

House was still regaining his composure when he asked, "Sure, Chief. Why, what did they do?"

"Assualt, unlawful imprisonment, interfering with government procedures and anything else that I can think of, and that's just for starters; I'll sign the complaint. Meanwhile, I want you to apprehend these bastards if you run across them. They are also armed and dangerous."

"I'm on it, Chief," House verified as he snapped to attention and reached for the radio.

House leaned closer to the radio and flipped a switch on the control panel.

"Unit two and unit seven, this is House. Report in, over."
Both units responded simultaneously.

"Keep your eyes peeled for a tan, Mercedes sedan with out of country tags. The occupants are three men; at least two of them are tall and blonde haired."

"Be sure to tell them they armed and dangerous," Paul interrupted.

House continued, "Approach with caution, as they are accused of felonious assault, and they are most probably armed. Request a backup unit prior to talking any action."

The response came through the speaker. "Anything else? Do you know what direction they were headed?" the voice inquired.

"No, that's all I've got. We think that they may be headed on the Simplon Pass Road. This is Haustein... out."

The inspector turned off the transmit switch and handed a complaint form to Paul.

"I'm going home to bed House. I'm exhausted. I'll bring the form back tomorrow morning... or should I say later this morning, as it's already after midnight." Paul grabbed the form and walked wearily out of the station house. It took him at least fifteen minutes to drive home, and fifteen seconds to fall asleep. He never noticed Gina's note.

<u>Chapter Twenty-Five</u> – Saturday

The sound of a wasp buzzing Gina's ear caused her to awake with a start. She sat up and looked around quickly, focusing on the aspen grove and struggling to get her bearings – she was not a morning person. Despite the early hour, she felt well rested and refreshed. She needed caffeine.

The early morning fog clung low in the the valley tenaciously, as the sun had not yet risen sufficiently to begin evaporating the mist. Gina reclined, allowing her head to rest while she stretched out her limbs. The exercise felt good. The air smelled clean and sweet and a layer of morning dampness blanketed everything including the outside of her sleeping bag. Her first thoughts were of building a fire and making breakfast. Camping outdoors made her ravenous, but hot coffee was the first priority.

Within minutes she had the beginning of a crackling fire, and she balanced a fresh pot of coffee to brew on the rocks near the flames. A gentle, but constant breeze began to blow as the sun warmed the air and the golden aspen leaves began to flicker. Gina finally poured her first cup of coffee and she strolled over to the stream. She was fully enjoying the gentle sounds and the peacefulness of the valley. Standing at the bank of the stream, she watched the clear water trickle between the larger stones and across the sandy bottom. Strands of water sedges, growing in tussocks in and along the sides of the stream were combed and waved by the rapidly flowing water.

She felt the ambiance of the pastoral setting and concluded that it would be a good place to write poetry, as soothing visual inspirations seemed to awaken her lyrical senses at every turn.

As she had done yesterday, Gina tried to imagine what the valley had looked like blanketed with fresh, deep snow. In a winter blizzard, the valley must be a brutally inhospitable place, she estimated. The outlaw's tracks would have been obliterated by the falling and drifting snow. Still, that obliteration might take some time. And with a posse in hot pursuit, the thief couldn't have relied on Mother Nature to cover his trail.

While Gina was observing a water spider negotiating a swift eddy in the stream the idea struck.

"That's it... **the stream**!" she yelled out loud. "The outlaw used the stream to conceal his tracks."

Gina raced back to her campsite and retrieved the old map from her sleeping bag. There was a notation, made by her uncle that indicated the outlaw's tracks ceased at a stream, or that the posse had stopped at a stream because there were no more signs of hoof prints in the snow. She examined the document and reconfirmed the notation. It appeared as though the outlaw had used the stream as a pathway, thus avoiding making telltale prints in the snow. He had simply managed to vanish, forcing the posse to give up the chase during the raging storm.

Excitedly, she poured the remainder of the coffee on the fire and buried the hot coals with dirt. Packing up hastily, she ignored her hunger and retraced her route back to the stream. Convinced that she discovered the correct trail, she reinforced herself with the belief that the outlaw had chosen travelling upstream as an easier alternative to plodding through deep snow drifts. The stream would have been lower in the early spring, and not deeply swollen to capacity with the late spring runoffs.

This was one clever outlaw, she thought.

Gina carefully followed the path of the stream, sticking closely to the right side embankment. Ultimately, she hoped that the stream would lead her to the remnants of an old shack or some structure that would indicate that the outlaw had used it as a source of shelter. She pressed northward, not knowing what she would find ahead. She was now positive that the outlaw had used this very stream to cover his escape a half century before.

The low hanging branches from the trees that grew on both sides of the stream were, at times, difficult to negotiate. But Gina rationalized that the dense growth would have offered additional advantages of concealment that the outlaw would have recognized immediately.

The major question that Gina now faced was where, exactly, had the thief emerged from the stream. She was hoping that the answer would come from something immediately recognizeable as a potential source of shelter. But after nearly a half an hour of walking, nothing seemed to be readily obvious.

Ten more minutes elapsed, and there was no sign of a suitable place to exit the stream. Gina was becoming a little discouraged, but she was convinced that her analysis and decision was the correct one. A desperate outlaw would not have turned back. On the contrary, he would have pressed on in the hope that his pursuers would become frustrated and give up. Turning back now would be a big mistake, and so she pressed on.

The branches whipped her face and arms. Gina had to duck quickly on several occasions or risk being struck in the face. As the stream meandered closer to the wall of the valley, large boulders began to appear to her right. There were also large trees that had been smashed by the huge rocks which had been weathered away from the cliff face over the centuries. The aspens had disappeared and Gina found herself within a dense grove of conifers. The green canopy seemed to cover everything. The sunlight which managed to penetrate the deep forest had an emerald green tint.

Finally, the stream began to widen and an opening appeared between the trees and the stream embankment. Gina understood that she had to check out every possibility where the outlaw's horse had had an opportunity to exit the stream. The pine trees in the grove were spaced sufficiently to permit relatively easy passage for a horse and rider. The ground was covered with a thick carpet of pine needles. Gina noted that she did not leave any tracks in the pine needles as she walked past.

She strolled slowly through the grove in the direction of the cliff. The large boulders scattered thoroughout the grove would have made ideal cover for the thief and his horse, she observed. However, there were no distinguishing features about any of them that would provide a good treasure marker – everything appeared unremarkable. Gina surmised that the thief would have only hidden his loot in a place easily recognizeable at some later date. As Gina continued through the thicket of trees, she continuously forced herself to think as a fugitive would have. She pretended to be half frozen and desperately in need of shelter from the blizzard as well as a safe haven from the posse. But nothing jumped out at her as a suitable place of refuge or to hide the gold. Nothing seemed to serve as an adequate shelter. She continued walking, paralleling the cliff.

The sun was approaching its noon zenith, and the grove was illuminated by bright, yellow rays which knifed through the spaces in the forest canopy. Alternating patches of bright light and dim shadows became irritating; making it difficult to distinguish any details in the shadowy undergrowth. It was only by simple, good fortune that Gina spotted the dark hole in the side of the cliff face.

Her heart lept when she realized that she had chanced upon a cave.

"That's perfect," she congratulated herself. *A cave would provide excellent shelter and a place to conceal the gold.*

Gina cautiously walked closer to the cave opening. It was large enough to permit a grown man to pass through, but she didn't know how deep it penetrated into the mountain.

It really makes no difference, she thought, *the outlaw would have seized any opportunity to protect himself against a raging blizzard. Any amount of good shelter over his head would have been welcomed,* she reasoned.

She picked her way carefully between the broken rocks and the tangles of broken tree branches that peppered the path to the cave. She felt that some of the sharp rocks and the broken, sharp limbs would have been very dangerous to the thief's horse. The dark opening in the cliff face also appeared ominous, like some giant maw poised to swallow unsuspecting prey. Despite her mounting excitement, she became aware of a tingling sense of fear in the lower portion of her spine. Her right hand confirmed the availability of the pistol which was holstered on her right hip.

Continuing to pick her way around the loose talus and branches, Gina did not notice the deep claw marks on the tree or on the ground; nor did the mound of freshly dug up dirt in front of the cave opening convey anything sinister. By the time that she reached the cave, she had passed all of the obvious signs made by its current resident. She peered inside inquisitively.

"Hello?" she managed. Although she felt a little silly announcing herself as she might do when going into someone's home unannounced.

Several insects buzzed her head, disturbed and curious about her presence. Gina was struck immediately by the fetid, musty odor emanating from inside of the cave. It smelled a little like a combination of spoiled, rancid food and cat urine – but stronger. Allowing her eyes to become accustomed to the darkness, she moved slowly inside, sliding each foot forward carefully in baby-step fashion. No sound or movement stirred from within.

Where the light was able to penetrate the interior, Gina could detect a brownish-black dirt floor littered with hundreds of rocks of various sizes. The floor appeared to be fairly dry, despite the dampness within the cave. She became impressed by the size of the cave's interior. There was a huge chamber that disappeared into the shadowy recesses. She wished that she had remembered to bring a flashlight.

Her right foot kicked something. She glanced downward and saw the flat hip bone of a deer lying on the floor. It was at that moment Gina began to realize that she might be trespassing into the lair of a wolf or a bear. Thoughts of the recent attacks suddenly came to mind, and Gina shivered reflexively. She now realized the potential dangerousness of her current situation.

But I've already come this far, and I need to see what else is in here, she convinced and motivated herself.

Gina soon realized that the cave was too deep and that there was insufficient light to explore it properly. She decided that building a fire would be the best way to illuminate the interior. In addition, the fire would be the best way to drive off any unwelcome predator types.

She left the cave and began gathering bundles of dead branches for the fire. A large pile was accumulated just inside the entrance. Soon, a small fire burned on the cave floor and Gina added more wood slowly and incrementally. She wanted to generate light without too much smoke, which would have made breathing inside of the cave difficult.

As the fire grew more intense, the dark recesses of the cave's interior succumbed to the steadily advancing illumination. The ceiling was ten to fifteen feet high in places, sloping to meet the floor at the rear of the cave. Water flowed in tear-like fashion out of cracks in the ceiling. There were several large boulders that originally appeared to be part of the ceiling, and which had dislodged from the roof at the back of the cave. Bones of different sizes and from various animals were strewn around in the soft earth, including the nearly complete skeleton of a deer. Gina wondered how many of them had come inside to die.

She noticed the ancient, Neanderthal art petroglyphs on the wall and walked over to examine them more closely. The petroglyphs depicted life thousands of years before and illustrated brave hunters, fierce predators and life and death struggles. She was drawn into the flat, two-dimensional picture writing, and she tried hard to imagine the Spartan life that was focused entirely on survival during that prehistoric era. The cave must have been used as a dwelling for a number of ancient peoples. She estimated that during the cold of winter, the lack of available game and the severe weather at this altitude would have forced the ancient dwellers to seek survival at lower altitudes.

A loud cracking sound coming from the entrance to the cave caused Gina to jump reflexively. She whirled around and stared at the opening. It was only the sound of a log popping in the fire. She regained her composure and decided that it was time to procede with an organized search of the cave floor.

She retrieved her metal detector and a small shovel from her back pack. She calibrated the detector, received a green signal indicating that her batteries were adequately charged, and then she tested the detector with the metal shovel. She received a loud tone in her earphones. Next, she turned the detector's sensitivity and descriminator to "coins", and tested her equipment by dropping a one franc coin on the floor. She obtained a signal from a distance of nearly eighteen inches away.

Employing the use of a sturdy stick, Gina marked off a grid pattern in the dirt. This would enable her to methodically screen every square meter of the cave floor without overlooking or covering any area twice. She placed the metal shovel on top of a small rock and unholstered her pistol, leaving it there as well. She did not want any spurious signals from the two, large metal objects to interfere with her detector.

She began her search at the cave's entrance, and swept an area two feet wide as she advanced forward. It took nearly ten minutes to complete the first line of the grids from the front to the back of the cave, and she found nothing. She rechecked the sensitivity and received a comforting hum, indicating that the instrument was functioning perfectly. She repeated the screening with the second grid lines. About half way through the third section of grids, the detector emitted a signal pulse of short duration. Moving the detector loop backwards, she located the area emitting the signal. Bending down, she loosened the dirt with a small, sharp stick and probed with the metal detector. The signal strength increased on the meter... she was getting closer. She continued to dig; alternately crushing the dirt in her fingers, probing and feeling for a metal object.

Picking up another handful of dirt, she sifted it between her fingers. Suddenly, she felt something hard in her hand. She walked over to the fire to examine her find more closely. It was a piece of lead – round and smooth on one side, and flat with scratch marks on the other.

A bullet, she concluded. It was a spent slug. *Someone had fired a pistol in here, and it must have been distorted when it hit a rock and fallen harmlessly to the floor.*

Instantly, she understood that some person had visited this cave sometime in the past one hundred or so years.

Probably someone doing some hunting or target shooting, she estimated.

As the day wore on, Gina methodically screened the ground in nearly half of the cave, stopping occasionally to add more wood to the fire to maintain adequate light with which to work. Suddenly, the detector gave off a loud whooping sound as she passed the loop across a small depression in the ground. She located the object easily, and gasped at her discovery. The ground had yielded a shiney, one hundred franc gold piece; dirty but untarnished after fifty plus years in the damp soil. She could hardly contain her excitement.

"**Yahoo,**" she rejoiced; her voice reverberating inside of the cave.

She examined the coin closely. "One-Hundred Francs, Helvetia" The date on the minting was 19**25**. Gina had her confirmation now that the outlaw **had** used this very cave as shelter fifty three years before.

The gold coin showed little signs of wear. The letters on the gold were sharp and every little detail, including the fine lines surrounding the Swiss cross, were distinct. It was not a fresh minted coin when it was dropped. Instead, Gina concluded that because the date of minting was 1925, that the coin had been stolen from a safe deposit box or from the case of a coin dealer.

Very curious indeed... I wonder what this must be worth. She mused.

A flurry of questions bombarded Gina's mind: *Why had the coin been dropped there? Where were the other coins? Had the outlaw buried the gold in the cave and then come back for it later, only to lose one coin?*

Preoccupied with her examination, Gina did not notice the fierce carnivore as it entered the cave – its cave. It was returning to one of its favorite, secure lairs where it could eat and rest undisturbed for a few hours. The animal had detected the scent of the intruder and had been alarmed by the fire. And being aggressively territorial, it had entered its home; its instincts compelling and demanding that it challenge the unfamiliar trespasser.

Gina heard a low growl coming from somewhere behind her, and she wheeled about to face the approaching animal. Crouching low against the ground and snarling vicously was a huge wolverine. Gina froze in her tracks as she recognized the menacing predator with a reputation for fearlessness and savagery. It advanced towards her threateningly. Its teeth bared in a menacing challenge. She reached for her pistol and remembered the empty holster. Her sudden movement compelled the wolverine to charge.

She dashed in the direction of the fire. If she could only get one of the burning sticks out of the fire, she might be able to drive the creature away. Now in a near panic state, Gina failed to see the depression in the ground ahead of her. The abrupt change in the level of the cave floor caused her to stumble and lose her balance, falling forward on her right arm. She heard a sickening crack as she landed, and she screamed as the stabbing pain shot through her arm. She had broken her ulna in two places and dislocated her right wrist.

The wolverine continued to advance towards her. Deep, throaty growls seemed to cough out of the mouth of the ill-natured, fifty-pound bundle of teeth and fur. Gina saw that she had another ten feet to crawl to the fire. The pain in her arm was excruciating, and she guessed that her shoulder might also be dislocated from the fall. Wincing in the throes of unbelievable pain, she managed to crawl towards the safety of the fire.

The wolverine covered the few feet between them in a second. It seized Gina's left boot in its powerful jaws and shook her leg violently from side to side. Gina screamed; the adrenalin surging through her system. She struggled hard against the power of the attacking wolverine, inching herself toward a branch, half of which was ablaze in the fire.

With an agonizing pain, the animal's sharp teeth tore through Gina's boot, pentrating her foot and part of her ankle. Exhausted, and afraid, she summoned up every ounce of strength remaining and lunged for the burning bough. Her fingers miraculously found the stick and in one fluid motion, she hurled it in the face of the persistent attacked. A shower of sparks and a tangle of burning twigs cascaded on the wolverine as it scrambled backward to escape the flames. Gina kicked and brushed off the hot coals and the burning branches which had fallen on her legs. The wolverine retreated to the cave entrance and continued to snarl at her, hunkering low to the ground and protesting his opponent's temporary victory.

Gina grabbed another burning log and tossed it at the badger-like animal. This time the wolverine realized that it was time to yield to the strange fire-tossing humanoid creature. It would never forget this encounter in that cave.

Satisfied that it had given a good accounting of itself the ill-tempered wolverine retreated into the forest, stopping momentarily to glance back and offer a last-word growl. It would look for another lair and return some other time.

Writhing in pain, Gina lay on the floor of the cave and bleeding profusely from the wound in her foot. With her right arm broken and her left foot injured, Gina understood that she was in very serious trouble. In her haste to get away from the fifty-pound ball of fury, she had dropped the gold coin. Somehow, it seemed to matter little now. Her primary objective had suddenly reprioritized to get herself off the mountain and to seek medical help immediately.

Chapter Twenty-Six

Paul was hotly engrossed in a conversation with Inspector's Meeker, Ferrigno, Casio and Haustein. His frustrations mounted because none of the deputies had succeeded in locating the tan Mercedes or either of the two blonde haired men. Also, because it was the weekend, he couldn't call any government agencies to inquire about animal radio-collaring activities in his area of responsibility.

"What do you mean there has been no trace of a tan Mercedes sedan? What happened to Willy and me up there was no mirage, gentlemen."

"Listen Paul," Meeker attempted to cool his boss' temper, "we notified Interpol and put out a description of the men and the tan Mercedes. They shouldn't be too hard to snare."

Paul could see that the men were doing their best, he could always rely on their efficiency in the past.

"Okay guys, I'm sorry if I got a little riled up. Keep me up to date if you come up with something… dismissed."

The four police inspectors left Paul's office.

*   *   *   *   *   *   *   *   *

Willy was dozing in a lounge chair in his home when an unexpected knock on his door roused him abruptly. Two men were visible, standing on the other side of the screen door. Willy recognized one of the men immediately.

"Doctor Levin… Mo, good to see you… what a surprise! Welcome to Brig," he greeted the men warmly.

"Willy, I'd like you to meet a colleague of mine, and an old school friend, Doctor Sydney Feller. He's the man I told you about. The fellow that does all of the DNA testing. I sent him your fur sample for identification."

"Very nice to meet you, Dr. Feller," Willy extended his hand.

"Sid, you can call me Sid," the man corrected. He was a short man with strong hands. He was stooped over like his friend Mo, but with a much warmer smile that grew into a continuous line from ear to ear.

"Sid came all the way out here with me, Willy, to speak with you about the fur sample that we submitted," Mo announced.

Willy offered the men fresh coffee to be hospitable, and then remembered that Mo liked tea. But both men politely refused his offer.

"We just finished lunch, thank you very much," Sid declined Willy's offer, and jumped immediately into the questioning.

"Willy, with reference to that specimen that you sent to me for analysis, can you be absolutely certain that it was obtained from a live animal?" Sid asked.

"I'm positive of it," Willy responded. Both scientists listened intently as the game warden detailed the circumstances surrounding the specimen's acquisition, and then related the events involving the bear's capture, the radio transmitting collar and the bear's subsequent release by the mysterious two men carrying pistols.

"You have absolutely no idea why this particular bear was collared or who was responsible?" Sid inquired.

"No idea whatsoever!" Willy affirmed.

Willy was becoming eager to know what the old scientist had discovered about the bear's identity.

"Warden… Willy, before I begin, I want you to know that this is in no way an official visit. I paid for this trip out here with my own money, ostensibly to visit my old friend. But you see, the real reason that I came so far, and got my allergies stirred up in the process is because of your discovery. I sincerely hope that all of this bear stuff is not an elaborate hoax."

Willy shot a glance at Mo, who was scrutinizing his friend's face intensely.

"**Absolutely not!**" Willy maintained avidly. "This bear has already killed at least three people. Believe me doctor, I sincerely wish that this whole blasted episode was a hoax and that it would just… fade away."

A few seconds of silence passed as both men measured the game warden carefully. Finally, Sid spoke up.

"Your bear is a living relic. If it proves to be what I suspect that it is, and as a scientist I must be certain of the facts, then this bear is a living anachronism… an animal out of its proper place and time in history."

"I don't understand what you mean exactly," Willy said, furrowing his brow.

"The sample that you sent for identification did not appear to be fossilized. It came from a living creature which is supposed to have been extinct for over twenty thousand years. In addition, the bear's skeletal remains are found in archeological digs all over this continent.

"What kind of bear are we talking about?" Willy pressed him.

"A cave bear… better known as Ursus Spelaeus," the old man said coolly, "or, as it is known here in Europe as Ursus Etruscus. He is one of the largest and most ferocious mammalian predators that ever roamed the earth."

A few more seconds of silence filled the room as Willy weighed the impact of Dr. Feller's comments.

"Well then, what the hell is it doing wandering around the mountains of Switzerland in 1998, and in my district?" Willy asked, feeling a little defensive.

"That's what we'd like to know, Willy," both scientists chorused.

Sid continued his explanation. "The bear, as a distinct animal form, has been on this earth for hundreds of thousands of years. The cave bear, was a direct descendant of Ursus Etruscus, and was thought to exist specifically in Europe, becoming extinct with the onset of the last ice-age. This was the middle Pleistocene era, just before the last ice age, and the animal lived in the temperate forests of western and central Europe. In the caves for France, for example, there are a lot of petroglyphs of cave bears, but there are few remains in those caves. In Austria, in the famous "Dragon's Caves", many bones of hibernating cave bear females were discovered.

"How is a cave bear different from, say… a grizzly?" Willy asked.

"Apart from its great size, it differs from a grizzly by a prominent, instead of a flat forehead; and a massive head in proportion to the rest of its body," Sid explained.

"How do you suppose such a creature could have survived without ever having been seen?" Mo inquired, turning to Sid.

"It is possible that some of the bears could have migrated through eastern Asia, and hidden out in the remote forests of northern Siberia. But how it managed to go undetected until 1998, is unbelieveable… impossible… unexplainable!"

The three men pondered all of the remotest explanations for the bear's existence, in silence, for several minutes.

"I will say one thing," Mo added, "when the word gets out that Urses Spelaeus may still exist in the world, it will be one of the most important scientific discoveries of the past hundred years."

"Well, it seems as though someone else is already aware of the cave bear's existence," Willy stated with an air of foreboding.

Chapter Twenty-Seven

Gina allowed herself to rest for several minutes. She managed to hoist herself onto a large, flat rock to catch her breath and to regroup her thoughts. She needed some time to better assess the seriousness of her predicament. Her right arm and shoulder hurt badly and the pain in her foot was sharp and throbbing. She worried about the possibility of rabies, and minimally, what kind of suppurating infection could she expect from the wolverine's vicious and deep bite. She began to wonder if she could make it down the mountain without being rescued. Gina thought of the outlaw, and how he may have experienced the very same doubts about his ultimate survival. Then the notion quickly faded as she concentrated on her own dilemma.

Suddenly, she realized that she had not told anyone exactly where she was going; only that she wouldn't be returning until Tuesday. She had shown Paul on the map where she was intending to explore, but she had the map with her, and what was the possibility that Paul would remember exactly where she had shown him? He wouldn't come looking for her until she was overdue on Tuesday morning – two days away. She carefully considered her alternatives, which weren't many. She could wait in the cave with the hope that someone would come looking for her, or she could take her chances with the mountain.

Gina decided that realistically, she had only one choice in increasing the probability of a rescue. She had to find a way of working herself down the mountain to where she had parked the Range Rover.

With great effort; her body wracked with pain, Gina managed to drag herself out of the cave. Realizing that she had to abandon her pack and tools because she could not carry any excess weight, Gina fashioned a sturdy crutch for herself out of a broken pine branch, which she snapped off to the correct length, using two big boulders wedged closely together. That effort alone nearly exhausted her.

As she plodded forward, her mind began considering her chances of making it down the mountain without damaging herself further..

What if I pass out?

She was losing a lot of blood from the deep wound in her foot.

What if I bleed to death? Then I guess it wouldn't be my worry any more.

Then she remembered the bear story, and what had happened to the young boys.

Boy...what an idiot I was not listening to Paul. I should have never come up here by myself. I should have waited for Paul to take some time off to join me.

Gina mustered up every ounce of resolve, and determined to survive she put out of her mind any thoughts of not making it home. She repeated over and over with every painful step, "I'm going to make it home."

    *   *   *   *   *   *   *   *   *

Inspector Haustein was making his Sunday afternoon patrol rounds in his freshly polished police cruiser. His routine was always the same: pulling up in front of a business establishment that was closed, and with a ritualistic, grandiose flamboyant style in case someone was watching, House proceded to check the security of the locked doors and windows. He rarely went around back to check the rear doors, having learned a painful lesson from a Doberman that had attacked him four years earlier. The dog, in its zeal to protect his master's property from anyone and anything, tore out the seat and the left trouser leg of House's uniform.

The Inspector had come around the back of the building, and walked right into the canine equivalent of the Tasmanian devil. The animal's toothy snarl startled House, who immediately turned on his heels and ran, triggering every aggressive instinct in the cursive canine's mind. The Doberman's speed and powerful jaws closed in on House's pants before the dog reached the end of his chain tether. Since that episode, House's backside always made it a point to avoid the backsides of buildings whenever he could.

As House drove around Chemin Street, he passed the parking lot of the Brighaus hotel; two blonde haired men were exiting the lobby. He observed them for a moment and then noticed the tan Mercedes. Haustein's heart lept as he realized that the men and the tan-colored vehicle fit the description that Paul had given of the people he was looking for.

A combination of fear, excitement, false pride and a sense of duty welled up in House's brain. He immediately went into overload as the adrenal glands above his kidneys began pumping out the powerful stimulant. He contemplated his next move.

What a feather in my cap...apprehending two armed and dangerous men... right here in Brig... in front of everyone. The townspeople will be talking about me for months... the other inspectors will admire my heroism.

Remembering Paul's warning about the men being armed, House found his hands beginning to shake and becoming sweaty.

What do I do? What do I do? What would the Chief have done? Call for backup? No, this is my collar.

House had never been in this situation before. He thought about Clint Eastwood movies: *What would detective Callahan have done under the same set of circumstances?* The suspects could not be allowed to escape.

In a split second, House decided to hit the lights and the siren, punched the gas pedal and rocketed his police cruiser up the gravel driveway into the hotel's parking lot. The two men were astonished by the sight and froze in their shoes. House halted the police vehicle and leaped out, gun at the ready, before he realized that he had forgotten to take the police cruiser out of "drive".

The car came to an abrupt halt amid sounds of of shattering glass and twisting metal, as his car struck and destroyed the small metal fence around the swimming pool. It came to rest after running over some glass tables and chaise loungers, with two wheels dangling over the side of the pool.

"Halt! You're both under arrest. Oh, Shit!" House yelled as he tried to concentrate his attention on the two men and the police car turned battering ram simultaneously.

The two men looked at each other briefly, astonished and somewhat amused by the policeman's comedic entrance, and then took off in the direction of the Mercedes. House sized up the situation quickly and promptly dispatched four, .44 Magnum rounds into the tires of the Mercedes. The two men halted immediately with their hands in the air.

House felt a strong sense of accomplishment.

"Go ahead, make my day," he challenged them.

He commanded the men to turn around and place their hands against the hood of the car. The heavy revolver shook in his hand.

The two men, now convinced that their captor would think nothing of blowing them both into oblivion, quickly complied with House's order.

By now, curious hotel patrons were pushing aside curtains and opening sliders to stand on their patios; all wanting a better look at all of the commotion. House was in his own personal heaven.

"My name is Inspector Haustein of the Swiss Federal Police," he yelled. **"Would someone please call the police headquarters for assistance?"** he purposefully avoided the words "help" or "back-up".

"You can all go back inside, it's all over," House barked. But secretly he didn't want anyone to miss out on his big performance.

Eight minutes later, Chief Inspector Soria turned his police car into the hotel's driveway and parked next to House, who still held the drop on his suspects. Stepping out of the car, Paul surveyed the entire scene rapidly. By now, a crowd of people had formed; intent on watching the developments, some were still running up the street.

Paul approached House, who couldn't contain his proud, broad grin, and then Paul spied House's police car dangling precariously over the swimming pool. House continued brandishing his big pistol at the two men.

"Did anyone survive this wreck?" Paul asked, rhetorically, whispering in his deputy inspector's ear.

House appeared confused at his boss's remark.

"Are you going to shoot them both, Inspector Haustein, or stand there all day?" Paul teased. "What did they do anyway… fail to pay their hotel bill?"

"These two guys fit the description that you gave us Chief," House stammered nervously. "There's the tan Mercedes over there, sir."

Paul glanced at the vehicle with the three flat tires.

"Well, it doesn't look like they were going anywhere," Paul quipped.

"They tried to make a break for it, and I shot out the tires," House stated smugly.

"Wonderful!" Paul leaned over and whispered into House's ear. "You'd better be right about these guys, or you'd better take a course in pool fence mending and tire repair, because you're not going to be working for my department by night fall."

House's expression changed to worry.

"Have they been searched yet?"

"No, Chief."

"Did you notice that the tags on the Mercedes are not foreign tags?" Paul noted as he continued whispering in House's ear.

House felt his heart sink in his chest.

"Here," Paul suggested, "give me that cannon you're wielding and get some I.D. from those guys."

House searched both men thoroughly, "No weapons Chief," he announced.

"Check their I.D.'s and let's get a look inside of that Mercedes."

Each man handed House their driver's licenses, and one man surrendered his keys to the Mercedes. A cursory inspection of the Mercedes turned up two, 9mm Lugers and a high-powered rifle. In addition, House discovered what looked to be radio-telemetry tracking equipment in the trunk of the car: a small, portable antenna and a narrow-bandwidth radiowave receiver.

"We were going to do some hunting," one of the men offered.

"Nothing is in season right now except bear," Paul retorted sarcastically.

Paul walked up to one of the familiar looking men.

"Tell me Herr whatever your name is, do you recognize me?"

"Nein," the man responded tersely and avoided Paul's gaze.

"You look familiar, and so does your car. I'd like to know how you switched license plates so quickly. Is this car gestolen, Herr big game hunter?"

The man said nothing more.

"I'm going to have to take both of you men in for questioning. I filled out an assault complaint on two men that fit your description, and who were carrying 9mm pistols exactly like yours, and driving a tan-colored Mercedes... just like yours. What a strange coincidence, wouldn't you agree?"

Both men were taken to the Brig station house, separated, and placed in two, isolated, temporary holding cells. A call was placed into Interpol, to confirm their identification, and that of the Mercedes.

The police station was buzzing with the news of House's great police work.

One at a time, Paul ushered a prisoner into separate interrogation rooms. Every eye in the police station scrutinized the men as they were transferred from the holding cells. This was surely the most important piece of police work that Brig had experienced in the last ten years. And together with the strange bear attacks, the two events would provid many opportunities for dinner table and bar-side conversations.

Paul was a by-the-book detective. He instructed the first man to completely empty his pockets onto the table in the interrogation room. He began his questioning in a casual manner, in a deliberate effort to make the man feel at ease. He started by examining their driver's licenses and credit cards.

The first man stood six feet, four inches tall. His name was Helmut Blaumen, and according to his license, he lived in Munich, Germany. Despite Paul's calm jail-side manner, Helmut was becoming tense and began figetting with the buttons on his shirt. Paul observed his behavior, but said nothing as he completed his examination of the man's wallet. He motioned for Helmut to sit down.

"Are you Helmut Blaumen?" Paul began his interrogation in a very calm but authoritative tone of voice.

"Ja, Ich bin." The answer came quickly and somewhat defiantly.

"This is a German driver's license. Are you a German national?"

"Ja."

"What are you and your friends doing in Brig, Herr Blaumen?"

"Vacation… sightseeing," he said, growing more nervous.

"Then why the heavy artillery?" Paul asked with a grin.

"Ve thought das ve might get in a little hunting or target practice," the man answered dryly.

"Exactly what kind of game were you planning on shooting?"

At this point Helmut shifted his position in the chair, as traces of perspiration began to bead up on the man's forehead. It was warm in the interrogation room - too warm. Paul knew that he wanted the man to be uncomfortable. It always helped to get at the truth.

"Deer mostly, perhaps a few birds."

"Red deer are not in season. Did you know that?"

"Ve vere nicht aware of dass."

"Do you have a hunting license, Herr Blaumen?" Paul was trying deliberately to keep the man off balance.

"Nein, ve had not gotten around to…"

Paul rose to his feet suddenly, the anger clearly visible on his face, as his prisoner was obviously lying.

"You hadn't gotten around to it!" Paul roared.

"You came into my country, my jurisdiction to hunt animals that are not even in season and you haven't got around to obtaining a hunting license? And what's with the radio-tracking equipment? You must take me for a fool Helmut. Do I look like a fool to you?" Paul was livid.

Herr Blaumen realized that this Inspector was no amateur and that he was rapidly becoming boxed in by the line of questioning. He attempted a concession to keep the Chief Inspector at bay.

"Look, Inspector, perhaps you're right. My friends and I didn't vant to pay zee stiff fees for an out-of-country hunting permit. Ve vere definitinely hunting without a license. Zo, there is no sense dragging zis out any further. Ve vill simply pay our fines and depart from your little hamlet. Ve don't want any more trouble than ve haf already caused."

Paul studied the man for several minutes. He was clearly lying through his large, perfect white teeth; years of police experience told him that. He was definitely hiding something or protecting somebody else. Paul decided to stop toying with him.

"Okay Helmut, I'll give it to you straight," Paul began his confrontation, "you and your friend were not picked up because of a hunting infraction... I believe you have figured out that part already. You were arrested because you and your friend and your Mercedes fit the wanted descriptions I provided for felonious assault and interfering with two government officers in the execution of their duties. Warden Wilhelm Redman is coming over here in a few minutes to make a positive identification of you two from a lineup. Until that time you will be detained in our wonderful jail accommodations downstairs in the basement. I hope that you enjoy our fine cuisine."

Paul motioned for a deputy to take the man away, and walked back to his office.

"House!" Paul called.

"Right here sir," he responded sheepishly.

"What's the deal with your police car and the swimming pool?"

"A tow truck is retrieving the car, and I ordered a contractor to fix the pool fence and to replace the damaged furniture."

Paul glowered at the junior Inspector for several minutes, while House waited expectantly for an excoriating bawling out.

Paul lowered his voice, leaned forward and said through clenched teeth, "The next time I tell you to call for back-up before you decide to play Clint Wayne, you'd better do what I say, understand?"

"That's either Clint Eastwood, or John Wayne, sir," House correct.

"**What?**" Paul missed Hausteins's point.

"I was just giving you their correct names, sir."

"Get out of my sight, House… right now," Paul commanded.

"Yessir… right away sir," House cowered.

As House was retreating out of Paul's office, Paul called out to him.

"Oh, and Inspector Haustein…"

Not knowing what his boss was going to say next, House answered feebly, "Yes, sir?"

Perhaps it was because of recollections of his own rookie year on the force that Chief Inspector Paul Soria remarked, "**Good police work, House!**"

House left the building with a broad grin on his face and a little more experience in his professional armamentarium.

PART   FOUR

UNBEARABLE   EVENTS

Chapter Twenty-Eight

Willy had been deeply engrossed in his conversation with Mo and Sidney when the call came in from Chief Inspector Soria's office notifying him that two men, who fit the description of the attackers, had been apprehended.

"All be right there," Willy told the deputy inspector on the other end of the phone. He returned to his parlor with his visitors.

"Well, it seems as though the Federal Police may have caught the two men that I told you about," Willy announced to his guests. "They're over in the lockup at the Brig stationhouse right now," Willy explained.

"They need me to go over there and identify them."

"Willy," Mo asked, "would you mind if we went along with you? Because, if these really are the men who are aware of the existence of this cave bear, then we would, as scientists, like to ask them some questions about it... assuming that would be possible."

Willy thought for a moment and then realized that Mo was right. There were many questions that required answering, and surely Mo and Sid could focus on a few of the correct ones. Willy was positive that he could convince Paul to allow his qualified friends to ask a few questions that could help shed some light this strange case.

"Let's go," Willy answered, as he directed the two scientists to follow him.

It took about twenty minutes to arrive at the police station. On the way, Willy pondered a notion that he thought might get at the truth quickly. If these were indeed the men who had interfered with the capture of the bear, then Paul had them in more of an advantageous position that he might have realized.

Willy, Mo and Sid entered the police station in Brig, and were immediately greeted by Deputy Inspector "House" who seemed elated to see Willy.

"Well, Willy," House announced proudly, "I captured your assailants." His grin portrayed a self satisfaction that went clear across his face. House held out his hand to be congratulated.

"How do you know they are the right ones?" Willy questioned solemnly.

"Easy; they both matched exactly the description that you and the Chief provided, and so does the tan-Mercedes that they were driving." House's extended right hand was not enjoined by Willy's. Instead, Willy just looked down and stared at it.

House was somewhat disappointed with Willy's response. He was anticipating a more animated level of gratitude and praise.

"We'll see," Willy told Inspector Haustein.

House returned to his chair, more than a little let down by Willy's lack of enthusiasm and appreciation for all of his skillful police work, not to mention his apparent bravery.

Willy went into Paul's office and introduced Doctors Levin and Feller to the Chief Inspector.

"I'm very pleased to meet both of you," Paul's greeting was warm and surprised. "But I'm curious. Why are you both here... and on a beautiful Sunday afternoon?"

"They are experts who are helping me with this rogue bear investigation, Paul, and I was hoping that you would allow us the courtesy of asking your prisoners a few questions."

Willy did not offer any more information than that, and he hoped that Paul would not press him for more until much later.

"I don't see a problem with that," Paul responded. "The more information that we can obtain from these guys... the better."

"Great!" Willy replied. Now, where are these two men that you need me to identify?"

Willy was anxious to get on with the matter at hand quickly, and avoid any opportunity for unnecessary questions from Paul.

"They are both downstairs in separate holding cells... this way Willy," he answered as he gestured for the three men to follow him.

The Noah's Ark Conception

On the way, Willy asked the Chief Inspector, "If you don't mind, Paul, if I do identify the two men as our culprits, I would like to speak with these men privately. I hope that will be okay."

Paul was very surprised by Willy's request, and pulled him aside.

"Willy, what the hell are you withholding from me?" Paul said as he gripped his friend's shoulder hard. Willy wasn't surprised at all by Paul's response.

"Why is it that you don't want me in the room with you when you make the identification? What the fuck is going on here?" Paul was becoming upset. "I thought we were a team."

"I'd prefer it if you weren't there at first, Paul... I have my reasons. I want to be sure about these guys, and I don't want you standing over my shoulder intimidating me or inhibiting any answers that these two men might be willing to admit to," Willy answered with a mild sense of conviction.

Paul wasn't buying Willy's excuse at all.

"What the hell are you trying to accomplish here Willy? Your reasoning is bullshit. I know it, and you know I know it. So what gives?" Paul pressed.

"You'll just have to trust me, Paul...that's all I can say for now. If I don't sign your complaint against these men, then you cannot hold them on a major charge. So, I'll ask you again, can I talk to at least one of them alone? Besides, they are much more likely to relate better to fellow scientists than to policemen."

Paul reluctantly acquiesced, and gave his friend a look of strong disapproval.

He led Willy to a room where Helmut Blauman was being detained, and motioned for the deputy who was guarding the door, to stand aside. Willy entered the room and Paul motioned for Mo and Sid to join him.

"Thank you, I'll call you if I need you," Willy said to Paul, as he heard the door to the room shut solidly behind them.

After instructing his deputy to remain outside the detention cell door, Paul walked back to his office slowly, pensively. He could not fathom what Willy Redman might be up to. He began to have very mixed feelings about his game warden friend.

<u>Chapter Twenty-Nine</u> – Sunday, p.m.

Gina mustered every ounce of strength she could find to move her battered and bleeding body out of the valley and started her perilous and exhausting journey down the side of the mountain. She retraced her steps; stopping frequently to replenish her strength, eat her last granola bar and to muster up the courage to continue. In her agony she found reserves that she never knew she had. The pain in her foot had become so intense that at one point she just wanted to lie down and die. It was worse than her occasional migraines.

She thought about her Uncle Mario, the café and Paul. Gina needed to see Paul again: to feel his hands, to smell his skin and to hear his voice – even if it meant listening to him tell her, "I told you it was a foolish thing to go traipsing up in the mountains alone."

As the afternoon darkened, Gina realized and resigned herself that she was going to be spending Sunday night in the woods. She had matches with which to make a fire, and she would locate a thick stand of pine, where the pine needles were dry and could be gathered up into piles thick enough to make a warm, dry and comfortable bed for the night. The simple satisfaction that came from knowing that she had a brain, intelligent enough to conceive that idea, bolstered her fragile confidence. She set to work preparing for her long, painful night.

* * * * * * * * *

As soon as Willy looked at Helmut Blauman he recognized him immediately as the man who had ordered the bear's release. The look on Blauman's face betrayed his anxiety as he realized that it was all over except for his trial. He knew that he was now facing serious charges and jail time.

The Noah's Ark Conception

Mo and Sid watched their friend's face for a sign of recognition. They found it in his eyes, but were both surprised at Willy's next move.

"Unless you want to spend the next five years of your life in a Swiss Federal Prison for assault on government officers and interference with government procedures, I strongly suggest Herr Blauman that you tell us everything you know about the bear that you made us turn loose up there on the mountain."

Helmut Blauman was sitting at the table; his hands were folded as if he were in silent prayer. The tough guy image had faded from his face, and now he appeared genuinely apprehensive by the prospect of a long-term incarceration. He looked pleadingly at the three men.

"Alright… alright, I vill tell you vhat it ist dass you want to know. But if I do, vill you let us both go?" he pleaded.

"I cannot guarantee that Blauman. But I can guarantee that if you voluntarily help us out, then I'll put in a good word for you, and I won't sign the outstanding complaint against you… believe me, that will help you a lot," Willy affirmed.

"I'm sorry I fired my pistol into the ground at your feet up there," Blauman's apology seemed genuine.

"Gunfire! You didn't say anything about gunfire, Willy," Mo said. He seemed very upset at the revelation.

Willy dismissed Mo's concern with a perfunctory wave of his hand.

"Depending upon how truthful you seem to be with us, Helmut, I'll decide on what charges I will agree to file with the Chief Inspector. Verstehen Sie?"

"Ja, Ich verstehe," Helmut agreed.

"Now, if either me or my colleagues here believe that you are lying to us, or not cooperating fully in any way, then you won't be seeing the light of day or your family… I'm assuming that you do have a family… for a long time."

Helmut nodded his head positively when Willy mentioned the word, "family".

"Am I making myself perfect clear, Helmut?"

"Ja, du bist." Helmut answered as tears formed in his eyes.

"Now, begin by telling us who the hell you are; who do you work for, and everything you know about this Cave Bear."

After a brief silence, Helmut took a deep breath and began his incredible story.

"My name is Helmut Blauman…Doktor Helmut Blauman, und my colleague in the next room ist Doktor Herman Schaffner."

"Doctors of what?" Mo interrupted.

"I haff a Ph.D. in physiologie and genetics, und doctor Schaffner has degrees in biochemistry und cell biologie. Ve both are graduates von der Max Planck Institute."

Sid and Mo appeared very impressed.

"Go on," Willy urged.

"Ve work for a privately funded genetics research organization located in Sweden, just outside of Goteborg. The name of the organization ist not important at dis time," he stated.

"I'll decide what is important and what is not, doctor Blauman," Willy interrupted.

"What kind of work does this organization perform?" Sid asked.

"Ve perform specialized applied research work fur an organization dedicated to reconstituting extinct species of animal life. They are trying to reintroduce animals that haff been extinct fur thousands of years."

"You do **what**? Why that's absurd," Sid maintained. "By the very definition of extinct, you've just contradicted yourself, doctor Blauman. Do you really expect us to believe…"

"Let me finish, please. Den you can be ze judge of ze truth sir," the German scientist continued.

"Ve are endowed by a very wealthy und concerned group of people who identify themselves simply as "Project Noah's Ark". Ve do not know their names, or anything about this secret group. Ve also have never met with them. But they pay us very handsomely for our research work, und supply us with anything that ve may require."

"How many of you work for them doctor?" Mo asked.

"Twenty-three scientists work at our facility in Sweden; all brilliant and dedicated people. There are also other facilities in other countries, but ve are nicht permitted to communicate mit them. Ve only get to work on one piece of the big puzzle."

"Then how did you get hired?" Mo pressed, his interest piqued.

"Each of us answered a "help wanted" solicitation in the back of prestigious scientific journals. They were looking fur experts in cell biologie, physiologie, biochemistrie, zoologie, genetics, reproduction, paleontologie and cryogenics. Ve all submitted resumes und were later interviewed in hotel rooms all around Europe, Asia und the U.S. by experts in each field. Ve were told that ve vould be working for a privately funded research project called "Noah's Ark", und which had as its primary focus, saving endangered animal species of the world from extinction. Our mission was ambitious and altruistic, but our instructions were simple: To find a way to preserve animal's from becoming extinct, und to ensure the reintroduction of species that had already disappeared from the earth."

"Put simply," Mo interrupted, "a high-tech Noah's Ark."

"Ja, precisely," doctor Blauman confirmed. "But ve had absolutely no idea when ve were hired that plans included **ancient** extinct animal species… like zis Cave Bear."

"Willy, this is astonishing," Mo said with amazement. "If what these men are experimenting with is true, then it **might** explain the existence of the bear. His explanation is certainly consistent with what we've observed so far."

"But he hasn't explained how they reconstituted a twenty-thousand year old bear," Willy kept the interrogation on target.

"That bear ist nicht twenty-thousand years old," Helmut offered. He seemed to be more relaxed now that he was aware that he was in the company of fellow scientists. And they felt a little less hostile towards him.

"The bear ist exactly eight and a half years from the moment of its conception, and approximately eight years from the moment of its birth. We haff detailed records of nearly every day of its life as well as the course of the bear's daily wanderings… und where she spent each waking and sleeping hour… almost."

"That explains the radio-tracking collar," Mo clarified.

"Precisely," Helmut agreed.

Sid and Mo were wide-eyed with scientific curiosity. At no time in their careers had science been more exciting. They had heard of experiments along these lines, but nowhere had any data been published confirming such a monumental success.

"Doctor Blauman," Sid continued to press, "I've tentatively and with a great deal of hesitation identified your animal as a Cave Bear... Urseus Spelaeus to be exact. No such animal has existed for nearly twenty-thousand to forty-thousand years, and yet you say that it was conceived and was born eight years ago. How's that possible, doctor?"

Doctor Blauman rubbed his chin and answered.

"It's a long story, doktors, but I'm going to try und give you the short version. From what I have been told und from the blanks that I've managed to fill in, the early research fur this project actually began just prior to Vorld Var Two in Rottweil, Germany. The Nazi's had undertaken the resurrection of extinct species of animals at a laboratory there mit very limited success. After it became apparent that Germany vas losing the war, they abandoned the project und the facilities... in a hurry. However, a few of the scientists, instead of burning all of the project's records as they were ordered to do, they removed all of the records and hid them away securely. Long after the war was over, sometime in the late 1960's, I was told das some of these scientists had done very well for themselves in post-war Germany's industry, and had decided to reinvestigate the feasibility of the Noah's Ark project. They set up a lab in Sweden that served as a front for what they were really trying to accomplish, und they staffed it mit some of the best scientists in their specific field of discipline. In short, they simply built upon what the Nazi's had already started, and took it to the next level."

"Fascinating! But, what about the actual implementation of their research?" Mo inquired; his tone indicating the intensity of his ever increasing interest.

"I'm sure you're familiar with the concept of test tube babies, doktor." Helmut stated.

"Yes, sir, I am. But that would require live sperm from a male bear and an ovum taken from the ovaries of a female."

"This bear vas quite simply a test tube baby," Helmut pronounced.

The two scientists were shocked by the implications.

"Where did you obtain the genetic material... the sperm and the ova from a species that has been extinct for so long?" Mo asked with great interest. He was practically leaning half-way across the table.

"Now you've hit on the real, how do you put it, crux of the problem. But I caution, not an insurmountable one gentlemen."

Dr. Blauman shifted in his seat. He was obviously more relaxed now as he delved into the specific explanation regarding the scientific foundation of his organization's research.

"Let me ask you this first," he continued. "Are you aware that today, right now as ve speak, there are frozen carcasses of mammoth und other animals, birds und plants that are completely preserved in the ice above the artic circle?"

"I've heard something to that effect," Willy replied.

"Well it's true, gentlemen. They are encased there, in the ice, perfectly preserved in nature's deep freeze since the beginning of the last ice age over twelve thousand years ago. Some northern climate native tribes, in Siberia, have been thawing and feasting on some of those remains. Naturally, such a find is a relatively rare event, but imagine if you will the following scenario." Helmut began moving his hands to emphasize his point.

"Two cave bears, one male und a female, are crossing an icy crevass und walking across a fragile snow bridge, in what is today northern Siberia or even Scandinavia, but two hundred centuries ago. They are migrating instinctively, compelled by inner stirrings that have induced them to den up for the cold, harsh winter that is inevitably coming. Suddenly, without warning, the snow bridge collapses under their combined weight und they plunge to their deaths hundreds of feet below. But instead of the normal decaying process taking over, the bears are quick frozen under tons of falling snow and ice that perpetually maintains their remains at sub-zero temperatures... frozen solid."

"And you've found a way to bring them back to life? You've perfected reverse cryogenics, is that it?" Sid interrupted.

"Not quite," Helmut corrected. "Vhat's dead ist dead, and I don't think anyone but Gott himself will ever breathe life into a dead carcass. However, if under controlled conditions, one can slowly thaw the sex organs of those creatures, und avoid the mechanical fractionation of the cell walls that is attendant with the freeze-thawing process; then one can obtain the sperm and the ova from each animal. Afterwards, und under very specifically controlled conditions which I cannot elaborate on, the offspring of the dead cave bear parents can be conceived in a test tube... in the same way that they have perfected the process with human zygotes."

"But wouldn't the sperm and the ova be completely destroyed during the freezing process?" Mo asked.

"As we have seen so many times today, definitely not! Ve can freeze human sperm in liquid nitrogen at minus 180 degrees centrigrade, for use at some later time. The motility of the sperm seems unperturbed by the deep freezing process. Und that temperature is significantly colder than those conditions found in the Polar Regions. Yet the sperm cells remain viable when thawed. If nature accidentally provided the correct freezing conditions, then the potential for conceiving the progeny of extinct animals certainly exists. It's all lying up there in the Arctic und in the Antarctic, und preserved indefinitely. All ve have to do is locate the right specimens. The local natives do that all the time... no one knows better about where the specimens are then they do."

Doctor Blaumen's voice began to reflect a pride of accomplishment. It was though he needed to get his achievement off his chest to someone who could appreciate the scientific magnitude of what he had discovered.

"Herr Doktors, we found two Cave Bears frozen solid in the ice, and ve initiated and achieved a successful fertilization. Und ve created a life form that has not existed in over two hundred centuries... the surviving embryo of an Urseus Spaeleus."

"Wait, help me understand, doctor Blaumen, "Sid stopped him from continuing, "How was the embryo nurtured? You cannot possibly keep a developing fetus of a cave bear in a test tube until it can survive on its own."

The Noah's Ark Conception

"That problem was slightly a less difficult one to overcome. Ve implanted the newly fertilized egg of the cave bear directly into the uterus of an Alaskan Brown Bear. Ve sedated a large female und implanted the embryo und returned the female back into the wild. Ve tracked her every move, including her denning activity, using a radio collar which ve had placed around her neck before her release. Und while the brown bear was in a state of semi-hibernation, the baby cave bear was born in the den. The adult female raised the baby as if it were her own; nursing it and teaching it to hunt and to survive."

When doctor Blaumen had finished his explanation there was dead silence in the room. Mo and Sid stared at him with a combination awe, astonishment and respect.

"Ve have also duplicated this same process mit a wooly Mammoth. In a large enclosure in Sweden is a live, breathing, eating, two-year old wooly mammoth. Its surrogate mother was an Indian elephant named Teala, who used to work for the circus and now she works for us. Teala is rearing a very healthy, well adjusted, but at times difficult, baby mammoth boy."

"What else have you developed," Willy asked with great interest.

"Ve are presently working on the fertilization of the giant, extinct Irish deer. This animal had antlers close to three meters across. Ve found two animals preserved in a peet bog. But this has presented us with some rather unique and challenging problems, und ve haven't achieved a successful conception at this time."

"Absolutely amazing! Incredible!" Sid expressed as he leaned back in his chair.

"Very impressive doctor Blaumen. You could probably win a Nobel Prize for your work."

"I could never publish this information; nor vould I vant to. Ve all took an oath of secrecy, und I hope that you'll keep what I told you in confidence, gentlemen."

Willy interrupted the scientific revelation. "Doctor Blauman, I think that we have lost track of why we're here. How did this bear get into this part of Switzerland?"

"That's the unfortunate part. It's the part of the experiment that went horribly wrong. The *Murphy's Law* factor that came into play and completely disrupted our plans," Helmut stressed, with sadness in his eyes.

"It is always the unexpected and unplanned events that happen. Simply put: Whatever can go wrong... **will**," Helmut emphasized.

*   *   *   *   *   *   *   *   *

Upstairs, seated at his desk, Paul was wondering about the progress of Willy's interrogation of doctor Blauman. It seemed to be taking a long time, which probably meant that Willy was obtaining useful information about the bear and its origins.

Paul was about to pour another cup of coffee, when Inspector John Meeker came into the room and presented him with Interpol's reports on his two prisoners.

"Thanks, Meeks," Paul said as he took the reports and spread them out into two piles on his desk.

He opened the first report:

"Helmut A. Blauman, Ph.D.   125 Kaiserstrasse, Berlin, Republic of Germany. D.O.B. 25 February 1957, Divorced - Remarried: Wife- Helga Blauman, two children: Martin and Siobhan, ages 17 and 14. Education: Max Planck Institute: Physiology and Genetics.

Criminal Infractions: None

Physical Characteristics: H: 6'-4", W: 195 lbs, HC: Blonde, E: Blue, R: Caucasian. No scars or tattoos.

Warrants Outstanding: None"

It appeared as though Herr Blauman was a model citizen.
Paul opened the second Interpol report:

"Herman P. Schaffner, Ph.D.   1414 La Terrasserie, Geneva, Switzerland.   D.O.B.   7 April 1955, Divorced: Wife- Carla Altschuller, one child: Herman, age 20.

Education: Max Planck Institute: Biochemistry and Cell Biology.

The Noah's Ark Conception

Criminal Infractions: Juvenile arrest for experimenting with explosives. Charges dropped.

Physical Characteristics: H: 6'-2". W: 185 lbs, HC: Blonde, E: Blue, R: Caucasian. Scar on right hand; tattoo on right bicep.

Warrants Outstanding: Traffic violation- Speeding-failure to appear – Geneva.

Paul was surprised that the two men's records were clean, and showed no indication of criminal activity. It tended to emphasize the incongruity of their actions concerning the release of the bear.

What is so important about that animal that these scientists would risk felony charges and jail time? Paul wondered. *This case is turning out to be very, very strange indeed.*

* * * * * * * * *

The conversation continued downstairs in the interrogation room.

"Ve had intended to keep the young cave bear in Sweden until it was old enough to be on its own. Next, ve were going to tranquilize the bear, und then transfer it to a secure facility in Germany so that we could study it as a living fossil. Ve had radio-collared the young cave bear, and for nearly two years she confined her wanderings to a remote area in Germany that ve had selected. She bothered no one, and lived an idyllic life hunting and foraging in the remote mountainous areas that ve had designated. In the meantime, ve were hoping to find another carcass of a male, so that we could begin to repopulate the species with a strong, genetic strain. Again, ve vould use the male's sperm to artificially inseminate the young female and to produce more Cave Bear offspring. It's a sound idea theoretically, however Mother Nature unexpectedly intervened."

"What do you mean… intervened… unexpectedly?"

"You should bring in doctor Schaffner now. This is his area of expertise." Helmut instructed.

All eyes in the room stared at Willy. It was going to be his call to decide in bringing the two scientists together in a single room. He decided to make that decision, as he could monitor what information the two men exchanged with each other.

Willy instructed the deputy to bring in Dr. Schaffner. He did so, and Herman Schaffner was instructed to take a seat at the table as far away from Dr. Blauman as possible. He complied and settled into his chair not knowing what conversations had already transpired among the men in the room.

"Herman," Dr. Blauman began, "I've already explained to these scientists about the origins of the bear. They have convinced me that if we are up front and honest mit them, then they will act as advocates on our behalf und put in a good word for us at our arraignment. My advice would be to continue with the same level of candor vhen answering their questions."

Dr. Herman Schaffner nodded his head in agreement and began to speak – hesitantly at first; collecting his thoughts carefully and methodically.

<u>Chapter Thirty</u>

Having had an exhausting trip out of the valley, Gina fell asleep quickly by eight o'clock. She rested in a nest of pine needles that she had crafted into a makeshift mattress. At least she was warm, dry and a little more comfortable under the dense pine thicket. The pain in her foot continued its unrelenting throbs, and she was starving. At least there was plenty of water nearby.

She was awakened suddenly by strange, deep breathing sounds coming from somewhere close. It sounded as though some large animal was sampling great quantities of air, analyzing the scents, and then snorting the air out of its nostrils in great bursts of exhalation. Gina froze in her bed. She knew enough not to make a sound or risk a movement. Her only fear was that if what she was hearing was indeed a bear then the animal might follow the scent trail right to where she was camped. Her fire was nearly out, and the dull orange light remaining was barely visible.

Listening intently to the sounds of the night and trying to discriminate the ominous ones from the benign, she heard some animal making scraping noises on wood. It was as though some animal was sharpening its claws against a tree. It sounded a little farther away now, but still dangerously too close. Suddenly, the sound of a terrifying roar pierced the air. It sounded like a lion's noctural bellowing as it changed into short, deep, staccato-like pulses. Something answered from a distance. She had never heard anything like those sounds before. Then a shrill cry followed. Gina remained rock-still. She began to seek solace and possible intervention from an entity larger than the earth itself. Gina didn't want to die this way: Injured and alone in the forest.

* * * * * * * * *

"Last summer, our cave bear female wandered into the territory of a local male bear, or a boar as they are called. We had no idea that any male occupied that area. If we had, we would have relocated one or the other bear immediately," Dr. Schaffner explained.

"Quite unexpectedly, our young female took up with the male and a courtship ensued; mating followed quickly. She was nearly six years old and in season. We had no idea what had transpired at the time, or we would have terminated the pregnancy. In fact, I'm really quite surprised that the pregnancy continued until full term. You see gentlemen, the cave bear is a much older cousin to the modern European bear. Technically, there shouldn't be any attraction between them. And equally surprisizing is the fact that they didn't try to kill each other. She would have won the contest easily because of her surperior size. I can only surmize that because the young female's surrogate mother was a brown bear; that the young Cave Bear was taught most of the courtship mannerisms and sexual behavior patterns of the modern day bears by her mother."

Schaffner wiped his head nervously with a handkerchief.

"In any event, sometime after the mating ritual, the young female began acting strangely. She began migrating south... perhaps attracted by the warmer weather. We had never observed this behavior before, and now, in retrospect, we attribute it to hormonal changes induced by her gestation. The bear continued to migrate southward, driven by instinctive urges, and at an incredible rate of speed. She often covered twenty miles a day."

"At first we decided that it was just a spontaneous outburst of migration behavior, but later we realized that we needed to intercept and to stop her from continuing her journey across the German frontier border and into Switzerland. We decided that she would have to be darted, given a complete physical examination and probably returned to the wilderness regions above the Artic circle."

"What happened, and why didn't you stop her?" Willy and Mo pressed doctor Schaffner.

A look of extreme frustration began to creep over Schaffner's face.

"Because, the radio-collar stopped functioning... we lost track of her. We were able to follow her movements as far south as the Swiss border, but once she crossed over into Switzerland we lost her completely. We simply waited too long to follow her and her trail went cold."

He took a long breath.

"The heavy snows of winter arrived early last year, and the female took the opportunity to den up early. We searched the area that we had expected her to forage by plane and helicopter, and turned up no tracks of the bear. Once she had dug her den and settled in, the snow buried any trace of her."

"And at that point you still had no idea that she was pregnant?" Willy asked.

"Absolutely not! We were more concerned that in the spring some hapless hikers might cross her path. Given the reputation that Cave Bears have had for ferocity, we wanted to avoid that possibility at all cost. And a female cave bear with cubs would have been incredibly dangerous to anyone."

"Then why did you allow the bear to cross into Switzerland, especially of you knew where it was headed? I don't understand," Sid pressed. "Why didn't you warn the authorities, at the least, so that the animal could be trapped or destroyed before it hurt someone?"

"In hindsight, that's exactly what we should have done," the visibly nervous scientists admitted. "We should have mounted a joint, international conservation effort, but we didn't. We thought that we could contain the problem ourselves, and preserve the secrecy of our project. If the news of this got out, our benefactors would have never been heard from again, and funding for our research would have dried up immediately."

"Then how did you discovery that your bear was here in our part of Switzerland?" Willy inquired. His voice seemed to reflect a growing sympathy for the scientist's predicament.

"We read the newspaper articles about the two boys who were mauled by a bear. The brutal way that they were attacked suggested to us that it was our bear."

Tom F. Dodd

"And how did you come to find out where we planned to trap the animal?"

"It was really very easy. Brig is like an open book. We had overheard conversations in your café, talked to people on the street, and even the gas station attendant was eager to tell us everything he knew about the bear. The rest was simple... it amounted to keeping you in sight as you drove out of town with a large cage on the back of a rented flatbed truck."

"Then why in God's name did you make us let the animal go after we had gone to all of the trouble to capture it for you? Why didn't you simply kill it, and end all your problems right there?" Willy pressed the scientists hard for an explanation.

"If we killed the bear at that time, you would have surely found out that the animal was a living fossil, and it would have been the scientific find of the century. All of our work would have been exposed, and our benefactors would have disappeared forever. But we thought that if we let the bear go, then we could dispatch the animal at some isolated spot and conceal the remains. Nothing would have been compromised. We would have chalked up the project as a temporary experimental failure. Our decision turned out to be a serious lapse of judgment."

Willy scrutinized both men's faces as Dr. Schaffner spoke. He was convinced that each man was telling the truth. At this point, each man hadn't anything to lose and everything to gain by being forthright. Willy realized that the scientists might be of immeasurable assistance to him in recapturing the bear. They would obviously be no help at all in jail.

Willy's primary responsibility, as was Paul's, was to eliminate the animal as a threat to the people in his jurisdiction. Quickly considering the alternatives, Willy could see easily that Mo and Sid were enrapt by the scientific impact of what they had heard. They were both in a scientist's heaven... that state of mind where only scientists who can fully appreciate the implications of the experimental results got off mentally.

Willy interrupted doctor Schaffner in mid-sentence.

"Look, I've got an extremely serious dilemma here. I've only a minimal understanding of the gravity of your scientific accomplishments, and given what effect that your revelation has had on several people in this room, I imagine that I'm appreciating it even less. I really don't give a shit about your funding or about exposing your Noah's Ark project... no matter how well intentioned it is. My only concern at the moment is getting rid of the problem that you gentlemen, who have been trying to play God, have created for the people in, and around Brig."

Willy saw the impact of his words on the faces of the two men, and watched them lower their eyes. They were feeling guilty, and could not look at Willy directly.

"We are truly very sorry about those boys who were killed and for all of the trouble that our experiment and our poor judgment have caused you, sir," Dr. Schaffner stated contritely.

"I don't want either of your apologies," Willy answered, "Instead, I want your help," he demanded. "And this is how it's going to be," Willy appeared authoritative and in control.

"There is a signed complaint against both of you, upstairs on Chief Inspector Soria's desk. All I have to do is to nod my head, and both of you go to jail. Understand? Your years of research go down the toilet, your project is exposed, funding dries up and about two dozen of your colleagues are out of work... their careers and yours probably ruined forever."

Willy waited a few seconds for his words to sink in.

"**Or**...I'm offering you a choice. You can help me recapture this creature, and we can destroy it or you can take it back to Germany with you. So, what's it going to be?"

"We'll help you, of course," Dr. Blauman affirmed.

"Good! Now I've got to explain to the Chief Inspector what we intend to do, and you'd better hope that I can prevail upon his sense of fairness and expediency. This is not going to be an easy undertaking," Willy warned.

Chapter Thirty-One

Chief Inspector Soria came out of his office, walked downstairs and eyed the closed door to the interrogation room suspiciously.

What was taking so long? He tried to imagine. The five men had been inside for nearly forty-five minutes, and Paul undertood that Willy only required a few minutes to positively I.D. the two men.

"They're all still inside?" Paul asked the deputy standing guard nearby.

"Yes sir... all of them," he responded officiously.

The door to the interrogation room opened and Willy came out first. He walked slowly and somewhat hesitantly up to Paul, who regarded him carefully. Willy was considering exactly what he was going to say to his friend and fellow police officer. The words came uncomfortably – almost sticking in his throat.

"These two are not the men who interfered with our work, Paul, and that's my official position."

"What!" Paul exclaimed, almost disbelieving his ears.

"Are you sure? They match our description exactly. They had the guns, the right vehicle... say, what are you up to anyway, Willy?"

"I simply cannot identify these men as the one's who had assaulted us," he reemphasized.

Paul could not believe Willy, and grasping his upper arm firmly, he ushered the game warden into another interrogation room. Paul slammed the door solidly behind them.

Studying Willy's face for several seconds, Paul looked for some sign that would betray Willy's inner thoughts.

"Look, Willy... you and I both know that these are most definitely the two men that turned the bear loose, and locked you and me up inside of the cage. What the holy hell is going on here? Would you kindly let me in on your little secret? Our friendship deserves more than this charade." The veins in Paul's face were beginning to show prominently, and his stare was boring into Willy's eyes.

"Paul... I'll give it to you straight... as a friend. Completely off the record, I need these guys to help me recapture this animal. They are extremely knowledgeable about this bear's habits and mannerisms, and I'm completely convinced that nothing good will be served by exercising your official complaint right now and locking up these two men. They are scientists, not crominals," Willy stressed.

Paul remembered the Interpol report that essentially agreed with what Willy was saying.

Then Paul thought about the administrative pressure he was receiving relative to resolving the rogue bear issue.

"Then what the hell am I supposed to tell the press; and how am I going to explain this new situation that you are suggesting to Haustein? This will make the Federal Police look like a bunch of morons... Keystone cops. I can't afford that right now."

"Paul, hear me out. Tell House that they closely resembled the two men, and reinforce his great police work. He'll live with that. My department will pay for any damages that occurred during the apprehension; and as an official peace officer of the state, I will take full responsibility for Blauman and Schaffner. They have both agreed to play ball with me in exchange for leniency... not forgiveness... leniency.

"Who the hell are they, Willy... really?"

"They are scientists who have a vested interest in seeing this bear caught and removed from here... just like I do."

"Then why the fuck did they release it back into the wild... in my territory... on my watch? Clarify that for me that, will you please." Paul's surprise and confusion over this new situation was causing him to become very edgy because he felt that he was losing control.

"Like I told you Paul, these men were not the ones."

Paul was furious with Willy and the stance that he was taking with two perpetrators. He couldn't believe that his friend would undermine his investigation by denying that the two scientists had anything to do with the bear's release. Still, Paul understood that the people and the press within his jurisdiction would hold him completely accountable for the outcome of this strange case – however it was resolved. Paul could not simply abdicate his responsibility for his role in the entire affair and pass it off on the game warden.

"Willy," Paul began with a strong resolve in his tone, "I can't hold these two men given your intractable attitude, but I am not going to let you take the responsibility for this situation alone. I can't. So, I'm going to say this to you in the clearest possible terms. Any assistance rendered by these men, who you maintain know the habits of this creature better than anyone, is going to be approved by me. They will work with me or they will be sent packing or to jail. Please don't try my friendship to the point where you will force me to threaten these guys with arrest for interference. You know that I'll do it. We either going to work as a team here, or we're all going to fail and be held accountable for this mess together. Do I make myself clear?"

Paul glared at the warden in a way that Willy knew he meant business. He had managed to push Paul to the edge of his patience and tolerance.

"Then you are forcing me to take matters into my own hands, Paul," Willy retorted resolutely.

"What the hell do you hope to accomplish alone, Willy? Why do you believe that you have to be a loner on this; why can't we work together?" Paul insisted.

"Because the way you have this all worked out, Paul, this bear is already dead. And I can't abide that outcome. That's all there is to it," Willy emphasized passionately.

"Whatever you say, Willy," Paul let Willy know by his attitude that he wasn't buying any of his maverick notions."

"Get out of my office, warden and let me get on with my job," Paul said disgustedly.

"This mess is both yours and my responsibility, Willy. I sincerely hope you know what the fuck you are trying to do."

Chapter Thirty-Two

Gina, after several more hours of torturously painful movements followed by short intervals of rest, had finally succeeded in making it down the mountain. Just when the pain appeared to be at its most unrelenting, did she peer through the trees in front of her and finally catch sight of her Land Rover parked in the clearing. She was so in need of seeing something familiar, that the image of the car sitting there, waiting to carry her to the nearest medical clinical, appeared almost surreal – like a mirage.

She reached into her pocket for the car keys. They weren't there. Shock raced through her body as she tried to recall where she had left them. Had she put them in her backpack that she had abandoned in the cave? Did they fall on the ground during her struggle with the wolverine and she had lost them?

Reaching around to her back pockets she failed to locate them. She checked her pockets again – nothing. Finally, desperately, she remembered that she had an inside breast pocket in her vest. She put her left hand over it and felt the uneven bulge. Her keys were safely there. She rarely used that pocket, and she had made the decision of storing her car keys in a place where they wouldn't accidentally be dislodged. Gina breathed a huge sigh of relief.

Standing on her right foot she managed to unlock and open the driver's side door. Shifting her balance again, she managed to gain purchase on the inside roof-pillar handle and swing herself onto the driver's seat. Her body, exhausted and tormented with pain began to shake uncontrollably as she sat back into her seat. Her hands were trembling so violently that she couldn't place the ignition key into the starter lock. Driving was completely out of the question. She waited for nearly fifteen minutes before she could calm down sufficiently, and still it required several tries to properly insert the ignition key into the slot.

The heat inside of the Land Rover was nearly ninety-five degrees when she started the car and turned on the air conditioning. Because of her exhaustion, the heat and the pain, she nearly fainted. Her eyelids began to close and she decided not to fight the anesthetizing sleep that was trying to overtake her.

The sun was shining on the windshield at such an angle that every scratch, chip and streak seemed to be emphasized in an exaggerated fashion. It was very difficult to see through it clearly. Tears from her strained vision formed in both eyes and distorted her perception even moreso. The mangled remains of insects collected under the wiper blades, and their dessicated juices marked the impact points on the windscreen's safety glass. Gina managed short shallow breaths which seemed to minimize the exacerbation of her pain. Her eyes wandered lazily over the instrument panel – everything seemed blurry. Perspiration from a combination of the heat and her ordeal down the mountain formed on her forehead, and dripped into her eyes: stinging and burning, and adding to the blurry transformation of sunlight streaked images. She felt like she might be going into shock.

Suddenly she remembered the golden coin that she had discovered in the cave. In her frantic haste to save herself from the wolverine, she had dropped the coin. Gina allowed herself to cry for the first time as the emotional impact of her entire ordeal began to overwhelm her for the first time. She felt like a depredated victim and yet somehow vindicated at the same time. She was confident now that the gold was buried somewhere in that cave, and when she recovered from her injuries she resolved to go back and find it.

As sleep mercifully deprived her of the painful sensations, the beginnings of a smile could be detected in the corners of her dried saliva encrusted mouth. Gina slumped in her seat for nearly thirty minutes as the engine droned on. The sun was lowering in the west when she awoke.

Chapter Thirty-Three

Earlier that same day, Warden Willy Redman had picked up the bear's trail from where it was released from the cage, and had been tracking it, on foot, for several hours. The large female with her two, half-breed cubs following close behind was still moving steady northwest and uphill to take advantage of the summer grazing opportunities high in the mountains. Willy had concluded that the only way to halt the bear's migration into the Alps would be to capture one or both of the cubs. And while it was still a highly dangerous undertaking, snagging one of the offspring was probably easier than recapturing the adult. He would have to remain downwind of the bears at all times or risk detection. Willy would wait for an opportune moment when the mother went off to hunt, leaving the cubs alone and unguarded.

He admired the great animal's spirit and courage, but feared the outcome of its inevitable contact with armed humankind. The bear would be regarded as an interloper; a dangerous threat that must be exterminated as would a rabid dog. Its great size and strength would never prevail against the impact of high-powered, semi-automatic weapons. A living anachronism out of its normal place in time, and existing in a world intrinsically hostile and intolerant, the survival of the mother Cave Bear and its cubs would be improbable.

Willy questioned the wisdom of his venture. Why was he willing to risk his life to help an animal that would never appreciate his efforts? There surely must be a higher purpose to his compellings, he reflected, though he knew not what it was. He only sensed a kinship with the bear. Minimally, they both shared and depended on the same earth for life. Willy's great ancestors were probably nourished by the bear's flesh and kept warm by its hides, as were they inspired to press on with their difficult life by the animal's courage. In some strange, distant way, Willy felt that he shared a connection with the bear – it was a kind of totem for him. And diminishing one life form had a finite deprivational effect on all others. He believed that it was all part of Nature's fragile balance; the will of God - a superior wisdom that should not be challenged.

The three bears' tracks were easy to follow in the soft earth, as was clear evidence of the animal's foragings. The bears' droppings were frequent and characteristic in appearance. Willy was also keenly aware of the wary mother's nearly supra-sensory ability to detect when she was being followed, and then to furtively double back on her pursuer. Bear's were masters of that tactic, and it often led to the death of any human who thought themselves clever enough to outfox a bear. The hunter simply became the hunted, as the bear masterfully turned the tables. Willy guarded attentively for any signs of this behavior and listened for any unusual sounds.

By mid-afternoon, the temperature had risen into the low 90's and the humidity was climbing. The sultry air was stifling, and there was little wind. Willy was now sweating profusely, and the insects tormented him relentlessly as he moved carefully, and as silently as possible through the underbrush. Soon he began to catch the unmistakable scent of the bear. It was close now – perhaps too close.

Willy sat under an overhanging laurel bush, quietly sniffing the air around him to better locate the bear. Had the ferocious animal detected his presence? Was the bear at that very moment lurking closeby in ambush? Fear slowly began clutching at Willy's nerves. Normally cool headed and always in control, he became very much aware of the awesome power in those terrible claws and rapier-sharp canine teeth. He knew that he didn't stand a chance, unarmed, against a ton of Pleistocene ursine fury. He strained to hear the slightest noise that might betray the presence of the ferocious carnivore, and that which would give him precious seconds to climb a tree and save himself from a horrible, certain death.

For several minutes he remained motionless in the crouched position, his ears straining to detect any sound. Only the incessant droning of the gnats and flies disturbed the silence. But the odor of the cave bear lingered.

Slowly at first, Willy began to crawl through a dense thicket of shrubs and dogwood, taking care not to break any branches or twigs which might betray his presence. Soon, he came upon a small clearing, well concealed by thickets of dense, thorny briars. He saw the dead body lying in the middle of the clearing. It was one of the cubs.

The notion that the female might be only a few yards away and hiding in the bush gripped him; causing Willy to shudder reflexively. He crouched motionless, eyeing a tall, sturdy cedar tree which might provide a hastily needed refuge in case the bear decided to charge. But nothing moved.

The odor of decaying flesh mingled with the residual scent markings of the bear. He perceived that the cub had been dead for several hours, perhaps a day. The hot sun had been accelerating the decay process and the fierce, biting flies were visible everywhere. He moved cautiously to examine the young animal.

It had already begun stiffening considerably, and there were no visible signs of violence. The young bear seemed to have died of natural causes. It was a young female. Willy then examined the head and the teeth. The head was much larger than that of a young grizzly or a brown of similar age, and its dentition was considerably longer. He noted the unusually large canine teeth as well as the over developed carnassial teeth, indicating that the species was more carnivorous than omnivorous. The young bear was clearly a different species from any that Willy had ever studied. He estimated its weight at two hundred pounds, and judging by the size of its feet and claws, it would have a lot of growing to do before maturation.

The fur was nearly identical to that of the sample that he had found in the clearing where the two boys had been killed. Gently rolling the follicles between his fingers, he could see in the soft ground the tracks which indicated that the mother attempted to get her expired cub back up on its feet. Willy noted the direction that she took after giving up the attempt to revive her dead offspring.

The flies were become far too numerous and bothersome, and the fetid stench was overpowering. Pausing to wipe the dust and perspiration from his face, Willy decided in was time to press on.

Chapter Thirty-Four

Drs. Blauman and Schaffner accompanied Paul back to his office. It was already late in the afternoon and he wanted to initiate the recapture operation as early as possible the next morning. No one spoke as they walked into Paul's office, and his mind strained to organize his thoughts despite the tension in the room.

Paul was both troubled and irritated by Willy's disappearance, and suspected that the game warden was up to something foolhardy – although he had no idea what that might entail. Willy had always been an enigmatic character who never allowed anyone to view his inner thoughts, yet his motives were always simple and never selfish. Willy seemed to be guided by fundamental, natural laws which the people of a technically driven society found difficult to perceive and to relate. Paul definitely required Willy's complete cooperation with this case, and he felt awkward without Willy's valuable counsel.

Paul's office in the old police building was drab and dingy. He had put in a request in his annual budget for a renovation and a paint job of the facility, but he had heard nothing from police headquarters in Bern. A rusty, one hundred foot, steel radio tower stood, bolted in concrete behind the building. It was obvious that a new antenna was required; frayed transmission cables needed to be replaced and all of the police vehicles needed refitting with more efficient, modern radios. His office was furnished in the simple, efficient, low-budget style of a satellite, low-priority government facility. Paul referred to it as functional grunge. The desk and chairs looked as if they had been purchased at a surplus military hardware sale. The walls were a faded light-green, and the paint was dried out, cracked and peeling in several places. Paul closed the door to his office so that they could converse freely. The scientists stared at Paul, waiting for him to speak.

"I'm open to suggestions at this point," Paul broke the heavy silence and staring directly at Dr. Blauman, who construed the remark to mean: *You created this mess, now what are you going to do to clean it up?*

Blauman's answer was quick, and to the point.

"I now believe das the optimal solution, fur all concerned, would be to destroy the bear und its offspring."

Dr. Blauman's remark startled the other men, who were surprised and visibly taken aback by the abruptness and finality of his statement. But none of them uttered a word.

Blauman felt that he needed to reinforce his point.

"After giving careful und analytical consideration to all of the alternatives, I do not believe das there ist any other workable option. The animal's presence here ist a direct consequence of an experiment which should have been terminated a long time ago. Minimally, the bear should have been restrained und studied under conditions of maximum control. It vas a gross miscalculation und an error in my judgement to permit this bear to be released into the wild. Und I accept fully the blame und the responsibility for the damage this creature has wrought; especially fur the deaths of all those innocent people. This experiment das has taken place under my supervision has been a gross failure," Blauman stated, as he appeared to be genuinely contrite and beaten down by the responsibilities of his work.

"But why destroy the cubs, doctor?" Schaffner seemed to be pleading for the young bear's lives. He had tacitly accepted that the mother bear, now an experienced killer of humans, had to be eliminated.

"I can empathize with your feelings fur those hybrid cubs, doktor, but you must keep in mind that they too are wild animals; genetically contaminated and quite capable of atavistic tendencies. As adults, they vould be as dangerous to human kind - or perhaps moreso, than their mother. They almost certainly have observed their mother killing those poor men, und have been nourished on the taste of human flesh. This is how a young bear learns to hunt, vhat to eat und to survive. Ve cannot take any more chances with these animals."

Dr. Blauman hesitated for a few moments and then drove home his point.

"Gentlemen, I am telling you in the clearest possible terms das humans are already regarded as prey und a normal dietary supplement by these young bears. This imprinting, or learned preference for human flesh is now irreversible. Consequently, those cubs cannot be allowed to reach maturity. I have made up my mind und my decision is final."

All eyes in the room fell on Chief Inspector Paul Soria, who acknowledged with a slow nodding of his head acceptance of Dr. Blauman's conclusion.

"I don't think that your experiment has been a failure at all," Mo Levin assured him. The paunchy, diminutive scientist sat rubbing his ruddy cheek with his stubby fingers. Up to that moment he hadn't said very much, but listened politely and pensively.

"Quite the contrary," he went on. "I think that your experiment has yielded valuable scientific information. But you are allowing this animal's recent activities to overshadow what would normally be considered a remarkable scientific achievement... namely, the resurrection of a completely extinct species. You have accomplished something which Nature herself could not. Through your knowledge, skill and scientific intervention, you have given a second chance to a life form that vanished from the earth over twenty thousand years ago."

Mo's eyes were wide open and twinkled as he emphasized his point.

"I think that you are being too hard on yourself doctor Blauman, and you are allowing your emotions to cloud your scientific objectivity," Mo added.

"I don't understand what you mean, sir," Blauman responded.

"Mo... please, call me Mo. Herr Doctor Blauman, wouldn't it be a better solution to trap these bears and transport them back to your facility for further study? To my way of thinking, that sounds like a far better alternative than terminating years of expensive and immensely important research with a single rifle bullet. There is so much more information to be gained from additional study."

"Such as?" Dr. Blauman sensed a certain kinship of purpose with the funny looking man who called himself Mo, and pressed him to provide a persuasive reason to save the bears.

Mo stood up and looked out of the window of Paul's office in pensive reflection.

"I'm a Paleobiologist by training," Mo continued. "And my studies are generally confined to dusty, ancient, dirt-encrusted fossil remnants, long since devoid of any life. I have to draw conclusions about the nature and behavior of extinct species by examining skeletal fragments, tooth surfaces and cranial development. Every theory that we advance is a supposition; to which we attempt to add credibility by offering corroborative evidence which is usually, if not always, conjecturable. Very rarely are we privileged to find irrefutable proof."

He stopped speaking to scratch his furrowed forehead, and to guage how well the other men in the room were following his reasoning.

"Perhaps once in a scientist's lifetime, if we're fortunate, someone finds a living fossil... such as the coelacanth, or the giant reptilian monitor lizard of the Komodo Islands. When this happens, that discovery offers bountiful opportunities for first-hand observation by scientists all over the world."

"What are you driving at, exactly?" Dr. Schaffner pressed.

"Well, for instance, we can now examine functioning musculatory, soft tissue... the circulatory, immune and reproductive systems and well as the digestive and neurological makeup of this animal... areas that were previously denied to us by the processes of decay and fossilization. We can learn how primitive systems cope with disease, infection and adaptation. What unique behaviors did it acquire? One question that I would be very eager to have answered is how does the Cave Bear's immune system, which stopped evolving twenty-thousand years ago, cope with twenty-first century pathogens?"

"You raise several excellent points, Mo."

The Noah's Ark Conception

Paul could easily see that Mo Levin was advancing a compelling argument to save the bears, despite the fact that Paul didn't quite understand all to which Dr. Levin was referring.

"Now wait a minute, gentlemen," Paul interrupted. "A few seconds ago we were convinced that these animals had to be eliminated. Are you now suggesting that we capture these beasts and Fedex them back to a laboratory somewhere in Germany, where they might escape again and come back here or go on a marauding spree elsewhere?"

"Not to Germany, Chief Inspector, but much further north... back to Sweden; to some remote place where there will never be a chance of them hurting someone again," Mo reinforced.

Paul glanced at the other men in the room. Tracings of a smile could be seen on Dr. Blauman's face, as though an idea that he never thought of before had struck.

Mo allowed himself the satisfaction of believing that he might have just saved the bears, even though he might not be around to see the inevitable scientific outcome of his suggestion.

"Wait!" Dr. Schaffner interrupted. We have to weigh our emotional tendencies of wanting to save these bears against the realities and the perils involved in implementing what you are suggesting.

"What do you mean, doctor?" Paul pressed him for an explanation.

"For example," Dr. Schaffner went on. "Does the potential scientific information derivable from studying these bears warrant or offset the attendant risks associated with their capture and transporation back to Sweden? And, once they are in Sweden, will the bear's immune system be robust enough to ward off whatever diseases may be indigenous to that area of the world?"

Dr. Blauman answered.

"Ve haff examined the animal's immune system almost continuously before its escape, particularly fur the concentration of lymphocytes. Blood samples vere drawn twice a month. The bear seemed to maintain its immune system in a manner similar to that of the polar bear. The ratios of red and white blood cells, the hematocrit and the hemoglobin levels are very similar in both species. In addition, the Cave Bear vas immunized slowly against several known bacterial und disease types over the months prior to the bear's release."

Blauman paused to answer any questions; none were forthcoming.

"In the weeks prior to releasing the bear in Germany, ve fed it on venison, wild berries, native grasses und other foods that it would find locally in the wild. The bear vas, ve believed, fully reintroduceable. The exact same acclimation process occurs whenever captive-bred animals from zoos are reintroduced into their native habitats. Normally, the extreme difficulties associated with most non-extinct animal reintroductions are overcoming learned behavior patterns while the animal was in captivity. Put simply, the animal becomes spoiled and takes the path of least resistance. Having never acquired hunting and foraging skills, the animal simply waits patiently for its keeper to bring it food at feeding time. In the wild however, the animal's acquisition of nourishment is a constant process; as well as sampling and learning what it can and cannot eat. In most cases, newly introduced animals lack the prerequisite learned skills to survive on their own in the wild. They become confused und lack the defensive, fight or flight skills to ward off the challenges of predators or aggressive members of their own kind. Consequently, they eventually die of starvation or they are killed. Fortunately for Cave Bears, they have no natural predators... they are at the top of the food chain."

"But having no predators," Mo interrupted, "it would seem to me that the bear would have a greater chance of survival than say... a tame deer."

"Its enormous size was one of the factors that we counted on to ensure the reintroduction experiment's success. However, the unknown factor in the equation was the cave bear's own instinctive behavioral patterns. No one had ever observed this species before, and very little was known about the bear's mating, territorial and migration habits. Once it began moving south and west, we couldn't stop it. In retrospect, we should have terminated the experiment that ve labeled as CBR101, the moment that it got out of control. But ve became so emotionally attached to the project und to the bear that our scientific objectivity became compromised. I suppose that now, the Noah's Ark Project will ultimately haff to be terminated."

Dr. Blauman's face continued to project the anguish of a broken and defeated man; guilt-ridden over the unnecessary death of three men. Paul seriously considered if he would bc any use to him in pursuing of the bear, or would he simply be in the way.

"Look, gentlemen," Paul took control of the discussion for the second time, but with a measure of respect. "I can appreciate the scientific merits of the situation that we have here, but discussing the methodology and philosophy of specie reintroduction is not going to prevent **your** bear from killing again. Now, I require a solid, workable plan from all of you. How do you propose to recapture this creature? After we have succeeded in accomplishing that objective, then you can figure out what to do with it. After that you can discuss philosophy all you want. I don't enjoy reminding you that you can still be guests in my jail."

The direction and the tone of the conversation changed immediately.

Paul walked over to the large map that hung, framed on one entire wall of his office. The map delineated the entire Brig Federal Police jurisdiction area – all of Paul's area of responsibility, including the remote sections of the Alps. The four scientists joined him at the map. Paul picked up a metal pointer and indicated the spot where the bear was last seen – the place where it was released from the trap.

"Here is the bear's last known position," Paul indicated; pointing to an area along the remote fire road.

"My guess is that the bear is still headed northwest in an acclivous manner," Dr. Schaffner indicated, along the rim of this mountain, here." He indicated the spot with his finger.

"There should be plenty of game and good water in that valley."

"That makes sense," Paul agreed. "So then we need to find a good place to intercept the bear when it comes through the valley in this direction."

"Precisely!" Dr. Schaffner concurred.

Paul was impressed by Dr. Schaffner's apparent willingness to contribute his assistance to the bear's recapture.

"There's another fire road… here," Paul followed a thin, dotted line on the map with the pointer.

"The road crosses the valley at the western perimeter of the mountain. The bear would be channeled through the valley and emerge right where the fire road crosses the edge of the valley…right here." Paul tapped the area with the tip of the pointer, and then drew a circle around the point with a yellow highlighter.

"Can you get in there with your capture cage, Inspektor?" Dr. Blauman inquired.

"I think so. The road really narrows at two points, and I'm concerned about a wash-out near this stream, where it passes under the fire road. We've had a lot of snow-melt and run off this spring and I have no idea what condition that dirt road might be in, but we'll have to take the chance that it's passable." Paul emphasized.

"What are you going to use for bait?"

"Oh, I forgot about that," Paul admitted abashedly. "We used a pig last time. But I doubt that the owner would let us have another one. The bear thoroughly mutilated the first one."

"What about using a dead deer?" Mo suggested. "You could suspend the carcass from the limb of a tree. The scent would almost certainly attract the bear."

"Good idea," Schaffner agreed. "The older the carcass the better the scent stream; our bear has proven herself to be a real opportunist."

"Do you have sufficient tranquilizer?" Mo inquired.

"Plenty," Paul insisted. "Two darts should sedate the bear for an hour or so, and we can use a quarter filled tranquilizer dart on each of the cubs."

"Ist there enough room in the capture cage fur the cubs?" Dr. Blauman asked.

"Yes." Paul answered firmly.

Then Mo introduced a new slant on the issue at hand.

"Have you gentlemen considered the possibility of bureaucratic problems with getting these bears back into Sweden?" Mo inquired, his eyebrows raised as if signifying some unique consideration needed to be factored into the equation. Then he continued to buttress his facts.

"Being well acquainted with government procedures and red tape, I can tell you that getting the bears through border inspection points will be very difficult without the proper authorizations. There will be mountains of paperwork and plenty of questions to be answered. I can foresee that these animals will come under the jurisdiction of many governmental agencies: The Departments of the Interior, Fish and Wildlife, Departments of Agriculture and the Customs Agencies… and not to mention private conservation organizations, assuming that they get wind of this. They could tie you up for weeks… or even months."

"We'll cross that bridge when we come to it," Paul stated, as he wanted to dismiss, at least for the moment, any negativism that might serve as barriers to going forward with the recapture process. He understood completely that regulations could become an issue later.

"My immediate problem is removing the threat of these animals from my jurisdiction; and the sooner that occurs… the better! Once that problem is eliminated, we'll concentrate on the next set of problems," he announced.

"I'll pick up both of you at the hotel, tomorrow morning at six a.m."

Paul turned to Mo and his friend, Sid, and as he spoke, there was a change in the inflection of his voice.

"I'm assuming that you and Doctor Feller will not be joining our expedition tomorrow."

The disappointment was apparent in Mo's voice.

"No, unfortunately we cannot. I have to take Sid to the airport tomorrow afternoon. He has to fly home and I have a regular job waiting for me."

"I wish that I were joining you," Sid admitted. "It would be a supreme opportunity for me to witness a living fossil. But, I'm getting a little too old and worn out for perilous safaris. These days, I confine my expeditions to the dusty, remote sections of the library. Besides, it's much safer," Dr. Feller remarked.

Paul smiled.

Paul drove the four scientists back to their hotel. And since the level of tension among them had diminished and was slowly replaced by a growing sense of comraderie, further conversation about the regeneration of extinct Pleistocenic species flowed more freely – particularly with Dr. Schaffner. Dr. Blauman remained quiet for the most part unless spoken to directly. Mo and Sid seemed to understand the senior scientist's inner conflict, and later, in their hotel room, had private discussions about it. They likened Dr. Blauman's conflict burden to that of the inventors of the atomic bomb. Unquestionably a scientific achievement of Nobel proportions, but also it was clearly a device with the potential capability of massive human and earthly destruction.

As the group separated to return to their rooms, Sid and Mo stopped Dr. Blauman for one final exchange of thoughts. They shook Blauman's hand firmly and looked deeply into his eyes. *There is real genius behind those blue eyes*, Mo considered.

"Doctor Blauman, we just want to say what an honor it has been to meet you. This may be very difficult for you to accept under the circumstances, but we sincerely believe that your efforts, motives and achievements are laudable. You have achieved creation – an accomplishment that until now, only God has been privileged to enjoy. If at all possible, you should not abandon your work or the Noah's Ark Project. Most humans, either by accident or design are contributing to the elimination of countless of animal or plant species every day. You sir, are among the very few who are making an effort to preserve them. In every heroic endeavor there is a measure of risk… and there is rarely any gain or forward progress without some setbacks."

Mo then let go of Dr. Baluman's hand.

"I greatly appreciate your thoughts, doktors, "Blauman replied, apparently moved by Mo's exaltation. Both men turned and walked in silent contemplation to their rooms.

Chapter Thirty-Five

Gina barely managed to steer her Land Rover into the asphalt parking lot of the Brig Infirmary emergency room. Completely exhausted, she picked the first parking spot available; aimed and nosed the vehicle into an awkward position between two yellow lines. She knew that the rear end of the vehicle intruded into the adjacent space but she did nothing about it – she had no strength remaining and she could barely keep her eyes open. She seriously doubted whether she could walk or crawl the final thirty or forty meters to the E.R entrance.

Two, white-coated attendants were lounging outside of the emergency room door enjoying a brief smoke-break, and Gina called out to them in a voice so weak that it required several attempts to get their attention. When they spotted her alerting motions, the two attendants walked towards her vehicle, slowly at first, but once they recognized the ashen pallor in Gina's face and observed her posture as slumped over the steering wheel, their responsive acrivities became more urgent.

"What's the problem, lady?" One of the attendants inquired.

"Hey, she's the woman from the café," the other attendant called out; recognizing her immediately.

The arduous ordeal of her journey did not permit Gina the energy to respond as her upper body continued to slump across the steering wheel of the Land Rover; her eyes were beginning to roll back in her head.

"She's going into shock! Get a stretcher and a doctor, fast."

Within a few seconds, the attendant had returned with the resident-on-duty and a gurney in tow. The doctor noted a weak, but rapid pulse and looked for any evidence of blood loss, injuries or broken bones.

"Let's get her inside. She's going into shock. We must keep her warm and start an I.V. immediately," the physician commanded.

The Noah's Ark Conception

The three men removed her from the front seat of the Land Rover, and placed her on the gurney. Within seconds, Gina was lying on her back on an examination table in the emergency room, the subject of a flurry of highly organized and well-rehearsed activity; doctors, nurses and attendants were administering to her in beehive frenzy.

"She appears to have a broken radius and ulna of the right arm, doctor, as well as a possible dislocated wrist and shoulder." One nurse called out.

Another nurse, examining the lower portion of Gina's body reported, "She has several puncture wounds to the left ankle and foot, but we'll have to cut this boot off to further assess her injuries."

Within two minutes, every piece of Gina's clothing had been removed, and her left boot was removed. It was filled with partially coagulated blood. An intravenous feeding tube was inserted in her left arm.

"Was any identification found with this patient?" the lead physician on the trauma team inquired.

"Her name is Gina A. Schmidt, doctor. She owns the Brauhaus café here in town. Some of the attendants recognized her."

"She didn't get these injuries working in a Café," the doctor responded sarcastically. "Not unless the café was overrun with a horde of vicious, giant rodents."

"Okay... notify someone at the café of her whereabouts. We need to know if she's on any medication or has any serious allergies. I want a complete series of x-rays on her right arm and shoulder...STAT! Then get someone from the lab up here. I want a complete chemistry profile, CBC's, electrolytes and also, while they are at it... a rabies test. Also, let's check on her myocardial enzymes. Get a blood type and cross-match on her because I think that she's going to need an infusion."

Gina lapsed in and out of consciousness. She had only a vague understanding of what was taking place around her, and the probing, bright light that seemed to be continuously shown in her eyes. There was a confusing and blurry array of shadowy faces making deep, voice-slurrying sounds like a 45 r.p.m. record being played at 33 and 1/3. The attendant's faces were defocused and appeared to have luminous auras around them. All the while the main examination room lights were almost painfully brilliant, glowing overhead. They were round and golden-yellow, she thought. Golden... yellow... golden......yell... Gina slept for the next twenty-eight hours.   When she awoke, she found that her right arm and shoulder had been immobilized, and her left foot was heavily bandaged and elevated.

She became aware of sunlight infiltrating her room between the slats of dark wooden blinds. She could feel a tube sticking out of the back and taped to her left hand. She could hear a soft beeping sound that seemed to be in sync with her heart beat, and muffled voices somewhere off in the distance. She wanted Paul.

Chapter Thirty-Six – Tuesday

It was early morning when Willy observed the bear cub frolicking in front of a small cave opening which was located about six feet up an embankment on the side of a small hill. The mother bear was not visible and Willy assumed that she was either inside of the cave bear-napping, or off on a hunting expedition. If the latter were true, then it would be the ideal time to attempt to capture and abduct the cub.

The wind was blowing from the northwest, and Willy knew that he was in a favorable position to approach the young animal. Willy's plan was a simple one. He would stalk the bear, allowing himself to get as close as possible. He didn't want the juvenile bear to cry out and to alert the mother. Next he would inject the cub with the same tranquilizer that they had used on the mother a few days earlier, and pray that the immobilization would take place quickly. Using leather thongs, he intended to bind the bear's paws and carry it back to where he had parked his pickup truck. He completely understood that his plan was frought with difficulty and peril, but he could think of no other way to prevent the cave bear's migration toward an area where it might come into conflict with more humans, and her inevitable rendezvous with certain death. He anticipated that the mother cave bear would follow the scent of her cub, and not leave the area until it was located. Willy counted on the intensity of her maternal instincts and hormonal drives to interrupt her urge to migrate.

The cub had discovered a large, furry, marmot-like creature and was amusing himself as the rodent darted in and out between the rocks. Using its powerful front paws, the cub would turn over a rock, exposing the terrified creature's hiding place, and then attempt to pounce on it before it found shelter behind another rock. Sometimes the rodent would run into a shallow hole, and dirt would fly in all directions as the cub excavated it with the ease of a backhoe. On one attempt, the bear managed to pounce successfully and the rodent instantly became a lifeless, oozing carcass. The cub delighted in the accomplishment and rolled all over the dead rodent; all the while uttering gleeful, triumphant little grunts.

Willy watched the animal for several minutes, captivated by the innocence and playfulness of the young bear. Like Willy, the bear was a direct descendant of fearless and powerful ancestors and carried forward the spirit and heritage of its family. And also similar to Willy, the bear was rapidly running out of living space and human tolerance for its naturalistic habits. Willy understood that he had a kind of kindship with the beast. And if this animal died then Willy and people like him, who were focused on the preservation of nature would ultimately share the same fate. In his mind the parallelism and destiny of their lives was powerfully irrefutable and compelling. He saw his own life path akin to that of the American Indian: fighting a losing battle to turn back the inexorable, selfish, polluting and contaminating forces of the human population incursion. At the risk of his own life, which was granted to him by God alone, he believed that he must ensure the preservation of the only surviving cub.

Willy's hiding place was about seventy meters from the bear; most of the distance between them afforded ample camouflage as it was well covered with high grass and dense underbrush. He began a silent low-crawl through the grass and under low hanging brush whenever possible; stopping every ten feet to listen for the mother and to confirm that the young bear was still preoccupied. At ten meters away Willy stopped. Traversing the next few yards between them would be crucial, and the ground cover ended about half-way to the bear cub. The final distance was across open ground that was littered with loose stones, gravel and broken brush. He would have to wait for an opportunity when the cub's back was turned, and then Willy would scramble as quickly as possible the final few feet uphill. He hoped that he could inject the young bear quickly, and then retreat, avoiding the slashing claws that would inevitably follow. Though the animal was young, it was still capable of inflicting a serious wound. He had no idea how much of the drug would be required to have the desired sedating effect on the cub.

If the mother was in the cave, she would emerge, enraged, in response to her cub's cries of alarm. He was well aware that outrunning the mother was impossible. Willy eyed an aspen tree would might make an ideal refuge should the mother bear attack. He would have to run fast and cover approximately twenty-five meters a few seconds. Then, and providing that the lower branches held his weight, he would scramble up the tree and out of the reach of the bear's lethal claws and jaws.

Willy reached into his backpack and slowly retrieved the syringe containing the powerful tranquilizer. Holding it in his right hand he watched the young bear intently, cautiously waiting for the precise moment. He was acutely aware of his precarious position – if the mother bear came back now she might take him by surprise. If the young bear detected his presence it would scramble for safety into the darkness of the cave's interior and cry out. He knew that his eyes would never become accustomed to the darkness inside of the cave in time to locate and to inject the cub. Finally, as if to make matters worse, the wind was beginning to shift. Willy could feel the quickly moving air evaporating the sweat on the back of his neck.

The opportunity came suddenly. The young bear thrust his head into the mouth of the cave as if distracted abruptly by something inside. His furry, almost comically positioned hindquarters protruded into the sunlight.

Willy stood up and glanced quickly in all directions – the mother cave bear was nowhere in sight. He began running on his toes, avoiding the broken branches and stones that could betray and hinder his approach. The cub never saw Willy approaching. In two mighty bounds he was up the embankment, and in one fluid motion Willy buried the syringe needle and injected the tranquilizer into the young bear's right flank. He quickly removed the syringe and ran headlong in the direction of the aspen tree; hesitating to glance back to observe the outcome.

Surprisingly, the cub let out a low moaning sound, signifying annoyance with the pesty insect that must have stung him. It slowly backed out of the cave and turned around, muttering the same sounds as it tried to get a glimpse of its hindquarters. Instead, the cub completed three complete circles as it tried to view and chase away what had stung him.

Willy witnessed the next scene from behind the tree. He was amazed that the cub did not detect him nor did it cry out in pain. Surely, he thought, God had seen the pureness in his heart and was blessing Willy's venture. He grew confident in that apparent sanction from the Almighty, and for the first time, he believed that he would succeed with his mission.

The young bear's hind legs began to wobble and then collapsed underneath him; disappearing under his furry undersides. Simultaneously, the rear weight of the bear began to pull it down the embankment as the young animal fought a futile battle to retain his balance. He rolled over and over the last few feet until his body came to rest safely, legs akimbo, at the bottom of the gentle sloping hillock. His tongue was lolling uncontrollably out of the right side of his mouth.

For a moment Willy became alarmed, as he thought that the tranquilizer dose had been too strong and the young bear may have died. But as he watched, the occasional twitching of the bear's tongue reminded him that his God would not permit harm to befall the cub. He would now have to move quickly.

He rushed over to the limp cub and securely bound its feet together with rawhide thongs. It was a young male, he observed, and slightly smaller than his dead sister – Willy estimated its weight at slightly over seventy-five kilograms. He was grateful for that as now he had the difficult and dangerous task of carrying the young animal back to his pickup truck.

Willy searched the immediate area carefully to make sure that the commotion had not alerted the mother cave bear. All appeared to be safe - for the moment. Willy leaned over and grasped the bear around the midsection and then hoisted the animal into a draped position over his right shoulder. The young bear felt like a hundred kilos of pure jelly as it tended to slip off Willy's shoulder. He had to keep adjusting his balance to prevent the cub from slipping and losing his grip on the animal.

Chapter Thirty-Seven

Eleven miles away, Paul and Dr.s Blauman and Schaffner were busy with the final preparations for the trap they were setting for the cave bear. The six-day-old carcass of a red deer, putrified as a result of nearly a week of decay, hung upside down from the limb of a large fir. The hind legs were bound together and the deer was suspended from the end of a sturdy rope. The pungent odor of death permeated the entire area and was swept eastward by a stiffening breeze.

Two rifles were loaded with the tranquilizer darts as Paul engaged the safety catches on each weapon and set them against the side of the truck. The cool breeze was refreshing – quite a change in the comfort level of the weather since the last time that he had waited in a stake-out for the bear. Paul watched the two scientists as they completed their preparations, and he wondered what was going through their heads. Blauman was the taller of the two men and didn't fit Paul's perception of a scientist. He was powerfully built and the energy he expanded rushing around the area suggested an athletic background. Dr. Schaffner, on the other hand, possessed the frailer frame of a man inclined to occupy himself with more cerebral exercises. The responsibility for the deaths of the three men by the cave bear seemed to add the heaviest of burdens to the man most physically capable of handling it. Paul could see the affects on Dr. Blauman's face. Paul thought it ironic how such a small oversight or an incorrect assumption could turn a Nobel worthy scientific endeavor into a nightmare of death, destruction and disgrace. He felt some degree of pity for the man, but the emotion was overshadowed by the urgency and the looming responsibilties of the moment. There was nothing to do now but wait patiently.

"I think we're all set," Schaffner stated.

Paul was beginning to take a liking to the junior scientist. It was clear that he was doing everything that he could to help.

"Good," Paul acknowleged. "Now comes the most difficult part... the waiting."

"I understand what you mean. The bear might show up in two hours, or it may take two days. Then there's always the chance that it might not appear all at."

"I'm trying not to think of that alternative," Paul replied, almost inaudibly.

Paul motioned for Dr. Blauman to take up a position inside of the cab of the truck.

"Dr. Schaffner and I will erect the tree stand, and then he'll join you in the truck. Meanwhile, you hang on to one of the tranquilizer rifles and keep your eyes open for any sign of our bear," Paul instructed.

Dr. Blauman dutifully obeyed Paul's command, and without a responsive word, picked up a rifle and climbed into the passenger seat of the truck, as Paul continued to observe Blauman's movements. He was now moving in listless fashion – almost shuffling like an old man. Paul noted that he had seen men, considerably older than Blauman, move in a more purposeful and animated manner. After Blauman assumed his position inside of the cab of the truck, Paul took the opportunity to quiery Schaffner about his senior associate.

"What kind of a man is Dr. Blauman? Does he have any hobbies, or is he totally wrapped up in his work? And does he always behave like this?" Paul asked in a volume slightly higher than a whisper.

Schaffner was not surprised by Paul's question – he actually had anticipated it.

"You are not seeing the Helmut Blauman that I used to know, Inspector," Schaffner responded as he made a furtive glance to the man sitting in the cab of the truck.

"I've known Helmut professionally, and to some extent socially, for many years... at least the past three, anyway. He has always been a very private person, but in the last few years our work has drawn us closer together and I've come to know something of his personal life. Yes, he's married... for the second time. He would tell you that he's to blame for the failure of his first marriage... extreme dedication to his work and all that. His older son ran afoul of the law, and the other boy, who is younger, was involved with drugs for a while. His wife bore the brunt of child rearing, and one day she told him that the boys needed a real father and that he should simply take his text books and get out. Dr. Blauman admitted to me one evening, after many lagers had been put away, that he had absolutely no idea that his relationship with his family had deteriorated to such an extent. And I really don't believe that he had a clue how disfunctional his family situation had actually become."

"I've seen that syndrome before. He must have been totally absorbed with his work," Paul interjected.

"Completely! But he is a brilliant scientific mind, and people like that generally find it difficult balancing the demands of a career, social obligations and raising a family at the same time."

"You were saying that he remarried?"

"Yes he did. After his first divorce, he literally immersed himself in his work. Totally in retreat from any social life, he'd spend twelve to fifteen hours every day, seven days a week in the laboratory. Sometimes he would sleep on the couch in his office. He lost about forty pounds over a six month period, and he never took a day off... he even worked over the Christmas and New Year's holidays. Finally, we all noticed that he was slowly killing himself, and so we threatened to go on strike if he didn't take some vacation. Then you know what he said?" Schaffner answered without waiting for a reply from Paul.

"He said that he would take off on Sundays and go home and rest."

"And so?"

"So his staff said, *nothing doing*. That was not what we had meant by a vacation. We demanded that he take at least two weeks. We never expected that a man with his mental drive would ever consider any more idle time than that."

"How did he react to your demands?" Paul asked as he pushed the tree stand higher into a sturdy European fir.

"Reluctantly he agreed, so we sent him to Ibiza for a vacation."

"You sent him?"

"We all chipped in and purchased an economy class air ticket for him, and his secretary made the hotel reservations."

"And did he go?"

"Yes… fortunately, and when he came back from vacation he was a changed man. The transformation was incredible."

"In what way?"

"Well… he was his old self again: outgoing, jovial, and a pleasure to work with. Everyone was completely amazed by the transformation."

"Did he say what happened to him?"

"He met his second wife. She was on vacation in Ibiza, too; also recently divorced and almost fifteen years younger than he. They fell for each other almost immediately."

"Hand me that nut and bolt would you please, Dr. Schaffner?" Paul requested. He needed to fasten the support base to the platform.

"They were perfect for each other, and more importantly, with her background in biochemistry, she understood and supported the importance of his work."

"But Dr. Blauman doesn't appear to be a very happy man now." Paul reinforced his earlier observation.

"You're correct, Inspector. Ever since this bear began migrating southwest we've noticed a significant change in Helmut's behavior. He grew very moody and quite pensive. Then he read the newspaper accounts of the deaths of those two unfortunate boys and he withdrew immediately. He became obsessed with putting an end to the experiment. We drove for two straight days to get here, and then we asked the local townspeople a few questions… the rest you know."

So you're saying that he's taking this whole thing pretty personally."

"Personally is only the half of it. He's riddled with guilt and blames his scientific talents on the deaths of the three men. He firmly believes that if he hadn't recreated the cave bear, then those men would have been alive today… and I haven't been able to convince him otherwise."

Once the tree stand had been secured in place, Paul checked out the purchase of the supports and made sure that its occupant would command a clear shot at the bear in a number of different directions. He instructed Dr. Schaffner to bring him the remaining tranquilizer rifle that was lying against the side of the truck. Paul took it with him as he climbed into position on the tree platform.

"You wait with Doctor Blauman in the truck, and signal me on the two-way radio if you see anything," Paul instructed.

"Good luck, Inspector," Dr. Schaffner offered sincerely; managing a weak smile.

Paul sensed the man's sincerity. "I hope that this won't take too long or require any luck," he replied.

Schaffner returned to the truck and Paul heard the door shut. Paul adjusted his position on the platform and placed the rifle across his lap. He wondered what was happening with Gina, and why he hadn't heard anything from her. He assumed that she was doing okay – probably wandering out of the woods and feeling dejected after a fruitless search for buried treasure.

Maybe now she'll get that silly fantasy out of her head, he thought as he peered through the dense foliage below.

The long, boring, tiring wait began.

Chapter Thirty-Eight

Using his strong legs, Willy lifted the young bear and stood up. Now his major problem became getting back to the truck and avoiding the mother bear at the same time. His progress would be slow and tedious. If the mother cave bear came back too soon, she would become enraged, follow his scent trail and that of her cub, and overtake them easily.

Willy followed the game trails and kept to the open, grassy meadows whenever possible. He understood that success required that he put as much distance between himself and the mother bear as possible. At the end of each meadow crossing, and before he reentered a wooded area, Willy turned around and checked to see that the mother wasn't closing fast behind him. If she were, he knew that he would have to abandon the cub and seek immediate safety in the branches of a tall tree. For the enraged mother would kill him without hesitation.

He would not put the cub down in order to rest. Instead, he would lean his body against a tree or a large boulder, or partially unload the weight of the cub on a low-hanging limb of a tree. He could not afford the time or the energy to keep lifting the cub from the ground.

A burning pain began in his right side, and then powerful neck cramps forced him to stop. He set the cub down gently on top of a large, flat granite boulder. Leaning his weight against the rock, he began to work out the cramp with his hands while looking around warily. Almost instantly he noticed that the forest around him suddenly became very quiet. Something other than he had disturbed the normal, noisy routine of the birds and insects. Willy froze instinctively.

Utilizing all of his senses and straining to detect any sign of a large animal, Willy slowly became aware of a dangerous presence nearby. He sensed that he was being observed which caused his adrenalin level to respond reflexively – knowing that he was in grave peril. Whatever it was was close enough to overtake him at will. He was being stalked and measured – singled out as prey by the unseen eyes and the unimpassioned brain of a large predator. His life remaining now might only be measured in seconds.

Inching slowly away from the rock and towards a large aspen he had observed nearby, he forced himself to make slow, purposeful steps while estimating how many strides it would take him to get to the tree, and then which branches he could rely on to support his weight. The young cub slept, oblivious to the unfolding drama. Immobilization would last for several hours.

The bear came out of hiding with the speed of an express train, tearing through a dense thicket of briars and roaring defiantly. A flock of opportunistic jays screeched as the bear attacked; their cries drowned out by the bear's thunderous growlings. Capable of short bursts of speed up to thirty miles an hour, the animal advanced rapidly on the game warden. In six or seven more long strides Willy would be at the tree. He could sense that the bear was closing the distance rapidly, but he dared not look back for fear of losing his footing. Reaching the tree he exerted a giant leap upwards, reaching beyond the lower limbs he had originally anticipated to secure his purchase. His right hand closed on a branch just as the bear grazed his left leg.

As the animal's momentum carried it forward it crashed, full-force into the tree. The tree recoiled from the force of the half-ton bear, shattering the branch enclosed by Willy's right hand. Fortunately, his left hand had located a sturdier limb and he managed to pull himself higher into the tree just as the bear recovered from the shock of the stunning collision. The bear raised itself up on its hind legs, its forepaws smashing the lower branches from the trunk and catching Willy's left boot just below the ankle. He felt the impact of the claws and climbed faster. Climbing another twenty feet before he stopped, he knew that the heavy bear could not follow.

His heart pounded as though it would explode; the excess adrenalin was making his spine pulsate and his arms and shoulders quivered spasmodically. But he was safe – at least for the moment. He sat resting on a sturdy bough.

Willy studied the bear, which glared at him with a wild, savage expression. The lips were curled back, threatening and exposing large, yellow-white ursine incisors. Blood, resulting from the collision with the tree, pulsed from the bear's nose and mouth adding malevolence to the ghastly visage. The great bear reached vainly for Willy with deadly, glistening claws. Finally, and in a fit of frustration, the bear pushed against the tree with all its weight, attempting to topple it. But the tree, despite a continuous rocking assault was well rooted and resisted the great bear's best efforts. Willy clung to the tree tenaciously.

As the bear began to tire, Willy suddenly realized what was happening. This animal was not the mother of the cub seeking revenge for the abduction of her offspring, but a hungry, ravenous, silver-tipped brown bear. And this new development presented an entirely different set of problems.

Bears, except females with cubs, are solitary creatures. The male plays no role in the rearing of the young, and their paternal urges begin and end with the mating ritual. To complicate matters, an adult male will not tolerate cubs in its territory, and will kill young bears if he finds them unprotected. Their mother however, motivated by powerful maternal forces will defend her cubs against a male twice her size and weight.

The male Brown Bear had not yet spotted the young cub on the rock, and unless the cub moved or made a sound, it might remain safe. However, the Brown Bear, like all ursines, possesses a keen sense of smell, and if it detected the young bear it would crush its neck easily in its powerful jaws.

The Brown was showing signs of becoming frustrated with the chase. It had tried several times to negotiate a tree climb without success, and the stubborn tree had resisted all attempts to uproot it. The bear's ferocious roaring had diminished to an occasional growl or a grunt as it paced, frustrated, around the base of the aspen. The inquisitive nose continually sampled the air, and soon its brain registered a new scent; very different from the lingering odor of the human. Willy quickly noticed the change in the bear's behavior and feared that the brown bear had detected the cave bear's cub.

Craning its neck to fix on the direction of the new scent, the bear rose slowly on its hind legs, the great head turning rapidly from side to side as it inhaled great quantities of air. Willy felt a sickening pain in his gut as the male Brown turned towards the young cub. The curious expression on the Brown's face turned malevolent and the snarling increased rapidly. It took three short steps forward and stopped, bellowing a roar that signaled a territorial challenge. The sound echoed loudly through the thicket and across the meadow. Willy fully anticipated that the young cub would be torn to pieces in seconds, but the brown bear remained, standing on its hind legs as if rooted in place; its head and neck were arched down and forward in characteristic ursine aggressive fashion. The Brown's challenge was answered with all of the savagery and fury that Willy had ever witnessed.

Chapter Thirty-Nine

The huge female cave bear barreled through the underbrush with the same unbridled abandon of a runaway steam locomotive. Instinctively, she knew that the male brown bear was a deadly threat to her cub, and she would furiously defend it with her own life. The two great animals collided with such force that the half-ton Brown was lifted off its feet and thrown backward. The female, not wasting any advantage, recovered and straddled the surprised male quickly; her powerful jaws attempting to locate a vulnerable area in his throat. But the Brown was quick to avoid the attack and slashed open an ugly gash in the side of his opponent's face with a right forepaw. The female howled in pain but redoubled by burying her teeth in the Brown's chest, ripping out a huge chunk of flesh. The big male managed to climb to his feet and backed away cautiously – head lowered and claws extended, measuring his foe and watching for an opening.

The great beasts were now on their hind legs, circling with claws forward; each waiting for the other's next move while bellowing threatening sounds. Blood oozed from the facial area of the cave bear, and dripped out of the ugly chest wound of the Brown male. The female, motivated by the sight of blood, charged savagely, her powerful hind legs digging deep into the soft earth. The Brown managed to adroitly sidestep the brunt of the charge, but caught the female's slashing foreclaw along its left side. A great wound was opened in the Brown with blood and fur flying everywhere – four white ribs were laid bare.

The female catapulted past the smaller Brown and tumbled forward in an attempt to stop, cleanly snapping off a ten-foot sapling. The male scrambled after her, and with eye-blurring speed delivered several gashing blows to the cave bear's back and hindquarters. She responded by savaging the male's chest with two deep lacerations, and by burying her razor-sharp canines into the brown bear's neck.

Locked together in what would inevitably become a death struggle for one of the bears, they tumbled into a small ravine. The violence of their fierce struggle sent clouds of red dust into the air making it impossible for Willy to observe what was happening. He could only imagine the ferocity of the murderous confrontation from the intensity of the raucous bellowing as the two animals disappeared into a dense tangle of undergrowth.

Suddenly, Willy saw an opportunity to escape with the young cub. The two bears were so intensely engrossed in their combat that they would not notice his retreat. And depending on how much longer the battle would rage, he might have sufficient time to cover the final half-mile to the safety of the truck. Then he could be guaranteed of his escape with the cub.

Willy climbed out of the tree carefully, listening to confirm that the two massive animals were still preoccupied with the struggle. He gathered up the sedated cub and moved off rapidly into the woods. The excitement of the two bears' hostilities and the brief rest in the tree had rejuvenated him, and he experienced a second wind. The young bear seemed to be lighter now, Willy thought, as he scurried off in the direction of his pickup truck. Fifteen minutes was all the time that it would take.

Hurrying as quickly as the dense foliage would allow, he was soon out of earshot of the bears' deadly combat. He assumed that one of them would ultimately destroy the other, or at least would succeed in driving it away. In either event, Willy rationalized, their efforts would consume several more precious minutes – minutes that he needed to ensure his escape.

After what seemed like an eternity, Willy broke into the clearing where the pickup was parked. The old truck had never looked better. He quickly placed the cub into the bed of the truck and then climbed into the driver's seat. Reaching under the steering column, he grasped two ignition wires and twisted them together hastily. The motor coughed and sputtered to an uncertain start. Almost as quickly as it had started, the engine died. After hundreds of iterations of twisting together and pulling apart the ignition wires, metal fatigue had taken its toll and one of the frayed copper wires had broken off in a cascade of sparks.

Tom F. Dodd

Willy pulled his knife out of its sheath and began to trim off insulation, exposing the fresh copper wire concealed underneath. Simultaneously, he saw a mountainous brown figure erupt from the forest to his left. The female had arrived in all her maternal fury. Willy saw instantly that she was seriously injured; bleeding profusely from several deep wounds and her left forepaw hung in grotesque fashion – now apparently useless. Willy felt a deep sense of pity for the creature, but was snapped back into reality and refocused on his original purpose of getting his vehicle started when the big female cave bear attacked. It stood up on its hind legs and charged the truck.

With two rapid cuts, the insulation on the wire came free. He reconnected the two wires and the engine turned over. This time it took several seconds for the engine to fire. By now the infuriated and gravely injured bear was next to the pickup; its right paw poised for the attack. Willy leaned right in the seat anticipating the deadly, six-inch claws that would surely come at him through the window. But the bear could not distinguish the human from the strange metal animal. The bear's first pass at the truck took out the left front roof pillar and part of the door frame; shattering the windshield in a spray of fine glass. With the second pass its claws hooked under the rear of the hood which was ripped open and peeled forward. The screech of tearing metal caused Willy to jump involuntarily.

He simultaneously depressed the clutch pedal and jammed the gearshift lever into reverse. He engaged the clutch and the rear wheels spun wildly. In his terror Willy had stomped the gas pedal to the floor. Red dirt, small rocks and twigs flew rearward. The bear was momentarily surprised by the unusual roaring sound of the strange animal. However it recovered quickly and resumed the attack.

Willy spun the steering wheel and executed a one hundred and eighty degree turn. Unfortunately he overcontrolled, and before he could straighten out the front wheels, the pickup tore into a thicket of wild blackberries. While slowed considerably, the vehicle had accumulated enough momentum to plow through the bushes and now it was heading on a parallel course with the road and picking up speed. The cave bear's cub, still sedated, bounced around the bed of the truck. The female was content that the strange intruder had been driven away, and she needed to rest before resuming her search for her missing offspring.

Willy finally connected with and accelerated down the dirt road, momentarily looking over his shoulder to make certain that the young cave bear was secure in the back of the pickup. It continued to lay there in a semi-conscious state. He drove directly to his home, stopping only to cover the cub and protecting its sensitive eyes from the intensity of the afternoon sun.

Chapter Forty

Gina rested comfortably in her hospital bed. She found it difficult to keep her eyelids open and understood that she was being medicated. The pain in her arm and shoulder had eased, but her left foot throbbed mercilessly. It seemed that whatever medication that they were giving her for the pain was not working well. And she now detested wolverines - passionately.

Not a big fan of mindless and mediocre television programming, she utilized the quiet time that confinement in the hospital had afforded her for reflection and to take stock of her life. Despite her slight stupor owing to the medication, Gina's mind was alert and she weighed her current situation with a great clarity, introspection and self-criticism. She had made one phone call to the Café to get an update on what was going on there, and to tell her friend Karen Aultschuler that she was safe, but recovering in the hospital. She learned that business had fallen off somewhat, and that a representative from the bank that held the mortgage on the Café had been by to discuss her shaky credit situation.

Just what I need right now, she thought when Karen told her the news.

Gina understood that unless the business turned around quickly, her costs were going to exceed her income sometime during the next fiscal quarter, and that she'd be forced to consider closing down the business. She also knew that if she could retrace her steps and go back to that cave, she might get lucky and find the rest of the treasure that she was now nearly certain was hidden somewhere within. Perhaps the value of the treasure was sufficient to pay off the debt that she owed to the bank, and that she could get out from under her burdensome obligation.

Perhaps, only perhaps, she considered.

Finally, she evaluated her relationship with Paul. He had a solid government job, and she loved him. But would Paul be a good partner in the long term? He was a dedicated policeman, but she understood that the divorce rate among police officers was statistically higher than many other professions. They had never talked seriously about marriage. In fact, they had purposefully avoided discussing the issue of wedlock. The realization told her something right there.

Gina knew that she enjoyed sharing her life with a man; but she was also keenly aware of the fiercely independent streak that she had inherited from her father's side of the family. On several occasions her need to be autonomous had clashed with Paul's tendency to be in control, and she could see where that might create potentially bigger problems with their relationship down the road. Still, she had to admit that their openess and their ability to discuss any subject with candor and intellectual honesty, except for marriage, was a strong suit. She understood that they could probably work through and negotiate any problem that arose between them. Most importantly, she trusted and respected him, and she knew that he loved and respected her. His actions had proved that unquestionably to her on several occasions. Paul had been very loyal, and she valued that quality in him highly.

Paul was a gentleman of the "old school": He held doors for her, pulled out her chair for her; he did not mind helping to clean up around the house and he was always polite and respectful towards all women. Better still, he was a great lover. He had taught her things about herself and her own body that she never before knew could respond in the way that only he could elicit. He was patient and gentle, and a good teacher. It made her wonder if she had succeeded in experiencing the private pleasures in life that her mother referred to as, "You'll find out, someday."

With all of that considered and plugged into a personal preference equation that only Gina could factor, she could not fathom or decide what the future held in store for her and Paul.

She did not want to end up with a roommate after twenty-five years of marriage. She wanted to "live" her life; not just to "exist". She was an active person, not a passive one. Could she find that kind of long-term relationship with Paul?

Chapter Forty-One

Paul filled in the tedious waiting moments on the tree platform by wondering what Gina, and then Willy were doing at that very moment. He believed that Gina had probably returned to the Café by now. But Willy was his chief source of worry.

He understood the game warden enough to know that he wasn't about to dismiss the idea of saving the bear and its cubs. The bear was too important, symbolically, to Willy to be neglected or ignored. But just what, if anything, Willy could or would do about the situation eluded Paul completely. What worried him more was that Willy might be killed in whatever undertaking that he might initiate. The vision of Willy's mutilated remains, lying partially buried in the forest somewhere, flashed shockingly in Paul's mind. He dismissed the thought by forcing himself to believe that Willy had far too much experience to allow himself to be surprised by the bear – no matter what the sub-species. Paul compared Willy's field expertise to that of Dr. Blauman's, and it disturbed him that Willy might make erroneous assumptions and oversights with the same tragic results as the brilliant Dr. Blauman had made. No matter how he rethought the situation, Paul always came to the same conclusion: Willy was in great danger if he tangled with the bear alone, but there was nothing that anyone could do about it. Paul's feeling of nervousness persisted until the overwhelming events later that afternoon.

The sun had declined to tree-top height in the western sky, casting long, shadowy figures in the tangled undergrowth. It was the strange laborious grunting sound that first attracted Paul's attention. It seemed to be coming from behind him. Two quail betrayed the animal's position with their blustery takeoff. Paul remained motionless except to close his hand around the stock of the rifle. He did not want to reveal his hiding place.

The Noah's Ark Conception

The cave bear limped carelessly through the underbrush, sniffing at the air as she moved forward. The snapping debris beneath her huge paws allowed Paul to guage the bear's approach without turning his head. Soon, she was almost directly beneath his platform. It was obvious that something serious was wrong with the animal. There was an apparent limp as the bear seemed to favor her left forepaw, and she swayed in an abnormal fashion as she moved. Deep gouges were visible in the side of the bear's face, and pieces of her hide flopped hideously as she struggled through the bushes. Paul realized immediately that she had been involved in a violent confrontation with another bear.

As she passed beneath the platform, Paul raised the tranquilizer rifle slowly and silently, pressing the stock firmly against his right shoulder. He disengaged the safety catch and aimed the rifle at a point midway between the animal's shoulders. The bear's sensitive nose quickly located the deer carcass, and the proximity of an easy meal. With great effort, the bear reached up, standing erect on its hind legs, to embrace the suspended carcass with its front paws.

Paul quickly readjusted his aim upwards, held his breath and squeezed the trigger slowly. Instead of the report that he anticipated, the rifle emitted a muffled click which was sufficiently loud for the bear to detect.

Had the rifle misfired? Paul guessed.

He checked the chamber. There was no tranquilizer dart present.

Astonished, Paul shot a hasty glance at the cab of the truck. What he observed next caused him to be riveted in place.

Dr. Blauman had emerged from the truck with a 0.44 calibre magnum revolver in his right hand, and with a look of intense hatred on his face.

"Blauman, **NO!**" Paul shouted.

The Cave Bear noticed the motion at the side of the truck and instinctively assumed that the human was going to steal the dead deer.

Blauman took five steps forward, and then with both hands he pointed the pistol directly at the female.

"I created you; developed you and now I must terminate you," he shouted at the bear. **"This experiment is now finished."**

A blood chilling roar emerged from the female as her lips peeled back revealing her deadly incisors. Foam lathered and fell away from her jaws in flocculent white globs. She turned on her hind legs and arched her neck forward; her claws extended menacingly; a clear indication to the human intruder that the carcass was hers and that she would defend it.

Dr. Blauman squeezed off three rounds in rapid fire succession. The first two struck the bear in the chest and in the shoulder. The third round went high and wild as Blauman failed to correct for the powerful recoil of the heavy calibre pistol. The bear was knocked backward by the force of the magnum's impact, but she recovered quickly. She charged Blauman ferociously as he fired two more rounds.

Blauman caught the full charging force of the enraged and mortally wounded animal. The bear clamped her powerful jaws shut at a point where Blauman's left shoulder joined his neck – the long, upper and lower canine teeth meeting somewhere deep inside the man's chest. Blood sprayed in all directions as two of the incisors shreaded one of Blauman's arteries. He was dead by the time that the bear wrenched Blauman's head from his shoulders. But the last bullets fired from the pistol had done their deadly work well. One had passed through the bear's left eye and lodged in her brain. The other had severed the animal's carotid artery. Bright crimson blobs burst from the bear's mouth as she uttered her last mournful bellow and collapsed on the mutilated remains of her creator. Almost as quickly as it had begun the confrontation was over. Blauman's open, but forever sightless eyes stared into those of his creation – both were now at peace.

It was several minutes before Paul or Dr. Schaffner moved a muscle. The Chief Inspector continued to sit on the tree platform, his hands sweating and quivering uncontrollably. Finally, Schaffner approached the pistol which Dr. Blauman had dropped in the struggle. He reached down and carefully retrieved it; pointing it at the head of the Cave Bear. The heavy gun shook violently in his hand.

The Noah's Ark Conception

"My God!" was all that Schaffner could say. He kept repeating the phrase until long after Paul had managed to climb down from his elevated perch.

The two men stared, in silence, for many minutes at the carnage that lay on the ground in front of them. Their minds almost refusing to believe what their eyes had just witnessed. Paul pushed against the side of the bear with his right boot, and as he expected, the animal was dead.

"I don't understand why Blauman did that," Paul said in a hushed voice that reflected the emotional impact of what he had just witnessed.

"Did you know that he was going to try to kill the bear?"

"I had no idea," Schaffner answered; his voice also betraying the shock value of the moment.

"He just pulled the gun out of his coat and calmly climbed out of the truck. I didn't even know that he had the pistol with him."

"Blauman must have removed the tranquilizer dart from my rifle, which tells me that he had no intention of letting this bear remain alive."

Schaffner commented, "I knew he was very distraught over everything that has happened, but I never expected that he would react this way." Schaffner wiped the perspiration from his face.

"What do we do now, Paul? What do I tell the institution... his family?" Schaffner managed, studdering his words.

"I don't know what you're going to do doctor, but I've got an official report to file which will state that a civilian consultant, who was an expert on large carnivores, was killed while attempting to protect us from a charging, rogue Brown Bear after my rifle misfired. As far as I'm concerned, the man offered his services to the Swiss Federal Police and died while attempting to save our lives. And that makes him a hero in my book."

Schaffner stared at Paul, without speaking, for several seconds; moved by the policeman's profound sense of understanding and compassion.

Nodding his head, Schaffner turned slowly to Paul.

"I have never known a true hero before, sir. But never in my lifetime had I expected to know two."

Tom F. Dodd

PART   FIVE

CONCLUSION

Chapter Forty-Two

Brig, Switzerland is a beautifully verdant place in mid-July. The quaint, rustic town, nestled in the bosom of the magnificent, snow-capped Alps wears the colors of summer well. The pace of life slows as the afternoon sun induces the residents to seek out shadier recesses. Bustling activity, a rare occurrence, is generally attributable to the tourists – vacationers who dart in and out of town in overloaded campers and sporty four by fours, creating long lines of traffic congestion and short tempers. The townspeople find consolation in the fact that the "sejoureurs" (vacationers) confine themselves to deep in the alpenglades, and mostly out of sight, except to reprovision, which mostly means buying huge quantities of beer.

Six weeks had passed since the rogue bear ceased to be a threat, and Brig's ubiquitous gossip mongers were keeping a sharp ear out for fresh material. Generally, it was great fun to relate stories about greenhorn tourists who had accidentally rolled their camping trailers down a ravine; found themselves stuck while fording a deep creek, or had discovered a long reptilian companion sharing a cool spot and curled up inside one of the park's portable toilets. That was always fun to hear and to talk about.

Today's edition of the local newspaper purposefully had no mention of the recent incidents of bear attacks, and noted that the number of visitors to the area were anticipated in record numbers this season – an obvious bonanza to the town's economy.

A cool, refreshing, pine-scented dampness hung in the early Saturday morning air as Chief Inspector Paul Soria walked out of his office. He exercised briefly with a sustained stretch and filled his lungs to capacity with the crisp, pristine mountain air.

"I'm really hungry this morning," he admitted to himself, and decided to begin the day with a hearty breakfast. But before he climbed into the police cruiser, he remembered to check the police station mailbox. He had forgotten to pick up yesterday's delivery, and since Maria was off, he knew that no one else had bothered to retrieve it. He rarely received anything but official notices and directives from police headquarters in Bern, and they usually were two months old.

Flipping open the mailbox, he quickly noticed the large white envelope sandwiched among the official government browns. The letter was postmarked in Basel. A smile crept across Paul's face as he realized that it was from Mo Levin. Eagerly he tore open the envelope and enjoyed the contents. He could hear the inflections in Mo's voice as he read the letter:

Dear Inspector Paul,

Just a short note to thank you for your generous gift. This letter cannot begin to express my appreciation adequately. Of all of the fossils that I have in my collection, this one I will value the most. The skull is much too large to place anywhere on my desk, so I'm having a special display cabinet made for it. I sent a picture of it to Sid. By the way, he says to say hello.

I was very sorry to hear about Dr. Blauman. Aside from being a brilliant scientist, he was a very brave man to do what he did. You are extremelyly fortunate to be alive. The newspapers here spoke very highly of him. I feel sad for his young wife.

If you get a chance, come up and visit me again soon. You have no idea how happy that you have made this old scientist.

As Always, your friend,
Mo

p.s. Dr. Blauman's secret is safe with Sid and me. We sincerely believed in his work.

Paul finished reading the letter and stuffed it into his shirt pocket. He tossed the other envelopes into the passenger seat as he climbed behind the wheel of the police car.

"And now for some breakfast," he declared as he turned the ignition key.

There were already several patrons in the café when Paul arrived. Through the window he could see Gina busily refilling empty cups with coffee; she spotted him pulling up and managed a quick wave. Her cast had been removed and her arm was nestled in a bright blue sling. Her smile made him feel good.

Opening the door to her café, his senses were immediately overwhelmed with delicious breakfast aromas. He took a seat at his usual booth near the kitchen door.

"'Morning, Paul!" Gina called out from inside the kitchen; her voice projecting a tone that was clearly affectionate.

"Mornin' Gina!" he replied.

"I'm mad at you," she said matter-of-factly.

"And what did I do now?" he asked, bracing himself for the answer.

"I haven't seen or heard from you in over three days, and I have to talk to you about something important," she replied in a voice that had suddenly been tinted with a testy tone.

"In case you hadn't noticed, miss, it's the tourist season. I've been busy keeping the campers from killing the townsfolk, shooting at our little forest critters, or from just burning up the woods around here. Besides, you know that you could have gotten in touch with me through Maria. Anyway, Gina, how's your broken right wing these days?"

"I'll be through with this sling on Wednesday. The doctors have given me permission to resume full-time duties."

"That's great!" Paul responded in a genuine fashion. "I'm sure that you're relieved. I hope you've learned your lesson about traipsing around in the wilderness alone?"

"Well," Gina began; her voice hesitant. "That's kinda what I wanted to talk to you about."

"Traipsing around the wilderness?" Paul answered sarcastically. "Haven't we covered that already a couple of months back?"

"No silly. Let me serve up this order and then I'll come over and talk to you. Meanwhile, help yourself to the coffee... you know where it is."

Paul poured himself a full cup of coffee as Gina raced by with an overflowing plate of French toast and sausages. The aroma made him reconsider his usual order of a ham and cheese bagel sandwich.

He watched Gina's buttocks sway seductively beneath her tan cotton dress, and the early morning sunlight that silhouetted her long, shapely thighs through the fabric.

It doesn't get better than that, he mused. *Well perhaps it does.*

He then lustily considered an alternative order but quickly dismissed it – as it was not to be found anywhere, and on any menu.

How long had it been? He calculated.

Gina hurried back and slid into the booth next to him, executing a quick peck on his cheek. "You look sharp today, Paul," she observed.

"Is that all I get after... I don't know how many days... is a quick kiss?"

"Listen Kemo Sabe, you are the one that moved out into your own place. You know where I live. Now, don't get me started again on that subject. Why don't you just come over and put out the fires in my part of the forest once in a while?" she whispered with a smile while chiding him.

Paul thought that everyone in the café had overheard Gina's admonishment, as the crimson blush on his face betrayed his embarrassment.

"Ohhh," she said, "the great Inspector Paul Soria has a touchy spot." Gina poked him as she chuckled.

"So, what is it that you want so desperately to talk about?" Paul needed to change the subject quickly.

Gina moved closer so that only Paul could hear her.

"I found it," she whispered.

"I wasn't aware that you had lost anything," he retorted with an indifferent smile.

"Paul... I'm serious. I found the gold."

"Gold! What gold?" Paul exclaimed in an unguarded voice. The other patrons in the café overheard him and cocked their ears. Rumor control was hard at work dredging up delicious new information to pander.

"Damn it, Paul... keep your voice down," she reproached him.

"I found the gold in the same cave where I was attacked by the wolverine," she stressed through clenched teeth.

"Where is it now?"

"It's still buried in the cave. After I was attacked, I had to get out of there in a hurry."

Paul was intensely interested now, and he grasped Gina's forearm.

"You actually saw the gold?" he pressed, astonished by her news.

"I held a One-Hundred franc gold piece, right here in this hand, 1925, fresh minted," she said proudly as she beamed.

"Gina... if you're putting me on..."

"May this café burn down to the ground if I'm lying," she stressed.

Her usual veracity and enthusiasm was proof enough for Paul to accept her statement as the truth.

"Paul, I want us to go up there together and recover the rest of it," she pleaded.

"You want us...?"

"Yes... next weekend... as soon as possible. I'll have this damn sling off, and I'll need your help," she said as she smiled and batted her eyes. "Besides, I'm sure that you and I could find things to do in the woods... at night... when no one else is around... in our sleeping bags... are you getting the picture..." she smiled seductively.

"What if that wolverine comes back and bites me in the..." he jested.

"Stop it! I'll split the gold with you, Paul, fifty-fifty," she was trying to sell him on the idea.

"No way, Gina. That's your gold. I don't want any of it. But I don't want you getting hurt again either."

Gina beamed. "Then you'll go back up there with me?"

"Only if you fix me a great breakfast this morning," he negotiated.

"Coming right up… and it's on the house." Gina ran off towards the kitchen.

"Wait!" he called out. "You don't even know what I want for breakfast."

"Yes I do. But it's not on the menu," she teased, laughing.

"Women," Paul muttered; avoiding the prying eyes of the other patrons.

Chapter Forty-Three

Willy drew a ladle of cool water from the hand pump and carefully filled the young bear's water bowl. The bear studied every movement that his human captor made; not daring to take his black eyes off of him for a second. Willy used a long pole to push the water bowl under the lowest horizontal steel bar of the cage.

At first, the bear did not drink. For the first few weeks the animal regarded everything that Willy had done for him as a potential threat, oftentimes growling and bearing his teeth. But slowly, the cub began to understand that this strange human was not a threat, and perhaps because of extreme hunger, the young bear began to eat canned dog food that was prepared, and shoved under the bars.

Willy sat quietly still on the ground and explained to the bear in a soft monotone the reason why it should eat the food and drink the water. As he spoke, the bear's ears stood upright and seemed to move as if trying to decipher what the man was saying. At times the bear would bite at the chain that secured him inside of the cage. As the days wore on, Willy began to see the young animal's resemblance to its mother. The cub had the large, prominent head – so characteristic of a Cave Bear. Emitting short cries that signified its annoyance with the tempered steel constraint, the cub attempted vainly to bite through it.

Willy had accepted that it was his responsibility to raise the bear to adolescence and then reintroduce him back into the wild. By then, its size would have increased three-fold, and as with any wild creature, it would become dangerous and unpredictable.

Except for humans, the animal would have no natural enemies other than disease.

There was a deep feeling of satisfaction that Willy experienced as he watched the young bear drink. He believed in his own way that he was doing God's work; facilitating the reintroduction of the animal into the wild. Whatever the fates had in store for the bear would be entirely in nature's hands – not mans.

The bear had every right to survive and create a life for itself, perhaps even to procreate, foraging in the vast expansion of real estate that was the mountain ranges of Switzerland, Italy and France. He wasn't trying to create another "Jurassic Park", or even a "Pleistocene Park". He just wanted the young animal to have a fair chance at a life that it hadn't asked to be born into.

Willy rested his forearm on a wooden railing and enjoyed the sight of the bear's playful movements.

"We are brothers, my young friend. Our destinys are interwoven like threads in a great tapestry," Willy said to the cub.

The bear tilted his head slightly as if trying to understand what the human was trying to communicate. Slowly, it lumbered over to the side of the cage closest to Willy and grunted. When Willy did not show any sign of fear, the cub reclined, close to Willy's foot, his eyes gazing upwards.

"We have a lot to teach each other," Willy pronounced. The young bear then looked away, seemingly content with the comforting sound of the man's voice.

Before the great orange ball disappeared below the western horizon that evening, the bear allowed Willy to stroke his head.

The trust that was developing between Willy and the young bear was encouraging, and made Willy feel good about himself.

Chapter Forty-Four – Wednesday

At two thirty in the afternoon, Gina watched as a shiney, new "Escapade Red", Aston Martin "DB-8" pulled up in front of her café and parked. The custom license plate read *"ELF-1"*, and a diminutive man with an imposing belly paunch slowly got out of the car. He appeared to be in his early fifties, with fly-away, mousy brown hair parted in the middle, and significant graying at the temples. He wore wire-rimmed round spectacles and a blue suit, and clutched a brown leather briefcase which he accidentally dropped before entering the café.

Gina had an uneasy feeling about the clumsy man, and in a few moments she would understand why. He came through the front door, allowing it to slam behind him. He jumped; surprised by the sharp sound.

"Gina Schmidt?" he asked as he approached her, after regaining his composure.

"Yes," she responded cautiously.

"My name is Eduardo Furto, and I am an agent of Deutchesbank. Here is my business card. Is there somewhere we can sit and talk privately for a while?" he asked as he carefully studied the interior of the café.

Gina read the man's business card: **Eduardo L. Furto III, Business Loan Consultant, Deutschesbank, Gmbh.**

She understood immediately that he was there about the outstanding loan on the café. Deutchesbank was the lien holder.

Motioning for him to take a seat at one of the many empty booths, she noticed that he seemed to regard her with sly, penetrating beady eyes. He appeared slightly nervous – almost edgy, as though he was at odds with himself, and most upsetting was his crooked smile and that he kept staring at her chest.

"You must know that the bank is becoming concerned Mrs. Schmidt... actually, more than a little..."

"That's Ms. Schmidt," she interrupted.

"Ms. Schmidt... sorry. The bank is concerned because your last payment is overdue by eight days, and the one before that was overdue by two weeks. I was sent here to take a look at your business, to make an assessment and make some recommendations that I... I mean, we feel, might enhance your business," he explained in a squeaky voice.

"What kinds of recommendations?" she asked with a measure of mixed curiosity and growing resentment.

"Well for instance, do you have too many people on your payroll? How are you controlling your food costs?"
He responded to her question with a pretentious smugness that irritated her.

"The bank has certain... guidelines that I... we, have developed over time that will ensure the success of your business, and our important investments.

"Except for a cook that comes in to help out on the weekends, you're looking at the entire labor staff sitting in front of you, and I will only buy the highest quality food for my customers," she answered somewhat defiantly. She could feel the petulance welling up inside of her.

"I understand, Ms. Schmidt, but the bank feels that in order to, lets just say, ensure the integrity of our loan that they generously gave to you, we need to be comfortable that you are implementing certain efficiency measures designed to minimize the probability that you will default on your debt to us. I'm quite sure that you would understand if you were in my... I mean... the bank's position."

Gina could feel raw anger building within her. How could this mealy-mouthed upstart of a man presume to tell her what to do with a business that has been in her hands for so many years? She felt like tossing him out on the sidewalk on his ass, and if he didn't stop ogling her breasts while he was addressing her, she might just do that. Besides, she knew that she could kick his fat-assed accounting butt with one hand tied behind her back, and pour whatever was left back into the front seat of his fancy English motorcar surrogate for his penis. At this point, the sight of his presumptuous persona in **her** café was rapidly starting to make her skin crawl.

Then Eduardo asked a question that Gina not only believed was a complete non-sequitor, but moreso, was highly inappropriate.

"You live here by yourself... am I correct?" he asked; with a tone in his voice that indicated something more was on his agenda.

Gina became incensed. Slamming his briefcase closed, she leaned across the table between them and said through her clenched teeth, "Get the fuck out of my business you pathetic little twit, and go back and tell your bosses that they will get their thirty pieces of silver. And if **you** ever come back in here again it will be too soon. Understand Farto?"

"It's Furto," he managed sheepishly. He gawked at her anger.

"Not in my book it isn't! You stink to high heavens, and **farto** how I am going to remember you. Now, O-U-T...out!" She yelled; indicating the way to the front door with her middle finger.

The nervous man gathered up his papers and put them back into his briefcase, and then hurriedly walked out the front door of the café. In his haste to escape the café, he neglected to latch his briefcase, and it fell open at the sidewalk. The breeze blew some of his important papers across the street and down the next block.

Gina smiled as she watched the little man running after them in an ungainly fashion.

Amazingly, she felt a little guilty about her harsh words. She had never admonished anyone so brutally in her café before. She needed a cup of coffee to settle her nerves.

Still, it felt kinda good, she thought.

<u>Chapter Forty-Five</u> – Friday Morning

Gina was busy packing sandwiches into separate, clear plastic bags when she heard the crunching sound of gravel from under the wheels of Paul's four-by-four as he turned into her driveway. She glanced at the clock – six a.m. He was always prompt. She hurriedly placed the sandwiches into an insulated plastic lunch container and then poured hot coffee, which had been brewing on the stove, into a large metal Thermos jug. Paul came in the side door just as she was turning out the kitchen light.

"Good morning, Kemo Sabe," she called out gleefully. "Are you ready to strike it rich this weekend?"

"I feel rich enough right now," he replied with a yawn, as he kiss her on the cheek.

"Funny, I'm really looking forward to this adventure with you... **Gina's quest for the lost gold**... the adventure continues," he stated with dramatic flair. "Besides, aren't you going to return all of the money that you recover to the bank here in Brig?" he said with an obvious tease.

"Oh, but of course I am, Inspector Paul... in a way," she retorted. "It's all going into an account with my name on it. The bank will still have the use of it... in one way or another," she smiled with that knowing look that Paul had come to understand.

"Okay, well, I guess I'm all ready to go," she stated with a look of anticipation. "All we have to do now is drive up to the Verplank farm, pick up the horse trailer and the two horses, load 'em up, and we're ready for a weekend ride into the high back country. Hmmm, that sounds almost like a movie."

"Saddle 'em up, pardner," Paul said, in his best feigned John Wayne accent. "Actually, I was hoping that we might get in a little horizontal enrichment before we left this morning."

Gina stopped at looked at him with an expression surprise and feigned exasperation. She put her hand on her hip for emphasis.

"Now Paul, you know that you always fall asleep afterwards. Besides, I don't want to be getting on the trail at noon. Now please don't get me wrong, I am truly grateful that you are giving up your long weekend to come on this adventure with me… and, I promise that I'll make it up to you. Okay?" Gina kissed him lovingly on the cheek and climbed into the passenger seat of the vehicle.

"Time to go, marshall," she beckoned. "Now that that's all settled, let's get this show on the road."

Feeling slightly discounted, but understanding she was correct, Paul slid behind the wheel and started the engine.

Forty-five minutes later, after connecting the horse trailer and loading the horses and their equipment at the Verplank farm, they were motoring along a narrow back road and headed up country.

The morning was clear and the snow-capped Alps were silhouetted against a cloudless, azure sky. A thin white veil of mist hung low in many of the deep valleys that they passed, but as the sun continued higher the mist evaporated quickly with an eerie stillness.

"The turnoff is about a mile ahead on the right," Gina indicated with her finger.

"I know exactly where it is, "Paul replied with a slight touch of annoyance in his voice. "You're forgetting that this territory is still within my jurisdiction. And I know this area like I do the back of my hand."

"Ooo, sorry," she answered, waving her hands in dramatic fashion. "We seem to be a bit touchy this morning. Didn't Paul get any last night?" Gina retorted sarcastically.

"Don't start," he warned. "You know damn well where I was last night."

"Okay, okay. I just didn't want you to miss the turn off, that's all." She squeezed his arm.

He braked slowly and turned the rig onto a dirt road. It took only a few more minutes to reach the area where they would have to park the truck and horse trailer, saddle up the two horses and prepare to enter the forest.

"How did you ever figure out that this was the correct trail to use?" Paul asked, genuinely impressed with Gina's ability to navigate.

"It was easy! I used the old map that my uncle gave me as an overlay on the geodetic survey map that you supplied. Then I calculated the location of the roads and trails that would bring me closest to the valley where the police lost the outlaw's trail that my uncle had indicated on his map."

"Good thinking!" Paul exclaimed. "You ought to apply for a detective's job on the force," he quipped.

They slowly rode the two horses up the winding trail for what seemed like hours; stopping occasionally to rest and water their mounts and to snack on some of the delicious sandwiches that Gina had brought along. The trail was steep, and as the day grew progressively hotter their pace slowed. Finally, they came to the clearing where Gina had made camp on her first night.

"It took me all day on foot to reach this place," she observed. "On horseback, we made the trip in half the time."

"It's very pretty here," Paul noted. "That stream will make a nice backdrop for our campsite as well as a steady water supply for the horses. He also noted that Gina had unbuttoned her shirt to mid-stomach, and he enjoyed the freedom in the way her unconfined breasts pressed against the fabric."

He also enjoyed the feeling beginning to stir in his loins, but he knew that Gina would not be interested in dallying until after camp had been completely set up and the horses were bedded down for the night. Since he had first come to know her, she had always struck him as a person who put her responsibilities first.

Gina piled up and then leveled a deep bed of pine needles whereupon she laid out the sleeping bags, because she knew that the needles would insulate them from the dampness of the ground beneath. Her mind soon focused on the events that happened a few weeks before. Next, she set up their tent.

"Paul, what do you suppose happened to those two cubs that the mother Cave Bear had? They were never found, right?" Gina inquired out of the blue.

"What brought that question on?" Paul responded.

"I don't know. I was just setting up the sleeping bags here in the tent and one of the bags has a logo of a baby bear on it. I just thought about the cubs, that's all!"

Paul hadn't thought about the cave bear in several days, and Gina's question had caught him by surprise.

"I don't know. They are most probably dead. Willy said that he found one of them, a female… dead in a clearing. He said animals that are immature will not survive without the mother to teach them and to provide nourishment for them while they are learning and growing. Nature has very strict and unwavering rules about survival. I do know if the remaining cub ever encountered another adult bear… or that the adult bear would kill the younger one. He told me that males will never tolerate young bears, even from another species in their territory. Bear society is not a friendly place except for when they mate.

"Speaking of mating…" Paul used the subject as seque.

"Wait a minute," Gina refocused him. "What do you mean another species?"

Paul explained, "The way that I understood it from one of the scientists, is that the Cave Bear female mated with a Brown Bear somewhere in her travels, and those cubs were a hybrid of the two species."

"Oh… I see. It's still a shame that they could not have been rescued and sent to a zoo somewhere." Gina suggested.

"You're right, of course. But no trace of the other bear cub was ever discovered. Willy's probably correct: the chance for the survival of the other cub is probably remote."

"I still think that's very sad," Gina added.

"One thing that we all learned is exactly how dangerous and unpredictable a sow bear and her cubs can be. I hope that I never have to go through an ordeal like that again. Four people killed in my jurisdiction will not look good on my record." Paul sighed. "I don't think that ever occurred in the town's history."

"But you're not responsible for those attacks on those people, Paul," Gina insisted.

"I know that and you know that, but that's not how the bureaucrats in Bern see it. We can't have marauding bears snacking on tourists in our national parks and mountain ranges. It makes no difference to my supervisors that the visitors are invading the bear's habitat; only that the bears should behave in a properly hospitable fashion. It makes absolutely no different to my bosses how ignorant, careless or foolhardy the tourists are… they are still taxpayers, and they pay **my** salary. Therefor, it becomes **my** responsibility to somehow keep all of the animals in my jurisdiction behaving as though they were all cute and cuddly Walt Disney characters. If I had known **that** from the beginning, I might not have accepted the position of Chief Inspector here in Brig, but remained in Geneva, instead," Paul admitted reluctantly.

"But then you wouldn't have met me," Gina responded.

"There, you see… there's a silver lining in every dark cloud," Paul added with a broad grin.

Darkness was beginning to enclose the forest around them, and Gina helped Paul gather kindling and firewood for cooking.

"How much further do you estimate that we'll have to travel tomorrow to reach your cave?" Paul asked, as he picked up one more piece of wood and added it to the huge pile that he carried.

"It's not too far to the cave, but we're going to need maximum sunlight to find the opening among the dense pine trees," she answered, as she broke out the cooking utensils.

Gina prepared a delicious dinner of cheeseburgers, home-made cole slaw, beans and a hastily thrown together salad. She had packed a bottle of red wine, and as the fire began to die into a cozy, orange glow, Gina put her head on Paul's lap and began to stare at the stars.

"Do you know what my mother told me when I was a little girl?"Gina asked rhetorically.

"Uh Uh… what did she say?"

"She said that if I was snuggling with a man that I thought that I loved, and I saw a shooting star… that I was going to marry that man."

"Did that ever happen?"

"I've never seen a shooting star… that is, when I've been with anyone. All of the meteors I've seen have been when I'm alone. Maybe that says something right there." She offered sadly and shrugged her shoulders.

"Like what… that you're meant to be alone?" Paul asked to clarify her statement.

"Could be! The only man that I have ever shared my life with… except for the short time that you and I lived together has been my uncle Mario. He's been gone for several years, and I'm not unhappy with my life so far. I've gotten accustomed to living alone. It doesn't bother me. But whether I'd want to spend the **rest** of my life by myself is another thing altogether," Gina speculated. "As for right now, I think I am where I'm supposed to be. Things work out for a purpose."

Paul thought about asking her if he qualified for one that she might consider living her life with; would he have made the "cut", but he concluded that now was not the right moment. Gina's instincts sensed that he was thinking along those lines and she decided to seque into her opinion of Paul. She felt that it was not only appropriate, but that it served her purpose.

"You are the only man, Paul, that I would ever consider forming a life-long partnership with. You are a very good man: sensitive, reliable, intelligent, considerate and perceptive. You are a very good lover, and… let's see… you are handsome and strong, **and** you can even be funny once in a while. Any woman I know would consider you a great catch," she explained with a genuine conviction in her tone of voice.

"But?" He asked, sensing reluctance on her part.

"But what… but nothing! There are no buts about it. You are what you are Paul, and that is a very attractive man from a women's perspective. There's nothing about you that I would ever suggest needed changing."

"Are you sure?"

"Of, course I'm sure. Are you perfect? No! None of us are. But any imperfections that we have are minor compared to the important qualities, and we can always negotiate the minor differences. You believe that... I know you do," Gina insisted.

Then she turned the tables on him.

"And what about me, Paul... could you see me as someone that you could and wanted to spend the rest of your life with?" "Nah!" Paul answered in jest; in a deliberate, matter-of-fact tone.

"**What!** What do you mean **No**?" She pressed hard on his leg.

"I didn't say no, I said "nah."

"Nah... what's that? Am I suppose to assume that nah is better than no?" Gina sat up and stared at Paul's face.

"I was only kidding... I was just demonstrating that I **do** have a sense of humor, contrary to your opinion of me."

"That wasn't funny in the least," she said.

"Okay, okay... you're right. Let me think about an answer to your question."

"You have to **think** about an answer?" Gina responded, the disappointment apparent in her voice.

"I have to think about everything... that's why I'm so sensitive," he answered with a look of stubborn defiance.

"Okay, that's it, Mister Chief Inspector. If you think that you're sleeping in the tent tonight with miss "Also Ran" here, then you've got another thing coming. You can sleep with the horses... I'm sure they are more your type."

Paul realized that the time had come to stop the deliberately facetious bantering and to be serious. He gave Gina a big smile and said, "Come here, please," as he held out both arms to her.

Gina could not resist that warm, loving, beaming smile that he seemed to reserve only for her. She sat back and leaned against his chest as he wrapped his powerful forearms around her arms and chest. She loved being in that position, because she always felt safe and adored by him. And when all was said and done, it was a refuge that she needed and welcomed.

The Noah's Ark Conception

"Gina," Paul whispered to her tenderly, "I have analzed my feelings for you on numerous occasions: while I was in different moods and at various emotional levels. And I always come back to the same conclusion. I have never loved any woman the way that I have come to love and to respect you. Sure, there are differences between us… but I celebrate, not regret those differences. I truly feel that we are very compatible, and that if I wanted to make a decision for a life-long partner… a wife… it would be you hands down. There aren't any "also rans", because you are the only person in the race." He squeezed her closer.

The moisture was beginning to form under her eyes, and she looked upwards through the blurring tears just in time to see what looked like a meteor streaking through the indigo sky.

"Was that a shooting star?" She called out excitedly. "Darn it! I didn't get to see it clearly because I'm all misty."

"I saw something go by out of the corner of my eye, but I was too focused on you to be sure." Paul answered.

"Gina, I don't believe that what happens with the stars in the heavens has any impact on our lives. While your notion may sound romantic, I'd rather believe that **we,** and not fate, make the decisions and choices that matter the most. I don't need an astrologer to tell me that I love you, and that you and I are nearly perfect for each other," he admitted as he allowed his hand to cover her breast. She warmed to his touch and took his hand and directed it under her shirt.

The moon, a thin, silvery smile in the night sky was becoming visible in the east but it was far too small to illuminate the meadow. The night would be very dark.

"You're not going to believe this," Gina announced. "But I'm still hungry. "Think I'm going to grab another one of our sandwiches."

Paul was disappointed again, as he was just getting into the mood for some serious romancing.

"I guess that being in the great outdoors, with all of the exercise and fresh air causes us to burn up a lot more energy, and we need to replace it. So, we consume more food. Everything

282

seems to taste better outside anyway, and with **your** cooking skills, food conservation becomes a serious challenge."

Gina attempted to get some extra mileage out of the compliment.

"Paul… is my cooking really **that** good," she asked coyly.

"It's excellent! How do you suppose that you have managed to stay in business for so long?"

"Well, maybe my appetite is not… for food right now."

She appreciated the sincerity of his answer and reclined her body; feeling even closer to him now, she reached up and kissed his lips. He looked downward, staring deeply into her eyes, allowing his hand to caress her hair as he kissed her forehead. Gina could see the reflection of the dying fire's embers dancing in his eyes, and for the first time she began to realize what a real treasure that Paul Soria had become for her. Here she was in the mountains, looking for buried gold, and what she had found was the real meaning of the word "treasure".

I'm already holding it in my hand, she thought.

"What do you have on your agenda tonight, Paul," Gina asked with a seductive flair.

He delivered a long, passionate, wet kiss to her mouth and she responded with such unbridled passion that he could not believe that she was the same woman he had met that morning.

The stars had all emerged to create a brilliant canopy of twinkling blue-white lights. The night sky was crisply clear and cloudless, and he held her close for a long while, with her head against his chest as they both stared skyward and marveled at the beauty and the enormity of the universe. They contemplated and discussed their insignificance in proportion to the vastness of the universe and felt drawn together protectively, by mysterious, unseen intervening forces. Yet Paul understood that despite man's insignificant stature, he still retained the power to alter detrimentally the delicate balance of the natural order of things.

"I want you to make love to me Paul… right here, under the stars and in a way that you have never done before… as though we are the only people on this panet."

Gina stood up in front of him with her back to the fire. The vision of her towering over him was more than intoxicating, and he felt himself succumbing to primitive, yet deliciously stimulating urges. Slowly, Gina began removing her clothes in a purposefully choreographed seduction that excited him in a manner that he had never experienced before. In rhythmic fashion she undressed herself; removing first her shirt, boots, jeans and finally her panties. The yellow-orange glow of the fire outlines and silhouetted every hair as she stood - legs apart before him. Never in his life had he seen anyone more beautiful or so incredibly exciting. The sight of Gina's complete nakedness in the middle of an open meadow was overwhelming.

He stood up, and without removing his eyes from the sight of her naked body, he quickly stripped off his own clothes. Paul wrapped her in his strong arms and they kissed her again and again; his tongue exploring her mouth, ears, neck, breasts and her belly as he sank to his knees before her. His hands embraced her buttocks as his mouth explored the front of her sex and she shivered involuntarily from the spasmodic pleasures that his tongue liberated from deep within her. Her knees were becoming almost too weak to support her weight. He sensed her weakness and held her tightly so that she wouldn't fall.

Gina gazed upward towards the heavens. Amid her waves of pleasure she saw thousands of eyes in the night sky watching her and blinking their approval of her shameless, natural ecstacy. Her ardor reached a new level at which she had never experienced as she found forbidden and primitive excitement in their outdoor wanton abandon. She felt young again, and nasty… and felt loved beyond anyone in the world. Paul was everything that she didn't know she had needed.

The erupting and strengthening spasms that came from within her became so overpowering that Gina was beyond any inhibitive cautions. She could hear herself crying out, "Oh my God… my God!" Her passion became animalistic, primitive, spontaneous, unbridled and deliciously sensual. It was as though a synergy of emotions was building and cascading within her; taking her emotionally through an entire spectrum of colorful passions, followed by recurring urges to continue her exploration into these previously uncharted waters. She wanted more of what he was doing to her, but she dared not hope that it could be possible.

Paul gently led her by the hand into their tent and attempted to make love on the sleeping bags. But Gina quickly found her second wind and reversed their positions by assuming the top, with her knees astride his hips.

"You're gonna feel real celestial fireworks, tonight," she declared in a voice that exuded control and raw sexuality. Paul had never heard that tone of voice before and it excited him. He enjoyed being subordinate in ways that he had never anticipated.

They coupled several times during the night, resting only for what seemed like short periods to rejuvenate themselves sufficiently and collect enough energy to begin afresh. Each time a new position was assumed and the dominant roles reversed. Every sexual whim was explored and sated until complete exhaustion and sleep became the ultimate respite. Paul and Gina collapsed; their naked bodies intertwined on top the sleeping bags. They slept without dreaming and enjoyed the most restful sleep that either of them could ever remember. The fire slowly evanesced into a warm, orange incandescence, and by daybreak it was completely extinguished.

<u>Chapter Forty-Six</u> – Saturday Morning

Gina awoke first. She could feel Paul's warm body pressed against hers and she smiled, as the images of the previous night's excitement flashed in her mind's eye. She thought about her unbridled erotic behavior and while she admired herself for "coming out" - the episode still caused a significant blush to appear on her face.

Her eyes opened slowly as the droning sound of some nearby insect compelled her to get up. As her eyelids parted, she could see that the morning sky was slightly overcast, but patches of blue were detectable through the waning mist. Everything outside their tent was covered with a layer of dew, and she knew that she would have to force herself to leave the warm comfort of the tent, and to dress in clothes that in her lust she had hastily discarded the night before. They were most certainly damp now, and she was naked. But thoughts of gold coins provided the needed inertia overcoming motivation to brave the early morning's damp and chill.

Moving quickly, she located her panties and checked them to be sure that no tiny, crawly critter had taken up residence in them overnight. She gathered up her jeans and her shirt that lay in careless fashion strewn about on the ground.

My mother would have had something to say about this, she thought, amusing herself with the absurdity of the observation.

Gina shivered as she fought her way into each garment.

I could really use a shower right now, she chided herself. *My hair is a mess, and I've been behaving like a slut. Maybe its better that mom is not here to have to witness this.*

It seemed to take a long time for her body to warm the garments.

Paul awoke to the sound of Gina's mutterings, "Brrrrrrrrrr!" she said with each garment that she put on, and he raised his head inquisitively to see what was going on outside the tent.

"Are we having fun yet," he jested.

"The worst part is already behind me, wise guy. But you still have to crawl out of the warmth and comfort of the tent and get dressed," she retorted.

"Aww, I was hoping to entice you to get my clothes for me."

"Entice me with what?"

"Maybe another sample of what happened last night," he answered with a grin.

"Oh, refresh my memory. What happened last night?" she teased.

"Frankly, I really cannot put it into words, but one of the participants kept crying out, "Oh, my God! Do it to me... more, more, more! Now did that mean she was having a religious experience?"

"No actually, overstimulation is a side effect of a prescription drug that I'm taking to relieve the residual pain in my shoulder and arm."

"You're full of what makes the grass grow green," he scoffed.

"You were a real animal last night... and loving every minute of it. You just won't admit it, that's all. It must be a girl thing."

"Okay, Kemo Sabe, if that's whats important to you... you were pretty darn good last night," Gina conceded in a condescending voice as she tossed him his clothes. Get dressed and I'll get the coffee going. Besides, we're going to both be wealthy people in about three hours."

"Three hours? I thought you said that the cave was just over there a ways?" Paul observed.

"It is, but don't forget that we have to locate and dig up the gold, too."

"Locate? You said that you had found the gold. What's to locate?" Paul attempted to clarify.

"I said that I found a fresh minted fifty-franc gold piece. The rest of the gold is still buried in the cave somewhere."

"What! I thought that you found all of it. If I had known that we were going to be digging up a cave looking for gold, I might have never come up here. You tricked me," he said in a voice that wasn't overly offended.

"No, you didn't listen to me. Instead, you only heard what you wanted to hear. I never told you anything but the truth, Paul. In your mind you had assumed that I found all of the gold, and I allowed you to believe it. Look, I'm sorry if I appeared to lead you on. I'll make it up to you… trust me."
Gina went to him and kissed his forehead.

"I need you here with me Paul, and I am certain that the gold is still buried in that cave somewhere."

Paul could see that she was being sincere and it convinced him.

"Well, okay. Even if we don't find any gold, last night was certainly worth the long ride up here… at least it was to me."
She stared into his eyes and saw the vulnerability that rested just below the surface.

"Paul, you were magnificent last night. I've never felt so satisfied… so much of a woman. And I mean that from the bottom of my heart."

"Okay, apology accepted. Now let's go and find your gold," he said with resolve as he jumped out of the tent.

An hour later, they were leading their horses on foot, upstream, and picking their way between the thorny bushes that overhung the narrow ribbon of shallow water. The trek was tiresome and Paul's horse particularly resented the narrow confines.

"We're almost there," Gina said encouragingly. I am pretty sure that the clearing is just around the next bend. I hope."

Her assumption proved to be correct, and they waded out of the stream onto the pine needle littered embankment.

"How did you ever stumble across this place?" Paul was taken with the area's remoteness and isolation.

"I just pretended that I was a thief, evading the Federal Police in the dead of winter, and I tried to imagine what **he** would have done. I just got lucky, I guess."

"I've got to hand it to you, Gina. That was a long shot."

"The cave is about a quarter of a mile... over here to the right," she said as she indicated with her hand the correct direction.

They reached the cave quickly, and Paul saw immediately that it would have made an ideal shelter for someone seeking a refuge from the harsh winter weather.

"You found the gold coin in there?" Paul asked; the astonishment was evident in his voice.

"Yep! That's the place. Isn't it exciting?"

They secured their horses and walked to the cave entrance. Paul did not see any fresh footprints or pawprints that would indicate recent usage by any two or four-legged animals.

"We're going to need some of this dead brush to start a fire. It's very dark in there," Gina suggested.

Gathering up as much dead wood as they could carry, they entered the cave cautiously, allowing their eyes to become accustomed to the darkness, and their noses to the fetid odors abounding inside.

"That's where I had the fire the last time that I was here, and that's where the wolverine attacked me." Gina pointed to the blackened section of the cave floor.

In a few minutes, they had a large fire burning. The smoke rose to the ceiling and wafted out of the cave's entrance.

"You get some more dead wood, Paul, and I'll get the metal detector and the shovels." Both returned to the cave quickly with their burdens and began to plan their strategy to find the hidden gold.

"Here's what we need to do." Gina assumed command of the exploration. "Using a shovel, we'll mark out a grid pattern on the ground. Each grid will be approximately one meter square. Once that is done, we'll scan the floor of the cave with the metal detector, beginning on the left side, and working alternately front to back and then back to front. In that way we'll make certain that every section of the cave floor is covered. There is some overlap, but we will not be duplicating our efforts. My estimate is that we can complete the scanning of the entire cave floor in less than one hour."

"Let's get going," Paul said approvingly.

Gina tested the metal detector and dialed in an audible, steady, but low volume tone in the earphones. After scratching out the grid pattern on the floor of the cave, she began sweeping each square with a methodical attention to detail. She poked at anything that caused the slightest variation in the signal's tone.

After covering about a third of the cave, a loud "whooping" sound was heard in the earphones. Gina carefully unearthed the same gold coin she had dropped when the wolverine had attacked her.

"I've found it, "she yelled to Paul, and he rushed over to see what she had discovered. Gina held up the gold coin proudly for Paul to examine.

He didn't know much about gold coins, but immediately understood from the newness and the heavy feel that it was genuine.

"You see, 1925, just like I said. And there's not a wear mark on it."

Paul was infected with Gina's excitement and was becoming bitten by the same gold bug fever. But something was still puzzling him.

"But why didn't you find any other coins at the same spot where you found this one?"

"Perhaps Van Traubben dropped it here." Gina speculated. "But even if he had, he would have bent down to pick it up and taken it with him... assuming that he left this cave alive."

"Van Traubben? Who on the world is Van Traubben?" Paul inquired, having not remembered hearing that name before.

"My uncle told me that some woman from Italy had filed a missing person's report about her husband... something Van Traubben... I don't recall his first name. Afterwards, some of the bank employees said that the thief matched almost perfectly the description of the woman's missing husband. Right down to the crescent birthmark over his eye...and... he owned a horse," Gina explained. "From what I came to understand from Uncle Mario, Van Traubben was never located."

"So maybe he left his wife, took the gold and just disappeared...forever. He began a new life on the French Riviera and lived like a Saudi prince all through the Great Depression Era," Paul suggested.

"That might have been what Van Traubben was planning, but he never made it out of these mountains alive, and the gold is still buried in here somewhere," Gina insisted. "I can feel it," she stated confidently.

Soon, Gina was back at work scanning the floor of the cave. As she was nearing the fire, another loud whooping sound was heard as the detector's induction coil passed over a depression in the soil. Stooping to remove the dirt, she soon discovered a metal object resembling a belt buckle, and connected to a rotted leather strand. Paul picked up a small piece of flaming branch from the fire to improve the illumination on the find.

"It looks like a belt buckle," Paul observed.

"Except for the spent bullet slug that I found last time, this is the only other thing, and the coin, that indicates that any human was ever inside of this cave," she explained.

"Let's dig around here a little further and see what we come up with." Paul suggested.

After several shallow shovelfuls of dirt were removed from the immediate area, Gina asked Paul to stop excavating and she began to probe the ground with her knife. She struck something hard, but the metal detector indicated that the item was not made of metal. Gina carefully removed the dirt from around the object and gasped at the realization of what she had unearthed.

"My God! It's a human skeleton," she stammered in astonishment.

"I think you may have just found your thief," Paul added.

"Do you think so? How can you be sure?"

"I'm just guessing, Gina. But I've never known Neolithic people to wear belt buckles like that."

"But if it's Van Traubben, who could have buried him here? He was supposed to have acted alone," Gina asked, puzzled.

"He's been in here for over three quarters of a century. Perhaps years of bat droppings and animal diggings, plus the action of the wind probably caused enough dust to accumulate over that period," Paul offered as one possible explanation.

"You don't think that someone could have accidentally stumbled upon this cave, buried the body and removed the gold, do you Paul?"

"That **is** one possible explanation," Paul agreed.

Gina felt disappointed. "Well, I've come this far and I'm not going to quit until we have scoured the entire cave," she said defiantly. She resumed her search and soon detected a large metal object near the back of the cave. She reached down and felt the cold, hard steel of a pistol.

"Paul, I found a gun," she said excitedly.

Together they walked closer to the light to examine the object. The pistol was an old, Italian-made handgun – army issue type. It was severely corroded from years of resting in the acidic soil of the damp cave, and the trigger was now nothing more than a thin metal sliver which disintegrated when Paul applied a slight pressure.

"There are no bullets in this gun," Paul noted. "Its owner must have emptied it at someone or something before discarding it. It seems a little unusual that someone would just toss away a good pistol," Paul reasoned.

"Something dreadful must have happened in this cave," Gina said.

"It would appear that way," Paul agreed. "But I guess that we will never know."

Gina asked Paul to bring more light as she probed around the large, enlongated rock at the rear of the cave. Suddenly, the metal detector emitted a loud, piercing sound that caused Gina to remove her headphones in hasty fashion, and caused the needle of the signal-strength meter to slam against the upper end of the scale.

"Oh my God!" she exclaimed, "Whatever it is it's huge!"

Paul rapidly went to work scraping off layers of earth with the shovel. On one of his efforts a dozen gold coins emerged from the ground and he scattered them as he tossed the dirt into a pile. Paul and Gina caught the glint of the lustrous metal immediately, and they stopped digging and stared at the coins in profound amazement; unable to speak for several seconds.

"We found it!" Gina screamed; her excitement uncontrolled as she threw her arms around Paul's chest and the two of them jumped up and down.

"We found the gold," Gina reiterated. "Uncle Mario was right all along. We're rich! The gold is all here. Thank you Uncle Mario!" Gina exclaimed as she looked heavenward and reached up with her arms.

Paul, while excited about the find, was able to control his enthusiasm sufficiently to unearth the remainder of the coins. He gazed in awe at the sizeable pile that they had collected on the ground.

"Unbelieveable!" He exclaimed cool-headedly. "Who would have guessed that all of this gold has been lying up here for all of these years?"

"I did, and so did my uncle Mario. In case you've forgotten about that," Gina stated proudly.

"There most be close to fifty pounds of gold here," he estimated.

"Twenty-one kilos, or forty-six pounds to be exact, Paul," she announced. "I did the math based upon what was purported to have been stolen."

"Thank God we brought horses, or I cannot imagine how we would have carried all of this weight down the mountain."

"I anticipated that the original sacks would have rotted out from seventy-five plus years in the ground, so I brought four, new canvas sacks with me."

"You've thought of everything," he acknowledged.

"When you've had as much time to think about the possibility of finding this gold as I have, you tend to leave no stone unturned. No pun intended."

"Well Gina," Paul stated, "You're a rich woman now. How much do you think that all of this gold is worth today?" He asked, only half-expecting her to know the answer.

"In gold bullion, at eight-hundred and fifty dollars an ounce on the spot market: approximately $650,000.00 worth. But numismatically, the coins are worth to collectors considerably more than that," she replied.

"Numismatically? What's that?"

"To coin collectors... these are fifty-franc, uncirculated gold pieces... extremely rare today in this condition. A coin collector will pay considerably more than the value of the gold bullion for each of these," Gina explained.

"Paul, I told you that I would share this find with you. There's a lot more than enough money here for me to pay off my bank debt, and for me to live comfortably for the rest of my life. I'm sure that there are probably things that you might like to have, and this money will allow you to afford them," she insisted.

"I appreciate your generous offer... but it's your money... not mine. Maybe some day, if I need it, you'll give me a loan. But for now, I have just about everything in life that I want."

"You're truly an unusual person, Paul Soria. I can't imagine wanting to change you," she said as she kissed him.

It took them another hour to load the canvas sacks with the coins, and to secure the four bags to each side of the saddles of the two horses. They made sure that the weight was distributed evenly for proper balance. The horses were led out on foot to the clearing, and were ridden by Paul and Gina back to the area where their vehicle was parked. They arrived back in Brig at dusk on Sunday evening.

When they arrived in Brig, they parked Paul's four by four at the side of Gina's cafe. The lights were still on and a few patrons could be seen eating at the counter.

"Willy's here!" Gina noted, and pointed out his faded old pickup truck parked in a corner of the lot.

"It's a little late for him to be out, isn't it Paul? Isn't he usually home and in bed at this time of the evening. I wonder if something happened again," she speculated.

"Oh God, don't say that," Paul cautioned.

They entered the café amid cheerful greetings by some of the patrons who recognized them immediately. Willy looked up from his dinner salad and waved them over.

"You people have been out camping, I hear tell. It's a pity that you missed all of the excitement around here yesterday," Willy announced.

They joined Willy where he was dining and sat down next to him. Paul asked the obvious question before Gina could relate her success story.

"What happened? What was all the excitement about, Willy?"

"Well sir, that crazy Deputy Inspector of yours is a bona-fide hero, that's what," he announced.

"**House?**" Gina interjected.

"Yeppers! A right nice piece of policework he did yesterday."

"What did he do?" By now, even Gina's interest was piqued.

"He captured an armed bank robber, single-handed," Willy explained. "Unfortunately, this town is not going to be able to live with that big boy's inflated ego the way it is now."

"Tell us about the bank robbery, Willy," Paul insisted.

"Well, the way that I heard it, yesterday morning this fella attempts to rob the bank across the street. While he's still inside of the bank, one of the tellers, I think it was Sarah, steps on the silent alarm which goes off over in your police station house. So, everyone over there believes that it's an alarm malfunction or somethin', and they put in a call to Haustein, who's on traffic duty in his sector cruiser. House goes tearing off to the bank, with no siren or lights. He insists that's the way that Clint Eastwood does it in Harry Callahan movies."

"Oh, good Lord," Paul says with understated exasperation.

"No wait... it gets better," Willy insists with a wave of his hand.

"So, House rushes into the bank with his usual macho bravado, both guns drawn, and he tells everyone to freeze. The bank robber, obviously **not** an experienced criminal, gets the surprise of his life as Haustein comes busting through the bank's front doors, and he immediately drops his pistol and surrenders. One of the bank patrons picks up the robber's gun and hands it to House, who still believes that the problem is only a malfunction of the bank's alarm system."

Paul and Gina began to laugh heartily along with Willy, and the tears begin to roll down their faces.

"The entire episode is comical... hilarious," Willy roared. "I don't know who was more surprised... Deputy Haustein, or this fellow Van Traubben...the bank robber!"

Silence befell the table instantly.

"Van Traubben?" Paul repeated the name Willy had mentioned and then looked at Gina in surprise.

"Yeah... Van Traubben," Willy reiterated the robber's name. "After he surrendered, he told the Inspectors that his great-grandfather tried to rob the same bank here in Brig about eighty years ago, and had disappeared in a blizzard while trying to escape."

Paul and Gina couldn't believe what they were hearing, and they stared at Willy.

"Hey! Why are you two guys looking at me like that? Do you know this fella?"

THE   END

EPILOGUE

Several years later, Brig remains the same sleepy, tourist town, changed little but for two barely noticeable exceptions. The café has a new coat of paint, burgundy-colored shutters and a completely remodeled interior. A few of the senior patrons occasionally protest the "modern" look; admonish Gina by inferring that her uncle would have never considered such "new fangled" fixtures. But most continue to savor her great home-cooking while seated in modern, plush comfort.

There is a large, internally illuminated Plexiglas sign on the roof, which now can be seen from the highway and the railroad station, and it beckons hungry tourists to stop and enjoy Gina's delicious home-style breakfasts, lunches and dinners, as well as an assortment of finely crafted desserts. Consequently, her little business has grown modestly and Gina now employs two waitresses, allowing her to concentrate on the activity that she enjoys most – her cooking and baking.

If one hangs around the "Bear's Den Lounge", a new local "Apres ski" watering hole that opened about a year ago, you might hear a delicate rumour that Gina is expecting a baby in the spring – but you couldn't confirm that by looking at her. Rumour control also has it that she is not marrying the father – so much for "Women's Lib in Brig.

Paul declined a transfer as an Aide to the Assistant Director of the Swiss Federal Police in Bern. He said that several things in Brig needed looking after, and he felt that he wasn't ready for such a large assignment. The truth be told – Paul hated all bureaucrats. The Assistant Director, named Weidener, took

The Noah's Ark Conception

Paul's refusal as a personal slight – so much for politics in Bern. But few in Brig were surprised by Paul's decision.

Willy Redman became an outspoken advocate for environmentalism and animal rights. This political stand has made him somewhat unpopular with his bosses at the Interior Department. But through his persistent efforts, another half-million acres of land adjacent to the Alpine ranges were set aside as permanent park sanctuary. All hunting was forbidden in that area.

The young, hybrid cub finally matured and consistent with Nature's plan sired many progeny – many of them living and thriving within the bounds of the very lands that Willy had rescued. The realization of the young bear's survival success has been very gratifying.

The Noah's Ark Project was ultimately abandoned; primarily, because it had failed to make any money for its original investors. The Scientific Staff were dismissed with generous severance packages, conditional on their sworn promise to keep silent. Today, they are all currently employed in a variety of unrelated endeavours.

I sincerely hope that you have enjoyed my story.

Warmest regards,

Tom F. Dodd

Tom F. Dodd

Tom F. Dodd

www.ingramcontent.com/pod-product-compliance
Lightning Source LLC
Chambersburg PA
CBHW031156020726
47499CB00002B/384